I0822535

<u>The Phoenix Chronicles:</u>

Amber Rhapsody

Fyra B Ginn

ISBN: 979-8-9883135-3-3
Published By: Phoenyx Honor Publishing
www.fyrabginn.com

Smoke clears, ashes lay on dead ground.
Time stills and we mourn
a single drop, the catalyst.
Something stirs, felt, not seen.
Hope seeps into the earth
a spark of life grown from grief.

From the ashes she ascends
her flame tempting,
a honed blade forged in hellfire.

Her phoenix, the fire bird,
her amber rhapsody unfolding
like ripples of fate upon the earth.
Each ascension, an aftershock
that propels forward, stirring the destiny of man.

Passion's double blade,
the muse or the lover,
controlled rage turned to turbulent desire.

Will it be she, the victim?
Who risks the flame consuming her soul?
Or the man who dares to chase her light,
As a moth to flame,
so a man to love?

-from the poetic works of Dr. Gregory Jackson

Prologue

It was more feeling than sight, here in the abyss. Her thoughts left before they could form. No heat nor cold touched her, but untamed energy swirled about her like celestial fireflies, racing forward, toward a red star. It pulsed once, twice, then exploded into pure valencian light.

As the particles reached her, they melded, giving her a new form. Then suddenly she flew, thousands of lightyears at once, slamming back into her body. A breath escaped her, and she remembered. She had ascended.

Opening her eyes, her grey irises looked wildly to the right, the left, forward, backward. She was in Tyrus's arms, his shirt covering her form.

"Nix, Tommy."

"Ann, you can't…"

Levi turned away and began to sob loudly, his rage and grief evident.

"He's gone." Tyrus said.

"So is she." Ann tried to be brave, but tears fell unbidden from her eyes. She reached toward the ashes of her mentor, the only sign that Nix had once lived a full and vibrant life. In grief and pain, she shouted, "she's GONE!"

Chapter 1

Shortly after the bombing…

He sat back on the plane in first class, one seat in front of Wills. They landed in London, and he waited to embark until she was gone. Smiling at the attendants, he walked forward into the airport, focusing on her features. Dark, dyed hair, quick pace, in observing her while she was helpful, he'd learned her gait, the way she moved. Spotting her entering the women's restroom, he grabbed a newspaper, waiting patiently for her to exit. He followed her from baggage claim to the taxi she ordered, always blending into the crowd. If he wanted to be invisible, he knew what to do. He knew no one would see his wings in the dark, so he waited until the taxi had turned the corner then he summoned his dragon, tailing them from above.

Even in the age of drones, no one tended to look up, easing the difficult task of surveillance. He kept to the shadows, avoiding any lighting, tricky, but this wasn't his first time. He firmly believed that it was best for the human race to keep their existence secret. The taxi, on her order, took many unnecessary turns, expecting to be followed.

Eventually, they ended their journey in front of a building that filled him with pure fear. Getting out of the car, he knew he wouldn't be able to follow her. It all made sense now.

Landing on a roof, he tilted his head. A few moments later, she exited her vehicle. The man himself came out to greet her with a hug and a kiss. Remembering both their faces, he chastised himself. He usually saw the connections between people. How had he missed this? Wills was the daughter of Europe's leading Genetics researcher, Dr. Henri Blanc. He'd never married, and publicly had no familial connections, but Rebecca Wills clearly mattered to him beyond a business relationship, the most likely being paternal. She was his daughter.

What he wanted was impossible. His memory told him to be cautious with this family. They were responsible for the divide in their group, for him severing Nix's connection to her bird. He couldn't do anything from here but get killed and give away their lead. Picking him up, his wings carried him home. It'd be a long fly, but he didn't want the record of him returning to the US in the system now. Better for Dr. Blanc to think he was right around the corner. Just in case.

He couldn't risk exposure, not now, when they were recovering. So, he seethed, silently, and returned, intent on preparing the Five for an impossible fight. Blanc had business connections on all continents, unlimited funding, and access to one of the three assassin Mythics. Tyrus, had a network, his family's land, and a broken director. His reckoning would have to wait.

He landed in NYC during the witching hour. He walked into an alley full of sleeping homeless veterans. He slipped a fifty into their coat pockets, careful not to wake them. He remembered Vietnam, too. Picking up a burn phone, he dialed a number. The person answered and he merely said, "Watch Blanc." He hung up before getting a response and tossed the phone into the barrel, its embers warming the alley. He watched the plastic degrade, then slowly, the metal components heated and became liquid. Now was not the time.

A year later…
80°F, Colorado, US

Ann stepped off the city bus, her stance wide. She stared down her large opponent, her right fist clenching slowly, the fire within her bubbling under the surface. A hint of smoke escaped, the only sign she was a Mythic. Today was a different kind of battle.

They'd been told, warned it was coming, from Nyx, Tyrus, hell, even Levi had counseled them. She knew what to do to succeed and her plan was solid, but she couldn't help but feel unease within her. No battle was ever assured, no success ever guaranteed, and she needed to stay balanced and focused to win today. Her heart pounded and she breathed out slowly, setting her shoulders wide and fixating on her goal. She stepped forward once, fought the urge to retreat, then pushed herself forward into the Chik'n Kitch'n for her first day of work.

It'd been a year since the bombing, and while she had access to resources they needed, the five had been cast out of the nest and told to move on with their human lives. In spite of having amazing abilities, things still cost money. No one got a free pass in life, and working with others was an essential skill. Or so she'd been told. As an introvert, she'd much rather work online. As work from home jobs were still rare in St. Blaize, she decided to try her hand at customer service in the fast-food industry. All the others seemed to adjust easily, so she doubted it would be too difficult.

She walked in with a wide smile and greeted the manager kindly. "Hi! I'm Ann, and this is my first day. What can I do?"

Two hours later, she sat on the steps across the street, watching it all burn. The manager ran around frantically, while the Kick'n Chick'n, their mascot, helped by miming, kicking the flames in his signature move, committed to the small amount he got paid for being ridiculous. The scene would have been hilarious were her uniform not singed from the flames. Not only was being around a fryer not a good idea, but she had made exactly fourteen dollars, if they paid her at all, and spent fifty on the uniform, which was not returnable in its current condition.

"Day 1, minus 30 dollars." She kicked the dirt as the manager glared at her harshly, to which she shrugged, then turned and walked away. "Definitely not getting a good reference." Her shoulders slumped forward as she sculked away. She rounded a corner to an alley and took a moment to breathe, but her eyes held her crimson flame when she looked up.

"It wasn't *for* you, anyway." Joy appeared around the corner out of nowhere and despite their friendship, Ann was startled.

"Don't scare me like that, Joy."

"Didn't mean to." Joy kicked a small rock down the alleyway. "How are you feeling?"

Ann sighed. "I'm upset because the rest of you all seem to have found the perfect job on the first try, and my fast-food work life seems to have literally gone down in flames."

Joy giggled. "Seth at the bank, Connor in college, Julius working security, my paintings…yeah, I can see where you might be a little lost, but I told you, no food."

"You did, didn't you?"

"We should add no oil too. No gas stations, hair salons, no massage therapy."

Ann felt defeated. "Too bad the government doesn't fund superheroes."

Joy giggled, but quickly looked sideways. "Not yet anyway."

Ann walked down the alley with Joy dancing around her. "So, what will we do for the rest of the day?"

Ann had intended to have a celebratory evening of pajamas and ice cream after a long shift in the May sunshine, but her time was open now. "Your call, Joy. Anyone need help?"

She froze, her eyes going wide for a moment. Joy had always been quirky, but since their change into Mythics, she was even more so. "Yes. We need help, though."

"Whose?"

She twiddled her fingers, and chuckled, vanishing from view. Ann waited patiently, the sounds of the firetrucks growing louder. A second later, Joy was back with Julius in tow, complete with his security uniform. He looked angry. She didn't blame him.

"Hey! What gives?" He nodded his head toward Ann, a greeting she returned.

"We get to save a life." Joy grabbed both of them by their forearm at the same time and the world swam before her eyes as they bounced from the streets of St. Blaize to another part of the world, instantly. Ann always hated the part after. When they could understand their surroundings again, she turned and emptied the contents of her stomach onto a conveniently located bush. Joy, more used to it, skipped ahead a few steps and looked around while Julius struggled and failed not to throw up himself.

"You almost did it." Joy patted his back while he growled at her. "Again, where the hell are we? And whatever happened to asking permission first? Didn't we talk about this, Joy?"

Joy stomped her foot. "No time. We have to go."

Ann looked around her, but she couldn't place where they'd landed. Shrubberies abounded, mostly rose bushes. This looked like someone's private garden. The sun felt slightly different here than in Colorado, but it wasn't familiar. She could hear faint sounds of traffic, but it was light. Not like the streets of St. Blaize. *Some rich suburb, probably.*

Julius gazed away, his nose in the air. "You're right. This way. Stay low and quiet."

Ann had learned how to trust the people around her in the last year. While she had always loved Joy and Seth, Julius and Connor were family, as well. If he sensed something, she knew it was in her best interest to follow him, even if she was scared. She held her questions for Joy as they rounded first one turn in the labyrinth, then another, coming to the middle of the grounds where a large pool lay. Toward the end of the pool, on the right, a woman sat sunbathing.

Ann wondered why they were being creepers in some woman's yard, but she heard Julius growl again. "It's her."

"It's who?"

Joy whispered, "betrayer."

Ann looked again, not seeing it at first. They hid as the woman stood, glancing in their direction, but the heels clicked away. Ann looked back, knowing that gait, that walk. "It's the former 'Dr. Wills.'"

Julius prepared to lunge, but seeing it, Joy stopped him with a firm grip on his arm. "No. That wasn't the point. Shh. Hide, and don't meet his eyes."

They looked back, and Wills was talking to an older man wearing a grey suit. She couldn't hear what was being said, but she felt the rage come. This woman had almost killed them, had destroyed an entire business and left without a word. She'd thought she was one of the few adults she could trust, and that trust had been snatched from her. Her eyes lit with her flame, but she hid as the man's gaze wandered toward her location.

Joy and Julius were on the other side of the hedge, and they began to hear steps walking toward them. They'd been made.

Joy held a finger to her lips, and vanished with Julius, leaving Ann momentarily alone as the steps grew closer. Her eyes, filled with her flame, grew resolved as her body became heat, spreading until her hands held her red spark. If she had to do this now, she would. The steps approached quickly, and she breathed once, twice, and a third time before clenching her leg muscles, ready to stand and avenge her people.

Before she could act, before the last few steps could reach her, Seth bounced in and, grabbing her arm, bounced her back out. The steps reached her position, but the only piece of her that remained were tendrils of smoke.

They were in an alleyway, back in St. Blaise. Ann sighed heavily as Seth leaned her against the wall, protecting her from view with his body. She didn't want to throw up this time, but she was a bit upset.

"Where is Joy?"

"She had…Joy things to do with Joy people. She knew I would get you in time."

"Her behavior is becoming…disconcerting."

"I know, but… she has her reasons."

"Does one of them include giving me a heart attack?"

He smiled. Seth was their leprechaun, and something about the smile soothed her, helped her breathing return to normal. "Why did she take me there? Where was I?"

"She said to go ask Tyrus. I'm to accompany you."

"Don't you have to work?"

"Small issue with the computers at the bank. Everyone has the day off."

She shook her head, trying not to say it, but it came out anyway. "Lucky break."

He chuckled. "Exactly! We can walk from here."

They left the alleyway and she realized where they were. In the green zone, an older part of the city that Nix called her home. She had lived with Nix last year while figuring out how to control her power, who she was after the bombing of their bus. She thought back to the kids that hadn't survived, including her best friend Marie, who she still regularly talked to in dreams. It still hurt, knowing she couldn't hug her, talk to her anymore, but it wasn't as overwhelming as it had been at the start.

"Heading to the penthouse?"

"Yes."

They kept stride with each other, passing several stores and open street kiosks as they walked along. She assumed Tyrus would be there with Nix, that this was Joy's way of telling them that it was passed time for an explanation. Tyrus had abandoned the operation to rescue her, had flown…somewhere, trailing Wills, and had returned, simply saying, "now is not the time."

Maybe that had changed? Joy had replied for the group, saying, "it really isn't, is it?" They'd moved on with their lives, but it still irked her that they hadn't gone after Dr. Wills.

They stepped into the building and into the elevator, hitting the button for the penthouse. Entering a pin, Nix came on the video screen, saw them, and said, "come on up." The screen went blank, the elevator closed, and they listened to the slightly cheery music on their way up.

"You realize you saved my life, just now."

He nodded. "You're welcome."

"How many times is that, now? I'm going to owe you in my next three lives."

He laughed. "I have a feeling you'll get me back. That's what friends do. Don't worry about it."

But the fact that he had a "feeling" made her worry. Seeing it in her eyes, he began to whistle a jaunty tune, and she felt at ease. The elevator doors opened, and they walked into the large white space. Nix and Tyrus sat on the couch with laptops and phones open. They were busy with something.

"Hey." She said it softly as she sat across from them in one of the large, white recliners.

Nix didn't look up, but Tyrus did. He smiled softly and nodded. "Hay is for horses. Hello."

She rolled her eyes at his dad humor. "We just had an interesting experience with Joy."

On cue, she materialized with Julius. "Be right back."

Julius scratched behind his ear. Grabbing two chairs from the dining table, he set them down near the recliners, creating a circle. Taking one more, he sat next to Seth in his chair. Joy returned with Connor, complete with his college backpack. "Joy! I'm going to miss math!"

"This is important, and your teacher is sick."

He glanced at his phone, scanning his notifications. "Huh. So he is. Class cancelled. Well, then, hey, everyone."

Tyrus turned to him, but Ann moaned out loud, and he looked at her, his eyes merry. "Just don't."

He shrugged his shoulders as they all took their seats.

"Are we waiting for anyone else to join us, Joy?"

She snorted. "No, of course not."

"Great. Then.... Why are we here?"

Joy looked at Tyrus. He ignored her, focused on his work. She sighed loudly, but he continued to ignore her. She bit her lip and furrowed her brow, standing up from her chair. She walked behind him and placed her hands on her hips, clearly upset with him. They all watched as she closed her eyes tightly and seconds later, his laptop became a white rabbit. After a moment of confusion, he sighed. He was obviously upset, but it was funny to see a grown man capable of dealing great pain tuck a bunny under his arm and start to stroke its furry head.

"I assume you want my attention, Joy." She walked back and sat down, pleased with herself. Nix looked over and chuckled low.

"I hope you saved that file."

He glared at Joy. "I had not."

Julius spoke up. "See, this is why they tell you to save often."

"In case your laptop spontaneously morphs into a furry critter?" Ann said it and everyone but Tyrus laughed.

Joy was still unhappy. "Enough. We need to know now, Tyrus. Spill it."

Tyrus handed the bunny to one of the deadliest assassins in the world, and Nix accepted it and looked it in the eyes.

"I left the scene to find Wills."

"Yes. A year ago, and you never explained."

"Yes, because I didn't explain. I needed to research strategies to protect ourselves as well as set up a network capable of watching Wills. I'm sorry it took me so long, but she is aligned with a powerful Mythic. I wanted us to stand a chance at winning when we go up against him."

He grabbed his phone, and seconds later, the TV in the living room showed the picture of the man from the pool. "This is her employer. Dr. Blanc. He runs Euro Genetics, a rival company of Dr. Jackson. We believe he is the one responsible for the bombing."

"And he's one of us?" Connor folded his arms, clearly unhappy. "What is he?"

"His Mythic is a gorgon." He tapped a couple buttons, bringing up another photo. "This is a statue of Medusa, a Greek myth I'm sure you're familiar with."

Nix continued. "She was raped in a temple and turned into a beast so men would never want her again. One of the Greek myths that enrages me the most."

"While we can't find any evidence of the actual existence of Medusa, we do know that Dr. Blanc is a gorgon. He lives in London but is originally from France. We aren't sure of his age, but he is older than me, younger than Levi."

"I don't see any snakes on his head." Ann said it to herself, but the others heard her. Julius chuckled.

"No, but I could smell the death around him. Like stone."

"Exactly." Tyrus brought up another slide. "This is a bird's eye view of Dr. Blanc's estate. You see the labyrinth?"

Ann looked to Joy, who winked back at her.

"We happened to be by the pool a few moments ago."

Tyrus' eyes grew wide, and he glared at Joy, who shrugged. "Don't take them there again without us accompanying you."

Joy nodded.

Ann was a bit upset. Tyrus still treated them as if they were fragile. They were powerful. She sighed, a little too loudly, and his gaze landed on her, before quickly returning to the screen.

He cleared his throat and continued. "You see the statues?"

Ann was beginning to see where he was headed. "Are…are they people?"

Everyone was instantly tense.

He nodded. "There are over one hundred statues in this labyrinth. You probably passed by at least one today. Yes, these weren't carved by an artist, but by Dr. Blanc, in death."

"Normal people? Or…"

"Mythics as well." He switched slides to reveal a dragon statue. "At least a couple of other Mythics have attempted to defeat him over the centuries. No one knows who this is, but we know he's taken down a dragon. When and if we go after him, we need to know how to take him down without losing anyone else."

"And you didn't tell us, because?"

He sighed. "In a little under two months, you'd had a shocking education. I thought it might do you some good to rest. To not have to worry about monsters for a while and regain a sense of normalcy. If I was wrong, I'm sorry, but I was trying to be a good mentor."

"Why bring it up now?" Seth's whisper sounded unthreatening.

"Because you have adjusted. Most of you have a rhythm going with your new jobs, or college, in Connor's case. You've grown, you're in control of your powers. I think we are ready to sit down and figure this out."

"Also," Nix used her phone and brought up another image. This was a contract. "This came through on the dark web two days ago."

Ann knew what this was. "This is one of your 'work' contracts."

Nix nodded. "It is."

"Who is the target?" Julius was tense, until Ann placed a hand on his knee. He smiled back at her. It could be any of them.

"Its Levi."

"Alive or dead?"

"Dead. With video proof."

The teens were silent for a moment. Connor was the first to say something. "Well, isn't this a good thing? Are we forgetting what this guy did?" The anger in his voice was clear.

"We are certainly not forgetting his nature." Nix touched her screen again and the TV went blank. "As a Leviathan, he is capable of destruction. However, you saw him pull me from the fire when Wills left me to die."

"Isn't he big and scary though? Can't he take care of himself? Why should we care?" Julius usually disagreed with Connor, but the two could also be thick as thieves if it was necessary.

Ann spoke up. "I think I understand." She waited a moment, while everyone looked in her direction. "You mean the code. You owe him as one human to another for saving your life, but there is also the code. Even my enemy is family. I think, in this case, it applies to Levi."

"Yes. There are three highly skilled assassins in the world who are active in the Mythic community. They are feared above everyone else. The contracts I take are small in comparison. This one out on Levi…it's huge. One of the two others will take it, or both. And that means not only could he be in danger, but we all could."

She swiped her phone once more and brought up a set of facts. "No pictures exist of the other two. While Tyrus has been creating a profile on Dr. Blanc, I've been tracking down their kills. These are their stats. We don't even have names, or their Mythic type. They are efficient. I'm almost, impressed at how little information exists on them."

"Based on Mythic listed keywords, I was able to find out some things. One assassin is male, the other female. We can start with the male." She swiped again, and the screen changed.

"This is a revered painting of a man at death. I'm sure you know the artist, Joy?"

"Yes! That painting is worth a fortune."

"I believe it was commissioned by the assassin to commemorate his kill. At that time, the man pictured, though unnamed, bears a remarkable resemblance to a notorious figure who vanished under mysterious circumstances. This painting, *Mort De Mon Ennemi, Mon Ami*, I believe, was commissioned by our male assassin as evidence of his, possibly first, kill. Although the subject is not known, you can see some evidence of who he might be in the painting. Note the sand on his boots, the pieces of wood around him. These are tiny clues that the assassin told the artist to add. This painting was sent from an anonymous source to a wealthy Englishman during the era of colonization who had a large trading company. It was common for those trading ships to be attacked by pirates. I believe you're looking at a depiction of the death of Henry Every, aka Henry Avery, aka-"

Tyrus interrupted. "…the pirate king."

"Yes. One of the few historical pirates who vanished without a trace. However, it is my belief that our male assassin was hired to find and kill this pirate, possibly in exchange for the loot. We know from other paintings at the time about what the pirate looked like. Joy, what is this painting famous for?"

"For showing a blurred face. Almost like modern day editing, you can't really make out the features of the person's face. It was ages ahead of its time. You think it was done to conceal this person's identity?"

"I do. There are also accounts of other mysterious 'disappearances' over history that I believe are at the hands of our male assassin. These include powerful figures from crucial times in history that lead to historic changes. This makes me wonder if he has access to someone like Joy."

Upon hearing her name, she squeaked. "Not this Joy." Then she crossed her arms, angry at the insinuation.

Nix smiled. "Other fortune tellers exist."

"How do we combat a lethal assassin whose victims just vanish with a Mythic sidekick that can see the future?"

"I am working that problem."

"And the second?" Ann didn't like the sound of any of this.

"The female. Unlike assassin one, this particular lethal lady leaves her victim visible, but with no apparent cause of death. They just…die."

Another new image came up. "Her latest victim, three years ago. This wasn't just a famous person or a politically influential figure." Nix paused for a moment.

"Do you want me to say it?" Tyrus was soft, sympathetic.

"No." Nix cleared her throat and continued. "This is a former colleague of mine and a Mythic. I used her as a source of information, an informant. I believe that she was killed in an attempt to send a message to me about my own contract killings, however, I haven't completed that particular puzzle yet."

"What kind of Mythic was she?"

Nix sighed. "She was a Pegasus."

Joy perked up. "Now I see it! Right!"

Nix waited for her to explain, but she didn't. She just went back to twirling her hair. "Moving forward…" Nix clicked on the next slide. "She hunts Mythics, specifically. I believe she sees it as a challenge. She's taken down a dragon, a Pegasus, an ifrit, and a chupacabra, that I know of."

The monitor went dark. "That is all I have on them, for now. I'll bring you more as I find it. It will take all of us to deal with these two."

Ann found the courage to speak. "For Levi, who kidnapped your nephew and double crossed us."

Nix eyed her a moment. "For yourselves, because you are connected to the thing that Levi loves most, and therefore, may be a target, whether you like him or not."

"What do you mean, what he loves most?"

Tyrus cleared his throat. "Assassins worth their salt don't just attack. They plan, they plot, they find weaknesses and exploit them. For Levi, his greatest regret is what happened to Nix, with her bird."

He placed a hand on her shoulder, showing support. Again, Ann felt the need to clarify. "Is that your greatest regret, as well?"

His face grew red. This time Nix placed a hand on his shoulder. "One of them, yes."

Ann looked to her mentor for clarification. "I just…don't think I'd be able to forgive someone who did that to me."

Nix nodded. "After the first decade, it got easier. Remember, we are older than we appear, and with time, you see the hidden threads, the manipulations, the ways that some people bend others to their will, and you learn grace. I won't say the anger is gone, but its fire has dimmed. Tyrus, especially, has changed since then. He's taken on your education, he's helping us all get through this alive, when other Mythics would much prefer the Five of you be dealt with."

"What harm are we causing?" Connor shifted his weight, uncomfortable.

"It's not the current harm, it's your potential. The fire that created you was synthetic, man-made. We still don't know in what ways you will differ as you develop. This can scare Mythics stuck in their ways."

"Are you saying that because we have a different origin, we could potentially face discrimination in the Mythic community?" Julius stood and placed his hands on his head. "Man. That just…sucks."

Tyrus walked over to him and patted his shoulder. "Mythics can't escape the bits of them that are human, and humans are programmed to fear what they don't understand. You have us, though, as imperfect as we are."

He glanced at Ann, but his smile was sympathetic. She felt her bird ruffle its feathers. She still didn't trust him, completely. He must have sensed it because he backed away. Ever since their encounter on the rooftop, he'd been very careful with her. The others trusted him, and Nix had forgiven him, but something pulled at her, made her uneasy around him, and she wasn't about to discount her gut, not yet.

"So, Ann, how did your first day of work go?"

Joy giggled loudly. Ann looked at her and rolled her eyes, and started explaining…

Nix listened intently then took a moment to think about her answer before she responded. "So, nothing with flammable materials? So, no gas station attendant work, no paint, no fast food, no bartending."

Ann sighed. "I wish I had the drive any of you do. I just don't feel it. I wish I knew I was a painter like Joy or college bound like Connor."

Tyrus spoke. "Your childhood may be influencing that a bit. While the others were busy asking questions like, 'who am I' you were busy doing something much harder."

She was surprised at his insightfulness. "Yes. I was worried about surviving."

"That goal, being over, now, we hope. Now is when you're asking those questions. Maybe some time alone to reflect on who you want to be may help you."

"You can stay here as long as it takes for you to figure that out."

Joy giggled. Ann eyed her sideways. "What?"

Joy bit her lip. Ann knew as a being that could see possible futures, this meant she was worried about saying not enough or too much. Ann let her debate that silently while she went to the fridge and took out bottled water. She downed it quickly, then took out another. By the time she returned, Joy was ready.

"You…can stay." She returned to playing with her hair. Ann was confused, and wanted to ask more, but knew better.

"So Connor, you've been updated. I know you have to get back to class. Julius and Seth, you're sharing space downtown for now?"

They nodded.

"Joy, still with your parents selling paintings online?"

Joy gave a thumbs up. "Good, then everyone has a roof over their head for the time being."

Joy giggled, again. This time, everyone glared at her. "What? Just… a lot of motion in the universe today." She was gone a moment later.

"I guess that means I'm taking you both back. See you soon, Ann."

She nodded at Seth as he touched both Connor and Julius on the shoulder, then they, too, were gone, and she was alone with the two older Mythics.

"I guess I get the couch for now?"

Nix nodded. "Ann needs her room back."

"Wait, he's staying here, too?"

They both seemed surprised. "Is that a problem? He can't teleport back and forth from the camp, so we just assumed…"

Tyrus spoke when she failed. "I can get a room, Ann, if you're not comfortable."

Ann felt instantly guilty. "No, I just, didn't expect it. It's fine as long as I have my own space."

Nix nodded. "Everything is just as you left it. I changed the sheets and everything this morning in case."

Ann sighed and gave a hasty, "Ok. I'll be going then."

She walked away before the blush formed fully on her face. She wasn't certain if this arrangement between Tyrus and Nix was platonic or not, but she had a sneaking suspicion regarding Joy's earlier mirth. She knew this would be awkward for Ann and hadn't said anything.

Shutting her door, she began to text her friend for an explanation.

JOY!

Ann?

You could have warned me.

Nope.

fr? Y?

???

Its awkward being in a house with a couple. Y?

Lol. He isn't with Nix anymore. You're fine. Use this time to deal w/ ur issues with him. We need him to be on our side.

Imma kick him out.

You will do no such thing! Deal!

Y?

He will save your life, one day. Just trust me.

*eye roll

Fine.

That's my girl!

She swiped over to another app and began to look through other open job postings. Financial independence just jumped to the top of her priorities. She filtered the results to exclude fast food and convenience stores. Two less possibilities, but there had to be something out there she didn't mind doing that she could safely do as a phoenix. And she'd find it. After a few minutes, her eyes lit up. This could be something…

The phone rang twice before Dr. Gregory Jackson picked up.

"Yes, Aunt?"

"The Five have been updated."

"Excellent. What is the next task on your agenda?"

"Tyrus and I are going to continue to plan. How are you?"

He cleared his throat, reflecting on the past year. After Levi left him in the middle of the state park on the night of the bombing, he'd had to suffer through dehydration, overexertion, sunburn, and begging to contact his aunt in the nearest small town. She sent a squad of Mythics to pick him up, taking him to a safehouse she used periodically.

Food was delivered automatically, left on the doorstep. While his usual diet consisted of lavish and tasty dishes, for the last year, he'd existed on simple meals he could handle cooking himself. He rarely went outside, and never during the daylight hours. A new burner phone arrived every month and the old was thrown away.

"I'm as healthy as can be expected. I'll be grateful when this charade is over. Any update on that?"

"I don't want it known that you survived the bombing until I have everything in place. We don't want him to be able to take you out."

He sighed. "I appreciate that you've spent the last year both protecting me as well as rebuilding our family empire, but you can understand how…small this feels, how much I want to reclaim my life."

Silence followed for a moment. "I understand. The building is going up, and as soon as it's finished, you'll have a state-of-the-art place to reclaim your life. I only ask that you give me time to secure it. Then you can announce your comeback."

"And the timeline on that?"

"Once the building is up, it should only take another couple of weeks to staff it, then you're good to rise."

"So, I still just... sit here and wait?"

"I'm sorry, Gregory."

She hung up. He sat down at the tiny kitchen table complete

with chipping white paint. He laughed, thinking of the extreme turn his life had taken. The bombing meant to kill him and destroy his legacy hadn't succeeded, but neither had it entirely failed. He was crippled, his network removed from him, unable to keep tabs on the enemies he knew were responsible. It fell to his aunt and Tyrus to keep him protected. His destiny hadn't before been in another's control, and the frustration he felt over this change was…difficult to deal with.

Unable to do much else, he walked out of the kitchen and through the tiny living room, opening the door to the one car garage. A punching bag lay at the back that would work nicely to calm those negative emotions. He slowly wrapped his hands then envisioned his enemy's face at the center of the bag, throwing his shoulder into the first punch.

The wafting scent of human was overwhelming for him after decades in the wilderness, yet Tommy was able to control his actions as he stepped off the bus into the heart of downtown St. Blaise. He swallowed hard as his mouth watered, and despite his best efforts, he found himself inhaling deeply the scent of perfumes and colognes that most twenty-somethings wore. To him, they were intoxicating, like the smell of pumpkin pie cooking in the stove, but more compelling. His stomach protested his control, but his willpower, the last of it he would show, was adamant. He needed to find a safe space away from the people buffet.

He turned to his right and walked along the towering buildings toward a small, cheap motel. People shied away from him as he walked, shivering at the sudden drop in temperature. The sun's warmth plummeted as clouds grew over the city, too quickly to be a natural occurrence. The wind picked up, cold and drafty despite June.

His sunken face looked starved, and in reality, he'd been on a strict free-range diet for decades. His once shiny green eyes looked lifeless and pale. You are what you eat, and he'd been surviving on the old, sick and dying since… Well, now was not the time to reminisce.

He walked into the hotel, and toward the clerk who sat browsing the internet, unaware of the strange man in front of him. He smelled of cigarettes and vodka. It turned his stomach.

Tommy cleared his throat as he approached the counter. The clerk didn't even look up. "Yeah?"

"I called about a room?" His voice was wispy, like the wind itself powered his vocal cords, his element showing.

The strange sound drew the clerk's eyes away from his phone. They widened as they took in the tall but slender figure standing before him. Tommy fought the smile that usually spread across his face. The clerk's fear was a sweet honey to him, almost enough to drown out the alcohol and cigarette smoke. Still, he knew he had to refrain from his nature, for now.

"Name?" Finally, the clerk spoke.

"It's under Tommy. Tommy Smith."

Fumbling with the keyboard, the clerk silently found the reservation. "ID?"

Tommy opened his wallet and produced his latest fake ID. "Here."

The clerk quickly copied it and produced a key card. "Room 143, last on the left."

Tommy smiled and whispered, "thank you" as the clerk shivered in the cold. That was part of his power, stealing the sunlight, encouraging all sorts of hungers in others. Walking along the hallway, he avoided a group of excited adults, keeping from taking in their scents. Young urban adults tasted like rare cuts of pork tenderloin. Juicy, healthy and flavorful. While he knew he would have to eat during his stay, his last remnants of humanity were haunting him.

Some Mythics got to shine, bright and vibrant like heroes in ancient tales. They were the Dragons, the Griffins, the Unicorns. Their psychic counterparts wanted to save lives and make the world a better place. It was in their nature to be "good." He'd always envied Tyrus, the Red Dragon. How simple it must be for him to worry only about which choice was the most right? Which was the greatest kindness?

For Tommy, his Mythic was more curse than blessing. He lived by a different set of rules, guided by a different, more primal existence. His Mythic bid him to eat, to savor, to devour all things in sight. His concern was not about good or evil, but the hunger, insatiable and fierce, that dominated his thoughts both in wakefulness and sleep. He knew how evil he was. For years, he'd refrained from feasting on human flesh, for decades he tried to tame his nature. Yet, it was inevitable that he fail, that the hunger would consume him. He wasn't in St. Blaise just to gorge. He was a prisoner of his Mythic, a powerful creature of greed, and this city was his last meal.

Chapter 2

72°F

FBI agent Ben Ryan, Tyrus's government contact, scrolled through his notifications until one caught his eye, a missing person reported in one of the lower economic areas of St. Blaise, just south of downtown. Though it wasn't his area, as he was working homicide, he routinely scrolled through those listings. Many were found alive, but a few could turn into a case. This particular report was less than twenty-four hours old, an elderly woman whose son reported her missing around 7 am. What was unusual was the temperature inside the house. He noted how cold it was, yet his mother was adamantly against air conditioning. He marked it for later, wondering if there was Mythic activity involved, an unofficial assignment he continuously completed for Tyrus.

He jumped as his desk phone rang. "Agent Ryan."

"Agent Ryan, can you please come to my office at your earliest available opportunity?"

Recognizing the voice of the Special Agent in Charge, he cleared his throat. "On my way directly."

He stood, adjusting his suit jacket and headed toward the elevator, wondering what Special Agent Stewart wanted. On his walk, a waving hand stalled his progress. "Yeah, Barnes?"

A short, plump data analyst with glasses smiled wide at him. "You get called up to see the SAC?"

"Yeah, headed there."

"Do me a favor and drop these off with his assistant?"

A stack of papers was handed to him. "Can't email these?"

"No, unfortunately. Need to arrive sealed."

He noted the seal on the envelope. "Gotcha. On it."

"You and your wife coming to the barbecue on Saturday?"

"I was planning on it."

"Great. See you then."

He didn't mind doing favors, but with continuously monitored secure servers, he wondered what he could possibly be delivering. He continued to ponder as the elevator rose to the top floor. As he exited, the receptionist greeted him.

"Go right in. He's expecting you."

"These are for you?" The papers were taken, the seal broken, and returned. "Actually, there for you. You'll need them in the meeting." They gestured toward the large double doors, and Agent Ryan strode forward, a bit anxious.

SAC Stewart sat at his desk, his eyes intent on whatever he was reading. Another Agent he was unfamiliar with sat on the right of three chairs. Agent Ryan walked forward and cleared his throat loudly.

"Take a seat. Almost finished."

He sat in the middle of three chairs and waited, opening the folder to view the contents for the first time. His voice caught, before he released a breath, the only slight sign of surprise. Looking back up, the SAC's gaze was intent and directed at him.

"So, you were surprised that we knew?"

Swallowing hard, not daring a glance at the other mystery guest, Agent Ryan felt very uncomfortable. "I can explain."

"Let me give you the full details, first." He picked up a remote, and the room went dark, shades drawing, and a large screen descending from the ceiling. "You see, we needed you here, specifically, to help us with this. Play your cards right, here, be honest, and you'll have a team working beneath you, something quite uncommon for a new hire. Lie to me in any way, and I'll know, and you'll be labeled a traitor."

Agent Ryan squirmed in his seat, ready to tell as much of the truth as needed. This could impact everything.

Ann walked into the building, a bit weary and self-conscious. Her grey eyes darted back and forth, taking in all the activity. Her business casual attire didn't quite fit perfectly, and she was suddenly aware that one of her stockings had a hole in the toe. After the virtual interview, she was showing up for work for the first time, and wanted to fit in. Searching for the correct name, she saw the office she needed, and walked forward.

The door was open, the HR rep sitting at her computer. Ann knocked on the door trim softly.

She looked up immediately, a huge smile brightening the room. Despite her awkwardness, Ann smiled back. Maybe this would work out. "Hello. I'm Ann Smith."

"Hi, Ann. Come in and shut the door behind you. Let's talk about your new responsibilities at Herbert Bank and Trust."

Ann shut the door and sat down. A lot was riding on this. After the failed attempts at jobs that didn't fit, she'd found an open teller position near Nyx's apartment. She desperately wanted this to work. "Sorry, I'm a bit nervous."

A tilt in the HR's head showed a bit of sympathy. "I have no doubt with your grades in math that you'll do well here. Now, tell me what happened at the end of your last school year."

Much like Agent Ryan, she was suddenly uncomfortable. Images of the bombing that changed her life floated in her head, but she knew she had to be prepared for those questions. Recounting the details carefully, she created a miracle out of a disaster.

An hour later, Agent Ryan left the office with his new companion, Mack, who was currently undercover, his pseudonym secret. There was an intensity behind his eyes, and a bit of grief that showed through during the meeting. For him, this assignment was personal. Agent Ryan respected someone who could remain professional and keep their emotions from clouding their judgement.

He waited until they were in the elevator to ask. "So where do we start?"

Mack pushed the button for the parking garage. "I'll fill you in on all of it, and the current assignment, but not here."

Agent Ryan nodded. They spent the entire ride in silence.

When the doors opened to the secure parking garage, Mack handed him a white card with an address on it. "This is my base of operations. Meet me there. Two hours from now. We can talk freely there."

Agent Ryan narrowed his eyes and turned his head to the side. The question was obvious, but silent. Mack responded, "no, we can't talk here. I won't risk it. Even if no one is involved. This... matters. I'll see you at that address in two hours."

He walked to his car, aware of the sounds around him, just in case. Getting into his vehicle, he pulled out quickly from the garage into traffic, then placed an earbud into his right ear and said, "call Tyrus." He would want to know this, and Ben wasn't keeping the smartest mastermind he knew out of the loop.

He felt the call radiate in his pocket as he sat outside a coffeehouse in view of Barnes Bank and Trust, watching and waiting, in case Seth's famous gut was right. He fumbled through his pocket and answered on the third ring.

"Yeah?"

"Ellie needs your help for dinner. Think you can stop by the new place?"

"Kinda sudden, though?"

"Yeah, well, newborn. Sudden dinner plans. Help me out?"

"Sure. When?" Tyrus heard the strain in his friend's voice. Something was up that couldn't be discussed over the phone.

"Seven thirty?"

"Will do."

"Thanks. See you then."

"Yep."

As he hung up, he glanced to his right and jumped. Seth was suddenly beside him. "So, this gut feeling needed backup? That bad?"

"Not sure. Here in case." Seth reached into his pocket and pulled out a twenty, setting it on the table.

"I can pay for a coffee."

Seth smiled. "Just in case you forget."

Tyrus glared but didn't object further. "Anyone else present at the moment? Or going to be here?"

"Julius is…around. Watching someone."

"So a luck element, two fire elements and an enforcer? Wouldn't want to be that guy."

Seth nodded. "Yeah, he is about to have a very bad day. Let's go."

Tyrus rose, forgetting to pay as Seth had predicted, and the two men walked toward the intersection separating the coffeehouse from the bank. Tyrus scanned the crowd, but a Mythic could hide well if they wanted to. No one in particular stood out. He began to doubt Seth, until they were halfway through the intersection.

Then he felt the wind. It whipped into his face, sharp and cold like ice crystals piercing his skin. It felt familiar, but he couldn't quite place it. The temperature dropped sharply as they crossed, the sun hiding away. Whatever Mythic this was, it was powerful. He suspected a water or wind element.

"Let's get inside the bank quickly." He said it softly, and they jogged, reaching the entrance just behind Julius, who smoothly held the door for them to walk inside. Tyrus nodded to him, and in response, Julius motioned to the right. Tyrus moved to the left and opened the second set of doors.

Ann glared at him from behind one of the teller booths, momentarily pausing, the money frozen in her hands. Before he could shrug his shoulders in apology, her head bent down, intent on counting the bills in her hands. He saw her psychic bird ruffle its feathers and take slight shape, hovering above its master. Neither of them were happy, but this was Seth's mission, not his. Getting into a line that wasn't hers, he nonchalantly waited for a signal, anything that told him he was needed. Julius got in line for an ATM while Seth sat in the chairs for a personal banker. Between the four of them, most areas inside the lobby were covered if anything happened.

Ann felt her heart pounding suddenly and knew her cheeks were slightly red from the change in blood pressure. What the hell was he doing here? Sighing softly, she resumed counting the till. Realizing she had lost her spot, she started over from the beginning of the stack.

"Excuse me, Miss?"

Forcing the frustration down so her eyes wouldn't show her flame, she smiled, fake and wide and lifted her eyes, ready to tell the customer she was just in training and couldn't help them quite yet. The words stuck in her throat when she saw the man before her. Dark, sullen eyes hid in the folds of a frail face. He didn't look old, but the taunt skin seemed to indicate food insecurity.

Worried this person needed her help, her demeanor changed. "Is there something I can do to help you?"

He smiled, but it didn't ease her. In fact, the smile only served to creep her out. He looked less desperate and more dangerous. "I think you may, indeed, be able to help me." He reached up and placed a too thin hand onto the countertop in front of her. "Your warmth drew me in, instantly."

She froze, seeing movement in her peripheral vision. "Is…that metaphorical?"

He tilted his head, and his voice came out strange, contorted. As if the wind were whispering something frightening to her soul. "Not at all. I came here for a snack, but instead, I find… resplendence in the form of a phoenix. Tell me, have you heard of a creature named 'Nix?'"

At the mention of her mentor, she breathed in deeply, but the cold air pricked her lungs. Coughing, she couldn't answer. As the other tellers turned to look in her direction, the man seemed to vanish into the crowd, and the cold along with him. Tyrus was at the window immediately.

"What happened?" His turquoise eyes met hers, full of concern. She shook her head, saying, "nothing. Just a strange customer. Please go. I'm working or trying to. No Mythic Madness right now, *please.*"

He looked a little wounded, but she couldn't help it. She needed to do this right. She gave him a sympathetic look but started counting again. Tyrus walked away from the counter, toward the ATM machines, where she saw Julius standing next to Seth. As she wondered what had earned the company of the three of them, she lost count for the fourth time, and frustratedly, started over again.

Her manager walked over at the exact inopportune time. "What, you're still counting that stack? I thought you had math skills? Here." Taking it from her, she put it through an automatic money counter. "Just do this twice and record the count as correct so we can move on." The annoyance clear in her voice, Ann bit her tongue to keep her frustration low. This was not going well.

Tyrus exited the Bank with Seth and Julius.

"I'd like you two to stay put, if you can. Something spooked her, but she won't tell me what happened. Just watch. We know how capable she is, but she may need support. I didn't like the look of the man at her counter."

"You thinking he was one of us?" Julius shoved his hands into his pockets. He didn't like the cold.

"Yeah. Considering the weather effects, I'm thinking wind or water. Water she can handle alone, but wind… she'll need the back up."

"Any idea who this is?"

"Too many puzzle pieces, not enough connected to make that assumption. Sorry."

"Is it Levi?" Seth didn't seem as bothered by the drop in temperature.

"I'll ask Nix to give him a call to see. Don't know what business he would have with Ann, though. Stay here and I'll see what's going on."

He walked away from the two and into an alleyway, where his

skin slowly morphed from human to his dragon scales. He removed his jacket in time for his wings to emerge and pushed off from the ground, too fast for most humans to see his climb into the sky.

He flew over the gathering clouds, above them. They were low hanging, which only made him more certain this was Mythic related and not a natural occurrence. While he would have preferred to stay himself, he knew he hadn't earned Ann's trust yet. The guilt tugged at his heart, remembering how he had been used to take down Nyx's orange phoenix. Locating her apartment building some moments later, he lowered himself just as quickly, landing on the roof of her building. Taking out his phone, he texted one word.

Roof.

OMW

He waited at the door until it opened, and Nix let him inside, then his dragon form merged back to human. Expertly donning his coat, he walked in front of her and said, "we need to talk. Someone is here."

Ann continued working, but she knew she wasn't alone. The air conditioning must have been turned up as all the employees kept shivering. Whoever that man was, he hadn't left for good, and unfortunately, she'd sent her support away. Looking around the lobby, she knew she may be on her own to deal with whoever was messing with the temperature. Calling her bird to her, she felt the warmth of it surrounding her, and she softly increased the heat until the other employees stopped shivering. Two could play with the temperature. The bird's claws gripped her shoulders, and though no normal human could see it, she felt supported and strong. If she had to, she could face this person alone.

Her manager came to check her work again. "Much better. I'm

going to let you shadow the drive through windows for the rest of the day. Come to the back with me. Remind me to get the heating and cooling checked out. This hot and cold is making it uncomfortable in here."

She nodded and followed her manager to the locked door, where she watched her manager enter her pin. As the door opened, she felt the cold force push against her warmth. She turned, facing the slim man with the creepy smile. He looked pleasantly surprised. Ann stepped between the man and her manager, a clear protective motion.

"I'll give you one thing, you're strong."

The manager began to turn away from the door to Ann. In the second it took for her to turn to Ann, the figure dissipated into air, the cold force of it pushing against her like a tidal wave of wind that slammed into her, stealing the air from her lungs. Try as she might, she couldn't breathe. Looking to her manager, seeing her in a similar state, they had seconds before they passed out. As a crowd rushed toward them, Ann saw the door to the back shut firmly just before she lost consciousness, annoyed that she'd been beaten.

She woke outside the bank on a bench, between her two peers, who both supported her waist. Breathing deeply, she let her mind steady itself before she spoke.

"Ann? Are you ok?" Seth's voice was soft and gentle.

"Who did this?" Julius was the opposite, aggressive and ready to defend her.

She cleared her throat. "It was a man. He went into the back room. He knocked my manager and I out to get back there. He just... vanished into air. What happened after I passed out?"

"We got back inside to see you passed out." Julius secured both his hands around her waist. "Seth went into the back, but he was already done. Everyone in the back room was out. We got you out of there and it took a few minutes for you to wake."

She felt her head stop spinning. "Ok. Thank you for that." She looked up. The sky was clearing, the sun peeking through the clouds. "I need to go back and finish my shift."

She tried to stand too quickly. It was as if all her strength was gone. Her legs were like jelly. "What the hell?"

"I'll go explain to the manager that you hit your head and won't be able to work today."

Before she could stop him, Seth jogged away. Julius stood with her, his hands holding her up, but her torso and his could touch. They were almost the same height, about half an inch difference between them. She helped steady herself by placing her arms around his shoulders, slowly increasing the amount of leverage placed upon her feet, and away from the warmth of his built chest. All of them had started weight training. It wasn't just your Mythic that could fight, and the difference in muscle mass may matter when evenly matched.

She felt the blush rush to her cheeks as she suddenly felt the contact too intimate for comfort. She avoided his gaze, looking down at her feet, which still felt too shaky for her to stand on her own.

"You ok, Ann?" His concern just made her blush deepen.

"Yeah, I'm just…awkward." She pushed away from him when she was able. "I'm ok, I think."

She glanced in his direction, but he wasn't meeting her gaze either. Was he blushing too? The awkwardness caused him to retract. Neither of them had ever thought of the other in that way, and the sudden shift was disconcerting. Ann sat back down quickly and focused on the event unfolding.

"This is not a great first day."

Julius chuckled. "Yeah. I can see why you'd be frustrated."

Seth came back out of the bank and walked toward her with his shoulders slumped, a defeated look on his face. She knew he had bad news. Handing her a note, the half-smile was sympathetic.

"I'm fired, aren't I?" She took the note and called her flame, which erupted in her palm, burning the small paper into ash.

He nodded.

Ann rolled her eyes. "Can someone take me home, please? No

reason to stay here." Despair set in, even though she was determined. She felt a tightness in her throat, feeling as if she'd failed personally, even though the attack was not her fault. She could feel the tears forming, and she didn't want them to fall. Distance seemed the wisest choice.

Julius patted her back, a silent show of support. Seth took her hand and they bounced to Nyx's apartment. Seth smiled at her before he vanished again. She sat down on the couch, listening to the phone call Nix was on. Tyrus came toward her, but she shook her head, unready for more conversation. He backed off and sat in a chair, giving her space.

"So, you aren't involved? "Nix sounded angry. Only one person in the world could bring out that level of rue in her voice. She must be talking with Levi.

"I believe you, we just needed to rule you out. No, don't…"

Ann felt the humidity behind her rise suddenly, a whirl of air following. She knew Levi had just used a water portal to transport into the apartment, but she couldn't work up the effort to look in his direction.

Tyrus saw her struggle and asked, "coffee?"

She nodded, her eyes silently thanking him for the courtesy.

His smile told her he understood. He walked away as Nix stood protectively near her.

"We didn't need you, we just needed to eliminate you."

"Well, now you have my attention. What can you tell me about it, Ann?"

She swallowed hard, not quite ready to speak, shaking her head.

"That bad?" Levi walked around and took Tyrus's seat.

Nix folded her arms in front of her. "Let her have a minute."

Tyrus returned with coffee. She gave a watery smile and accepted the cup, sipping the hot liquid a bit too quickly and burning her tongue. *Coffee hot, self.* Still, the slight pain helped reorient her thoughts, brought her out of her emotional state.

"Yeah, just give me a few minutes to reorient. Just got back."

Levi gave her a sympathetic look, which was disconcerting coming from someone so deadly. "I'll go check out the Bank, then. Be back soon."

Another rush of water and wind, and he was gone. Nix growled low. "He infuriates me sometimes."

Tyrus nodded but didn't say anything. "How is the coffee?"

"Hot." She took another careful sip and focused on her breathing. She felt the well of emotion crawl back a bit more. "So, when you left, the manager took me to the back, to the door with the pin code. The guy waited until she'd entered her pin, and the door was open, then…" She fumbled for the right words. "Stole the air from our lungs. I passed out. Woke and came here." *Leave the awkwardness out. Good job!*

"Air element, then." Tyrus looked at Nyx.

"Damn." Nyx's sigh caused Ann to worry.

"Why is that bad?"

"So elemental discussion. You know that the three of us are fire elements. Levi is water."

"Yeah."

"The four basic elements are fire, water, earth, and air. Any mythic with one of these abilities is termed an elemental. There are other kinds of Mythics, like Joy and Seth, who are both considered luck Mythics."

"Right."

"The four elements must always be in balance with each other. Think of it like an extension of the scientific principle, 'for every action there is an equal and opposite reaction.'"

"So…" she was still confused as to where he was going.

"So, Levi is a very powerful being. He's lived a thousand years. His power in water must be balanced by our power. Including several others. Omega Flame will keep creating fire elements to balance the power of water Levi controls until the elemental 'scales' are even."

"A way of keeping each elemental power in check?"

"Yes. A natural system of checks and balances."

"Ok. That I understand. Now explain how that has to do with air? Water and Fire are opposed, so air would balance with earth, right?"

"Yes, but also, there's another level. Fire and water compose one side, as air and earth compose another, and the two sides are dynamic with each other. So not only do water and fire have to balance each other, but together, their combined power must be balanced against earth and air."

"So all of us fire elements balance Levi, and fire plus Levi must balance all air and earth?"

"Yes."

"I'm still confused as to why that makes Nix irate."

Nix chuckled and sat down. "The balance was upset when the fire became synthetic. We aren't sure if the scales accommodate you, or if the Five of you are anomalous. Tyrus and I are trying to figure out a couple of possibilities with little to go on. Either, the scales consider you, which would mean air and earth get stronger, and create more Mythics."

"Which would be bad."

"Exactly. Or, you're not considered, whereas this Mythic may have already existed, be someone we know of."

"Which is…"

"Still bad."

Tyrus opened his laptop. "According to the Mural, the only place in North America where Mythic names are recorded, three air elementals exist. Only their names show, but it gives us a place to start."

"What are their names?"

"Chimera…"

"Hasn't left Asia in over a hundred years, and commands all four elements, not just wind."

"You keep tabs on them?" Ann was constantly amazed at her mentor's abilities.

"Have to."

"So not Chimera?"

"Not likely, no."

"Second name is Raijin."

"If one of the Three were given a contract in the States, I'd have been warned."

"The three?" Ann tilted her head.

"Three Assassins. Levi, Raijin, and I."

"There are only three?"

Nix smiled and Tyrus had a sudden coughing fit to hide his laughter.

"Only three of us at the top. We get first dibs on special contracts. Had to earn the right to be in the "top three" so to speak."

Ann swallowed hard with new respect for her. "Ok. So its not likely to be him either?"

"No."

"So who is left?"

"Either someone we don't know and can't anticipate, or…" Tyrus sighed and looked at Nyx.

"Tommy." She said it softly.

Tyrus nodded. "Tommy."

The silence that followed perplexed her. She let it linger over a few sips of coffee, but when the two remained so, she asked, "who is Tommy?"

The collective sigh only served to add to her frustration, and she sipped again, waiting.

"Tommy…" Nix began.

"Is a problem, because he was once a friend." Tyrus finished for her.

"Exactly," she continued, "he was part of the group before my phoenix was taken. Part of that manipulation."

"Which side was he on?"

"Neither. He was so young, the escalation just... destroyed him. We lost track of him after the fact. Me because I was healing, Tyrus and Levi because…"

"Because we were seeking retribution. Honestly, I haven't talked to Tommy in years."

"Neither have I. Which means this could be a huge problem."

Silence again.

"Why?" Ann asked, a bit too loudly.

"Because of his mythic."

"An air element?"

"Yes. But more than that… he is one of those Mythics whose connection is all curse, no blessing."

"Can you elaborate?"

"He's a Wendigo." Tyrus clicked a remote and the screen lit, allowing her to see various pictures online of Tommy's Mythic.

"What's a Wendigo?"

"A wind spirit of greed, based in Native American myth. They consume, never feeling satiated."

"Is that why the bank got cold?"

"Yes. When they grow in power, they can affect the weather, removing the warmth of the sun, the happiness from life. They also increase the appetites of others around them."

"What does that mean?"

"Urges grow, hungers grow. People prone to overeating overeat more. Those with gambling addictions gamble more."

"All hungers grow."

She felt her cheeks turning red again. That would be why she'd reacted to Julius. "Got it. So, he's pretty powerful now."

"Yes. But worst of all…"

Tyrus set the laptop down and looked at her intently. "Worst of all is the actual hunger."

"So, he has an increased appetite like Nyx, and I do?"

"Worse. He..."

Nix stepped in. "He's a cannibal."

She felt the surprise and shock overwhelm her for a moment.

"HE…eats…" Tyrus tried to explain.

"I get it. He eats people." Her stomach heaved at the thought.

"I'm going to find something without flesh to eat. I don't think I've had enough food today."

She stood and walked into the kitchen, grabbing carrots. She chomped away, turning her thoughts away from what human flesh must taste like.

"I'll take one, too." Tyrus stole a carrot from her and chomped. She appreciated the solidarity. She didn't feel alone in her awkwardness.

"So, what do we do? Now that we know it's either a new unknown or an old friend?"

Nix sat beside her. "I'm sorry, but the fact that he went after you specifically means something. You have to pause your search for a job for the time being, until we know more."

She felt her spirits drop, but she understood. "Ok. I get it, but it just… sucks."

Nix handed her a credit card. "Use this for now."

She felt a bit like a little child, but she took it, grateful she had a mentor that could give her that option to be safe. "So, I stay in the apartment like last year?"

Tyrus chimed in. "Not necessarily. We just don't want a repeat affecting your work references. We can draw him out."

"You want to use Ann as bait?"

"How else are we going to know how to deal with this problem?"

"She's not prepared for that."

"I can speak for myself, Nyx." Ann placed the coffee cup on the table and squared her shoulders. "Today, whoever this was, they made me feel… scared, small, and vulnerable. I got a taste of this Mythic's power. I deserve the chance to repay the favor."

"Give him a taste of yours?"

"Taste, shove down his throat, same thing, right?"

Nix bit her lip but Tyrus laughed loudly. "You've created a monster, Nyx."

"No, she didn't create me, she just showed me what being a

strong phoenix means, and it's time for this mystery Mythic to learn that, as well."

"I agree with my young protégé."

The two women looked to Tyrus, who held up his hands. "Far be it from me to disagree with either of you."

"Smart man." Nix smiled at him, and Ann felt awkward again, not knowing if they were being friendly, or if they were "more than friends" again. The stupid blush rose to her cheeks. She glanced at Tyrus, and he seemed confused, so she simply said, "let's make a plan."

"On it." He got to work, and she returned to sipping lukewarm coffee. She'd shown very little power at the Bank, and she felt a renewed sense of self, having a goal to work toward. With the full force of her phoenix, she'd make him regret every second she'd lain there, unconscious. She felt the heat of her flame enter her eyes. She looked at the glass wall of the balcony that stood across the room and saw red flame filling her irises. *Regret, indeed.*

Chapter 3

65°F

Tommy felt invigorated after that encounter. It'd been years since he had tested his powers against another Mythic. He'd heard of the Five, synthetic manmade younglings with incredible powers. The ego boost knowing he'd so swiftly derailed one of them, was giving him an intense high. Walking into Pierside Park, he eyed someone young and fresh, reading a book near a tree, the nerdy in the herd of athleticism. His Mythic was hungry, and it was time he started feeding it, before it completely took control.

He surveyed the environment, a plan forming in his mind. A twisted smile summoned a cold wind that blew over the girl's pages, as she lost her spot. It lifted her scent to him, and he tasted notes of strawberry moisturizer, coconut, and carrots with a hint of kale. Vegans were the salad of humans. Was he in the mood for Vegan? He weighed his options, the cold wind sampling others at the park like a fresh bakery. Athletes were lean cuts, no fat and strong muscle tissue, healthy and filling, but he didn't want to have to marinade or soften the meat. One human could feed him for up to a couple of weeks. You had to be in the mood for the person you chose.

As he was about to exit, a tantalizing scent reached his nose. His eyes and smile widened as he smelled pizza, French fries, and soda. Enriched with high blood sugar, these humans tasted extra sweet, the equivalent of fast-food desserts like donuts. He turned and saw to his delight a slightly overweight middle-aged man that would make a tasty snack.

After seeing a small child run up to him, he decided against it. Humans had gotten quite advanced in communicating over the past decades he'd been sequestered in the wilderness. With alerts sent directly to their phone nowadays, he would have to navigate both social and governmental networks in order to eat as he wished. It wasn't impossible, but their love of mini sized morsels often rendered that task too complex to waste time on. He'd find another with a similar scent without a micro version of himself.

A bit disappointed, he walked the back trails to the ancient building that housed the Mural, a secret record of the Mythics that came before, the only place the list was allowed to exist. A magical realm of its own, he sent a soft wind to open the portal. Soft, shimmering light reflected a thousand fractured shards, the world beyond unclear, revealed only in pieces. As he passed through, it took shape, and he stood suddenly in the dark halls of the timeless temple. If he couldn't get a meal, he could at least view the record. He walked without the aid of light into a large room, the only source the small hole from which sunlight drifted onto a platform. Walking up the steps as he had done in his youth to write his name, he took out his phone and turned on his flashlight. He was hoping to see the names of the Five written, but finding those spaces not filled, his good mood deflated. They'd not yet chosen their names.

He searched the ancient stone for the symbol of the phoenix, moved his hand slowly over the name "Pride," Nix's preferred pseudonym for those unfortunate enough to be the target of a contract, or the hopeless ones who crossed her.

He stood at the Mural, the name "Pride" not quite as faded. He scribbled his name down under the sign of the Wendigo, his self-chosen, "Tommy." Much better than his given name, innocent despite the pull of his Mythic. He could hear the older members of the group chatting away as he chiseled his name into the stone.

"Spit it out, Ty."

"I don't even know what to say. Too many pieces."

"I'm aware." The heat in her voice caused Tommy to glance over at them for a second, before resuming work. She looked irritated, but not angry.

"I did nothing to earn your ire. I'm trying."

She sighed. "I know. I'm nervous, too."

"Has he been in contact with you?"

"No. Has Amanda?"

"No, unfortunately. That's why I'm worried."

"They're luck Mythics. There could be something going on."

"You're not wrong, but I have a bad feeling."

"Me too."

"I should talk to him."

"NO!"

"Nix, consider it before you forbid it."

"We have too much at stake to upset the balance by watching the two of you get into it again."

Tyrus leaned inward, placing a familiar arm on her shoulder. "I'll behave."

She snorted. "No." She cupped his face in her hands. "Please let me take care of this."

Tommy felt a real and visceral reaction to their intimacy. Nix had just risen to her orange flame. It seemed to be having the same reaction to other people in the vicinity. Levi and Tyrus had gotten into it just days before, leading to a fracture in the group he didn't quite understand. She'd earned it by saving him, and he felt both guilty and grateful to her for risking her life. The image of her, burning to ash before him was still fresh. They hadn't known for a few eternal seconds whether she'd combusted or if she would ascend. Thankfully, as Tyrus knelt beside her ashes, a flicker of life rose from the smoke, a small orange flame igniting from complete carbon. As he watched in wonder, the flame grew, a fiery portal that returned her to them, her flesh taking shape in the orange light, turning to human as the glow slowly faded, reborn.

He remembered that vulnerable moment while the two of them hid her frame from the others, Tyrus removing his shirt to cover her quickly. How could he not care for her after seeing that? She was the bravest person he'd ever met, and he'd vowed to defend her life until his death, despite the dire prophecy surrounding his little known Mythic, something new in the world. He could do this. Finishing his name, he sighed, resolved to do and be better tomorrow than he was today.

The memory faded as his mind swept him viciously forward through the horrible war that followed and its aftereffects, the most striking of which was the loss of the group, his isolation and abandonment. He didn't blame Nix, she'd lost her bird, her loves, and her network. She was as broken as him, but he hadn't taken it well. He'd hid in depression and despair, living off of the animals that tasted like unsatisfying diet shakes, and had avoided feeding off of others for as long as possible, waiting for her to remember him, waiting for the group to recover.

What a fool he'd been, a misguided young twenty-five-year-old in a world of intrigue that lay beyond his understanding. How naive to think that with all her options, he would ever be one. The hand softly touching her name balled into a fist, smudging the letters. Upset that he'd done so, he found the symbol of the dragon, and without hesitation, smashed it with full force into his future victim's name.

Tyrus walked into a small home in one of the newer subdivisions of St. Blaise. The mountain view was gorgeous, though it was a good hour drive into the city with traffic. Still, with Ben Ryan's upgrade to FBI agent, his friend's small

had been able to finally own a small home and move out of their starter apartment. With the housing market so inflated, they got lucky to receive the call, and the pride his friend felt at finally being a homeowner showed as Ben walked him into the small backyard, where he continued to grill steaks.

"Have a seat." Ben motioned to the chair next to him and opened the grill.

"I appreciate the invitation."

"Ellie misses you, and so does Hannah. It was time."

"I agree."

Ellie came out wearing an apron, clearly still in the honeymoon phase of home ownership. He smiled at all the struggles they would face, the hard times that would bring them closer as a couple. No need to burst their bubble. Happy times were so rare.

"Hey, Ellie!" He stood and gave her a hug. She laughed and hugged him hard in return, walking back toward the house. "Let me find Hannah so you can see her. She's getting bigger every day. Do you want a beer? Of course, you do. I'll grab one."

He merely smiled. A moment later, Ellie came back out with a small child in her arms and his smile widened. The tow-headed youngster was wary until her mother said, "Ty." Then she beamed and pointed toward the house.

"We keep a picture of you up there so she remembers your face."

"Sorry I don't get out more often."

"Understandable. Completely. We just want Hannah to know who loves her."

The small child waved toward him and he stood, holding out a finger which she grabbed tightly, her hands still very small compared to his. A wave of sadness swept over him for barely a moment. There'd been a time when he'd longed for exactly this, ages ago before Omega Flame upended his life. Still, he was happy that someone would get to live that life, and he'd do whatever he could to protect the tiny family that had adopted him without condition.

"Oh, I need to get your beer. Here. Hold her." She was unceremoniously thrust into his arms, where she smacked him in the face and giggled, grabbing his shirt with her tiny fingers. With one eye open, the other watery from the smack, he rocked back and forth softly as she snuggled to his chest.

"She just takes to you." Ben whipped out his smartphone and took a picture. "There. Sent it to you so you have memories."

"Thanks!" Ellie returned swiftly and smiled seeing Tyrus care for her daughter. "Here you go. One for you and one for Ben." She set them down and held out her arms for her daughter. The baby gratefully exchanged hands and Tyrus rubbed his injured eye.

He picked up the beer and opened the can expertly. He took a quick swig and nodded his head, a silent thank you. Mythics couldn't get drunk off of alcohol, but after his service in several wars, he appreciated the taste and the memories, sometimes.

Of course, his human friend, Ben, knew only of Iraq, where'd they'd met years before. He'd found the younger man impressionable and had made the effort to secure his safety, sometimes at the risk of his own.

But those were memories neither of the men preferred to dwell on, so he focused, grounding himself. Fighting for so long had given him numerous issues despite his eidetic memory, including PTSD. He smiled at Ben and breathed deeply, inhaling beer and steak seasoning.

"Steaks are almost done. Want to grab a plate from…"

Ellie came out with a wobbly toddler behind her crying. "Sorry, sweetie, these can't be dropped."

Tyrus looked at the decorative plates. "Good China? For a barbecue?"

The look she gave him lowered his head. "It's very pretty, Ellie. Thank you." He set it carefully down as a steak was unceremoniously dropped onto his plate. "Medium Rare, right?"

"Yeah, thanks Ben. Let's eat!"

After the meal, as the sun began to set, the two men stayed outside next to a small firepit while Ellie put Hannah down for a much-needed nap.

"This was great, Ben. Thanks for making this happen. I needed this more than I wanted to admit."

Ben turned up the volume on the stereo system suddenly.

"I'll have to be honest, this wasn't just a family visit." Ben set his beer down, all business now. "Some things I've recently discovered that you should know about."

"Always back to work too soon, huh?"

"Yeah, unfortunately."

Tyrus set his empty beer down, as well. "Ok. Lay it on me."

"I have a new partner getting into Mythic related activity. I was pulled in from my SAC because he kept noting the patterns in my browser history. No one has asked specifics yet, but they know something."

Tyrus took a moment, pondering the implications of the

government finally verifying the existence of Mythics. "It's been one of our best kept secrets, but with the advent of cell phones, it was bound to happen."

"Looking into a string of disappearances stretching from Canada to St. Blaise over a span of two decades. When I know for certain whether it's related or not, I'll let you know. Just warning you that you should tread extra softly. Let everyone you care for know to lay low on the powers, unless you want this guy's attention."

"Got it." He didn't mention the incident with Ann, but he was beginning to put some pieces together. "I appreciate the heads up. Let me know what you find, but don't jeopardize your career to do it. They could be watching you, too."

He smiled, revealing a tablet with security systems in place, complete with detection software for hidden bugs. "Nothing yet. Some new tricks."

Tyrus smiled. "You're always adapting."

"Have to. After you saved my life, I owe you."

"You don't really." Tyrus looked back at the house. "Seriously, look out for your family first. I'll take care of mine."

He sauntered into Nyx's apartment a couple hours later, smiling softly to Ann, who looked away too quickly. As much as he'd tried to tread lightly with her, she seemed less eager to accept his presence than the others. Considering the heat that one fire element gives another during their first meeting, he didn't blame her. She had probably never experienced it before, and those types of interactions can be confusing when you can't put them into perspective. Sitting across from her but in her view, he gently folded his hands and placed them on his knees, an attempt to look non-threatening. She looked down at her phone, biting her lower lip and he couldn't help but smile a bit. When she cast a glance his way and glared, he quickly neutralized his face. She didn't need any help from him in feeling awkward.

He quietly cleared his throat before he spoke. "Is there

anything that we need to discuss?" Maybe an open-ended question would seem less threatening.

Her face turned pink. "No. I'm good."

To push or to comfort? Before he could decide, Nix walked out of the kitchen. He watched as Ann glanced in her direction, then back at him, her red face darkening. *Ahhh.*

"So, Nyx," he began carefully, waiting for the older phoenix to stop and look at him, "how is the research progressing on the assassin?" Out of the corner of his eye, he could see Ann's body relax a bit. *Good.*

"There isn't much of a trail online. I'm waiting on some contacts. If they show their face, I'll know where. What about you? What did Ryan say?"

Nix sat on the other end of the couch, allowing him to view both firebirds at once, though his focus remained away from Ann. "That's a conversation for the whole group, but if memory serves, they're unavailable at the moment. Next time Joy intends to get everyone together should be around two days from now. Do you have any job interviews to go to, Ann?"

"No…" she said, defeatedly.

The idea planted, Nix continued. "Then maybe this would be a good time to get some training in. Roof in 15?"

"Sounds great to me." Tyrus smiled at Nix. As she turned away, Ann glared at him, but he skillfully ignored it, reaching into his bag. She walked away and into her room, not quite slamming the door. She clearly didn't want to be around the two adults, but she needed to see how they interacted with each other to overcome her embarrassment. That, he could do without a confrontation. Besides, she would need the focus, because they had no way of knowing the next time the air element would strike.

The wind whipped Ann's hair in a flurry around her head until she pulled it back with a ponytail. She stood at the center of the roof of

Nix's apartment building, the two fire elements surrounding her.

Tyrus breathed in too much air, and the memory of his dragon shout caused her to draw inward, but his voice was merely louder to cut over the wind. "I'm sure you can guess why we're here. You're dealing with an air elemental that stole your breath. While we don't know the exact species, this is the perfect place for you to practice dealing with some aspects of that element."

She had to shout loudly for him to hear her. "And how do I do that?"

"Simple. Don't let the wind touch you."

She laughed. "How in the world would I do that?"

"You have to figure it out. Mythics are bound only by their imagination. You control the flame, but your mind determines what you can do with it."

Nix stepped in front of her. "We may not always be here to tell you how to do everything. You need to problem solve this yourself."

Ann nodded, frustrated but understanding. "This is a puzzle, and you want me to solve it."

Nix smiled wide. "Exactly."

"That doesn't seem too difficult."

The two adults eyed each other, and she felt like she was missing something. "What is it?"

Tyrus spoke again, the sound seeming to come from everywhere around her. "You have ten minutes before Nix attacks, and twenty before I join her."

"Uhm.... what?"

"You need to think on your feet. Like a diamond, you don't grow without pressure. We are going to provide just enough to make this a challenge for you, but not enough to put you in any true danger."

Nix reached into her pocket, removing her phone and setting a timer. "Begin."

Ann swallowed hard, looking back and forth between the two. She'd sparred with them both, before, but never at the same time. She'd beaten Tyrus days after she'd been reborn, but he hadn't fought back. It was best if she focused and tried to complete the objective prior to their involvement.

"Nine minutes, thirty seconds."

Ah, she was going to make it worse by counting down. *Great.* Focusing, she tried to drown everything out, calling the calm ocean the way Seth had taught her…

"I don't see you doing anything." Tyrus sounded around her, interrupting her peace.

She opened her eyes and eyed him harshly. "That's not fair."

He placed his hands into the pockets of his pants. "You're right, it's not."

She sighed. She closed her eyes again, trying to ignore his voice.

"Nine minutes."

Uuuugh. She eyed Nix who shrugged. At this rate, she wasn't going to be able to complete anything. The fear came on the end of that thought. She really didn't want to spar with the both of them, even if she was stronger. Something about the synthetic resurrection of the Five gave them access to power that organic Mythics needed years to create.

"Eight minutes, thirty seconds."

"You gonna do anything today, Ann?" His tone was purposefully mocking, and she didn't appreciate it. She felt the heat in her eyes and knew her red flame was visible, the first indication of power she'd shown. For one with control, she didn't seem to be showing much of it today.

"Eight minutes."

She was no longer frustrated with them, but with herself for her lack of focus. She'd wasted two minutes of her time already. She breathed deeply and released it slowly, holding out her hand. Her flame was already activated, she just needed to start small.

"What's your hand going to do against the wind?"

The flame crept from her hand moved toward him for a split second before it was returned to her. Nix chuckled.

"Seven minutes, thirty seconds."

"Are you even going to let me *actually* try?" Her voice came out altered and ethereal, like her phoenix.

His eyes changed, the dragon in them appearing. She heard his growl, low, and tangled in the wind, which whipped harshly against her and pushed her a few steps off center. She looked back and he had leaned against the edge of the building, waiting silently.

Her emotions were just beginning to bubble up. She focused on the flame in her hand, watching as the wind flowed over it, trying to snuff out the light. In the next instant, the flame stabilized when the wind died down, only to grow subtly as it was caressed by it more gently.

"The wind causes my flame to become unpredictable. It's much harder to control." Tyrus nodded, smiling.

"Seven minutes even."

Ann compelled her flame to grow, until it surrounded her entire hand, down her arm to her elbow. The wind howled again, and she focused on trying to keep the flame steady. She failed to do so and her flame was gone.

Frustrated, she called it again. "This is tricky!"

She called the flame and focused, but the wind snuffed it out.

"Won't work like that." Tyrus was no longer mocking her but reminding her of something she'd forgotten. Indeed, her strategy of concentrating on the flame and focusing was not working.

"Six minutes even."

"Come on, baby bird."

Her flame reacted to that, alive with rage. She felt it creep down her arm, strong and fierce against the wind. The warmth traveled down her other arm, her whole upper body filling with red light.

"Five minutes."

The flame waivered, and she tried to force it back, but it died again.

'Uuugh! Why isn't this working?"

"You're focusing on the wrong thing."

She gave him a sarcastic look. In frustration, she released a fireball at him. He absorbed it easily, his hand turning momentarily to dragon scales, a reminder he was fireproof.

"Want me to attack now?"

"No!"

He shrugged his shoulders and relaxed again.

"Four minutes." A glance at Nix showed her that her mentor was prepping her orange flame to do battle. It lit her dark features, from her head to her feet, a subtle glow, barely any flame, more like a soft halo of light.

Now or never, self. If force wouldn't work, then she needed to try something else.

"Any ideas yet?"

"Three minutes."

She thought back to her days in foster care, attempting to summon a memory to inspire her emotions. If she could summon her rage, her flame would follow. She looked back to the days when she was helpless and young, the memory flooding over her as if it were yesterday…

The trees were giants, her stature small, her running slow. Her five-year-old body filled with fear as the monster behind her cried out her name.

"ANN!" Its howl drove fear deep into her chest, its claws gripping her heart. Her little legs moved faster away from the source of pain on her heels. This was different than the other times. This time, he might just end her life.

Her eyes opened, and her bird was there, beneath the surface of her soul, ready to defend her. The fear melted away, replaced with rage at going through something so terrifying at such a young age. No one deserved that. With only a little urging, she would protect Ann with her life.

Tyrus must have felt it, because he stepped to the side, just in case. In their last match, he'd fallen from the roof, three stories down. Neither of them wanted to repeat that fiasco.

Holding her hand outward, the bird landed, a mix of the most dangerous birds of prey and red fire. Rage filled her chest, and the bird reacted, their minds linked and their goal certain. From the center of her being, the flame expanded, the wind inconsequential. It surrounded her as a perfect orb, a shield against the onslaught of the wind. As it whipped, her bird protected her, the flame undisturbed by the force of it. Though it was less sophisticated than Nix's orange light, it did its job.

Tyrus was suddenly there, a confused look on his face. He stood just outside the circle, focused on her completely. She locked eyes with him sternly. She just started succeeding. She didn't need him screwing this up for her.

Yet her warning look went unheeded. As she watched, his body changed, red scales crawling along his skin as he stepped through her orb of red, returning to flesh as the danger passed. He took two large steps forward, and before she could even ask, his arms wrapped around her as he embraced her fiercely.

She had an instant to decide what to do with her flame. To let it go, or pull it in. The fear of hurting him, or Nix, caused a momentary pause, and she chose both options at once.

Her bird, confused, vanished, as the flame split, moving outward and inward with a giant pulse. She felt his skin shift to scales against hers, felt his chest expand far too much as he took in her fire, trying to absorb the pulse before it could cause any damage. She felt the siphon, the heat flowing away from her and into him. She'd known he could nullify her flame, but she didn't know he could absorb it, let alone this much.

His arms like steel around her, she couldn't back away. His chest filled with her power, three times as large as it should have been. When all of her flame was absorbed, his eyes met hers, turquoise mixed with red embers. Without loosening his grip, he looked toward Nix, and began to release the flame from his lungs in a huge breath.

Nix released her flame, and as Ann watched, orange and red mingled, fire cancelling its twin. Ann's flame was potent red, but orange was the hotter of the two, and the energy released as heat that safely ascended to the heavens.

When all her flame had been extinguished, she assumed he'd

release her, but he did not. Instead, with a sympathetic look on his face, one of his hands gently cradled her head against his chest. Confused, she attempted to push away, but Nix was there, too, both holding her.

It took a few more seconds before she felt wetness on her cheeks, before she understood why he'd taken such a huge risk. The tears flowed from her eyes and down her face freely, the memory too potent to control. She'd chosen unwisely.

She felt her chest heave in spite of her unwillingness to be vulnerable. She hated the tears, hated the memory, hated the fact that they still controlled her behavior after so many years. Her hands balled into fists, gripping his shirt. Her body began to shake as she struggled for control.

"I…don't…want….to…"

"*Shh.*" His soft voice caused her throat to close.

"No one but us ever has to know. Whatever it was, you're safe now." In spite of her best efforts, the tears kept flowing, as she stood between her two mentors, and they formed a wall protecting her from the world, so a piece of that five-year-old child could begin to heal.

Joy wiped away a tear from her eye. That one had been intense. Overall, this was what she had hoped for. They needed Tyrus on their side in the end, and this was the best way to ensure his loyalty. Was it uncomfortable for her bestie? Yeah, but without the pain of the memory, no Tyrus, and no Tyrus, no win. Only darkness. She took the small orb and placed it back into her pocket, the light inside it fading to black as the memory vanished. She watched a moment while Tyrus and Nix comforted her, a slight smile playing on her face.

Seth bounced in behind her. "Was that a necessary cruelty?"

"We took the memory from her so she could become powerful. It was only a matter of time before it needed to be returned. Or have you forgotten how bad exploding memory orbs can get?"

He shivered, remembering their first attempt. "Still, this feels manipulative."

"She can handle it now. Look." She pointed toward the triad.

Seth sighed. "My gut tells me to trust you. You see things I can't, but I hate seeing her like this."

"I hate it too, but you know we only have so much time."

"If she finds out…"

"Odds are she won't. We are the only two fate Mythics, save an auger or two."

"Well, on this plane anyway."

"The others shouldn't concern themselves with Ann. They don't know what we know."

He nodded. "Can she really do this?"

"She *has* to do this." Joy looked back at her friend, watched as Tyrus and Nix helped her get back inside. "Not just for us, either."

She smiled at Seth, who produced a single wildflower from his pocket. Joy's eyes widened, a smile brightening her face. "For me?"

"Always."

She giggled and took the flower, hugging him tightly. The golden glow that surrounded them both caused the entire roof to slowly fill with the same wildflower, seeming to grow out of the very concrete. A moment later, Seth bounced them away, off the roof, and the garden slowly faded back to the in-between.

Chapter 4

55°F

Ann pulled herself out of bed a couple of hours later, when her emotions had calmed, and her clear head had returned. She walked out dreading that the conversation she was about to have would return her to a state of emotional upheaval, but she knew she would be required to explain.

Nix was busy in the kitchen, while Tyrus was buried in his laptop. She cleared her throat a bit too loud, and Tyrus glanced in her direction. The look was familiar, sympathy mixed with apology.

"I guess I should explain what happened…" Her voice raspy, she took a deep breath.

Tyrus was up and close to her in seconds. "No, I think Nix and I have a pretty clear indication of what went wrong."

"I'm not used to being…overwhelmed like that." She played with the hem of her T-shirt to keep her nervous hands busy.

"I gathered that. The memory surprised you."

"Yeah, I was five and…" Tears threatened to fall again.

"You don't need to describe it. Remember, I'm a war veteran. I get being overwhelmed by crazy life situations."

"I just… wish I could get it out without the tears."

"That will come, eventually. Maybe you just need more processing time."

"I just have no clue where all that emotion came from."

"Welcome to the life of a Mythic. Fire elements are often tied to their emotions. I know the red flame of the phoenix is characterized by anger and rage. I'm assuming the memory drew more out of you than you were prepared for."

"How did you absorb it?"

He smiled. "Dragons breathe fire, right?"

"I've only ever seen you nullify it."

"For me, I have no real reason to let the anger out. I've had time you haven't, been through experiences you can't imagine. Anger fuels itself. The more you feel, the angrier you become. Knowing this, I choose to not let it out. It gets easier with time to gain emotional control. While you're powerful, you're still only nineteen. Give it time and lean on the people you trust."

"What exactly did I do? Splitting my flame?"

He nodded. "You saw how some of the energy went outward? Some went inward."

"I felt… paralyzed. I wasn't sure what to do."

"So before you could decide, the flame split."

Nix walked out. "Took a long while for me to learn that. Controlling one flame is different than dividing your magic. It was impressive, if unintended."

"I've seen you do different flames in both hands."

"Yes, but there was something… intense and unusual about your power."

Tyrus nodded. "It felt like a shockwave of fire. Part explosion, part implosion, a dangerous combo. Which is why I intervened."

Ann gave him a quizzical look.

"You know the myth, how a phoenix can rise from the ashes?"

"Yeah. That's how Nix got her orange flame, right?"

Nix nodded, heading back to the kitchen.

"Right. Well, there's a right and a wrong way to change, or what we call, ascend. Basically, when the energy is given out to the universe, when you 'let go' so to speak, the universe returns it to you, a balance of sorts."

"An explosion."

"Correct, or what half of your flame did today."

"And if it implodes instead?"

"The energy goes within the phoenix, burning up its soul from the inside out. The universe cannot give back what it isn't given. The phoenix takes the flame into themselves, and it burns through their very essence and their bird, destroying them forever. Instead of ascending, we call this combustion."

"Which is why you intervened. You were afraid the inward

force would destroy me?"

"What you did on that roof, it was powerful."

Nix returned with a bowl in her hands. "Indeed. I'm sure you felt it, as did Ty."

Without warning, the blush returned at the use of his pet name. She turned away but she saw the confusion on his face.

"Ann," Nix said, "what's causing the embarrassment?"

Unlike Tyrus, she was much more direct with her pupil. Ann usually respected that tendency.

"I just… know of your history and…if you two need privacy I can find a place…"

At their blank stares, she felt her cheeks redden even more. She was about to ramble.

"I mean, I know you two are together, or whatever, but not really together, and I know it's weird for you with Levi, and I'm not sure how to explain it all but I'm sure it's weird being here with a teen when you have adult relationships and I don't want to be in the way of anything or to see anything for that matter so if you need me to go live with Joy or find an apartment it's ok because I need a job anyway-"

Nix snorted, out loud, while Tyrus merely walked away. Setting down a bowl of dip, knowing Ann would need to replenish calories after that shockwave of fire, she motioned for Ann to sit next to her.

"I think you embarrassed him."

"Why? I was trying not to." She glanced in his direction but he was hidden from her vision.

"Ann, Ty, I mean, Tyrus and I are friends. We've known each other for decades. There was a time when my orange flame was rowdy and we were more than that, but it faded quickly."

She placed the bowl into Ann's lap, handing her a chip, as if to say that she needed to eat, now. Ann bit into the fried potato and realized how ravenous she was. No wonder her emotions were a bit wild.

"We are just friends now. Even if we weren't, we wouldn't…" Nix purposely cleared her throat, "we wouldn't dream of inconveniencing you with that in any way. We are both very old adults."

Through the chip and dip, Ann murmured, "the orange flame?"

"Yes. Each flame goes with an emotion. Red, as you know, is rage. Orange is the double sword of passion, for art and for people. It can be intense, and uncontrollable, and have real consequences for people."

"That sounds awful." Chomp, chomp.

"For you, it will be less so. I didn't have another phoenix to help me control my flame, to keep others safe."

"Was that when you and Levi…"

"Yes, that too."

"Do you regret it?"

Nix's eyes went wide at that, unprepared. She took a long thoughtful moment before she answered. "The short and appropriate answer is no. I don't. Even after losing my bird, I don't regret those nights."

"I don't think I could forgive someone after that. I find it astonishing that you're strong enough to."

She smiled softly. "Ann, as Tyrus has stated, anger is a furnace. The more you fuel it, the more it destroys you. There comes a point where you have to let things go for you. I reached that point sometime after the bombing of my nephew's building. Seeing the lengths that they both went through, for me, for you, for the Five, you see the good. Plus, I know what it's like to be manipulated. They are responsible, yes, but they didn't maliciously intend to destroy me. I suppose it's difficult to explain. I've processed the pain, and it doesn't hurt like it used to. Maybe your bird is healing me."

Nix took her hand, and her bird fluffed its feathers somewhere within her. She felt the pull, and almost cooed out loud. "I guess we are of the same flock?"

"Odyssey, if you want to talk about a group of phoenixes, but yeah, different origin, same family."

That made Ann smile. Tyrus conspicuously brought out some

cake and she smiled wide, silently thanking him for his sensitivity. He gave the plate to Nix with two forks, and the girls dug in happily.

Tommy wiped his mouth, the blood fresh from his kill. It was sweet cherry flavored savory goodness to him yet tinged with the drugs the man had pumped into his system. Looking at the dead meat that would be his next week of meals, he didn't bother closing its surprised eyes. He merely slung the man over his shoulder and walked into a back door close to his hotel room. At the early hour, no one walked the halls, no one darted in with a questioning face. No one to knock unconscious, no repercussions. He'd waited days to eat, and his patience, though thin, was a sign of his age. When he was younger, there was no way he could have shown such control. The door swung open from his wind as he walked toward the two double beds, one covered completely in plastic. There was a correct way to prepare *homo sapiens*, and an incorrect way. Over the years he'd learned from his mistakes, learned to live light, to take what he needed from a city, to make his footprint small and his kills undetectable.

Ignoring the bed, he walked into the bathroom where various tools and equipment lay ready for him. If he did this right, no one would notice. He could disguise the scent through his element, smoke the meat under their noses, and have tasty people jerky that could last for days. Taking off the man's shoes, they weren't his size, *shame*, he tied rope around each of his ankles and used the reinforced handicap shower bar as leverage to lift the man up and into the shower, head down. Around his neck went a tourniquet he could use to control the outflow of blood. Beneath the head he placed a mason jar, cheap and easy to find. Cutting a small slit in the man's throat just above the pressure point, he began to drain the liquid into the jar. A human body contained upwards of 150 ounces of blood at a time, and the jar held a mere twelve to sixteen. He could stack some in the minifridge, have some tonight, though the drugs would make him giddy.

When one jar was full, the tourniquet was tightened, and

another placed beneath. He wasn't a wasteful person. Over the next several days he would section off the various organ systems, using his knowledge of rigor mortis to his advantage. The human body could spend 1-4 days stiffened, and if the muscles were carved during, the meat would be stiff. The trick was getting the corpse to last until it vanished. While the muscles would stay fresh longer, the juicy inner organs would suffer bloat the following day, limiting the amount of time he had to work in the abdominal cavity.

Still, it would be worth it to assuage his hunger enough to consider how he would reintroduce himself to Tyrus, Nix, and Levi. He needed to at least *appear* controlled at first, or his plan wouldn't work. He needed them to understand, before they felled him, what they'd put him through. Snapping one of the little fingers backward, he let the anger wash over him for a time, until the next jar needed to be replaced. A long night ahead of him for a great reward. He allowed himself a sip or two of the first jar, and an eerie giggle escaped him before he covered his mouth. What fun it would be to see her again!

Julius walked into the night shift at his security firm, ready for his random assignment. With outsourcing technology, he could be at one of several different businesses within the city, that took contracted security work as needed. He'd found the change of pace each night exciting, having worked at everything from armored transit to stadiums, to private security for wealthy citizens. He hated monotony.

He checked in at the front desk with a nod, the receptionist aware of his name. He'd had a couple of kerfuffles already on the job, and with his superior senses and strength, the normal human bad guys never stood a chance. It felt good to be the hero, get the flirty eye from the girls at reception. Tonight was no different.

"Hey, Julius." A blonde smiled widely at him and leaned against the counter. He struggled to keep his eyes on hers. "Here for your schedule?"

He winked at her. She giggled. "What do you have for me

tonight?"

The brunette chimed in. "Sorry, printing it now." He noted her fresh lipstick and foundation. They had access to his schedule and knew when he'd be in. "Why don't you tell us how your day was, while we wait."

He smiled back at the two of them. "Well, I guess I can spare a couple of minutes." As the two of them leaned in, he saw someone bounce in behind them, near the printer. His smile never faded, but he didn't get why Joy was meddling with his job. She wasn't supposed to.

"So, I ever tell you about the time I survived this bus crash?"

They both widened their eyes at him. "You have not! How could you keep that from us?" She pouted demurely.

He tried his best to ignore Joy as she switched a couple of papers around. She glanced at his direction and smiled, softly wading one into a ball and tossing it at a garbage can. She missed.

His smile froze in place, his heart began to speed up. What was she doing?

"Oh, yeah, me and some of my friends were on a trip to the museum here in St. Blaise. As seniors."

Joy picked up the paper wad and tried to score again, this time doing a dance as it landed in the bin. Julius needed to distract the girls.

"Picture this." He turned toward the entrance, making certain to flex a couple of his arm muscles in the process. "I'm at the back of the bus with my friend Marcus, right?" He pointed and curled his biceps, making the girls red in the face. Joy stopped her dance and placed her arm on the printer, the other propped so her fist was under her chin, clearly ready to listen to the entire story.

Cursing her silently, Julius continued to explain the circumstances of their change into Mythics, civilian version. At least until Joy was gone, which she took her sweet time. Seething silently, when she finally disappeared, he ended it quickly.

"So, you know, explosion, fire, flames. Where am I working tonight?"

He already knew it would be a long shift. Looking at the job listed, he resisted the urge to groan. What was Joy doing? Walking out of the building with a goodbye to his admirers, he made sure he wasn't being followed before heading into the alleyway between buildings, where he abruptly whispered, "*JOY*!"

She appeared with a giggle. "They thought you were handsome." Her teasing tone didn't help him.

"Explain to me why you meddled in my job when you agreed not to?"

She kicked at the cement beneath her, a rock rolling toward him before swaying back and forth. "Because reasons?"

"Do those reasons include life and death?"

She smiled. "Possibly."

He was suddenly terrified. "Am I going to die?"

"Well, of course you are."

He stared at her dumbfounded until she giggled and added, "we all die. Just not tonight. I think."

With that she faded from view, while he kicked the rock back at her now empty spot. Three deep breaths and he strode to the parking garage to grab a vehicle. *Damn unicorns…*

He pulled up to the hotel twenty minutes later, and stopped dead halfway to the lobby. That's when he smelled the death lurking around the building. The chill in the air, too cold for the normal summer weather already gave him goose flesh, but his hair stood straight up from this. His Mythic, Cerberus, growled softly in warning from within him. Born of the underworld, he knew the nature and sensory experience of death better than most. Though a normal human would walk right by, his hellhound was instantly alert. The hair on the back of his neck stood erect, and he crouched slightly into a defensive position out of instinct.

The smell reminded him of…something. It was faint, but familiar, and it took a few moments for him to place it. Blood, the ending of a life, the ethereal severing of soul from body, these were all intimate smells to him, but something else, deeper. Breathing in too deep for his frame, he struggled to place it. Top notes were woody, the head almost of pine, with fungal base notes.

He walked into the lobby, nodding to the reception desk and began to walk the halls of the first floor. It was late, midnight long since come and gone. The scents of chlorinated water and takeout eased his mind. He started to whistle a song stuck in his head and turned the corner near the back alleyway.

Then the smell became overwhelming. He opened the side exit, the smell of iron ripe in the air. It wasn't just familiar but threatening. Walking toward the first door, he felt the death in the room from the hallway. His heart pumped hard in his chest as he debated confronting what lay behind the door to room 143. He reached slowly toward the handle, about to use his key card, when something made him pause and just listen.

Shuffling feet… the curtain in the bathroom opening and closing… a giggle….more feet…the stab of a knife into flesh…

He backed away and considered his options. Should he go in there alone? If it was a human killing another human, it wouldn't be a difficult fight. If it was a Mythic, he was underprepared. Something about it seemed more than human but he couldn't place it.

"*Joy…*" Silence. "*Joy…*"

The footsteps moved toward the door and he continued walking down the hallway. He heard the door open, felt the chill creep up his spine from his gaze, but skillfully kept his shoulders relaxed and his pace even, though his hands were balled into fists and prepared if he heard him running forward.

But no footsteps followed, and the door shut behind him. He kept his breathing even until he could exit a side entrance. He walked behind the building and toward the alley, where Joy stood, wringing her hands, sitting on a stack of old tires.

"We…have a guest in our little city, it seems."

Joy nodded. "He's a big problem. Did you get his scent?"

Julius smiled. "Yes."

"Good. We'll need that soon."

"Joy, what's really going on?"

She stood and paced back and forth. Her usual quirky smile absent. "It's hard to know what to tell you and what not to."

"So, this has to do with celestial odds?"

"Yes." She said it too assertively. "So… some things I've done have gotten the attention of…people… who don't like that I was able to do those things."

"You got yourself in trouble with fate?"

"Yes." That seemed to settle her a little. She stopped pacing. "That's a great way for you to say it and not me."

"Ok. Trouble with the universe, but what does that have to do with our guest?"

"There's like…" she sighed, struggling for the words. "Think soccer."

He was more confused than ever. "Soccer?"

"Yeah. And other teams come to town and you play them, right? Well, we are the home team, 'The Five,' and another group are coming, we'll call them…what's something you don't like to eat?"

"Tripe?"

"Right. So we'll call them 'Tripe.' So Tripe is coming because The Five managed to score one too many goals, and if they murder us on the field, quite literally, the entire soccer community with die in a dumpster fire."

"That's… bad."

"Yes. But it gets a bit convoluted, because Tripe doesn't know they're scheduled to play in St. Blaise, but the umpires are on their way and the concession stand is out of ice and don't get me started on the balloon animal guy-"

"I think you lost me there."

"Essentially, we need to stop the team members of Tripe individually before they create a team the umpires can use to throw us off the field."

"And this guy is on that team."

"Yes."

"And what do we do next?"

"This. I get all the elements in place to create a play so unexpected that all the bases are covered when the umpire tries to throw us off the field."

He couldn't even… "What?"

She thought a moment, before she looked at him, defeated. "We hope that I chose the right person to pay the price of the magic I stole."

Ann sat on her bed, looking through various listings. She hadn't found another job opening that fit her criteria. She desperately wanted to be independent of Nix, but being a Mythic and having a regular job seemed a monumental task at the moment. She rubbed her eyes and stared at the screen, willing the perfect solution to just appear. It didn't.

Looking at the time, she groaned. She'd been at this tedious task for hours. She set her laptop down and walked out of her room, intending to find food in the kitchen.

She stopped on her way at Julius sitting in the living room. "Hey."

He froze for a moment, then faced her. "Hey."

"Why are you here?"

"I miss my friend, Ann. Why don't we hang out for the rest of the day?"

She thought back on the awkward encounter at the bank, where they'd been momentarily thrown into some "will they, won't they" tension. Did he like her? How did she even *feel* about that?

"Uhm, yeah, I mean, I was just job searching. Couldn't find anything. Would be nice to do something…else."

Great, self, make it more awkward. She walked into the kitchen, needing food to think. Julius followed her.

"Are you hungry? We could grab lunch. My treat?"

Well, that escalated quickly. "Sure. Where did you want to go?"

"There's the new brunch restaurant downtown. They have outside seating. We could go there."

"Isn't that kind of far, though?"

"Eh, I have a craving. You ready?"

"Sure." Maybe it would be good to do something normal for a change, regardless. She smiled. "Let's go."

Thirty minutes later, they sat down at an outside table, menus in hand, jackets on. The weather was still unusually cold, getting chillier each day. "What were you craving?"

She watched his eyes dart across the street to the hotel on the other side, but when she looked, there was nothing there.

"Something with chicken, I think. You?"

She glanced at the menu, unsure. She set it down and took a sip of her water, seeing his eyes move again. Maybe it was time to ask.

"So what are we really doing here?"

He met her gaze and smiled. "Joy told me to stick with you for a bit, but I also need to watch a guy in that hotel, so I figured this would be perfect. You were gonna eat anyway, right?"

So she had misunderstood his intent. She tried to hide her embarrassment with a napkin, but he noticed.

"Everything ok for you?"

She smiled, feeling the heat creep into her face. "Yeah. I'm ok. Restroom."

She practically ran to the girl's room inside. What was up with her? She splashed some cold water on her face and patted it dry, and calmed herself with breathing exercises. She reminded herself that they were just friends, that it was ok they were, and that she wasn't really attracted to him anyway. Then, she stepped out of the bathroom.

When she came back, he was seated so he could easily watch the hotel. "I ordered an appetizer. You ok?"

She really didn't want to feel those feelings again. "Yeah, I'm ok."

He looked back to the hotel, and she felt comfortable in that he seemed totally oblivious to her right now. She took a few more deep breaths and tried to think of a polite topic of conversation.

"How's the job search going?"

She sighed, relieved it wasn't on her to think of a topic.

Joy smiled, watching them from a distance. Now that Julius was watching the hotel and Ann, she could focus on the next piece. She walked out of the alley, careful not to disturb the couple making out on the corner.

When she was a block away, she bounced to the penthouse. Upset that Tyrus wasn't where she left him, she stomped around the apartment, looking for him. When he was clearly not there, she sighed. Taking a small bracelet from her pocket, golden and engraved with emeralds, she asked, "where is he?"

The bracelet began to vibrate, then a picture was projected above showing Tyrus running through a wooded area. "What… ugh."

She bounced again to Pierside Park, near the trails. She walked to the middle of the trail and stood, her hands crossed in front of her, a stern look on her face. Tyrus jogged up to her and took out his earbuds.

"What is it, Joy?"

She stomped her foot. "You run in the *morning*."

He looked at her bewildered. "Yes."

"This isn't morning."

"No, it's not." He placed the earbuds in his pocket. "I couldn't run this morning, so I was making it up."

She sighed and walked to him, worried the extra seconds would cost them. She took his wrist and bounced with him to the hotel area.

He rounded, ready to admonish her, but she didn't have time to explain. She bounced again, this time feeling a bit nauseated. She stood on a tropical beach with a man bathing in the sun, nude. With this, she could have some fun.

She giggled, watching the man tense up, making herself invisible. The man stood, his long platinum hair covering his back side, but not his front. He wrapped a towel around himself and looked in every direction. Joy was silent until he turned away from her, then giggled again.

The man called the very ocean with his hand, swirling water around him until it hit her, revealing her form in the negative space. The water receded and she appeared again, as he covered himself with a towel.

"Do you have an extra one?" The water had soaked her.

"What do you want, Joy? How did you find me?"

"The better question is why are you sunbathing a la birthday suit when you know people like me can pop in at any time?"

He sighed. "I've gone to great lengths to be hidden and anonymous, for obvious reasons. How did you find me?"

He towered over her, yet she was not intimidated by him in the slightest. Sure, he'd killed a lot of people, maimed Nix, destroyed Jackson Genetics, but she knew he was the good type of chaos.

She placed her hands on her hips. "We need you. You need clothes."

"What's going on? Is Nix in trouble?"

"We are all in trouble if you don't get dressed right now." Sure, it was a white lie, but it did make him hustle into the house that sat fifty feet inland.

Tyrus stood there, confused. He lifted his shirt to wipe the sweat away from his face, noting the couple making out across the street. Something seemed, off, about their behavior. For being in a public place, they were *really* into each other. Something at the back of his mind fluttered, but Joy reappeared before he could pull the memory out.

"Here you go. Gotta run." She handed him a water gun and disappeared again. He looked around, wondering if she'd return, but he was on his own, in an alley, holding a child's toy. He squirted a little, worried it held more than water. It fell on the ground in front of him and began to swirl upward.

"Oh, no." He backed away as the water became larger,

eventually forming the shape of a man, then Levi fully appeared.

"Any idea why we've been summoned?"

"No. You?"

"None." Levi looked at his surroundings, then back at Tyrus. "Don't you usually run in the morning?"

Joy bounced next to St. Blaise University, watching Connor on the football practice field. She watched as he threw the ball to someone downfield, who caught it easily.

"Ok, that's a wrap. Head to the showers." The coach began to walk off the field, and Connor moved to go to the locker room. She did not want to repeat earlier, so bounced so she was directly in front of him.

He jumped backward. "Joy? What are you…"

"No time. Sorry."

She grabbed his wrist and bounced again, back to Tyrus's location, looking over her crew. Tyrus stood in shorts and a tank top, Levi in his trench coat attire, and Connor still in his practice pads. She looked to her left, and on cue, Seth showed up in a suit, with an extra T-shirt, handing it to Connor.

"Great, you're all here. We can chat now. Question one, is it *always* wrong to use your bestie as bait? Discuss."

Ann laughed out loud at the dad joke, every trace of awkwardness gone. "Here's one. There's a new species of ant that cohabitates with other animals."

"Oh, really?"

"Yeah. The ants get protection and in exchange they make necessary repairs to the dwelling."

"Huh."

"They're… mainten-ants."

"That's…just…so, so bad." They both chuckled. "Thank you

for helping me surveil this lead."

"No problem. It was nice to go somewhere and not have to pay for food."

He smiled wide at her. "Looks like there's some movement. Hang on." He focused away from her a moment, the silence stretching between them. "Not the right person."

"Care to share who we're watching?"

"Your breath stealer."

Her eyes grew wide at that. "What?"

"The guy from the bank."

"Right. But he can steal breath from people. Won't he recognize me?"

Julius looked at her intently, taking her hand to hold it gently. She felt the magic flow down it, and she felt protected and calm.

"That's exactly the idea."

Tommy watched the couple, a bit curious as to how they wound up in his path again. In such a large city, it wasn't often that he encountered the same individual twice, not unless he wanted to. He was suddenly interested in the former bank teller. Their first encounter had been bracing. Something about her was interesting, though. He was drawn to her. He could feel the pull. And here she was, right in front of him.

He jaywalked toward the restaurant, each step measured carefully to avoid walking too fast or too slow. He'd become an expert in being unrecognizable, average and unassuming in every way. It was the only way one could hunt a human successfully. Standing out caused them to run, and though he might win the chase, he preferred his kills to be quick and painless for the prey. *Most of the time, anyway.*

He walked in and sat at the bar, ordering a vodka martini. He could watch them through the mirror above him without drawing any extra attention. When the drink came, he paid the bartender with a large bill and while he was distracted, placed a single drop of his victim's blood in the glass, to flavor the otherwise tasteless alcohol. The olive, he dipped into it and savored the flavor on his tongue before sipping slowly and watching, waiting for something he wasn't quite sure of.

Connor entered the restaurant after their guest, watching him while he watched Ann and Julius. Joy was insistent that he watch and not interact, waiting for the right signal. She'd forgotten to tell him what signal, but apparently, he would "know it when it happened." *Unicorns…*

Levi knew the instant that Tommy went to wash his hands, though he was positioned as directed, to the left and away from the epicenter of the operation. As a water element, he rarely suffered from moral obligation, especially considering his long life. However, he found himself wondering if he should involve Nix. This was *Tommy,* after all.

Joy appeared in front of him instantly. She placed her hands on her hips and glared angrily in his direction. He met her eyes and shrugged his shoulder, the question silent but effective.

"No."

Levi sighed and tilted his head forward, raising his eyebrows.

Joy narrowed her eyes. "I need you to trust me. Do not involve Nix, or this gets much worse." She disappeared, then reappeared behind him and grabbed his cellphone. "You can have this back when you can be responsible with it."

He was torn, a feeling he didn't often suffer from. Joy understood the odds of success, of fate, but she didn't know Nix like he did, didn't know their history. Even unicorns don't get access to everything. "His moral compass is as changeable as his element." He'd once overheard Nix say that to Ann. It wasn't far from the truth. He'd lived so long, been through so much, nothing mattered anymore.

Except *her*. Except Nix. How would she feel if she was left out of this? How would she feel if this went down wrong? If Tommy died today and she didn't get to say good-bye? They'd gotten to the point that they could finally stand in the same room without the resentment on her face. It was a gift he cherished, and he wasn't giving it up. Not for Joy, not for Ann, not for anyone. He couldn't risk her thinking he had lied.

He created a portal and walked through it, landing in Nix's apartment, where she was on her laptop, facing away from him. He reached out a hand, water swirling around them both, moving them back to the scene instantly.

She turned and glared at him. "What was that about?"

"We don't have much time." He leaned in to explain and a loud ethereal scream, like sandpaper scraping on chalkboard, hit them with full force. Covering their ears, they dropped to the ground, still in sudden silence, as birds in the area fell from the skies with them.

Chapter 5

Levi came to on the concrete moments later, shaking his head to clear it. Unsure of how much time had passed, he focused his attention on Nix. Maybe Joy had been on to something, but the damage was done, and he couldn't take it back. He could help from here, though.

He placed a hand on her head where she lay, breathing but unconscious. His eyes lit with bright blue water as he used his powers to move the water in her body. Finding a little bleeding in her brain, he sped up its flow, so that she recovered what would take weeks in a matter of seconds.

She came to promptly, breathing deeply. Her eyes popped wide open, and she looked at him.

"Explain."

"We need to go see the others."

She pulled herself from the ground, accepting his help. She walked forward carefully at first, until she felt sure of herself. Then, she began to run.

They rounded the corner a second later, to see devastation before them. Julius lay bleeding out in the middle of the street. Levi went to him, trying to seal his wounds. Nix didn't have time to stop to help him, because Seth and Tyrus were also on the ground, and neither was moving.

She ran into the restaurant, Connor dead from wood sticking out of his chest. She gulped as panic filled her mind. She walked with trepidation slowly toward the sound of slurping coming from her right. She rounded the wall and gasped, watching as Tommy, dripping in blood, bit into Ann's throat.

She fell to the ground, the shock too much for her. She watched as the light left her protégé's eyes…

Levi found her some moments later, assuming the charred body was Tommy.

"We were too late." Nix let the tears flow from her eyes freely.

"They're.... gone. They're all gone."

Levi knelt next to her, wrapping her in his arms. The guilt dropped his stomach as he realized he could have been responsible for all of this.

"It's my fault."

"How is this your fault?"

"Joy told me not to include you. Had I not lost those precious seconds, they may still be alive."

Nix shook her head. "Nothing could have stopped this."

Her chest heaved from the sobs, and he held her tightly. The sound of emergency vehicles could be heard, drawing closer. "We need to go."

"We have a few more seconds. Let me stay with her. Just for a few more seconds."

"Ok."

For those precious seconds, she leaned forward and brushed the hair out of Ann's face, closing her eyes. His draining of her blood had left her body already cold.

"What do we do now?" Nix forced the words out.

"We live, for them."

She nodded, giving him the ok to create a portal, and they both vanished through it just before the police arrived.

"Well, that was all wrong."

Joy, watching from the in between, cursed Levi for not listening. This explosion, that had knocked all her chess pieces off the board, was unavoidable, but the addition of another piece resulted in an additional rule. She sighed, letting her shoulders relax, and did what she did best, she worked the impossible problem.

"Ok, self, new rule. Levi will always go for Nix first."

She waved her hand, and before her, from the infinite void of magic, appeared a bird's eye view of the scene. In the front row for the good guys, Ann, Julius, and Connor. In the next, Tyrus and Seth. In the last row, Levi and Nyx. On the other side, Tommy, alone, but as a powerful wind element, physical attacker and cannibal.

"This essentially means they will attack as a unit." She waved her hand again, a line of light connecting the two. "But that also means I can't use Levi like I wanted for a double assault with Tyrus. Meaning the water-fire explosion is unlikely to occur, at least, at the correct time."

She rubbed her eyes, feeling a slight headache coming on. "Ok. New scenario one. Running…now." She touched Tyrus and the board came alive, Tommy exiting the restroom as the adorable mini-Tyrus crossed the street. She watched as he tried to talk Tommy down in an adorable chipmunk voice. She touched Connor, who then moved to intercept Tommy from behind. "This may work."

A minute later, Connor was dead, Ann, Tyrus, and Julius were unconscious, and Tommy was uncaptured.

She bit her lip. "I can only raise one friend at a time, or I'll run out of power. Yet we can't attack one on one, or Tommy wins. Maybe if I start with Ann, first?"

She touched tiny Ann, who began throwing flame instantly. She watched as the scenario played out, again over a minute of time, and the results weren't much better. Connor was still dead, Ann and Julius unconscious, and Tommy uncaptured.

"Ok, can't lead with our heroine, either." She cracked her knuckles then her neck. "Not giving up yet, though."

She reset the board, trying Julius, Connor, and Nix in the lead position with similar results.

"Let's get a bit crazy then." She chose Levi first, then Tyrus. Levi revived Nix so she didn't have to, expected. Tyrus tried to talk him down. Good so far. She felt her spirits lift for a moment. She watched the others wake and join the fight, but felt her stomach turn as it ended with Connor and Julius dead, Nix eaten, Tommy addicted to his first taste of phoenix blood, and everyone else unconscious.

"Ok. Three steps back." She stretched her shoulders and reset the board. She knew that there was a near perfect solution, she only had to find it, and do so within the next several minutes or be discovered. "No problem."

For fun, she squished little Tommy out of frustration, and the mini piece looked at her and waved a fist. She flicked him off the board and into the void, but the piece instantly returned, hopping up and down angrily. Well, yeah, that wouldn't work, but at least it was satisfying. She reset the board again and got down to business.

"Ok. Rules. One. Levi and Nix come as a set and can't be first or second. Two. You, Joy, can only revive a single person at a time. Three. Tyrus will always play peacemaker. Four. You have two physical attackers that are essentially useless without a magic shield but would be very powerful last. Five. You can't raise Tyrus or Ann first. So, who is left?"

Suddenly excited, she reset the board again, watching the solution play out. Letting out a "woo-hoo" she vanished, just before light entered the chamber from behind her.

Tommy took a few moments to gather himself. Letting loose that amount of wind energy to knock everyone in the area unconscious had cost him, but he knew when he walked out the door, everyone around him would be down. It was desperate, but the girl…unnerved him. He needed to get her alone and find out why. For the first time in a very long while, he felt renewed, as if maybe his death wasn't the only inevitable fate playing out. Something about her gave him…hope, and while it was foreign to him, it was powerful.

As he walked into the main dining room, a shift in the air bristled the hair on the nape of his neck. Someone else was conscious within the vicinity.

Joy used those precious extra seconds to enact the best version of her plan. She bounced first to Seth, the only other person that had the ability to both create portals and wake others without getting lost by their heart.

She knelt beside him and quickly touched a hand to his head and chest. He woke instantly. She cupped his face in her hands and said, 'no time. Tyrus, Connor, Levi. Repeat it back."

"Tyrus, Connor, Levi."

"I'll get the rest. Go wake them, in that order. Now. Quickly!"

They both disappeared with a shimmer of light.

In the seconds it took to revive Seth, Tommy walked forward through the restaurant, first toward Ann, then toward the entrance when a surge of power caught his attention. Passing an unconscious Connor, he didn't realize he was walking into a carefully constructed trap. He reached the entrance right after Seth revived Tyrus. The luck element disappeared, and Tommy confronted his prior mentor.

"The Red Dragon in all his glory!" He made a show of bowing sarcastically. "I was wondering when you'd finally acknowledge this lowly knave. Do you even remember me?"

Tyrus squared his shoulders, making his stance non-threatening. He placed his hands at his sides but refused to put them into his pockets. "I remember you, Tommy."

He twitched at the mention of his name. "To what do I owe this pleasure?" He growled the last word.

"I take it you know I didn't come alone."

Tommy smiled. "I felt so many Mythics so quickly. I hope you don't mind the…pretense."

Tyrus tried not to snort at the massive amount of unconscious and vulnerable bystanders currently lying on concrete around them.

"What is it going to take to resolve this without bloodshed, Tommy?"

The twisted man smiled sadistically. "I'm so glad you asked."

Joy revived Ann as Tyrus distracted Tommy. She put a finger

to her lips, as her friend looked up at her. She carefully mouthed the words, "do not attack him." Then she was gone.

Ann looked at Julius, who still lay unconscious, but her attention was drawn to her right where she could hear two men talking.

"I take it you know I didn't come alone."

That was Tyrus. Slowly, without making much sound, she stood, and walked back into the restaurant, where she locked eyes with Seth as he bent to revive Connor. Within seconds, Connor was awake, and he looked at her.

"Do not attack." She mouthed the words Joy gave her. Then, they each silently took a sheltered spot near the door, where they could strike in an instant if Tyrus failed to talk him down.

Tommy walked forward a few steps, wondering if Tyrus would retreat. Seeing him unmoving, Tommy instantly recalculated. He could feel the presence of two more behind him, but he didn't want to let on that his powers had grown that much. Someone was undoing his hard work, hoping to overpower him. They were foolish.

"I want one very simple thing." His voice shook a bit despite his efforts to appear formidable.

Tyrus changed his stance. "What is that, Tommy?"

Control. The word whispered through his mind as he struggled to keep the anger in his chest from overwhelming his senses. He knew his arms were elongating, becoming claws. He wasn't ready yet. He felt the power rush to his eyes. Saw fear in his mentor's as they began to glow yellow.

"I want you to admit what you did."

Joy and Seth both arrived at Levi and Nix at the same moment. She smiled as they revived the couple at the same time. Levi and Nix woke instantly. Joy put a finger to her lips and reached a hand out to Seth, who took it. A glow enveloped the four of them and she could reach their minds.

"We have no time. Seth and I will come from the sides. Levi, you need to support Tyrus. Nyx, stay back unless I come get you. If Tommy sees you, something horrible will happen."

The glow faded as she opened her eyes, and everyone nodded. One more person to wake, then they'd be able to strike. She just hoped Tyrus said the right thing. This whole plan could crumble in the span of a second, if he didn't.

"You'll have to give me some context."

Tommy snarled at him. "I tried, you know. I tried being good. For the first couple of years after what you did to Nix, I tried. Living in the woods, surviving on animal kills. It worked for a while, then, well… *it didn't.*" He let out a maniacal laugh.

Tyrus was beginning to understand. "You want me to apologize for abandoning you."

Tommy was instantly in front of him, his claws digging into Tyrus' shoulders. "Yesssss. The kind, wise, patient dragon. Always the hero." Tommy chuckled. "Where were you for me? After you and Levi killed her…" Tyrus hissed in a breath as Tommy's claws ripped through his skin.

"Did you even care what I was going through?"

Tyrus fought the pain. "After the battle with Nix, when Levi and I found out how we'd been played…"

"The great mastermind? Being played? That's a funny…twist." Tommy curled his fingers under Tyrus's flesh, torturing him. He watched his mentor's face begin to change, his eyes turn bright green. "There's the dragon."

"Tommy, stop. We tried to fix it."

"Fix? There is no fixing me." In his rage, Tommy's awareness of his surroundings faded. He lost track of the Mythics surrounding him as he focused his ire on the man in front of him.

Joy waited for that very moment to slip into the restaurant to revive Julius, the fuse to the bomb she was about to purposely set off. If anyone could be counted on to attack fiercely, it was the man lying on the ground in front of her.

She knelt carefully beside him and placed a hand on his muscular chest. The other went to his temple. His deep brown eyes opened swiftly, and she sought his mind.

"*Go.*" Then she vanished.

The stage set, Joy bounced into her position, to the right of combat placed to both save Julius and support Ann. Everyone had their assignment, and if luck was on their side, they'd all survive. She had done all she possibly could. With a breath and a protesting stomach, she waited for Julius to attack.

Tyrus felt his hands begin to change. The claws and red scales moved from his fingertips to his elbows. He was close to losing control, but he knew he had to keep Tommy talking as long as possible.

"You know I cried the first time. Did you know that?" Tyrus watched Tommy's yellow eyes fill with tears. The guilt hit him, twisting his chest and stomach into knots.

"She was lost. In the woods. She came to me smelling like birthday cake and strawberries and sweat."

Tyrus moved his hands toward Tommy's head, slowly as the younger Mythic flinched. Tyrus touched his shoulders gently. "For that, I am very sorry."

The yellow power dampened, his eyes returning to normal. "She was a hiker. Lost. And she found me. *ME*! What rotten luck did she have? To come into my home seeking help but finding…"

Tyrus squeezed his shoulders. "I'm sorry."

"I told her to go. Even then. I was *good.* She wouldn't go. She touched me and I was so…hungry and deprived of contact. I couldn't resist. Cake, and strawberries, and sweat."

Tyrus's stomach rolled, but his face remained calm and sympathetic. Tommy lowered his head. "What bad luck to step on my door, poor Gretel."

Tyrus saw Julius ready himself out of the corner of his eye. "It's ok. You're home now. I'm sorry I couldn't help you then, but I can now."

"Fix?" Tommy tilted his head, still for a moment. "No, Tyrus. There's no fixing a monster."

Tyrus braced for it. He knew what would happen, and was helpless to stop it, other than saying, "Tommy, don't."

But his protégé was already throwing him away, across the street, and into brick.

Julius struck just as Tyrus was out of Tommy's grip. He sank canine teeth into the Wendigo's shoulder, his murder paws pinning the Mythic's arms, trying to hold him still as long as possible. Tommy struggled against his grip, just as the others attacked. A low growl escaped him as the wind hit his back, sharp as knives, cutting into his flesh as he dug his claws and teeth in further.

Connor's griffin wings were out, and he used his momentum to attack just after Julius. The force propelled all three men forward, Tommy hitting the ground the hardest., Julius on top of him. Connor recovered and turned against the same brick wall Tyrus hit seconds earlier.

The glow around Tyrus meant Seth had protected the Dragon, and Connor was able to help him to his feet. Both men rushed to the center of the street as Ann walked forward, fire burning in her hands. The others closed in as Tommy used his wind to propel himself and

Julius up from the ground, flipping them in the air, hoping to crush Julius against the concrete. Ann looked at Levi across the street, her brow lifting, trying to tell him what to do. She then aimed and fired a volley at Tommy while Levi reached a hand out, water suddenly underneath Cerberus, creating resistance to their fall.

Tommy had to concentrate on too many things at once. While he was powerful, his mind was still far too human. He wouldn't allow the beast to take his mind, not yet. As he battled to force Julius to hit the ground against Levi's will, the fire hit him. He screamed and twisted, the water extinguishing the flame, but placing him in the inferior position. Julius let go for only a second and he took advantage of that, flinging him away.

Connor and Tyrus were in the air, Tyrus colliding with Tommy while Connor grabbed Julius by the waist, saving him from a bad fall. Levi swirled the water around the two, hoping to keep Tommy from lashing out at any civilians. Ann, seeing his idea, reinforced the barrier with fire.

Joy and Seth appeared at their sides, each placing a hand on their elemental, reinforcing the barrier. "Just keep going for a few more moments."

"Tyrus is in there alone." Ann's ambivalence toward him faded.

"Trust him. We've got this."

Ann didn't think Joy sounded convinced. Her usually upbeat and cheery friend was so serious. Still, she focused her fire toward the ball of swirling mythic power. She watched as the fire and water mingled, sending sparks of energy flying wildly around it. "This can't hold forever. It will only get worse."

"Just a few more seconds. Trust me, Ann."

Inside the destabilizing orb, Tyrus and Tommy both grappled with each other.

"Tommy, stop!" Tyrus screamed as Tommy ripped through the skin of his dragon wings. He punched the younger man in the face once to break his concentration and tried again. "Please!"

Tommy's laughter sounded over the roar of power. "I will never stop. Don't you get it? You know what I am." Tommy punched into Tyrus's stomach, feeling his skin give way. "Give up or kill me. This was inevitable and you know it."

Blood gushing from his mouth, Tyrus fought against the darkness that tried to swallow him whole. A roar from his throat shook them both, Tommy's hand in his stomach stilling. Claws ripped into Tommy's shoulders where Julius had begun. Tommy cried out, sandy chalkboard against a dragon's shout.

Tyrus couldn't stay in this battle any longer and live. His vision was already darkening around the edges. With his remaining wing, he dove, shoving Tommy through the barrier and slamming him into the concrete below.

Levi and Ann dropped the barrier as they saw the two figures hit the ground. Everyone, including Nyx, began to surge toward the two men. Joy watched it in slow motion, before she tried in one last effort to stop the inevitable. She saw Ann and Levi take a running step as Connor and Julius came from the other side, gathering their muscles to lunge forward.

Seth bounced forward and took Tyrus's hand, slowly gripping the dragon claw to remove him from the fight. But Joy was more worried about Nix. She bounced to her swiftly, as time sped back up.

She grabbed for Nix's arm, hoping to stop her from her fate. This jerked the firebird backward, and her feet flew in front of her, and Nix hit the ground with a thud.

"Dammit." Joy moved, desperate to stop the flow of blood from her head. She didn't want Tommy to smell it, or this whole situation would get so much worse.

But at that moment, two pivotal events took place simultaneously. Levi felt Nix fall and dropped from the fight, his water suddenly absent on the battlefield. And the sweet smell of phoenix blood reached Tommy's wind, flying toward his face rapidly. As her intoxicating scent hit him, his eyes lit bright yellow. It stimulated his mind beyond the depths of his control, the smell an instant addiction that promised renewal, rebirth, and sweet redemption.

The beast surged through his mind, taking over completely, and with it, power rushed over his body and outward, another explosion of wind throwing every player away from Tommy, slamming them far away where they could do no harm.

The beast rose slowly, a clicking growl coming from its changing, vinelike throat. It floated over the street toward Joy and Nix, arriving instantly.

"NO!" Joy screamed, throwing her power at him. He shoved it back at her, and she flew, hitting the ground ten feet away, not moving.

Taking his former crush into his arms, the clicking growl became a purr. He sucked in air, her delectable blood filling his senses. "Ambrosia, apricots, and…peace." A second later, they were both gone.

Chapter 6

When Ann came to on the concrete, she stood abruptly, her head swimming a bit. She steadied herself and walked forward, taking in the scene around her. Everywhere she looked, people were beginning to wake up. It was hard to tell where her team was among the crowd. Everyone seemed confused, and the distant sound of sirens told her help was on the way.

She walked into the alleyway where Levi and Nix had been, finding nothing except a few drops of blood. She circled around the building and looked at the street in front of the restaurant, where the fight had occurred.

It looked as if a tornado had touched down only for a split second, wind damage evident from the torn shutters and flung garbage cans. Branches had fallen from the trees that lined the sidewalks and chairs and tables were overturned in disarray.

A hand on her shoulder caused her to jump. Her eyes lit with red flame as she rotated her body to see who it was. Julius greeted her.

"Julius." She hugged her friend, careful to avoid the bloody stains coming through his shirt. "You're ok, at least. Have you found anyone else?"

He shook his head. "Unfortunately, no. What do you remember?"

"Being shoved backward by his wind. Then I was out."

"Me, too."

"Can you use your sense of smell to find them?"

He sighed, "already did. I don't know where they went, but they aren't here any longer."

"I guess we regroup at the penthouse? Do you have your phone?"

"Busted."

She reached into her pocket and produced her own destroyed smartphone. "Mine too. I guess we walk until I can fly us there. You good?"

He nodded. "Hurting, but I can walk a block or two."

"You need my shoulder?"

"Nah. You go ahead, Fenix. I'm ok."

She walked away from the crowd, trying to make a path for Julius to follow. In spite of his bravado, she knew he was hurting and needed to be healed. She just didn't understand why her friends hadn't waited for them. Usually, no one was left behind. She turned into the first alleyway they came to and held out her arms.

"Ready?"

He chuckled. "No, but we need to get there…soon."

She gripped underneath his arms. "Once we are airborne, remember to wrap your legs around mine."

He blushed. "I should be saving you, not the other way around."

She bit her lip to keep from laughing. "I'm saving you because you took so much damage saving me earlier. You did your job, now I'm doing mine."

He nodded, an apologetic smile on his face. "Weird to worry about what other guys would think of me, yeah?"

"They'd think you're quite dashing with a woman in your arms. Now come on, Romeo, let me get you home."

A few seconds later, they were interlocked and she allowed her phoenix in, calling to the bird that was always beneath the surface. She didn't so much ask for her wings to spread, as she simply whispered to her, "*take us home*."

Her fire wings stretched out from her torso, red flame dancing in the slight shape of feathers. Ashes fell from them slowly as they stretched, then retracted, lifting them off the ground. They were flying away from the scene seconds later, toward the penthouse as quickly as possible. Julius wrapped his legs around hers to keep from falling, struggling to stay conscious with the change in air pressure.

"Just breathe." Ann said it over the roar of her fire wings. "Five minutes to go."

He clenched tightly, focusing on breathing in and out, while she tried to steady her flight path. It was difficult to carry a muscular man without dropping him. Reaching to her bird, she said, "*help me hold him.*"

Giving up a little more control, the phoenix within came out, talons of fire wrapping around Julius to steady her. Ann didn't try to control her, she just watched as her bird piloted them to the roof of the penthouse.

It was a hundred feet away when she felt him go limp. The change jostled her bird who dived slightly to keep from losing him. Luckily, they had enough space to gain altitude back to land on the roof of her mentor's apartment complex.

Her heart pounded in her chest and her head, from the near-death experience. She calmed herself and her phoenix flew back into her mind, the wings vanishing. Some burnt ash fell to the ground as she picked up Julius's head, feeling for a pulse.

It was faint, but it was there. "I'll be right back with help."

She left him on the roof, walking to the stairway, burning the lock off the handle and heading down a floor to her mentor's apartment. Hopefully, someone else made it out. Hopefully, they'd be able to help her keep Julius alive.

Tyrus wanted to search for them, but the hole in his stomach took priority as he woke. He was lucky to be alive. He struggled to turn onto his back, groaning at the immense pain. He knew if he could change into dragon form, his wounds would heal, but the severity meant he would need to stay changed for a long while. Taking a series of quick breaths, he concentrated on calling to his beast. His hands changed first, becoming scales and claws, which moved up his shoulders and down his chest. As they grazed over the wound, the pain became blinding hot, piercing as his tissue changed form.

He whimpered as it receded, as the change moved down his legs, and able to stand, he allowed himself to fully transform, for the first time in a long while. He felt the ground beneath him with his four claws, felt the wings protrude from his back. One was weak, but he couldn't risk being seen here.

The sirens were drawing closer, and it would be a few days before he would have the energy to return to human form. He worried about the new Mythics, but he had to take care of himself first. Hoping the wing would last for a short flight to his family land, some three hours away from the city, he gathered his body, and lifted off the ground with his wings.

The instant pain told him it wouldn't be an easy flight, but he let out a soft growl and half climbed, half lifted himself to the roof of the alleyway building. There, he prepared for the pain for a few seconds, and lifted off, traveling away from the city. As he flew, he calculated where to go from here, but in his heart, he had very little hope left.

Seth rushed toward the hospital doors, carrying a limp Joy in his arms. Try as he could, she wouldn't wake. After everything failed, he thought it best to make sure she was getting as much help from modern medicine as possible.

"Can someone please help me?" He shouted it, disturbing the emergency staff, but he didn't have time to care. Someone in scrubs rushed over to him, stethoscope placed onto her chest. "What happened?"

It was removed, as the attendant checked her pulse. "Steady heartbeat, strong pulse."

The truth wasn't an option, so he simply said, "she won't wake up." His gut was telling him this was the best course of action. "Where can I put her?"

She motioned to an orderly who ran off, presumably to produce a gurney or a bed. His knees began to shake. While he wasn't a tall man, he should have been able to carry her, but the stress from the event was making him unstable.

The orderly arrived with a bed, and he set her down just as his knees began to give way. “You need one too.” The attendant checked his pulse at his neck. “Your heart is racing. We can get your info later. Let’s get you both to the back.”

She motioned to the orderly, who placed one hand around Seth’s waist, supporting him by slinging his hand over his shoulder. “It’s ok, we got you.”

In spite of his best efforts, hearing that he was ok stopped his adrenaline from spiking, and the darkness took him over. Hopefully, they were speaking the truth.

Ann began to panic as she searched the penthouse, finding it empty. This was their emergency meeting spot. If not here, they were to go to Tyrus’s farm outside the city. She couldn’t imagine anyone choosing to do that. Her family was just… gone.

She took a quick breath and stilled herself, calling the ocean to remain calm. After a moment, she asked herself, “what is top priority right now? Right. Finding help for Julius.” She searched for a smartphone and found a burner near the couch. Looking quickly through the numbers, she tried first Joy, then Seth. When both calls didn’t go through, she tried Nix and Levi. Then Tyrus. All were sent straight to voicemail.

“Dammit!” Her eyes began to tear up thinking that Julius might die, that there was no way to save him. Begging the universe for an answer, she dialed Connor.

When it began to ring, she gained a little sliver of hope and her stomach muscles unclenched. “Hello.”

“No time. Julius is dying. Can you get to the penthouse?”

She heard him moan. “Yeah. Just give me five minutes and I’ll be at the roof.”

She knew he was hurting too. “Ok. Just…get here and we can sort it all out. Please hurry, if you can.”

“Will do.”

With the call ended, she grabbed a blanket off of the couch and rushed back up the utility stairs. Opening the door, she walked out to see Julius where she had left him, a small pool of blood forming on the concrete beneath his body. She quickly closed the distance and began to rotate him to his side, so she could place the blanket over the wounds on his back.

By the time the blanket was in place, the wind picked up, and she knew it was from Connor's wings as he landed. She faced him, worried he was injured too.

Connor, however, was ok. "Thank god you're alright. Help me help him." Her voice shook.

He knelt beside her, placing a supporting hand in between her shoulders. "How is he?"

"He was conscious at the restaurant but he passed out during the flight."

"How long ago?"

"About five, ten minutes. Give or take. I'm not sure. I ran down and tried calling everyone. You're the only person that answered."

"I checked the area before you called, and no one was there. That's a good thing. It means they were able to leave."

That helped calm her. "Right. How do we help him?"

"Can you use your fire to seal his wounds?"

"Won't that hurt him?"

The hand between her shoulders patted her back while he checked for a pulse. "Dying will hurt more. His pulse is uneven and faint. We have to act now."

He turned him over onto his stomach. "Seal the wound while I go get something."

She did so, raising the blanket away from his back, trying not to notice the blood flowing from the wounds. She called back the ocean and held out her hands, her firebird just beneath the surface and said, "help him."

Inside her mind the firebird fanned her wings, and she felt the heat of her magic flow from her mind to her fingertips. She watched as the flame scored her friend's back, as his body twitched and moaned from it. Seconds later, no more blood flowed.

Connor came back with two hot wires. "What are you doing?!" She covered her friend's body with hers.

"He has to turn to heal."

"He hasn't done so completely yet."

"I'm aware, but I know of no other way to force him to while he's unconscious. If he turns, he can survive."

She sighed, but seeing no other Mythics floating toward their destination, she knew this was all they could do.

"You get three tries, before we stop."

"Got it." Using the wires, he placed one on each side of his friend's chest. "God I hope this works."

He touched the wires onto his friend's skin for a split second before pulling them away. His body jerked, burns forming at the site. No change happened.

"Two more."

"Right." He moved his hands slightly and carefully touched the crackling ends to his friend's sides again. One, two. And pulled them away. A growl sounded from Julius.

"Talk to him. He may be awake enough to change."

Ann rushed forward and knelt beside him. "Julius? Can you hear me? You need to transform. If you don't, you'll die."

He moaned out loud, and his hands began to form large, black paws. "He's trying." However, the change stopped at his shoulders.

"He lost consciousness. Once more, and hopefully he can finish."

Connor moved forward and gently touched the wires to a third spot. His friend convulsed, and he pulled away, running back toward the power supply to shut off the breaker.

Ann watched as Julius quickly finished transforming in front of her, first his legs then his torso, and finally his head. It was quick, almost instantaneous. She was about to breathe a sigh of relief, but then his dark brown eyes landed on hers.

She stopped moving, realizing they'd angered a three-headed hellhound on a roof with very little maneuvering room. If he didn't remember who she was, then this could get deadly, fast.

A low growl escaped his lips as his two other heads focused on her. She remembered to breathe, slowly letting out the air from her lungs. His teeth bared, he snarled at her. She blinked, and swallowed hard, hoping to speak.

"Julius." She said it carefully, hoping a small portion of his mind was alert, that it wasn't just up to the beast inside him. "It's me. Ann."

He was black, sleek, his body doubled in size, larger than any wolf, more like a bear. His paws were huge, more than triple the size of her own hands. Staring into his three heads, she looked back and forth, one set of eyes brown, another green, the third blue. His ears were pointy and large, his face too square for a wolf but not blocky enough to be a bully breed. His fur was long over his neck but short along his body, which was muscular, his gait wide.

How did this even work for him? Did he suddenly have three brains? Was he seeing through all six eyes? Or just the middle? Frustrated she had not thought about these things earlier, she repeated her request as he snarled again. "Julius, it's me. Ann. I'm sorry we had to hurt you."

One of his giant murder paws stepped toward her, but his snarl was gone. She couldn't hear Connor, so only assumed he was standing as still as she was. Her body tensed as his paw hit the ground near her, and he tensed as well. When she didn't move again, the three heads began to sniff the air around her.

She took that as a good sign. "Yes, it's me, Ann."

The middle head tilted its satellite ears and sniffed again, into her hair where she smelled most like her. The other two buried their noses into her neck and her side. She felt his back end move rhythmically, and knew his tail was wagging.

"Yes, Cerberus, it's Ann."

The sniffing heads knocked her to the ground, and she was

suddenly being licked by three rough, wet tongues.

"Connor!"

She heard footsteps and Cerberus noticed him for the first time. The licks stopped and she was able to slide her body away, while the two stared each other down, frozen in place.

With their track record, this could easily escalate, but Connor seemed to have complete control over his beast. It was known that the two shared a rivalry like siblings, getting into fights only to resolve them moments later.

Cerberus growled at the man in front of him. Connor turned sideways, trying to take up less space, and slowly lowered to his knees. "It's ok. It's Connor."

Cerberus was just as wary with him as with Ann. He looked to her, seeming to ask if this was a friend. So she walked slowly toward Connor and placed a hand on his shoulder. When the beast saw he wouldn't move, he walked forward slowly, a growl sounding a little louder.

Connor stayed still while the beast sniffed him as well. Recognizing him, Cerberus turned back to Ann, who he seemed much more interested in.

He wagged his tail, crouching, showing he wanted to play. Ann and Connor both collectively sighed, relieved this hadn't turned into another battle.

"Ok. Now we have an alive but huge dog to get down a staircase and into the penthouse. Ideas?"

Connor shrugged, as Cerberus walked over to the door and marked his territory.

"Wakey-wakie!" Someone was slapping her cheek, and Nix groaned. "It's time to wake up, Nix."

The voice was deeper than she remembered, but through the haze in her mind, she recognized it as Tommy's. This startled her, and her eyes flew open.

The dim light made it hard to see at first. She felt cold steel around her wrists and ankles. She was sitting upright, probably chained to a chair. Tommy leaned against a table in front of her. She heard birds, but no traffic. That meant they most likely were no longer in the city.

She glanced at the walls of the room, noting they were made of rounded log. They were in a cabin.

"Hello, sleepy head! Half your friends are probably dead!" Tommy laughed as she glared at him. "Just kidding, I think most of them are alive. I don't know about the one boy though. The canine. He and Tyrus might be dead. Not sure on that, because I left with you before anyone could stop me."

She took a few seconds to breathe, to sort out her thoughts. "Why didn't you gag me?"

He smiled. "I don't need to worry about anyone hearing you scream out here. In fact, I kind of want to enjoy the sounds I know you're going to make."

She swallowed hard at that. "What are you talking about, Tommy? Why are you going to hurt me?"

He looked wounded. "Hurt you? I mean, it will hurt, but you'll live. I promise. I'd never do anything to kill *you.*"

"Why did you take me?"

He stared at her as if she were stupid. "You don't know? Well, of course you don't." His expression changed, his pupils dilating. "You are… the best of us." He wiped one of her dark bangs out of her eyes. She flinched as he touched her skin.

"Don't do that. Please."

The intimacy he was showing didn't match their past, and Nix was confused. "Tommy, just explain to me why I'm here."

"You're here…. because of…. apricots, and ambrosia, and peace."

She opened, then shut her mouth. "Is that what I smell like to you?"

"Smell isn't strong enough a word. And not you, but your

blood. I can't believe in all our interactions, I never smelled phoenix blood before. Forgive me for having a little taste while you were unconscious. Your head wound has since been cleaned. You should heal yourself."

That's why the room kept turning. "Let me go, and I can heal myself."

"No, no." Tommy leaned back against the table. "No, you stay chained with stainless steel. Your orange flame burns at around 1300 degrees Celsius, and this metal is strong enough to resist you."

"So, I just, have to heal myself here?"

"Yes."

"Do you have a way to cool me down?"

"Oh, right, you probably can't see, but yes. There's a shower above your head and a drain at your feet."

She didn't want to think what he used those for. "Fine. But leave me alone until I'm finished."

"Agreed." He stepped back, and Nix let her flame fill her eyes. Without her phoenix, she had to be extremely careful when she used her fire to heal. Too much, and she'd combust, and without her bird, would be a pile of ash for eternity.

Still, the head wound was serious, and she knew she needed to try. Closing her eyes, her whole body felt hot. She focused the flame toward her head, and the heat collected there. She could tell she was surrounded by orange light. It filled the dark and she felt the burn fade the pain over the wound. When the pain was gone completely, she knew she was healed.

She let the fire release, let it die, and the heat faded. However, her body remained hot. "Shower, now."

She heard his feet walk toward the right of the cabin, the squeak of a neglected spout being opened. Seconds later, cold water poured over her body, steam rising from her flesh. It filled the room quickly, a dense fog that both of them couldn't see through.

She looked around wildly, wondering if there was anything she could use to escape. Unfortunately, the walls of the cabin were bare.

The chains were attached to the ground, so she couldn't use them, and the chair beneath her felt like metal. She probably couldn't burn through it. If she killed Tommy now, she'd be stuck here.

As the fog faded, along with her hope of escaping, Tommy clapped his hands together slowly and stepped forward out of the fog. "Magnificent, as always."

"You can turn the water off now." She was beginning to feel cold, and her teeth chattered.

"Oh, right." He moved to do so, then returned to her side. "Unfortunately, no towels. But you should know I value you more than my own life."

"Why?"

He sighed. "Why." He looked away from her. "You were always the most honest. Levi, Tyrus, they always feared what I could become, but they acted like it wasn't a big deal. Back when you had your phoenix, you were always truthful with me. I value that honesty. If you were afraid, you dealt with the threat, made sure I knew you'd kill me if I went too far.

"Because of you, because you were honest, I could keep the monster in check. Because I knew there *was* a monster, because you told me it was there. Tyrus, Levi, the others, they all wanted to treat me as a human. As a boy. And if I gave into that, I'd forget that I was a monster. And if I forgot, the monster would overwhelm me. Don't you see?"

He knelt in front of her, and she struggled not to tense. "Your fear kept me grounded. In acknowledging the monster, you help keep me in balance. Your honesty meant I could trust you. Trust you to kill me if I got too bad."

"You, want me to kill you?"

He chuckled. "When I got here, yes, I was looking for a phoenix to end my life. Your younger one, Ann.... I ran into her at a bank."

"I remember."

"She's strong, but not too wise, yet. She was out in seconds flat."

"I remember that too."

"But you." He smiled slightly. "Even without your bird, you are still being *honest.* And that means everything to me. I…don't want to die anymore."

"What do you want then?"

He gazed at her as if she were food, rather than a friend. "I want…" He sighed, as if he couldn't find the words. Walking away, he reached into a backpack and turned toward her, holding a knife.

"Tommy, what are you doing???"

"Shhh. It's ok." He held his hands up as if he wasn't going to harm her but strode forward slowly.

"Tommy, please don't do this." She could feel her heart beating out of her chest, her stomach was tight with fear. Her breath sped up and her whole body tensed.

"It's ok." When he reached her, he held out his wrist, and slowly swiped the blade across his own flesh. She calmed, watching as his wound instantly healed.

"How?" She didn't recall Wendigos having that ability.

He knelt beside her again. "Just a taste. And this is the result. Don't you see? I don't want to *kill* you. I *need* you."

She was beginning to feel a different, slower kind of dread fill her. "My blood, did this?"

He searched her face. "So, you didn't know, either? That phoenix blood can heal other Mythics?"

She gulped and began to breathe too quickly.

"Shh. Shh. It's ok. Nix, its ok." He stroked her head as if she were a child. "I don't want to hurt you, unless I *have* to. Don't you see? You're my redemption."

She bit her tongue, hoping the pain would stop the panic from building in her chest. "I can't be that for you. Tommy, friends aren't food!"

Tommy retreated as if she'd burned him. "No, no no. You're not food. Nix you are so much more to me than food. You're…" he searched for the word. "You're a friend. And a mentor. You're a healing power. You're…

"Listen, I know that we didn't get off on the right foot this time. I know the chains aren't ideal. I'm hoping, that with time, you'll understand that this is really the best option. I don't want to eat you, just…drink some of your blood so I can heal. I…haven't felt this clear-headed in a long time."

The panic threatened to overwhelm her again, and she chuckled hysterically.

"It's really ok. Look, eventually, you'll get used to me and I can release you. That's the plan. You'll stay with me, and I can use your blood to stop the cravings. One drop, one taste, and it's like the beast went quiet. I've fed and fed and fed until the hunger consumed me. Until I was nothing but flesh and bone, and need.

"But you, Nix, your blood. One drop, and I was *me* again. I don't want to hurt you. I want to protect you. Keep you safe. Keep you fed and happy, and healthy. I want…" He tilted his head to the side and closed his eyes, as if he were debating with himself.

"I want you to see me as you used to see them."

"You." She steadied herself. "You want me. To…love you."

He smiled, boyish and innocent. For her, it was horrifying. "One day, hopefully, yes."

She closed her eyes, as thoughts raced through her mind. *This is crazy. How am I going to get away? Did the others survive? How will they find me?*

Out loud, she said, 'then you need to get me food. Now."

He thought, and then said, "yes! See? Cooperation! The start of any good relationship. And *communication.* Of course, you need food. I'll be back."

He opened the door of the cabin and light rushed in, but it was quickly shut and bolted behind him. Alone, Nix prayed that they found her, before this monster could do much damage.

Marie turned away from the too bright sunlight cascading into her room in the tower. Joy was bouncing up and down on her cot, merry despite the events that had just occurred on earth.

"Why are you dreaming now? Shouldn't you be there, helping them pick up the pieces?"

Joy stopped, tears instantly falling from her eyes. "I can't go back yet. I messed everything up."

Marie felt sympathy for her friend, who visited often, but didn't understand everything about this realm. "No, you took every precaution you could. We often can't make perfect outcomes. We just try to make sure fate wins over chaos. And you did that. You found a way to save everyone."

Joy kicked her feet into the air off the side of the cot. "But Tyrus is hurt. So is Julius. And the one outcome I was trying to avoid happened anyway."

"Nix is still alive. They're all alive. Because of you."

"I can't face them yet. I'll cry. They'll feel bad. I'm not ready."

"You can stay for a few days, but we both know that your work isn't done."

"I know."

Hoping to ease her friend, Marie opened the door. "How about I get you some pastries. You always love those."

"The rose flavored ones?"

"Sure."

"Ok." She stood and began to jump on the bed again. Marie closed the door behind her, walking slowly down the alabaster steps of the great hall. She couldn't give away the fact that Joy was staying here. In this realm, she was currently a fugitive, and Marie's standing was necessary for the group's success on earth.

With a blank face, she nodded to the other similarly robed initiates as she walked into the kitchen, grabbing overly large and colorful pastries laden with bright butterfly fondant in rainbow bright colors. Rose, jasmine, and peach lily, Joy's favorites. These would bring a smile to her friend's face and peace to her soul. The sooner Joy recovered emotionally, the sooner they could get back in this fight, and it was incredibly important to do so.

Humming quietly, she avoided the stares. Though you never really felt hungry or full here, many of the residents of this realm still disapproved of gluttony. Marie didn't care, as she loved the pastries just as much as Joy. This would seem odd, but not unusual. Making sure no one was around, she opened the door to her room carefully and closed it behind her, as Joy ravenously attacked the tray of pastries. Marie chuckled and sat next to her, hoping Ann was ok. Thoughts of her father drifted to her, but he was beyond her reach. She'd tell Joy to check in on him for her, when she returned.

After finishing the first tasty treat, Joy asked, "so, while I'm here, why don't you catch me up?"

Marie smiled, and began to share what she knew of the In-between.

Ann and Connor eventually used some meat to lure Cerberus into the penthouse, and an hour later, they realized he couldn't stay here, forever.

"He's already destroyed the couch." She looked at the tattered white fabric and dreaded the chastisement she'd receive from Nix. "We need to get him out of the city."

"Where?"

"Didn't Tyrus have land somewhere?"

"Right. But we don't know where. Even if we find it, how do we get a giant three headed dog out of the apartment without being noticed?"

She watched as Cerberus chewed through an armchair like he was chewing a bone. "We need a portal."

"Exactly. So we need to find Joy, Seth, or Levi."

"No one is answering their phone."

"Have you tried calling them again? It's been an hour. Maybe someone will answer now."

She sighed, but knew he was right. Taking her phone from her pocket, she tried Joy, then Seth. Neither answered. "Ok, lastly, Levi."

She hit call and was surprised when he picked up on the third ring.

"Ann?"

Not expecting him to answer, she collected her thoughts.

"Ann? Hello?"

"I'm here." At the sound of her voice, Cerberus moved and sat on the opposite end of the couch, his large body half on the cushions and half on the ground. He leaned into her as he continued to chew his bone chair.

"He's going to choke on those splinters." She said it to Connor, but Levi heard.

"What?"

Connor shook his head as if to say, "*I'm not telling him 'No.'*"

"Sorry. We have a bit of a problem on our hands, and we need help. Seth and Joy aren't answering."

She heard his silence on the other end. She knew he was calculating something. It seemed pensive, instead of peaceful.

"Where are you?"

"We need a portal at the penthouse." The phone went dead.

A few seconds later, Cerberus alerted, his ears and heads turning toward the bedrooms. "He must be in there."

Connor stood, and walked slowly around Cerberus, greeting Levi in the hallway.

"Please don't make any sudden moves." Connor asked Levi before he could see Julius.

Levi looked confused. Behind Connor, Cerberus hopped toward Levi, and seeing the intruder, began to growl.

"Nice, hellhound. Good puppy."

With a whirl of water, Levi produced a large bone. Cerberus looked at it with interest. "I bet this bone tastes much better than that chair."

Cerberus barked in agreement and wagged his tail.

"Just promise not to eat me and it's all yours."

Another bark, and Cerberus even sat. Levi walked around Connor and handed the massive hound the bone. He walked away and sat in the corner, growling and chewing, his three heads fighting for a spot of the bone to gnaw.

Connor eyed him strangely.

Levi nodded. "Not my first run in with hell hounds, although the first three headed one I've seen. Has a good temperament, for being one."

Connor and Ann nodded. "We think he's still young."

"Yeah, he'll grow into using his hell fire."

"His… *what*?"

Levi saw their scared faces and thought it best not to elaborate. "Never mind, anyway, I take it he needs to stay in this form until he can conserve energy to change back?"

"Yes. And we can't keep him here."

"Where are we taking him?"

Connor and Ann looked at each other. "Doesn't Tyrus have a family farm or something?"

Levi thought of his last visit there, when he'd left Dr. Gregory Jackson tied to a tree instead of killing him outright like the contract had specified.

"I'm familiar with it."

"Can we go there? Soon?"

Levi nodded. Water swirled around all of them, and they were transported to a woodsy area near the mountains, three hours east of St. Blaise. A couple cabins and a dock lay next to a lake, a great snow-capped mountain rising up in the distance.

Cerberus, at first confused, walked to Ann for pets. She gave him a good ear scratch and then he walked away with the bone still in his mouth, sniffing the trees.

"Great, he's going to mark here, too."

"Better here than the penthouse. Speaking of Nix…"

"I'm on it." A roar sounded in the distance. "You get to deal with that, while I watch Nix until we make a plan to save her."

"Save her from what?" She tried to ask, but he was already gone.

Levi stayed well out of range of the cabin. He'd tracked Tommy there after the fight. This was his fault, and he intended to stay by her side until a moment when he could strike. Wind unfortunately trumped water, even though he was stronger than most. In addition, he couldn't risk Nix getting hurt if he chose to attack.

Staying downwind, where it was least likely for him to be scented, he was glad he had an excuse to bring more of the Five to Tyrus. They'd watch over the changed Mythics so he didn't have to.

The luck elements, Joy and Seth, were out of play for now. Guilt washed over him. This was happening because he hadn't listened to Joy. At the time, it seemed like the right decision, but he knew that the right decision didn't always lead to the best outcome. Still, he hadn't anticipated this. No one had.

Forgiving himself a little, he felt the ground beneath him. Inside, a shower turned on. He felt the water wash over her body, felt her cool at its touch. For now, she was whole, unharmed, and alive. He'd wait until the time was right, then the last thing Tommy would see was his eyes as he ripped him apart.

Chapter 7

After realizing that Cerberus would do what he wished, Ann and Connor followed him at a distance, more to make sure others were safe from him. They had tracked the hellhound through the woods around Tyrus's land for several hours, before they spotted the dog perched low, as if it were focused on prey. His hair stood up and a low growl emanated from him.

"We need to see what he sees."

Connor nodded, instantly spreading wings and flying to the front. Circling back, he landed next to her. "He's near a cave."

"I don't see one." She looked around trying to spot it.

"It's behind the waterfall."

"So, whatever was roaring is in there?"

"I take it, yeah."

"He shouldn't go in first."

"I agree. I'll take the lead."

"Considering his size, maybe we should both 'go first.'"

"That's fine by me. Then no matter what we find in there, we can have each other's backs."

"My thought too. Let's go."

Cerberus allowed them to pass, then followed when he realized they were headed into danger. A large river spanned their right with a waterfall to the west. They walked along the rocky shoreline until the cave appeared. Claw marks and water made it clear something large had recently headed inside.

"Slowly, carefully."

He nodded. They helped each other over the rocks, avoiding the water falling from a large crevice in the mountain. The cave entrance was large enough that they could walk in side by side, big enough for Cerberus to fit easily.

As they walked into the dark, she lit a flame so they could see. Letting it go, the flame danced with a life of its own ahead of them slightly. Cerberus was entertained by it, so to keep him occupied, she made another he could chase behind them.

They walked inward slowly, about fifty steps before the cave turned and the walls gave way to a large cavern. Several holes above allowed small drips of water and sunlight to invade the dark. It was very large, with a small pool of water in the middle. To the right was a dark corner, something breathing evenly from inside it.

She looked to Connor, who nodded, silently agreeing with her. Producing another flame, she launched it forward, watching it as it slowly made its way toward the beast. A low growl caused Cerberus to rush to their side. He growled in return.

She touched between his shoulders and calmed him. "We don't need another fight so soon."

Though he sat, he stayed where he was. The light got close to the beast, and they could see red scales glistening.

"Tyrus?" She said his name loudly, hoping his mind was intact. From the corner, his head popped out in full dragon form.

Cerberus barked, and the dragon backed away into the darkness. Ann turned to Connor. "Let me go. Fire elements recognize each other."

"I'll try to keep Cerberus back."

"Thanks." She walked forward, while Connor wrangled the hell hound. She stepped around the pool of water and toward him slowly. When she couldn't see anything anymore, she lit another flame, and gasped, his large dragon head close to hers, his green eyes staring at her intelligently.

"Tyrus?" Something about his eyes made her bold. "Are you ok?"

He nodded slowly. She reached out her hand and touched between his eyes, allowing their flames to recognize each other. It had happened once before. She felt liquid heat flow over her body, knew he felt something similar. Flame recognizing flame.

"It's ok. We've got you now."

The red dragon lowered its head and sighed loudly.

She knelt next to him. "How many days will it take for you to change back?"

He tilted his head at her, then sighed twice in a row. "Two days?"

A soft purr escaped him. "Ok. Just be careful. Julius changed, too. And I think his mind is less intact than yours."

That caused him to look outward, lifting his head and standing on all fours.

She got nervous. "Tyrus, I don't think that's a good idea."

He paused, hearing the quiver in her voice. Lowering his head, he stared at her, maintaining eye contact. An intense pull drew her to stare back at him. His eyes glowed bright green, and he seemed to whisper directly into her mind.

"*I can help him.*"

The sensation faded quickly. "Ok, but it's on you, now." He nodded again and began to walk forward toward the center of the room where Connor was rubbing his belly.

Connor jumped at the sight of the Red Dragon. "Oh, hey, Tyrus."

Cerberus got up and growled low at the large dragon. Tyrus reacted, lifting his head and flaring his nostrils.

Connor rushed to her. "Is... this ok?"

"Tyrus thinks so. He said he could help."

The two circled the cavern, sizing each other up. Their body language was relaxed, so she knew they weren't a threat to each other yet. Cerberus took a step forward, and the dragon tilted his head. He tried another step, and Tyrus mirrored him. Cerberus backed up and barked loudly, its three heads all focused on the one potential threat in front of them.

Tyrus froze, allowing Cerberus to come to him. Ann held her breath, worried first that Julius would claw Tyrus apart, then wondered who would actually win.

"Who wins in dragon versus three-headed hellhound?"

Connor chuckled. "I don't want to find out."

She nodded her head in agreement.

Tyrus ended up lying down, letting Cerberus sniff him while remaining absolutely still. Knowing he was in control of his mind, she admired the way he seemed so patient with the younger Mythic. She realized this probably wasn't a first for him.

An hour later, Ann and Connor exited the cave, followed by Cerberus, who jumped along the path and drank from the water of the river. Tyrus came out of the cave, through the waterfall, flying away from them, Cerberus following after him barking excitedly.

"I guess they're ok with each other now."

"Without having gone through this, I don't think either one of us could understand what Julius is experiencing. It's probably the best that they bonded. Hopefully, as he recovers, his mind will return."

"What do we do in the meantime?"

"Make sure they're safe, I guess."

He nodded, and his stomach began to growl.

"Sorry, I guess I'm starving. Haven't eaten today."

"Let's go see if there are provisions in the cabin."

"Do you remember how to get back?"

She nodded, turning toward the trees, where a small burn mark lay on each one, showing the way back. "I didn't forget the breadcrumbs."

Seth checked out of the hospital twenty-four hours after the incident at the restaurant. Joy wasn't waking, despite being perfectly healthy, and his gut told him it was time to leave. His friends needed him, soon.

When he was out of sight of the hospital, he created a portal and went with his gut, landing at Agent Ryan's home. He strode to the door and knocked quietly.

When Ben Ryan opened the door, surprise lit his features, then worry.

"As far as I know, everyone is alive, but I feel the need to make sure you're up to date as our unofficial liaison of the state. Mind if I come in?"

"Not at all. I wondered if the restaurant was Mythic related. Come on in."

Seth closed the door behind him and followed Agent Ryan into the living room where he took a seat beside another agent, light hair, blue eyes.

"I'm Mack. I work with Ben. I don't think we've met?"

"Seth."

"Seth. Gorski."

He was beginning to become suspicious. "Yeah. How did you know?"

His gut, however, was completely silent. Something about Mack wasn't right, but it wasn't concerning either. Just a man, keeping secrets.

He looked at Ben, who gave him a nod.

"I've been keeping up on your group's progress since the bus explosion. Ben and I are working on a new unit of the F.B.I. We investigate…"

Ben took over. "…activity related to superhuman or miraculous feats. Like you guys surviving that day."

"Ah. Well, yeah. Seems so long ago now. I'm just lucky to be alive."

"Lucky indeed."

There was more to those words, but Seth couldn't tell what that was.

"How long have you been on this project, Ben?"

"A couple weeks now. Didn't Tyrus fill you in?"

"No, we were…in the middle of…something."

"But everyone is ok."

"Yeah."

Ben smiled. "Ok, we are all tiptoeing here and it's wasting what could be precious time, so I'm just going to drop the veil. Seth, Mack investigates Mythic activity discreetly for the F.B.I. Their division has existed for several years. It's the government's way of slowly gaining intelligence regarding what being a 'Mythic' actually means. It's not a catch and release program, if you know what I mean. Purely observation. He knew about your group before I was brought on."

"So you know we are…different."

"Yes."

Seth waited for him to elaborate, but he didn't continue. "Ok. So I can talk freely?"

"Please do." Mack clicked a pen, indicating he would be taking notes.

"This is strange, but if Ben says it's ok, then I'm ok. I need to catch you up. The restaurant? Was us."

He left an hour later, convinced that Ben and Mack would support them as best they could. If anything happened, they'd call his new smartphone. Creating another portal, he stepped through and bounced to Tyrus's campground.

It took a couple seconds to adjust. Noises came from the cabin to his right. He walked up the steps and into the large kitchen, where Ann and Connor sat chopping vegetables.

They stopped what they were doing, and Ann rushed toward him, hugging him tightly.

"Where were you?"

"Hospital. Joy is still out."

"What happened after the restaurant?"

"I'll catch you up but I'm starving, and you look like you're making food. Is there enough for me?"

"Yeah, just pasta and wild vegetables. Some mushrooms."

"Great." He sat on one of the stools near the kitchen island looking at the two cooks. "Where is everyone?"

A roar in the distance caused him to jump.

"Short answer? Tyrus is still a dragon, Julius is a three-headed hound of the underworld with no control over his mind, and they're friends."

"How much longer before they return to normal?"

"We are hoping less than a day from now, they'll be ok. Why is Joy out?"

"I think she feels guilty over the whole thing."

"Why?"

He sighed, not wanting to share the depth of her involvement. "She…had a lot to do with how the restaurant played out. She was hoping for a better outcome. Have you heard from Levi?"

"Briefly. Nix is still MIA."

He nodded. "I filled in Ben Ryan. Was going to update Tyrus but I guess it will have to wait until tomorrow."

"Yeah. Here, help me with these."

She placed green onions in front of him on a cutting board along with a knife. "Start chopping."

Connor and Seth built a fire that Ann promptly lit after the sun had vanished. Both turned Mythics came at the sight of it, lying down near the three teens close enough to warm themselves. Ann looked over them both, making sure there weren't any injuries. They both looked fine, so she went back to Seth and Connor.

"The weather seems to be warming up again. After that bitter cold spell, it's nice. And if it's warm here, it's warmer in St. Blaise."

"The effect of the Wendigo on the environment has stopped, yeah. Though considering how things were left, I'm not sure that's a good thing."

"Do…you think he has Nix?"

"Oh, he does." Levi came from the shadows. Neither Cerberus nor the dragon stirred. They were both asleep.

"There you are."

"Yes. I'm here, as are most of us."

"Where is he?"

"Not far."

When he didn't elaborate, Ann asked, "do we go get her now?"

Seth and Levi both said, "no."

Levi continued. "That would result in more death, I fear. We…" he looked to the two transformed men. "We need them back. Where's Joy?"

Seth sighed. "I'm afraid she won't be joining this particular rescue mission. However, Ben Ryan may be able to provide government support if we wait until tomorrow."

"Then wait, we shall." Levi looked deep into the fire, avoiding eye contact with all of them.

"Is…she…ok?"

He sighed, and if she didn't know better, teared up a little. "She's alive. He's keeping her that way."

"Is he hurting her?" Her voice shook thinking of it.

"Don't make me tell you that." Levi looked at her then, and instead of the witty cowboy he usually was, he looked dull and tired. This was devastating for him.

"Ok. Tomorrow, then?"

He nodded. "Tomorrow." He stood, and walked back into the trees from wherever he came. The three teens called the evening soon afterward, the foreboding silence too much for casual fireplace conversation. Locking the cabin for the night, they slept on couches inside, where they could watch over their two friends.

Ann woke first, grabbing a hot coffee and walking outside to check on the two of them. She froze when she saw them returned to human form, but…without any clothing. Turning beet red, she walked back inside and searched the drawers, trying to find some shorts or jeans they could put on.

When she found some stretchy pairs, she shook Seth awake.

"What is it?"

"They're…themselves again."

"That's great. Can I sleep?"

"No, they're…themselves without clothes, and you need to go

give them some."

"What makes you think I want to see naked men?"

"What, should I just leave them out there?"

"Yeah." He rolled over and went back to sleep.

So much for help. She walked outside quickly, not looking in their direction and left the two pairs of shorts on the railing of the small front porch. Then she went back inside, focusing too much on her coffee.

It wasn't long until she heard their voices, and she gave them more than ample time to dress. Then she meandered to them, slowly.

The two men looked at her and smiled. "Thanks for the shorts."

"The tidbit about returning to human form unclothed would have been helpful to have prior to…this morning."

Tyrus nodded, blushing. "Sorry. Just wasn't prepared for any of you to change fully yet. You won't age anymore, so get used to looking like you're twenty."

"Hey, I'll be my beautiful self for a long while then."

He winked at her, making her feel more awkward.

"We need to catch you both up."

Tyrus stretched, his muscles apparent without a shirt. "Got it. Let's go inside, eat and catch up."

They followed her in, and she suddenly missed having another girl around. She'd be the only one in this operation and surrounded by all the maleness didn't make her feel comfortable.

They began to discuss the plan in earnest an hour later.

"So, Levi is near her, watching." Tyrus wanted all the details before they talked strategy.

"Yes. He popped in last night to let us know we should attack today."

Seth added, "the F.B.I should be on their way and are arriving to support us by sunset."

"So that's when we'll get into position, around twilight. We need to plan not just for ourselves, but for them to support us without putting them in harm's way. As well as not getting Nix killed."

"He listened to you, at the restaurant. Will he listen again?"

"Maybe. I can try."

"Physically attacking him didn't seem to work. Should we go with elements this time?"

"I think that's the best option. Though we lost our concentration, the orb you and Levi created appeared to contain him. I'm hoping we can form a sort of net with it, reinforced with more power."

"Julius and Connor can't help with that." She looked to them, adding, "no offense," when she saw the look on their faces.

"No. No they can't. But they can direct the agents."

"And Seth?"

"Adding luck to the equation never hurt. I'll be making sure every random element reacts in our favor."

"How?"

"Oh, you'll see it when it happens. I'll need a bodyguard though."

"So, Levi, Tyrus, and I are on the net. One of you guards Seth and the other directs the agents."

"Connor should guard me. Julius is the one with Tommy's scent. He needs to find the cabin for us and track him quickly if he moves."

"Got it." Julius cracked his knuckles. "I am so ready for this dude to get what's coming to him. You weren't there at the hotel. It was…a lot."

"Hopefully, after today, he won't be a problem for anyone anymore." Sympathetically, Tyrus rested his hand on the younger man's shoulder.

"So, we have our roles, our time, we will find the where. Now we need to discuss the take down." Ann was focused.

"Here's where I want to go with it." Tyrus leaned in a began to explain his plan.

The agents arrived an hour prior to sunset, and after being briefed on the plan, Ann opened a bottle of water and "called" Levi. Sticking her hand into the liquid, she said, "Levi, we need you."

He appeared, startling some of the agents.

"No weapons!" Ben shouted at his men, who began to take aim, but they lowered their firearms and followed his instructions.

Levi looked over the camp, walked up to Tyrus, and held out a hand. Tyrus shook it, and Levi pulled him in close. After a moment, the water dragon vanished, leaving Tyrus alone.

Ann didn't hide her confusion. "What was that? Where'd he go?"

Tyrus nodded, walking toward her, lifting her hair and whispering, "*in case Tommy is watching.*" His whisper caused goosebumps to travel along her arms, and she shivered, both from fear and the unusual sensation. Tyrus seemed to ignore it, though, as he walked over to Seth.

After whispering something to him as well, he nodded to everyone else. "Seth will make a portal, on the road. Agents, you'll drive through first. Be prepared to vomit on the other side. I believe Ben supplied the bags?"

Ben nodded. "I remembered."

"Good. The Mythics will follow after the agents are through. On the other side, we are running silent. So, directions will need to be conveyed with the hand signs I showed you. Any last minute questions? Because if you have any, this is the time and the place to ask. We don't want any fatalities on this."

One of the newer agents raised his hand, and Tyrus walked over to him. Ann couldn't hear what was being said. Rather, she watched his demeanor. He looked less like the relaxed mentor they all knew and more like the soldier he'd once been. She realized she was proud of him, in fact, proud of all of them, for how far they'd come and how capable they were. Thinking back to who she was before that fateful day, she'd grown and changed without realizing just how much.

Looking to Connor, Seth and Julius, they all nodded back at her. They may be a couple members down, but she had faith that this time, they'd be successful. No more doubt, no fear crossed her mind. Then she looked to Seth, who looked away. Was he helping them feel connected this way? Helping them *feel* lucky?

Tyrus walked back toward the center of the crowd. "Anything else?"

As the crowd stayed silent, he nodded. "Alright. Let's get started. Everyone, into your vehicles."

He nodded to Seth, who walked toward the small dirt road that led out of the clearing. She watched as he concentrated, and the blackness around the road began to sway and shimmer. Tyrus saw it, and said, "roll out."

The government vehicles went first, followed by a few on foot agents and Julius. Tyrus placed a hand between her shoulders. "Our turn." They walked through the portal together, with Connor and Seth walking through last.

On the other side, she struggled with the nausea, proud of herself for not throwing up. After a moment, she nodded to Tyrus, letting him know she was ready. She looked at the changes in the flora as they moved. Because of the size of the trees, and the lush green, they had to be in the forests in Washington State.

Tyrus led and she followed, slowly moving forward until they stopped abruptly. Tyrus pointed to the ground and used the wait signal. This was where she would begin the net. She just had to wait for him to be in position. He began to walk away from her, and she readied herself, calling the ocean to remain calm. They could do this.

Tommy stroked her head, as Nix sat unconscious. She was still chained, still defiant, and he was losing his patience. He'd used reason, logic, and appealing to the hero in her, but to no avail. As long as he kept her against her will, she would fight him. So, he made sure to knock her out at night, so she got her sleep, made sure she had a bucket to go in, and food to eat.

Pricking her finger, he let the blood pool there for a moment until a perfect drop formed. Then he savored it. It was amazing how her blood calmed him, removed the hunger, the fury. He'd always had a crush on Nix, but now, it was more like goddess worship. He'd do anything to protect her. She was the road to his salvation.

The brightness of the headlights hit him all at once. All around the cabin, it filled the dark room from windows and holes, like the sun had risen just above him. It was seven at night though, so this was manmade.

The megaphone sounded, Tyrus's voice ringing clearly through it. "Tommy! We have you surrounded. Come out now and surrender. Repeat, you are surrounded. Come out with your hands up and surrender immediately."

Well, well. They'd found him sooner than he'd hoped. No matter, with his power he was capable of dealing with them, as he'd proved twice before. A bit amused, he slowly opened the door and obliged, walking down the steps with his hands in the air.

"Tyrus! What a pleasant surprise!" He shouted it back at the megaphone. As he did, a plethora of laser sites trained on his torso.

"So, you've given up defeating me yourself, and you called in humans to do it for you?" He laughed out loud.

"No need to make this any harder than it needs to be, Tommy. Kneel, on the ground, now."

He began to obey, one knee touching the earth, where it began to sizzle. He was a wind element, and dirt was a weakness. With one knee burning, he said, "this won't work, Tyrus. You know I could take these agents out with a flick of my wrists."

"Tommy, get on the ground, now!"

He placed his hands behind his back, almost as if he was going to obey the order, but his lips pursed, and he debated. "Nah, I think I'd rather just kill all of you."

"Tommy, don't do this."

"Agents! This is the bad guy." He let his voice spread on the wind, so anyone within a mile would be able to hear him as if he were standing next to them. "This is your last chance to back off. Do so, and I won't kill you. Back off, and run, and I'll let you live. Whatever Tyrus has told you, he doesn't know how powerful I am. Go home to your families, and live."

Many of the dots that were trained on him, went off, but none of the vehicles moved to exit. "Shame. Your snipers seem to be smarter than the ground troops. Give up now, Tyrus. You've lost your best advantage."

"On the ground! Now!"

To himself, Tommy whispered, "*so be it.*"

He slowly moved his arms away from his head, outward, while the megaphone continued to shout at him.

Then, *snap.*

With the flick of his fingers, the vehicles began to overturn, one after another, in a circle, leading toward the megaphone. The air shifted and he felt the bullets from the snipers propel toward him, but a gust of wind blew them off course. Walking slowly forward, the cars honked, beeped, and lights flickered as he closed the distance to Tyrus.

He smiled wide as he got within a few feet of his voice, and flung the wind toward his former mentor, hard enough to sweep him and his megaphone into a tree. When nothing greeted him, he walked passed the lights, and confused, looked at the megaphone lying smashed on the ground. No one lay next to it.

Then, he looked up. "Shit."

At the sound of the megaphone, the three began to create the magical net that would contain Tommy's wind. Levi made sure to intersperse the water he used with bits of dirt, so between the three, the other elements could contain his wind. They began close to the ground, so the net would be hidden by the headlights of the agent's vehicles up ahead. They walked forward, steadily, adding more and more power to the net.

Tommy's voice came to her, and she faltered. It sounded as if he was right next to her. As the net gave way, she refocused, ignoring the warning he gave the agents to retreat. Getting back into position, she continued walking slowly toward the center, the net building toward the sky. If they arrived at the right time, they could trap Tommy without Nix getting caught in the net as well.

When the magic suddenly began to move faster to the center, she picked up her pace. Levi and Tyrus were full on running forward to close the net, and she wasn't going to be a failure. She'd become better equipped at exercise since their run into St. Blaise the year before, never wanting to feel so out of shape again. She ran as often as she could, and the difference showed.

She glided forward, using her fire to move above the brush and roots of the trees. Running through the air with fire feet, they quickly closed the distance, reaching the clearing just as the last of the cars overturned.

That was the signal. She pushed her fire out, calling her bird, saying, "it needs to be an orb." Her bird flew to the top of the scene and fanned its wings, and her fire interlaced with the other two, perfectly capturing Tommy within it.

The cabin was now safe from his influence, and Julius moved forward with the other agents to surround and enter it, to save Nix. Their job was to hold the net in place until they were clear.

Looking toward the cabin, she saw a golden glow over the entire area, and knew Seth was working his luck magic on them. A feeling of safety came over her, just as they felt Tommy push back.

The force of the air knocked all three of them back six feet. Gaining her footing, she concentrated, calling the ocean, telling her firebird to help. From behind, she felt her fire wings unfold, flapping furiously to move her forward, so they could close the net. This wasn't a battle of strength, but a battle of willpower. The three of them, against him.

As they walked forward, one slow step at a time, the net began to spark. Lightning formed as a storm of magic was created, the elements colliding. The maelstrom began to take on a life of its own as they moved forward, and she had to avoid the pockets of sparks that were escaping. One hit a nearby tree, setting it ablaze. Another hit an agent in the leg as he fled the cabin, his scream testing her concentration.

Then, Tommy's voice came through the holes in the net. "*Stop! Why are you doing this?*"

Ann felt guilt plague her and suffered a crisis of conscience. Were they doing the right thing? Was he really a monster? Did he deserve to die this way?

From Tyrus's position, she heard, "DON'T LET HIM GET IN YOUR HEAD! PUSH!" His voice held that dragon quality, lower and louder than a human could. The net closed another step, its diameter about ten feet now. Tommy must have been feeling the sparks too, inside.

"*Stop! I only want to live! STOP! I WON'T HURT ANYONE, ANYMORE!*"

From Levi, she heard, "PUUUUSH!"

Another step forward and the circle closed in. Now it was around eight feet, just enough to contain Tommy, with very little room. Julius, Connor, and Seth appeared at their side. From behind her, she heard him shout, "CLEAR!"

Tommy let out a scream as they closed in, shoving their magic against his with all their might. After a moment, he must have given up, because all resistance stopped, and the fire and water rushed inward.

While Levi's water and Tyrus's flame receded immediately, Ann couldn't pull back from her power. It became the entire net, and something kept her magic funneling into it, even though there was no one to fight anymore.

Tommy's voice had gotten to her, but not in the way they had thought it might. All her frustration, at the unfairness of life, fueled her flame. It was a great release, her anger and rage from the events of her short life in foster care coming forward. The abuse, the abandonment, the emotional pain all left her body through the flame.

She called to her firebird, and said, "Stop!"

But it only fanned the flames harder. The net was now a molten hot ball of dense fire, a small sun in the middle of the forest. Tyrus rushed up to her, and she screamed at him, "GO! GET AWAY!"

Her voice had changed. It rang of a wisdom and depth she didn't normally possess. Her firebird was warning others through her.

She watched them run, hoping it would be far enough away. She held the ball of flame for as long as she could, pouring all her memories of anger and rage into it. When she was sure they were out of range, she simply gave into her firebird, and said, "*save me*," then let it all go.

Hazy at first, Nix woke on the outskirts of the net, seconds before it exploded. She stood groggy, and Julius rushed toward her. "We have to get back. Now!"

Nix looked at the fire, and unlike the others, she recognized what was going on. She remembered, in that split second, how awful her ascension had been, how alone and lost she'd felt. She remembered how she struggled to find herself, again, and she made a split decision.

"GO! I'm going to help Ann."

"What are you talking about? It's going to blow!"

"I won't leave her to go through this alone!"

"Nix!"

"Go!" She shoved her orange flame at him, and he ran away. Nix began to walk forward, into the clearing, where Ann stood, creating a small red sun. She smiled as she realized how different this was from her ascension, yet the power was similar. So was the cost.

As she was inches away, Ann let go. She felt the sun explode, and she didn't fight it, touching Ann's shoulder as they both began to burn away to ash.

The tiny sun pulsed once, twice, then exploded outward, the force propelling them backward. The cabin was torn to splinters, the trees cracking as they blew apart. Ann's firebird wrapped around her as she fell backward, burning bright red, her call a scream of victory as Ann felt her body become fire itself. Her hands, feet and body all burned with it, yet there was no pain. She felt herself give into the transformation, knowing this was her first ascension. With a final breath, she sighed, the world going dark.

And in the middle of the wreckage, their ashes fell, glowing red to dark carbon against the dirt of the campsite.

The others rushed toward the remnants of the cabin as soon as the explosion was over. Tyrus and Levi arrived first, recognizing the signs. The others approached seconds later.

"Nix!" Levi called out to her. "Where is she?"

Julius spoke through quick breaths. "She...came back...to help…Ann."

The two older men were silent for a moment. Tyrus looked at Levi, who looked at Julius. Watching his hands form fists, Tyrus stepped quickly between the two.

"Why didn't you STOP her?"

Julius stepped back. "I tried, she wouldn't listen."

Tyrus held Levi around the waist, as the other man swung wide. The others were confused, but the two older men knew exactly what happened.

"You should have stopped her! All this, for what?"

Levi crumpled, tears staining his cheeks, and he went limp in Tyrus's grasp. He helped the other man to the ground, struggling not to cry himself.

The other three came closer when they realized he wasn't a threat. "I don't understand," Connor began, as gentle as possible. "Isn't this what phoenixes do? They ascend?"

Levi couldn't answer, so Tyrus looked to the younger men, swallowing hard so his voice was steady.

"Yes, normally, a phoenix burns to ash, then ascends, her flame hotter and brighter, her abilities stronger."

"Then why the tears? Won't they come back."

Levi's voice came out rough and tight, but he was able to add, "not Nix. She doesn't have her bird. *She can't come back*."

Julius felt awful, falling to his knees as well. "Then, why would she…"

Tyrus answered. "For whatever reason, Nix wanted to make sure Ann didn't go through this alone. To the point that she-" His voice caught.

Levi ended it, "sacrificed her life."

The quiet settled in then, no one understanding what to do, and the men sat in the clearing, waiting to see what would happen.

Somewhere "In-between"

After a moment of darkness, she came to, kneeling on a red rock, and Ann slowly lifted her head to see maleficent magnificence. Sand and stone lay ahead, dry and cracked, orange flame rising from the ground in random spots. The sky was covered in black clouds, smoke filled the air. It reminded her of the bus crash, the fateful day she became a fire bird. She was dressed in black leather and heels, the outfit more likely something Nix would wear over Ann, who preferred to move quickly and inconspicuously.

"Looks good on you. Must be my influence."

Ann looked in the direction of her mentor's voice, and seeing her, remembered the cabin, the explosion. It clicked, and she asked, "we aren't on earth anymore, are we?"

Nix shook her head. "No. No, we are…somewhere else."

"What is this place?"

"I called it the "trial." This place is a challenge, a rite of passage. I walked this hellish path when I ascended to the orange phoenix. You make it through, you'll ascend as well. I have no clue if your experience will be the same as mine."

"Why are you here?"

A shadow of pain crossed her face, but she only said, "be grateful. I had to walk here alone. Step forward, Ann."

She slowly descended from the red rock onto a broken, fiery path, confused as to how she was able to glide so easily in the tiny heels. As she stepped on the path, it glowed, flowing forward, apparently showing her the way. "Follow the flame-charred road?"

Nix chuckled but stayed behind her. She moved forward carefully, the red rocks igniting around them. "Is this a dream?"

"Not exactly." Ann came to a fork in the road, one dark, one bright. "Which one do I choose?"

"Honestly, I chose at random. It ended up being the light path."

"What was down there?"

Nix swallowed hard. "An…aspect of myself that…. I had to overcome. I doubt the road chosen makes much difference, really. Either way, this next bit will get tricky."

Ann swallowed and wondered for a moment. She closed her eyes and tried to feel which road beckoned her strongly. "Hurry, Ann. The fire behind us is growing."

She could feel the heat press on the nape of her neck. She was not meant to stay indecisively in this moment. Sighing loudly, she chose. Her mentor was with her, and had chosen the light? Fine. She would face the dark.

She turned left toward the shadows and walked away from the light. The darkness grew thick, so it was difficult to see, but the flames were still randomly burning around them, giving glimpses of the hellscape they traveled. Ann sent up a beam of red fire, as Nix sent up an orange one. They traveled around the two women, tiny guides lighting enough of their path so they didn't trip. Every now and then they heard something scurry in the dark, but it never faced them. "What do you think that is?"

Nix shivered. "I'd rather not find out."

Ann agreed. The landscape was changing. The fire began to

wane, the darkness so thick the flames seemed faded and worn. The bursts of orange flame no longer lit their way, only a faint glowing light at the end of a great distance remaining. Ann snuffed out her red ball and Nix did hers. They weren't helping, anyway.

The rocks gave way to the bark of trees, dark columns rising, the path crooked with roots. It was harder to walk forward now, and the scurrying sounds were louder, closer. At one point, she could feel its cold breath on her neck, and she turned, her flame lighting up the area, and it screamed, and vanished back into the abyss. With more light, the shadows pushed forward, trying to snuff out her flame.

"This almost hurts."

"It was the same with the light path, but the opposite. The light was harsh, my flame unable to react without piercing my mind. This path seems to eat the light. Let's keep moving."

She motioned for Ann to continue forward, and she did, the roots three feet tall now. She had to sit and swivel her body around and jump down to move forward. She helped Nix over the same root. The light was changing, turning to shades of orange again. Huge trees the size of buildings stood, fire popping up from between the roots. Ann stepped into what appeared to be a clearing, and Nix tried to follow, but couldn't. A solid wall of energy blocked her path. Ann called her flame, but her mentor shook her head.

"I'll be fine. The only way forward is for you to defeat your challenge."

"Which is?"

Nix motioned behind her, and Ann turned, seeing a red figure standing before her. It twitched when it moved, not human but not animal. It wore red rags, from which flames flowed. Its hands were gnarled like tree branches, with red skin and broken nails. Its hair lay over its face, covering her from view. A growl, familiar, but too low, came from her throat.

"You." It spoke. "You…."

It lifted a twisted hand up, pointing at Ann, then was suddenly next to her, rotten breath making it hard for Ann to breathe. "You…"

Ann felt it, then. The twisted creature's emotion. Anger, bubbling up out of this horrendous creature as it bubbled from her own stomach. "YOU!"

The figure flung her across the room, and Ann landed on her arms, rolling the way she'd been taught. She was up quickly, but the demon instantly there. "You let them hurt ussssss." It hissed it out, vicious and damning.

Ann was beginning to understand. The voice wrapped its hands around her throat and began to squeeze, and Ann struggled to remove them, forgetting her power in a moment of fear. A cry from above came, an orange firebird descending swiftly, knocking the assailant away. Ann was surprised. She hadn't called her bird, and as she watched, she felt no connection with her. Then she remembered and looked at Nix, who held tears in her eyes. They locked for a moment, and she saw the pain in her mentor's gaze, but Nix quickly recovered, "quick! Before she gets back up. Act now!"

Ann tried to call her Rage, but it only made the figure stronger, the flame growing as Ann let the emotion flow through her. Confusion lit her features. How could she call a flame if her rage only fed the demon? Calming herself, she envisioned the beach Seth had mentioned, and the creature's fire lessened, but its words were just as harsh.

"You let them hurt usssss. You don't deserve to live." It snaked close beside her again but didn't touch her. "You did this to usss…"

Flashes, memories came unbidden to her mind, that threatened the calm. She saw herself as a toddler, being returned to the foster care system. Saw the black garbage bag full of toys. Children being adopted while she sat, alone with her few belongings. The necklace from her birthmother tightly held in her hand, tears streaming down her cheeks.

"You…. they took us back because you weren't good enough…."

Ann kept calm, but stated, clearly, "NO. I was given back because they couldn't afford more than one child, and they were pregnant with their own. It was their miracle, and it broke them to give me back."

"LIEEESSS!" The demon grew closer but couldn't touch her if she remained calm. A light began to surround her. "They beat us because of you!" Another flash, another image, a rainy day, where she hid in a closet to escape the pain, but the pain came anyway, in the form of a belt buckle against her tiny arms and legs. The rage came, her calm interrupted, and the demon chuckled. "They hit us because you couldn't follow the rules."

The hand crept close to her throat, but Nix's bird descended again, grabbing the figure, and throwing it away from her. The calm returned as she realized that she wasn't alone. "No, I followed the rules." The rage was right there, below the surface, but she didn't call it, didn't let it control her as it controlled the creature. "I could have followed every rule, but it wouldn't have made a difference. He was a drunk who was so pathetic and weak that he had to beat his foster children to feel control over his existence. That man went to jail because we spoke up. We stopped him from hurting other children."

"I did. You cowered and hid. I saved usssss." The creature puffed up her chest, preparing for another strike. With a scream, it came forward, a full force assault on Ann, trying to snuff out her light.

Ann held up a hand and called her phoenix, who instantly blocked its path, her red wings outstretched, the orange bird mirroring her, a united front. It hissed, but didn't move. The flame may take her rage, but the bird she commanded confidently. A smile lit her face as she understood, tears forming in her eyes. "Yes, Rage, you did save us. So many times, when I had nothing left, you kept me alive. You kept my hope floating when everything else was lost. And I will always be grateful. But we aren't a helpless five-year-old anymore. We no longer need to live with the anger. We can let it go."

"NOOOOO!" The creature shrank, to the size of a child, its voice rising in pitch. "NO! You need me!"

"Indeed. I need you, but I don't need to *become* you any longer. Come home with me." It shrunk even more, to the size of a doll. Ann walked forward and picked up the tiny demon, as it bit her hard, a vicious little monster. "Hush, now." She looked at the orange firebird in front of her, a hand reaching out to pet her, but she flew away, wild and fearless. She looked to Nix, and told Rage, "we aren't alone anymore. We can survive on more than anger and revenge."

Rage became stone in her hand, the mouth still trying to break skin. She placed it in her pocket, and the barrier between her and Nix vanished. She rushed forward, looking in the direction of her bird. Her breath heaved in her chest, and Ann understood some of what she must feel. "She's alive!"

"Can you call her?"

"No. She's…wild and beyond my reach."

"But alive."

"Yes." Her voice broke, and Nix turned from her, wiping tears away that fell down her cheeks. Ann let her have a few moments before she said, "we should keep going."

Nix nodded, and Ann walked forward, the orange light growing bright. The trees around them grew flowers, and they began to fall, cherry blossoms falling to the earth, incinerated by the fire. Ann reached out to touch one, but it popped like a bubble. "Strange to see something so beautiful in a world so ghastly."

She looked up, and the blossoms began to fall all around them. "Why do you think they're here?"

Nix smiled. "A reminder that this isn't the end, Ann. That you have more work to do."

Ann stepped forward through a barrier and felt her bird leave her. She felt completely alone for a moment, without her soul companion, and looked to Nix just two steps behind. Is this what she feels every day? The weight of it crushed her, feeling as if the entire universe had faded until she was left, existing in complete solitude. A cry, somewhere between an eagle and a condor sounded, and her bird returned, bathed in orange light. She'd ascended, and she was flying to Ann to help her return to the world.

Ann looked at Nix, who shook her head. "This is the end, Ann. The end of my journey. I'm no longer alive on earth. You have to return alone."

Ann felt tears stinging her face as her bird came closer. The blossoms fell, so thick now that they carpeted the roots of the trees. She stepped over them, back toward her mentor, who held out her hands. "It's ok, Ann. If I stay here…." She looked at the phoenix circling a single mountain. "Maybe I can tame her."

Ann didn't have time to convince her, but something at the back of her mind felt that this was wrong. That Nix couldn't stay, not really. The bird was here, but this wasn't where Nix was meant to be. She looked suddenly to her right, and saw Joy bathed in light. "She can't stay here, Ann. She wasn't meant to be here at all. You have to take her back."

"Is there any way?"

Joy shook her head. "Not from here. If she stays, we are all doomed."

Ann watched her mentor walk away and made a decision. She silently prayed she'd be forgiven, but she wasn't ready to watch her mentor die. Not now, not here. Her bird was seconds from joining with her, and Ann rushed forward, reaching Nix as her bird reached her. She wrapped her arms tightly around her mentor, against her will, and felt the orange fire consume them both, until she lost consciousness and returned to shadow.

Joy stood, breathing a sigh of relief. Nix's phoenix landed next to her and cooed. "Someday, my friend." She reached out and began to pet the bird, who accepted the affection lovingly. "Someday, we will find a way out for you. Until then, I'll keep coming to visit." Joy vanished a moment later, and the firebird flew away, back to the great mountain.

Levi and Tyrus moved toward the pile of ashes, knowing that if there was any hope, they had to do what was necessary from this end.

"We still try to bring them both back." Tyrus gripped Levi's shoulder supportively.

"Always. If this doesn't work, I'll spend the rest of my life finding a way."

Tyrus pulled a knife from his pocket, as Levi did the same. "Maybe one of the others would be a better catalyst for Ann."

Levi chuckled. "Phoenixes are drawn to Dragons. I think the fact you are one will be more of a powerful draw than her childhood friends."

"And you're sure this is all her brother did? When Nix ascended last time?"

"Yeah."

"Alright then. At the same time, since we aren't sure which is which."

"Ready."

"One, Two, Three." The men both drew their knives across their palms, allowing the blood to drip down into the ash. It burned, a small flame forming.

"The catalyst has been presented."

"Stand back."

As the group watched, the small interaction between the blood and the smoldering ash caused a new spark to ignite, orange in color. As they backed away, the spark became a flame, growing rapidly to the size of a woman. Slowly, it changed shape from teardrop to hourglass to human, the fire binding skin and bone from the ash of a previous life.

After a few moments, the fire began to fade, until Ann stood before them.

Tyrus rushed forward, already removing his shirt, and placed it over her form as the light faded. As the fire left her, she fell forward, temporarily disoriented. She breathed deep, as if it were her first, the air filling her lungs, new life flowing through her. Tyrus helped her to the ground, and she took only a few moments to orient herself.

"Nix."

She shoved away from Tyrus, toward the other pile of ash.

"Ann, you can't..."

Levi turned away and began to sob loudly, his rage and grief evident.

"He's gone." Tyrus said.

"So is she." Ann tried to be brave, but tears fell unbidden from her eyes. She reached toward the ashes of her mentor, the only sign that Nix had once lived a full and vibrant life. In grief and pain, she shouted, "she's GONE!"

The grief flowed quickly through her, and she managed to touch her mentor's ashes. A tear fell from her face to the earth, igniting her mentor's remains. To her bird, she whispered, "*save her, whatever the cost.*"

Her bird cooed, then flew toward the ash, to the dismay of the older Mythics who could see her. It disappeared within, and something within Ann caused her new orange flame to flow from her, scorching the ashes.

Tyrus and Levi moved away, as Ann's flame began to grow, a repeat of the process that had risen her. As they watched in disbelief, the flame grew and changed slowly into Nix, fading away until the light was gone.

Levi was ready with his coat and caught her as she toppled forward. Ann fell to the ground, unconscious as Nix breathed deeply, fully alive and upset.

"What did she do?" Nix was angry.

"She…saved you."

"I was done. I was ready."

Tyrus picked up Ann as the agents came back onto the scene. "Apparently, she wasn't ready to let you go."

"It could have killed her."

"She's alive, but asleep. Probably exhausted."

Ben walked up to him. "Charred remains his, I take it? Over there?"

"Yeah. Chop them up, bury them in iron. Just in case."

"Will do. Glad we could support you. Nix. Welcome back."

She nodded, overwhelmed. "Levi?"

"Yes."

"I'm going to pass out."

"I've got you."

"Good." She went limp in his arms. The other three rushed forward, eager to help.

"What can we do?" Julius asked.

"We need a portal back to the campground. They can recover there."

Seth nodded. "On it." He created one, and the others stepped through, back to the campground.

They walked in silence until Tyrus tripped over a log. Ann stirred in his arms, and he whispered, "shh. You're ok." She settled and began to breathe evenly. He looked toward Levi and the fear was plain on their faces. No one knew how much power Ann had gained with her ascension.

"Treat them both like dynamite." Levi said it, and Tyrus nodded, but honestly, dynamite would have been more predictable than a newly risen phoenix.

Dr. Gregory Jackson paced back and forth in the small kitchen, his usual half empty. It'd been three days passed the deadline for Nix to check in. He'd been silently debating with himself over the correct course of action, but not hearing from her brought up the possibility of extraordinary circumstances. If she were incapacitated, or somehow compromised, then she may need him. But contacting anyone would start a chain reaction that would lead to more violence.

His mind had been fighting his heart for days. He knew how important it was to stay quiet, but she was family. He dialed once, hung up, and put in the number again. On the third time, he let it ring.

"Hello, Isaiah. I'm alive, and I need your help."

Every element had its own way. Water elements could sense

each other through the drops of the water table that connected them, wind elements could whisper, sometimes control the minds of others. Earth elements could feel vibrations no one else could.

And fire recognized fire. In handshakes, or with more powerful beings, from the different signature of explosion felt from its blast. They'd had a very long life, and walking through the scene of the Wendigo's death, he felt a new fire here, burning, that was…interesting. Different, even than the fire elements that had come before. It was intriguing, both the signature and the tiny seeds of fear that creeped into them. Not enough to be threatening, just enough to wonder.

Picking up the soil, they held it to their mouth, licking just a morsel of it. Dragon blood, and phoenix ash. As they'd suspected. What had the humans done now.

Chapter 8

Levi sat near Nix's side until she woke, late during the night. He smiled wide as he looked down at her, expecting her to smile back, but she didn't. Instead, tears came to her eyes.

He was alert and attentive instantly. "What is it?"

"Tommy. He's dead, isn't he?"

Levi let his face show his confusion. "Yes. I thought that was a good thing?"

Nix sighed. She took his hand in hers and squeezed. "It is, and it isn't."

"I don't understand. What happened in the cabin?"

"Promise you won't tell anyone?" Her voice shook, and he found anger building inside him, thinking through all the things Tommy could have done to her.

"I promise." He touched her short hair, ran his thumb over her forehead. "What happened?"

She swallowed, hard. "Have you ever heard of the blood of Mythics being special?"

He tilted his head. "In what way?"

"Tommy…tasted my blood."

He struggled again to keep the anger out of his voice, but his eyes began to dance like water. "And the effect of that was?"

"It…healed him. The crazy cravings, the endless hunger… It was gone."

Levi thought through his response. "So, he was Tommy again, and we…"

"Yes." Tears fell from her eyes and were furiously wiped away. "But, if he had lived, then…"

"Others. Our enemies… would have found out about your blood."

"Yes. And without my bird...."

"You'd be prey for them."

"So there was no right solution, but I'm still sad."

He handed her a tissue, and thought it through, silently.

She squeezed his hand. "Something else."

"Yes?"

"In the hellscape, the place in between. Where Ann and I went. She was there."

"She who?"

"My bird. She's alive. You didn't kill her."

His eyes widened. "I'll use every contact I have."

"No."

"NO?"

"Not yet. I need to rest, and Ann will need help with her flame. Research, yes, when you can, but promise me you won't stop helping the group. When I'm ready, I'll let you know. And we can figure out how to get her back."

He sighed, frustrated. He had finally found a path to redemption, for him, and possibly for Tyrus. The fact he was denied walking it was frustrating, but Nix was right.

"I promise." She smiled then and his heart healed and broke all at once. She turned away and was out some moments later, while he continued to think. There had to be a compromise in there, somewhere…

Ann woke, breathing heavily, unsure of how long she'd been out or the nightmare that had forced her awake. Uncertain of where she was, she stretched, feeling as if she'd slept forever. It was dark out, the moon high in the sky, but this wasn't the main cabin. Why was she here?

Walking outside, she saw Tyrus sitting on the step, sleeping soundly.

As she approached, he woke. "Ann?"

"Yes, I'm awake now."

"You slept for two days."

"Two days!"

He rubbed his eyes and looked at her. "Sit down. We need to talk."

She did so, looking up at the stars. It was a beautiful clear night. Thousands of twinkling lights lit the sky. The moon was full, hovering low over the mountains in the distance. She wondered how Nix was recovering.

"Have you been…tortured?"

He sighed. "It's not something that I like to talk about, but yes. I was."

"How long?"

"Months."

She turned to him, tears welling up in her eyes. For Nix, it'd been a few days. She couldn't imagine what it was like for him, being dealt pain on a daily basis for months. "How did you not go insane?"

He knew he had to answer, but he didn't know what to say. Thinking a moment, he answered with, "I went, I just came back." He reached for her hand, giving it a squeeze and a wink.

She laughed then, and her eyes began to glow. Taking his hand away, he stood, and said, "Ann, we need to talk about your powers."

The glow left her eyes. "I've ascended. My flame is stronger."

"I know that. You know that. But there's more to it."

"What do you mean?"

"Rage and anger sum up the red flame. It took Nix years to control hers, but you had a natural ability to control yours. It was almost, magic. For Nix, it was three years of hard work on controlling her emotion, her rage."

"She mentioned that, yes."

"Rage is the red flame. Yours is orange, now."

"Right. Nix said it earlier. The emotion that controls it changes with the flame."

From a distance, she heard Nix's voice. "Passion." She walked over to Tyrus who was failing marvelously at his explanation. "For others and passion for creative pursuits."

She blushed. "Uhm, you mean…"

Nix laughed. "I mean both sides. Some people see the side of the muse, where passion is what they love to do. There are also the people we love that we feel passion for. The orange flame is a double-edged sword. You will need to learn to wield it."

Ann was silent for a few minutes. "Okay."

Nix sat next to her, Tyrus leaving the area. "It's alright. We'll practice all the meditation techniques that I've learned over the years. I'll give you tips and tricks that I used to control my amber flame. I'll help you. You don't have to do this alone."

"What can you do?"

"I can block your flame with my own. If you lose control, I can keep others from your flame. Tyrus can as well."

"So, I should stay close by either of you?"

"For the time being, we'll be your chaperones, yes."

She sighed, relieved. "This is embarrassing."

"Not as embarrassing as waking up next to Levi, let me tell you that."

"Oh, that's why…"

"That's why. Him and Tyrus."

"Oh." Ann blushed.

"Let's start with a run, now that the weather is getting better. It's in the seventies today. You up for one?"

"Does exercise help?"

"Yes."

"Then let's run. A lot. I don't think I'm ready to deal with this…flame."

Nix laughed before they both stood and walked to the gate. They did three laps before the sun began to rise. Collapsing on the ground, the two women breathed heavily and watched the world wake.

Tyrus stood watching, hoping that Nix would have more success with Ann than she had with her own ascension. If there was trouble that they didn't need, it was hormone driven newbies who weren't focused on their objectives. Turning away, he walked into the main cabin, intent on taking a long, cold shower.

◆ ◆ ◆

The next morning, Ann walked into the main cabin and helped Nix with breakfast. Sitting down, she ate before any of the others woke. Nix had gone over the rules with her, personal rules she'd learned while adjusting to the flame. Ann was going over them in her head. No touching. Touch made everything worse. No eye contact. She had to stay with her or Tyrus, always. If she felt unstable, walk away. Lastly, if something did happen, she had to forgive herself.

She felt capable. If she kept exercising, kept to herself, she was sure she could conquer this.

There was a tension between herself and Nix, and now was as good a time to try to clear the air.

"You know I had to bring you back."

Nix froze, the knife chopping the onions silent. "Yes. It was just…" She continued chopping. "It was a relief for a moment, that life would be…finished."

Ann said nothing, at first, contemplating feeling that way. "I…you're the only other phoenix I know. Joy, Marie, they were my found sisters, there for me, and I love them. I always have them, but we are…" She searched for the words. "Sisters in Flame."

Nix thought about that for a moment. Then she smiled. "I suppose that's a great way to put that."

"You've also given me so much. You've protected me, even at the cost of yourself. You're selfless. And that…"

Nix chuckled. "I care deeply about you too, Ann."

She smiled, then, satisfied that her mentor understood her. She walked away and sat on the couches near the fireplace. A door shutting and footsteps told her the others were awake, save Joy, who was still comatose.

"Hey, Ann." Connor tried to sit next to her, but Tyrus and Nix were suddenly there, blocking access to her on both sides. Getting the hint, he sat across from them. "What's wrong?"

"Ann has new powers and caution is the solution. No contact, no time alone."

Connor looked at Ann, then at Tyrus. "Seriously?"

Tyrus nodded. Ann felt very embarrassed. "It's because of my new flame."

Julius asked, "what about it?"

"She'll tell you if she's ever ready, but it's her choice. Just, for now, keep your distance, or you'll deal with me."

Connor changed the subject. "What are we doing today?"

"Lighting the candle. We go to the mural, and Ann decides whether to keep or give up her name. Julius, too."

Her plate empty, she stood and washed her dish. She felt like everyone's eyes were on her as she walked out. She would be grateful when this was over.

They walked into the park, turning away from the water and down the path to the memorial. Nix's flame opened the portal and they all stepped through into the darkness.

Turning left, Nix lit the flames and the room came into view. It was brighter this time, and Ann could see the whole room.

The stairs at the center were familiar, but the rest of the room was covered in paintings, but something ancient, of mythic creatures she'd never encountered before. The stone tablet held the names of people whose creatures she knew. There were a lot more on the floor, on another tablet, all corresponding with names and dates. In the middle of the room, was a circle of flame that matched the outside entrance. Ann looked at it, and at Nix.

She shook her head. "Not today. What's down there is for seasoned members."

Walking away, she accepted that, and started up the stairs. It was time for her to choose a name. A name like Nix had. Something all her own, that summed up somehow who she was, who she wanted to be. Ann was so plain, so ordinary. While she'd had the name since birth, it didn't feel like it was who she was inside. She walked up the stairs, and running out of room, sat on the floor cross-legged, waiting until she thought of the perfect name.

An hour passed, then two as she sat, the others growing restless. "How much longer?" Connor whispered to Seth.

"She knows what it is, she just has to realize it."

"Should we make suggestions?"

"No, then it wouldn't be hers."

"Right."

Connor sat next to Julius, who waited for his turn. "Have you made a decision on yours?"

"Yeah, but this…seems like her time. I'll let you know after she's done."

Nix sat next to them. "Was it hard for you to change your name, Nix?"

She snorted. "No. It took only about five minutes. But I had years before my ascension. I had more than ample time to think it through. Ann…this happened so quickly for her. She needs the silence and time to be certain."

Tyrus walked up to Ann and sat next to her. She briefly meet his gaze. "What was your name, before?"

Tyrus looked at her then, noting her concentration. "It's not important, because I'm not that person anymore."

"I'd just like to know."

He smiled. "I'll tell you one day. Today, is your name day. You choose who you are."

"How do I know it's the right name?"

"When you think of it, you'll know."

He walked away, and she watched him go. Resolved, she thought about what summed her up as a person. What did she value? What was most important to her? Truth, honesty, of course. She liked it when people showed follow through. She was devoted to her friends. She had a code that she lived by….

Suddenly, it came, and she knew what to write. Scrawling the word underneath "Pride," she turned and stood.

Nix and Tyrus walked to the bottom of the stairs and asked in unison, "What is your name?"

She stood, tall and said, "I am the phoenix, Honor." She felt the weight of her decision creep into her chest, as if the universe was adjusting to her choice.

"From now on, this is what we shall call you. This name you have chosen is who you are. You are a Phoenix, of Honor."

Her friends cheered as she walked down the steps. As she did so, she felt her name change as if by magic. She was no longer a blank slate, an empty book or a lump of clay. The fire had changed her, forever, and her name would change with it.

When she reached the bottom step, the transition was complete. She didn't know what had happened, but she felt alive. She felt whole. She felt complete in a way she never had before. She was happy, healthy, and loved. She was Honor.

Everyone looked toward Julius, who walked up to the podium slowly. Now was his turn, since he'd fully transformed. He elbowed her as he passed, whispering, "*nice one*."

Honor smiled as he walked up the steps. She was grateful she wasn't the only one choosing a new name, and a new life today.

But when he reached the landing with the stone, he simply wrote his name, turned, and announced, "I'm keeping my name. Ann-Honor, sorry, chose to change hers, and I respect that very much. It seems to fit her, but…Julius already fits me. I'm fine with my identity, and I don't need to change it. For now, I'd like to stay me, as much as possible. But I wrote it down."

He scratched his head, a sign of awkwardness. Tyrus spoke quickly. "Then you are Julius, a fully transformed Cerberus, and that is what we will call you."

Honor wondered if the walk down the steps was as revolutionary for him as it was for her. If there was magic in his steps, for confirming his identity. When he winked at her, she smiled. She sincerely hoped their experience was the same, even if they had made very different choices.

When Julius reached the bottom, Connor shook hands with him, and he smiled, saying, "you know I won on this, right?"

Then he gripped his frenemy in a headlock and messed up Conor's hair, while the others laughed.

Nix walked away, taking out her phone and checking voicemails. She knew her nephew had come out of hiding, assuming the worst when she'd been taken by Tommy. While the building wasn't completely up and running, she did have a full security team on him, a list of safeguards in place, as well as surveillance on all his properties. Things change, though, and she understood why he'd come to the forefront. Pursing her lips together, she opened an email from him, with a news article touting the miraculous recovery of the missing director.

This…was bad for him, bad for her, and possibly bad for the group. Her heart a little heavy, she turned back, wondering how long she could allow the smiles and laughter to continue, before revealing that in addition to the assassin they were still tracking, there would be another threat.

She walked into his office for the first time in days. Her botched attempt was public now, obvious. She knew why he was calling her in. She waited outside until his personal assistant, Amile, said, "He will see you now, Rebecca."

Taking a deep breath, she walked into her father's office. The door shutting behind her, she stared at the opulent room. Two stories of office stood before her. Gold lined everything. Exotic woods framed marble floor. She thought about the modest upbringing she had, tucked away from the London business and resentment flooded through her. He cared about showing off his wealth more than he cared for his daughter.

Approaching his desk, she began, "Papa?"

Turning, she looked at her father. Grey hair from stress lined his features. Hard, cold blue eyes stared back at her. A long, straight nose and angular features mirrored hers. His suit was perfectly cleaned and pressed, nothing out of place.

"Daughter. You disappoint me."

"I know, Papa." She hung her head.

"I thought I made it clear that the family was supposed to be wiped out. Killed. Then I see young Gregory, boasting about rebuilding. What happened?"

"The man sent to do the job didn't finish it. I was too busy getting the data back to you to oversee it."

"This is exactly the reason I taught you to take these things personally. Too many things can go wrong. What do you intend to do about it?"

"Yes, well, "she straightened her jacket. "I've already posted a contract for the previous employee."

"Has anyone accepted it?"

She hung her head again. "No, Papa. Everyone is afraid of him."

Thinking for a moment, he said, "I'll make a call. You'll go back and personally oversee this one. I want proof of death. A video will do. You will not see me again until it's done."

"Yes, sir," she said, turning to go.

"Rebecca," he said, "I realize I'm hard on you. If your mother were alive, it'd be different. Remember, everything we do, it's for her."

Tears in her eyes, Wills said, "I know," without turning back. She was going to fix this. She was going to make her father proud of her. She may officially have her mother's maiden name, but in her heart, her father's legacy burned brightly. She'd do better this time, be smarter. When she killed the leviathan, he wouldn't see it coming. A sadistic smile spread across her face. *I've got this.*

Two women landed at the airport from two different countries. Both stepped off the plane intent on involving themselves in the events that unfolded here. Both were powerful, both were beautiful. Two women touched the ground, their steps bringing ripples of change. Only one, though, was their ally…

Wills would not meet her in person. She would contact her via phone and arrange for her to fly to Colorado at the first available opportunity. She had contacts in place, the best private investigators she could buy. They would alert her to any opening they could take advantage of.

Opening her phone, she dialed the number. It took a moment before a synthetic voice answered the phone. "Yes?"

"I'll send you directions to your apartment. Welcome aboard."

A pause before she continued. "We're not friends. I'm doing a job and I'll do it my way. No more contact, no apartments. I'm leaving for Colorado now."

"Wait, we have to talk- "

"No, no we don't. I'll contact you when it's done."

The phone went dead, and Wills slammed it down. So much for being a handler. In mere moments, she'd managed to cut herself out from the whole project. Still, she had the eyes she needed. Sitting back, she decided this was a good thing. If her operative failed, she could blame the lack of communication. If she succeeded, Wills would be back in her father's good graces. It wouldn't matter how she handled this. Liking that idea, she sat back and picked up the hotel phone. "Hello, room service?"

They arrived back at the camp, exiting the vehicle. Honor would practice with Nix, working on meditation and exercising. They left the group, leaving Tyrus with the others.

"What do we do?"

"Stay out of trouble. Leave Ann-I mean, Honor alone for now."

"What are you going to do?"

He'd received a phone call that morning about a potential threat. He needed to investigate that. "I have some calls to make. I'd like the four of you to work on your fitness. Scout the camp, everything I've taught you to do, do it. You're adults. It's time you started making your own choices."

Turning away, he picked up the phone and dialed the number. "Agent Ryan."

"Hey."

"Hey. You got my call?"

"Yes. What have you got for me?"

"Transcript from a phone call. Sending it to your phone. Also got eyes on her, but not the operative. Two choices. Trailing them both."

"Thanks for the help, Ryan. Keep me updated."

"Tommy's remains were disposed of, as you requested."

"You've been busy."

"My baby girl has to eat."

"How is your daughter?"

"I swear she said, 'Dada' the other day. My wife thinks I'm crazy."

Tyrus chuckled. "Glad to hear it."

"I'll catch up with you later. Meeting with the boss."

"Will do."

He hung up and Tyrus placed the phone in his pocket. Walking toward his cabin, he decided to review the transcript, see if he could determine who was coming after them this time. If he stayed one step ahead, if he could figure out who it was, then maybe he could stop this before the Five were any further involved.

For Honor, those awful events were not over. She kept envisioning what she thought Nix had gone through while taken.

"I can't stop thinking about what happened with Tommy."

Nix smiled. "I've been tortured before..."

"How long?"

"It always seems like eternity."

"How do you cope with it?"

"Sometimes grounding works."

"What is that?"

"Your body reacts to what it thinks is danger. That means your whole system reacts when you feel fear to keep you alive. It's part of our evolution. Digestion slows, your breathing quickens, adrenaline rushes through you. All those things happen to keep you alive. The thing is, your body can't tell the difference between a real threat and a memory. That's where all these techniques come in.

"When you start to feel yourself being pulled back into the memory, open your eyes and describe what is around you. It's called grounding. What color is the grass. Do you see animals. Verbally describe what you see. This helps your brain remember where you are, helps it calm itself from fear. Eventually, when you can talk about it, your brain will be able to adjust, hopefully, and you'll be stronger for it."

"That's a lot of information."

"It'll help you if you ever end up in that situation."

"Is that what Tyrus does too?"

"Who do you think taught me?"

They walked back to the others, hours later, Honor exhausted. She turned toward the main cabin, but Nix stopped her. "You've got your own cabin for now. Tyrus gave you his. Go rest up there." She pointed. Slowly, Honor walked away and up the small hill to his place.

Walking inside, he was busy on his computer. She didn't want to disturb him, but she needed rest, so she lay down on the bed and drifted off to sleep.

Tyrus noticed her an hour later, as her dreams activated her flame. He turned and felt the pull from her strike him. Summoning his own, he pushed hers back, creating a fire cocoon around her so she could sleep. Nix walked in a moment later, and seeing his control, left again. He began to meditate, so his flame would remain.

◆ ◆ ◆

When she woke, her body was drenched in sweat from sleeping during the day. Tyrus was still inside the cabin, meditating. She sat up and he opened his eyes.

"Did something happen?"

"When you're dreaming, you're vulnerable. That's all. Don't worry. Nix and I have got you." He smiled at her.

She stretched and walked out. She needed a shower. Walking into the main cabin, she saw Nix making dinner and Connor helping her. The smell of the food touched her nose and she breathed in deeply.

Her flame was around her before she could control it, and it was shoved at Connor and Nix. For a moment, everyone froze, then they were moving again as Honor watched. They'd see what this new flame was capable of.

Connor took out a piece of paper and began to write something. She glanced over his shoulder and realized it was…poetry. Strange…

Nix was opening the cupboards, looking for ingredients. "Go shower before you inspire everyone to greatness."

Honor walked away, wondering what she'd done. It happened so quickly. That was scary. She didn't have the control over this flame she had over her red. While she didn't harm anyone, there's no guarantee that she wouldn't in the future.

She walked into the bathroom and got in the shower. As the hot water washed over her, she meditated, concentrating on keeping herself levelheaded. She focused on the now, on the water, its sound as it fell.

Finishing, she walked out in a towel and grabbed a pair of clothes from her old room. Refreshed and dressed, she came back out to the chaos she'd created. Nix had made…Thanksgiving. Connor's poem was being recited. It sounded like words, being randomly spewed out.

Seth was observing. Julius was in the corner looking uncomfortable. He walked toward her, and asked, "What the hell did you do?"

"I…inspired them. Apparently."

"He's…reading poetry."

"We get to eat like, *all* the food tonight, too."

He laughed. The sound of it, the smell of the food, the warmth from everyone flowed to her, and her power activated again. It hit Julius, then Seth. Nix turned. "Dammit, Honor, get out of here and go see Tyrus."

She rushed out, not even looking to see how it affected them, but she couldn't help but listen to Nix.

"Julius, what are you doing?"

"I have to draw."

"Not on the walls!"

She laughed, and her flame lit up again. Tyrus saw it coming out and his magic surrounded her. She walked to him and said, "sorry."

He shook his head. "It'll happen. Honestly, the more you're exposed, the more control you'll gain. What's happening inside?"

"Uhm, everyone's…crazy."

"Stay here. I'll see what I can do." He walked inside. From her spot on the porch, she could hear what was said.

"Seth, Joy's unconscious. Stop…sniffing her."

"But she smells like coconut."

"NOW!" He must have listened because she heard footsteps "She got you too? Stop cooking, Nix. We have enough food for three thanksgivings in here."

"Fine, but don't come crying to me when you realize we've run out of pie."

"Connor, no one cares!"

"Aww."

"Julius! Julius!" She heard footsteps. Then a loud smack.

"Hey!"

"Stop drawing on the walls. There's paper in the desk."

"It's art. It happens where it happens."

"Go!"

He walked back out a moment later. Sitting next to her, he said, "we never really know what creative aspirations our friends hide until they're inspired."

"At least it wasn't all bad, right?"

"That poetry was pretty bad."

They laughed. She could see her eyes reflected in his. They were glowing orange.

"Honor…"

"Yes?"

"No eye contact."

She looked down. "Sorry."

"Stop apologizing for what you are. None of this is on you. You are a phoenix, and sooner or later this too shall pass."

"Why couldn't Nix stop me?"

"It happened so quick that she was already…under the spell of the muse. They'll come out of it, once they realize what it is. Joy and Seth though… that's a different story."

"He likes her. Did I…make him feel that way?" Tommy was able to bring out people's desires, needs, their hunger, to even control and manufacture what he wanted them to feel. What if she was the same, forcing people to do and feel things they wouldn't otherwise.

"It's more that you brought the feelings that were there to the surface. You can't force people to be attracted to someone they just aren't. If that's what you're asking."

"Yes. That's what I was wondering. They like each other."

"Yes."

"Oh, Joy and Seth. Hmmm."

"Is it strange?"

"They're my two best friends, so yes." She wrung her hands nervously together.

"It happens."

"You and Nix…"

He laughed. "What about us?"

"So, you were attracted to her?"

"That was a long time ago, but yes." He smiled wide at her, a sign of ease.

"How long did it take her to control this?"

"A year."

"Great." She rolled her eyes sarcastically.

"It'll be okay."

"How do you know that?"

"Because you've got us. Others who can help you get through this gracefully. What happened to us won't happen to you. I promise."

She grabbed his hand. He held it for a second, and squeezed, before pulling away. "No close contact."

She nodded. "I know, but this is a lot to take in."

"You feel calm now?"

"Yes."

His flame dissolved, until nothing remained. Honor stood. "I'm going to take a long walk. Really long walk."

She walked away, worried about her control.

Tyrus watched, more intently than he should have. He recalled the last time a firebird had stretched her wings near him. Flashes of Nix came to him, but he pushed them away. They were ancient history now, anyway. He was worried that the cycle would repeat itself. Worried that the old tales would come true again, as if fate itself were intervening.

Shaking his head, he turned away. He was older, wiser. He was in control of himself, and he knew how to protect them both from the flame. At least, that's what he told himself as he walked away, cursing fire birds.

Chapter 9

A week later…

Though she had gained a bit of control, Honor still required the protection the flame of others. Nix and Tyrus were great mentors, but she was concerned that by not challenging herself, she wouldn't gain more control. She knew she could be impatient, but she thought now was a good time to move to the next step. She hoped they agreed with her.

The storm outside made it impossible to train, but she wanted to have the conversation, at least. Sitting down with the both of them, she said, "I think, given the control I've shown, that a challenge would now be appropriate."

Tyrus and Nix shared a look. "Oh? What sort of challenge?"

"I…need the pressure of more people. To help me gain control. I know most of my friends and you two, will be forgiving. I need to try to be around others who wouldn't be. I think I'm ready to attempt that."

Nix looked at Tyrus, who shrugged. "I'm going to make something that smells delicious. Prove you have the control to focus your flame, while I bake, and if no incident occurs, we will discuss moving on to the next challenge."

"Ok." Honor summoned the ocean, the calm, and when her bird appeared, she asked for a single flame. When she opened her eyes and held out her hand, her orange flame burned steadily above her palm.

"Like this?" Her voice was a bit deeper than normal, but otherwise, she was the same.

Tyrus cleared his throat. "Good. Just continue to stay exactly as you are. I'm right here beside you in case."

The sound of the others was her first possible distraction. They came into the cabin, the three younger men, and chuckled. Seeing what was going on, they fell silent.

Until Seth asked, "it feels ok to stay today. Are we welcome?"

Tyrus nodded. "Progress is being made, it seems. We are testing control, and yes, you can help Honor by staying."

Julius moved into the kitchen with Nix. "What are you making?"

"Oh, just a buffet of Honor's favorite foods. One by one."

"Oh! I get the idea. Food is a trigger."

"A possible one. Starting with garlic bread."

The oven opened, and Honor felt her mouth water. Tyrus encouraged her when the flame flickered, growing a bit bigger. "Don't give up. You've got this."

She refocused and continued to ignore the smells.

Connor sat across from her, concern on his face. "How long does she have to sit there, doing this?"

Tyrus smiled at him. "Until Nix is done cooking, and the both of us are satisfied she's passed."

The younger boy nodded. "You can do this."

Julius, however, was playing devil's advocate. "Oh, man, this smells so good!"

Whether he was attempting to tease her or not was unclear. She sighed, convinced she had all the support she needed, and focused. This would be a long day.

A few hours later, after she'd been mostly successful, she dug into a plate of her favorite foods with Seth. "Oh, my God this is so *good.*"

Nix chuckled, pushing aside her plate. "I didn't have this level of control for months after my change. I'm proud of you. And I think it's time we assess our intelligence and move on to a bigger challenge for you. I'm glad you felt comfortable talking to us about your progress, or this would have waited, and with everything going on, we need you all at your best as quickly as possible."

"What do you mean?" she mumbled it through the food in her mouth. Nix nodded at Tyrus.

"Right." Tyrus rose and paced back and forth. "I feel I need to update all of you on what I know about the big picture. Wills is back now, in New York. I got confirmation today from Ryan."

"Now that Gregory is out in the open, again, I'm sure they have a contract out on Levi."

"The real issue isn't with her. She's an arm of the giant."

"Who is the head?"

"The Director of the European Genetics Institute."

Nix kept her face carefully blank. "They're in the pact."

"That didn't stop them from destroying your building."

"Why would they do something so stupid?"

"It wasn't stupid at all."

"What are you talking about?" Connor interrupted.

"We are talking about Dr. Henri Blanc. He's old, he's a Mythic, and he's been the head of the company for a very long time.

"What's his connection to Wills?"

"I'm not sure yet, but I believe she may be a relative of sorts."

"And she's in New York?"

"Yes."

"You know where?"

"Yes."

"Why don't we go kick her ass?" Julius chimed in. "It's what she deserves."

Tyrus looked at the young man. "No, she deserves much, much more. Unfortunately, I don't see it ending well for us were we to strike without more information. Without Joy, we don't exactly know the odds."

"My gut is saying the timing is wrong to strike." Seth bit into the garlic bread. "This is delicious, Nix."

"Thanks. I've had a lot of practice."

"Right." Tyrus smiled. 'That year in Italy."

"Well, going to the source usually gives the best result."

"Italy." Julius thought it over. "That's a romantic city, right?"

Nix raised an eyebrow at him. "Mmhmm."

"Were you…alone? In Italy?" He was clearly probing. The transformation had left him with much more confidence.

Tyrus eyed him now. "Not your business."

Honor would usually blush, but the food tasted too great for her to care. "Stop probing, Julius."

A sudden knock on the cabin door alerted them all. Honor's flame returned to her, lighting her eyes a bright orange. Tyrus squeezed her hand. "Stay calm."

Nix walked toward the door. Outside, in the rain, stood a woman dressed in a white gown, no coat to protect her from the weather.

She motioned to Tyrus, who stood and walked forward, peeking out a window. A silent glance was shared, and Honor almost understood what they were trying to say.

She could be normal.

She could be the assassin.

We can't just leave her out there.

Nix sighed, and held up a hand, telling the younger Mythics to stay back. "I'm opening the door."

She did so, but the woman was gone. Nix stepped outside, wondering what had happened.

"Hello?" All eyes turned toward a figure emerging from the dark near the back door. 'My apologies. No one answered at the front." She slowly walked toward the light, and Tyrus moved to block her access from the others, just in case.

He looked at the unknown person, a girl with brown hair, with blue eyes that danced like Levi's, as if they were made of water. She shivered suddenly, her body cold from the weather outside.

"Connor, would you mind getting her a blanket?" But Connor stood still, enamored by the visitor.

Nix shut the door and said, "I've got her." Producing her flame, she lit the fireplace with it, and motioned to the girl to draw near while grabbing an Afghan off the back of a chair. Placing it around her shoulders, she asked, 'do you need anything?"

She shook her head, and said, "just a moment, please."

They all sat down, waiting to see if she would explain.

"Some welcome you've given me. My father didn't prepare me for this." She smiled sweetly at them. "Hello. I'm Maiden."

Tyrus held out a hand, but she didn't shake it. "And who is your father?"

"The Mer King."

The surprise showed in his face. "I thought the water people were extinguished before the pact?"

"We remain, although in truth we don't mind if land walkers believe us dead."

"I understand why. How did you find us here?"

She looked at the lake. "You have water, so we can hear you. My father sends a message for you, Tyrus, the Red Dragon."

Connor touched her hair, brushing a leaf out of it. Tyrus narrowed his eyes at the behavior. "And what is this message your father sends?"

She turned, looking at the others. "Are these your allies?"

"No foes lurk here."

"Then I may speak freely?"

"As if they were stone."

"My father sends this message: The third coin seeks to swallow the world."

"Is that all of it?"

"No." She struggled, trying to remember. "There was more, but after the chill, I'm sorry, I can't recall. He did say that he wished me to learn about you, and the Five."

"Now, when you say the Mer king is your father…"

"He's my biological father."

Tyrus and Nix shared a look. "A mythic bore a child?"

She nodded. "I am the daughter of the Mer King and the Queen Selkie."

"And you are Merfolk?"

"I take after my father."

Tyrus turned and sat. "I didn't think any of us could have children."

She shrugged. Connor looked at her and finally spoke. "You're pretty."

She smiled at him. "Thank you, land walker."

"Connor," Nix said, "go check on Joy."

"Her state hasn't changed…"

"Now." She lit a flame ball and shot it at his feet. "Okay, okay." He walked down the hallway, to the room where Joy slept, and out of sight.

"My apologies, Maiden. We have not been hospitable, and on behalf of the land walkers, I invite you to choose a room where you may recover until you're ready to share more."

"It is rare to find one familiar with our ways. Thank you, Red Dragon."

She walked down the hallway, peeking into the doors, until she found one suitable. She came back and said, "the last, on the left."

"It is yours until you leave. That one has the adjoined bath, I believe. No one will invade your privacy, should you need it."

She smiled. "Until a later time, then."

"Until then."

She walked away, while the younger Mythics stood, a bit shocked.

It was Julius who first said, "*Holy shit!* Mermaids are *real*??"

They watched from the shadows as the scene at the camp played out, cautious of drawing attention from the dog or the lion. The rain could hide one's scent from them. It was easy to walk in a cloak of anonymity.

It was true, what they had felt. A new phoenix had arisen. One that put even Nix to shame. Their heads tilted as her flame grew, a small sign of her potential. Unlike the Mythics in the cabin, so young, so hopeful, they knew her true meaning, her true power.

The figure opened a portal to the other side of the world. Stepping through, night became day, as they walked along a beach, their body now transparent in the sunlight. The boats had landed, and the lemmings were lining up to leave. Here, an empire could grow without fear of interruption for at least a year, the only threat the chimera.

They looked at the figures, bones frail, skin grey, and delighted at their enterprise. They'd waited for technology to catch up to their genius, and the day had finally arrived. A new facility, a new chance to change the face of humanity forever.

One by one the thousands left the ships, turning and following loyal soldiers without a word. They shuffled in their bonds with entropy, their limbs taunt from strain and lack of food. If one could have seen a face, they would have seen a smile, but twisted, dark, delighted in pain. And they did. This was just the beginning…

Dr. Jackson looked at his new building, after having fired the previous manager, the foreman on site was now working miracles. The outer frame was finished, windows were being installed and the ground crew was clearing out debris from the bottom of the structure.

With the preliminary work done, now they would begin to make it professional, installing sleek and industrial décor. Walking over to his foreman, he shook his hand and said, "Glad I hired you instead."

He smiled at the man's firm handshake. "Thanks boss. Finally getting stuff done."

"When you're finished with this, I'd like to talk to you about another project for your workers."

His smile grew. "We like work."

"Good. I like to reward great workers. Keep in touch."

Walking away, he approached his limo, his driver running to open his door. As the driver turned wide on the back corner, it suddenly exploded, knocking the two men away.

After a long, stunned moment, workers rushed to drag them both far from the deadly flames.

Dr. Jackson looked down at his driver, bleeding from a head

wound. "Someone call an ambulance. Now!"

He checked himself for blood. Finding none, he sprang into action, opening his phone and hitting a red button in an app he'd designed himself. As he did so, cameras, hidden on all of the nearby buildings, began taking snapshots of everyone and everything around them, with their flash function turned off. He would not allow this harassment to continue. He'd been prepared this time. Whoever this was, he would have their head on a plate or their ass in prison.

Wills walked away from the site, upset that her bomb had diffused early. Her agent was on Levi, but she still had to end Dr. Jackson. She'd have to be more careful. Walking through an alley, she entered a black vehicle and drove away.

A phone call startled her as her driver turned toward the airport. No way was she staying here when she had a penthouse suite in New York.

"Yes."

"Daughter, what have I taught you about bombs?"

"You *already* heard?"

"He got you on camera."

"Dammit."

"You'll have to revise a new strategy to achieve success. What are your options now that you've been sighted?"

"Third party, but that didn't work in the past."

"No, it didn't."

"I could use poison."

"That's so blah. Surely you can do better."

"I could make it look like an accident."

"Or…"

"Natural disaster manipulation?"

"I think that would be best. Simulate a mudslide on his home, make sure he's in the center. If they believe it was an accident, they won't even investigate."

"Thank you, papa."

"Until then."

"Until then." He hung up his cell and she placed hers away, her cheeks red in embarrassment. It was bad enough that she missed her target, but to know her father was this close, watching her fail, was unbearable. The next time she dared to cross Dr. Jackson, would be the last. One of them, preferably him, would not make it out alive.

Marie looked at her friend, as Joy read through another volume on the history of their realm. "You need to go."

She pointed at a mirror, through which they could see the events play out, the fires of the bomb displayed.

"I know. I'm just ashamed."

"I understand this was in your eyes a failure, but, my friend, remember, nothing is ever one hundred percent in our favor."

"I know. I just…" She struggled to find the words. "What do I say? How do I explain it to them?"

"With everything going on, you won't have that conversation for quite a while. Now is the perfect time to go. They won't question you when they need you."

She let one tear slip from her cheek. It dropped to the ground, and a rose began to bloom. "You aren't wrong. I need to go."

"Waking now will be optimal. I'll see you again soon."

"Keep at it from this end. We need that information."

"I'm aware. And I'm on it."

Joy vanished slowly, and Marie continued searching through the volumes in the large library.

Nix stretched in bed and looked at her phone. Listening to one of a few messages, she sprang into action. Walking outside, she yelled, "Tyrus! Tyrus!"

She turned to the water, noting it was early enough he may still be swimming. Walking toward the dock, she yelled once more. He rose from the water, quickly. She approached him as he rushed to towel himself dry."

"Tyrus, we have to go to the city."

"Why?"

"Gregory's limo was just blown apart. We need to bring Joy to heal his driver. He's going to be in a coma."

"Did she wake yet?"

"Yes, I did." Joy's voice came from directly behind him, startling Tyrus.

"Don't do that, Joy."

She giggled. "We need to go. But not Honor."

Nix thought a moment, "I'll take you and Julius then."

"Okay. I'll take Honor into the nearest town, see if she's ready for more training. She's doing well. I think she's close to the control she needs."

"Fine. I have to go. Joy, grab Julius for me."

She disappeared. From inside, Nix heard Julius shout, "*Jesus Christ*! Don't sneak up on me like that!"

Tyrus felt sorry for him. Joy was awake, and her idea of funny was controversial.

Honor was surrounded by flame. It was everywhere, on every surface of the cabin. Standing, she walked outside, to a forest set on fire. She tried to scream, and she couldn't form the words. Her voice was gone. Searching for anyone to help her, she came up alone. Panicking, she turned toward the lake, trying to run, but her legs were like stone. As she finally approached the dock, she saw the others on the opposite side. They stood waiting to die, and as the flames tread closer, she waved her arms, trying to signal to them to run, to hide from the flame.

When the flame reached them, she turned, sobbing into her hands. Cold hands cut through the flame, and she lifted her head to see a shadow.

"This will be their fate if you stay. You are far too powerful a creature to be caged by a code."

She was mesmerized by the voice. "What…what are you?"

"This is their fate if you stay. You must leave to allow them to live."

"How do I know you're telling the truth?"

"You'll know when the time to leave has arrived. The moon will turn red, the water will boil and the one closest to you will betray you. Then, you'll come find me. For their sake." The shadow stroked her hair, but it's touch chilled her to her soul. Whoever this was, they weren't her friend.

The shadow drew away from her as the flames grew around her. A tree toppled as she tried to flee, falling and crushing her under its weight…

When she was finally conscious, she struggled against pressure to her chest. She opened her eyes, fighting from fear, and saw a face before her. For a moment she struggled, unsure of where she was or who was around her. As she regained her awareness, she saw Tyrus above her, pressing a knee on her chest, holding down her arms. His flame surrounded the both of them, the cabin alight with the mystical fire.

"Are you awake now?" He asked, straining, his eyes glowing with flame. She looked down, his hands, talons, his scales slowly spreading up his arms.

She worried her flame would go wild, and the fear lessened her power, as the fire dissipated and Tyrus released her. "I thought you had better control, now?"

She sighed. "I do. I just had a strange nightmare. It felt real, like the world of ascension."

"A nightmare? What happened?" At her guarded look, he added, "well, talking helps sometimes."

"A shadow. Death. Warnings. It's really just…silly. I'm ok now."

"Good. Get ready. I'm taking Seth, Connor and you into town."

"Are you sure I'm…"

"We have to keep slowly pushing your boundaries. Other than that nightmare, you were right about making progress. I'll be there in case."

"Ok." She rose as he left, dressing quickly.

The boys were excited to get into the SUV that would drive them an hour to a little town on the way to St. Blaise, off the highway. The entire town consisted of a few blocks, much smaller than the large city they were now used to. Still, being surrounded by people felt comforting.

They walked into the only real restaurant that served the area, a combo diner/bar whose inhabitants included a host of regulars and a few seasonal hikers. The regulars ignored them, until they saw Tyrus. Then they were all smiles and cheers.

Honor set aside the shot of whiskey they'd given their group, not quite ready. Conor and Seth downed theirs, coughing loudly. Tyrus didn't drink his, either.

A waitress with dark hair and red lipstick came to wait on them. "Tyrus, honey! Welcome back to Verity. Do you ever age?"

"How ya doing, Harry?"

"Harry?" Connor asked.

"Got a problem, kid?" She eyed him sternly. "It's short. For my full name. Which I'm not keen on divulging."

"No problem. None. At all." Connor smiled wide, and Harry seemed to accept that.

"Now, what can I get you?"

Honor was handed a menu, gazing at its contents while her

stomach growled. Tyrus must have heard, because he said, "round of fried pickles, for the table, and some chips and salsa. We'll order soon."

"Gotcha, cutie pie." She winked at him and sauntered away.

Seth asked, "is she…"

"Dude." Connor elbowed him.

"Is she what?" Tyrus took a sip of the whiskey, now.

"Yep, never mind, I'm not touching that."

Connor chuckled and looked at the pool table. "Tyrus, do you shoot?"

"Pool? Yes."

"Wanna play a game?"

Tyrus laughed. "No. You don't either."

"Why not?"

"Because it happens to be a Friday night."

"So?"

"So, look at the people around you. Half the town is in here, yet no one has touched that pool table. Why would they avoid it?"

"Not…following. Is there a league or something?"

Tyrus nodded. "Something. Yes. The only person with the luck to get near that table tonight is Seth."

Connor looked discounted, and eyed his friend, who smiled broadly and shrugged. "You and your luck get all the fun."

"Remember, while I want you to have a good time, for Honor, this is a test. You are back up, bodyguards, support. Keep the safety of this group in the front of your minds."

All three looked to Honor, who was so interested in making a decision about the menu that she had missed the whole interaction. She murmured to herself, clearly trying to choose what she wanted to eat most.

She looked up as they stopped chatting and said, "do you think they'll judge me if I order more than one meal?"

Tyrus smiled at her and took the menu from her gently. "Order as much as you want. It's on me."

She smiled back as the fries came to the table, but Tyrus

squeezed her hand and said, “remember, food is a trigger, and you’re being tested.”

She nodded, focusing on keeping her growling tummy from igniting her power. She slowly grabbed a fry and they all watched it make its journey to her mouth. Before she ate it, she said, “this is weird.” They chuckled and everyone grabbed at the food, happy to be out.

An hour later, Honor still picked at the plates of food while the others sat with very full bellies.

“Where does that all go?” Connor asked as she bit into a burger.

Tyrus chuckled. “Her phoenix takes most of it and stores it for later. Honestly, being full is a good thing. A hungry phoenix is a reactive phoenix.”

Honor nodded and took another bite as Harry approached the table. She smiled wide and added, “good to see a girl with an appetite. Chef will love it. Anything else I can get you?”

The boys groaned. Tyrus reached into his pocket and pulled out a credit card. “No, honey, you put that away. On the house tonight.” She pinched his cheek as she walked off.

“Seth, you think you can leave her a great cash tip?”
Producing a wad of twenties, Seth placed them on the table. “Already ahead of you.”

“Good. Because the second challenge of the night is about to enter the bar.”

Harry arrived with another round of shots, and Honor debated having one. They couldn’t get drunk, but the others seemed to like them. She lifted one to her lips and smelled the strong whiskey, then with a twisted face, set it down. Locking eyes with Tyrus, she said, “nope.”

Tyrus took the drink from her and emptied its contents in one gulp. “That’s ok.”

The door opened and a group of people walked in. Honor continued to chew her burger while the group boisterously caroused.

Tyrus seemed interested in one of the members, his eyes trained on one in particular, who came to the table and held out a hand.

"Tyrus. Long time." The words rolled out so smoothly, sounding eloquent. Honor stopped chewing her burger for a moment as the man's green eyes landed on hers. Framed against his long black hair, it was insulting to say he was gorgeous, but she couldn't find another word. She did wonder what Tyrus was up to.

"And your taste in companions is impeccable as ever." He smiled at her, with her mouth still full of beef and ketchup. Was that an insult, or a compliment? She looked at Tyrus, silently asking if she should be angry or pleasant. He placed a hand on her knee under the table in support.

"He means it." She smiled, without showing her teeth, then looked back down at her burger.

"Mind if I pull up a chair?"

Tyrus nodded, and the large man came back with a chair that seemed much too small. He turned it around and sat leaning on the back. "What brings you here?"

Honor finished her burger and wiped her mouth. Without thinking, she asked, "what's your name? How do you know Tyrus?"

Connor and Seth looked at her strangely. "What?"

"You don't usually speak up so easily."

She shrugged her shoulders, looking at Tyrus. "I guess I'm full and happy."

The large man chuckled. "My name is Kayden, but everyone calls me Kayde. A pleasure to meet you all."

"So what are you?" Ann asked, interested.

"Beg your pardon?" Tyrus squeezed her knee firmly, but she wasn't deterred.

"Your Mythic. You're one of us. I just wondered what kind."

"You're perceptive."

"Sometimes."

Kayde and Tyrus shared a glance. "I'm a metagot."

"*hmmm*." Seth didn't add any explanation to his murmur, so she did.

"What is that?"

"Essentially an animal spirit that can bring luck, both good and bad, to the environment based on how well they're taken care of. I, like your silent leprechaun," he nodded at Seth, "am a luck element."

"What animal?" She sipped some of her cola.

A smile lit his features. "A metagot usually has a primary form, but I have two."

"Oh, interesting."

Connor and Seth shared a look, clearly not agreeing with her.

"You've probably heard of the negative stereotype of black cats being bad luck. Well, when the luck runs toward the positive, my Mythic takes a similar form, like a large panther. When the luck runs bad, it's an oversized grey fox."

"I *love* foxes."

Tyrus chuckled, and she glared in response. "What?"

Kayde stood, removing the chair. "If any of you wish to play me at pool, let me know." He winked at Ann then left with his group.

Tyrus looked to Seth. "You're the only one that stands a chance against him." Reaching into his pocket, a wad of twenties came out. "Use this to bet with. Have some fun with your serious gift."

It was tossed and caught, as Seth stood and walked away. Connor leaned in to talk quietly. "I don't get how Ann plays into the environment tonight? Or me. What exactly do we do?"

"You and Ann have the hardest job, as both of you tend to be serious minded and can't play him in pool. You need to find a way to have fun in this environment."

"Our job is…to relax?" Connor smiled and laughed loudly. "Got it."

He pushed away from the table and walked over to Kayde's group, ready to begin to mingle. Ann watched her friends adapt and worried. As an introvert, places like this could get overwhelming.

"I would like you to let your hair down, so to speak, as well, but you have another objective."

That made more sense. "One you couldn't share with Connor."

"Exactly."

"What do I do?"

"Karaoke starts in an hour. I want you to use your power to inspire yourself to sing."

"I've…never told anyone about that." Normally, the thought would terrify her, but for some reason, she was only mildly nervous at the thought.

"There were signs."

"What signs?"

"You hum to yourself, sometimes, obviously without realizing it."

"And you noticed?"

He leaned back, trying to get comfortable in his seat. "It's my job to notice those things. You seem to be ignoring a talent you have. Your flame can help you, you've gained some control… I'd like you to try."

"Ok." She took another sip of her cola, and added, "can I have dessert first?"

He chuckled but waved to Harry as she smiled.

An hour later, she stepped up to the microphone on the small stage behind the pool tables. She'd picked a song she loved since childhood and knew very well. As the first notes of a piano poured from the speakers, she took a deep breath, and prepared to accomplish her objective.

Her vocal chords hummed to life with the first low notes, and she allowed the energy from them to summon her bird. Tyrus was correct that she hummed every so often, when she was focused on a task, or in the shower. She knew her bird listened to her, enjoyed the notes, but to do this, in public, was a huge step for her. She allowed the heat of her magic flow along her skin, and the notes flowed easily from her lips.

Swinging down from some magical realm, her phoenix sat on her shoulders. As the melody grew more intense, Ann closed her eyes, focusing on the song and her power. The flame grew, spreading with the song down her arm and into her hand where it leapt to another. Who, she couldn't see, but she let it flow from her and into the crowded bar.

The chorus began and her birds flapped its wings, fanning her flame as the melody rose higher, moved more quickly. Her power poured out of her in strings of fire, matching the movement of the song, the rhythm, melody and chords vibrating to life. She began the second verse alone, but by the second chorus, she began to hear other voices joining in.

Opening her eyes, the entire bar began to first hum, then sing with her. Whether they knew the words or not, they followed, some tapping pool cues to the beat like Connor and Seth, or outright singing like Tyrus and Kayde. When the song ended, and the last piano notes were done, a silence hung heavy in the air for a few long moments, as everyone felt a certain melancholy at its too quick end.

Ann walked off of the stage in that silence, and down to a waiting bar stool near the pool table, Tyrus and Connor standing on either side. Only when she sat did the bar burst into applause, and she blushed furiously, happy and embarrassed all at once.

She looked to Tyrus who winked at her, silently thanking him for helping her come out of her shell that night. In the search of her professional identity, singing may not make the best career, but at least she had developed a small piece of herself. This was something she did now. She sang. *In public.* And it was validating *as hell.*

On a silent cue, Tyrus followed Kayde outside the bar some hours later, as her voice drifted out to them. Kayde lit a cigarette and offered one to Tyrus.

"I know we can't get cancer after our change, but I stopped anyway."

"Ah. No problem." The pack was placed back into his jacket pocket. "Interesting group you've got."

"You haven't met the others."

"Oh?"

"A unicorn and Cerberus."

"Nice. Quite potent magic, too."

"A nice meal for you."

"Oh, indeed. I haven't fed that well on power for quite a while."

"I thought it would interest you."

"And help an introvert come out of her shell. Did she know I influence the environment like that?'

"No, I kept that one to myself. She overthinks, can't help it. Had I told her, she would have fought it tooth and nail."

"Is her nature, the phoenix, right?"

Tyrus just nodded at that.

"How…" Kayde shook his head, placing the cigarette to his lips. He let out a breath, unable to finish his question.

"How what?"

Sighing, he added, "Oh, *come on*. The question is obvious. Do I have to say it? Are we acting like the dichotomy of phoenix and dragon doesn't exist?"

Tyrus swallowed, hard. "You know that there are caveats to that. It doesn't always end well and doesn't always take the same form."

"No, no it doesn't. I get it. You don't want to be the older guy crushing on a girl too young for him."

"Not at all. It isn't who I am."

Kayde nodded, looking off into the distance. "Thing is, not everyone is as noble. You know there are monsters in the world, some of them dragons stronger than you, Mythics who are uncomfortable placing their name."

Tyrus sighed, a bit frustrated. "She's safe here, between Nix, the Five and me."

"Oh, yes. Bodyguards, all around. I noticed that. I'm just saying, old friend, that a phoenix not bonded is potent magic, and some dragons will be drawn to it. She won't be able to hide here forever in your little corner of the world."

"Her fate will be her own."

He chuckled. "I just don't understand how your dragon is controlling itself. If I met a potential bonded mate, I wouldn't hesitate to make my intentions known. Life is too short, and that kind of love, too rare."

He placed his hands into his pockets. "Not hard, with my past experiences. You know what I went through."

"I can't imagine losing a mate I've bonded with. It's a singular pain few have had to survive. Levi's situation, and yours, just…tragic."

"Something you probably shouldn't mention."

"Did it hurt, when Nix's bird chose him?"

Tyrus let the glow of his power reach his eyes. "Again, probably not something you should mention."

"I find it quite curious. Some dragons go their whole lives without meeting a single phoenix. You've had the luck to run into not one, but three."

"What are you implying?"

"Not sure if it was just luck, that's all."

Tyrus tensed at the potential accusation.

"Oh, I know you're not *that* twisted. Just, wondering why the universe seems to keep you blessed."

"*Blessed*?" Tyrus laughed, the irony obvious. "Blessed to be surrounded by an odyssey of gorgeous firebirds I couldn't love? The better question is why the universe seeks to torture me." He kicked at the stones near his feet.

"See it as you will, I can't stop you. You know I'm just… compelled to ask sometimes."

"You've always kept me honest with myself. I appreciate the reality check."

The absence of her voice drew their attention. "She'll be looking for you."

He nodded. "Best get back in there."

When he opened the side door, though, she wasn't looking for him. She was on the bar, along with Harry and several others, doing a line dance, while the rest of the bar joined in, wherever they were able. As the cheery country song played, he couldn't help but smile as she twirled around, her hair wild.

Kayde finished his cigarette and patted his friend's back. "Best of luck with *that,* mate."

Chapter 10

Nix stepped out of the car with Joy and Julius. The three entered the hospital, avoiding as many people as possible. Walking directly to the elevator, they went to the third floor, where her nephew was located.

She walked into his room to see him hooked up to tubes. The argument with his nurse stopped abruptly as he saw his aunt.

"Hey. You didn't have to come."

"Yes, I did. Where's your driver?"

"I'm trying to find out." He glared at the nurse.

"I'm sorry but he's still in surgery. His head wound was quite severe. We can let you know how he's doing once he's clear."

"Can you tell us if he's critical?" Nix asked.

"He is. That's all I can say."

"Thank you." Nix smiled and waited for her to leave. Joy and Julius stepped forward.

"So, we wait?" Joy asked.

"We wait." Taking a seat next to her nephew, the other two found spots to bide their time. "Did you install cameras?"

"Yes."

"Do you have the photos?"

"Here." He handed her his phone. She combed through the photos as they waited. An hour passed before she found what she needed. "That's Wills." She showed him a photo of a blonde in an alley walking away. "Clear as day. We've got her leaving the scene."

"Now what?" Julius asked.

"Now," Dr. Jackson's eyes were cold. "Now we wait and hope she's stupid enough to do it again. I'll send this to all my guards on the estate. They'll know who to look for, now."

"If she's smart, she won't use herself as an operative. Keep a look out for signs of mythic activity."

"She has that much of a network?"

"She was sent from Blanc."

"Oh." His face grew angry. "They broke the pact."

"They did."

"Should I start legal proceedings?"

"I'm already on the surveillance, but it might be a bit early yet."

"Just let me know." He flexed his knuckles and his shoulders. "Do we have her location?"

"I don't know. I'm on it though. We've got Ryan tracking down leads. She'll make it known one way or the other."

A nurse walked in, halting their conversation. "Dr. Jackson? Your driver is out of surgery. He is alive, but I'm sorry to say he's in a coma. We have to let him wake up to know the full extent of the damage he's suffered. I'm sorry, but the doctors don't feel he will wake up. You may want to contact his family."

Dr. Jackson nodded. "What room number?"

"347."

"I'll go check on him for you." Nix kissed his forehead and the three walked out of the room, avoiding contact with any cameras. Reaching 347, they entered, shutting the door, closing the blinds. Nix locked it softly. No need for anyone to be suspicious.

Joy got to work. She placed both hands over the driver's body and concentrated. For a moment, nothing happened. She'd only done this a few times before, and never on a normal human.

Nix waited until, after some time, her light finally shone. It surrounded her body and slowly then the driver. The light pulsed softly as she worked. It began to shine brightly, until it filled the room with blinding power.

When it faded, they left quickly, as if they had never been there. From the hall, she could hear the sound of the driver choking on his breathing tube as he woke. Nurses were already running to help him. She smiled as they got into the elevator and rode down to the first floor. Another good deed under their belt.

Looking at her phone, she saw a text from Tyrus and shook her head. Texting back, she told him they were on their way back. It would take several hours to drive back to camp. Hopefully, he could hold down the fort until then.

◆ ◆ ◆

Tyrus stood and walked over to the two friends. They were laughing at some joke he hadn't heard. They grew somber as he approached. "Today was an interesting turn of events. How are you doing?

She sighed. "The bar was great, but I still messed up earlier, when I woke. What was that?"

His half smile was sympathetic. "The energy I felt then, it wasn't all you. Someone was pushing it out of you. You might not have been entirely at fault."

"Who would do that?"

His eyes grew dark, distant. "Tommy taught you that not all Mythics were kind. It's a powerful lesson.'

"Am I safe here?"

He placed a hand on her shoulder. "Now that we know that you can be contacted like that, we can take precautions. You'll be safe."

She followed Tyrus into the cabin. Connor and Maiden were sitting in the living area talking.

"Hey, Honor. Maiden's a mermaid." Giddiness dripped from his voice.

She laughed. "I kind of thought that the way Tyrus was talking last night."

"It's cool. You really transform in water?"

"Yes, I can." She said it as if it were only natural.

"How did you get here?"

"We can make portals in the water. I came through the lake."

"What else can you do?"

She laughed. "I can talk to sea creatures."

"Sweet. What do fish say?"

"Mostly, they just want food. Dolphins are very…quick-witted though."

"Anything else?"

Tyrus turned to Honor and motioned that they should sit. Taking her hands in his, she felt the pull of his power. "What are we doing?"

"I'm going to give you a memory. It's not a pretty one, but you need to understand how to control your dreams. You will see one of mine, and you'll learn how I wake myself. Ready?"

"Yes." She looked into his eyes, which glowed green. The talking, the room, everything faded away until she saw nothing but the image he sent to her mind…

He was standing on a ledge, in the middle of a desert. Below him was a vacant dirt road. Two vehicles were coming from the left toward him. He sat down, waiting for the vehicles to slow. As they reached the middle of the road, near the cliff, he stood and started to wave his hands. There was a bomb in the middle of the road, and they were heading right toward it.

No one saw, and the two vehicles approached. The first vehicle exploded as it hit the bomb, and as it did, he was suddenly stepping out of the second vehicle, walking forward toward the wreckage. He saw the pieces of bodies and metal covering the desert. As he watched, gunfire suddenly came from the right, someplace high up. He watched as men around him kept falling to the ground, dying.

This is a dream. The thought came to him quietly. Instead of engaging in the memory, he turned his weapon on himself and fired.

She was jolted back to the present, free from his memory. She stared at him a moment before he reached out and wiped a tear she didn't feel away from her cheek. He smiled weakly, and said, "Not a memory I like sharing, but you get the idea."

"How did you know you were dreaming? It seemed so real."

Sad eyes looked back at her. "It happened, but in the dream, I was on the cliff first. I knew I hadn't been there, so I knew I was dreaming."

"Oh."

"Your most powerful weapon is your mind. There's always something in your dream that is off. If you can use your logic to find that and focus on it, you'll realize you're dreaming and hopefully, you'll be able to wake yourself up."

"By unaliving myself out of my dream?"

"That's what I have to do. You can choose to do other things."

"Oh."

"Just keep it in mind. Dreams shouldn't control you."

"I will."

He was still holding her hands, even though the moment had passed. He didn't seem to realize he was. She was debating pulling her hands away when Seth bounced into the room with an unconscious woman.

"Help me." He held her head on the ground. Tyrus rushed toward him, examining the woman quickly.

"What happened?"

"I don't know. She was there, waving at me and a force just threw her off a twenty-foot drop."

"Did you see what it was?"

"No."

"Grab a pillow, let's not move her. Hopefully she will survive long enough for Nix to get back with Joy."

"I may be able to help." Maiden stood and walked to her.

"I didn't think Merfolk could heal…"

"Not exactly, but we can control water."

"How does that help her?"

"I can help keep her blood circulating or from collecting in her brain cavity. I can keep her stable." She placed one hand on the woman's head, another on her belly and a blue shine surrounded them both. "I'll just stay here and help her as long as I can."

An hour passed, then two. They paced back and forth, waiting for the others to return. The moon rose and fell, night growing closer to morning. They heard the tires of a vehicle roll to a stop, and minutes later their friends walked inside.

"Long day," Nix said, "and I guess it's not over."

"No, no it's not." Joy walked toward the woman and knelt. "I *told* you to go faster."

"Yes, Joy," Nix rolled her eyes, "you did and I should have

listened."

Joy, tired from the long day, focused her energy, trying to heal the woman who lay unconscious. The same light filled the room, but it wasn't as bright, and sweat dripped from her brow. "Just a little more."

The light stopped, and Joy fell to the floor. Seth rushed to pick her up. "Is she okay?"

Nix touched her forehead. "She's probably just tired. Let's get her to bed." The two left the room.

The woman was still unresponsive. Whatever Joy had done, it hadn't been enough. Maiden placed her hands on the woman again and examined the blood in her veins.

"She was able to repair the brain injury, but her body is tired. She should wake after a long sleep."

Standing, she addressed Connor. "Cool." He took her hand and began to talk with her about her life some more.

Tyrus picked the woman up and set her on a couch. "I guess we'll find out who she is in the morning."

Honor nodded, glad everyone was safe and home. She walked outside with Julius on her heels. "You ever wonder what we'd be doing now, if our lives were…normal?" He asked it softly.

"I imagine we'd be at jobs in the city, never really getting to know each other. You'd have Markus. I'd have Marie."

"Yeah, I still miss them."

"Me too."

"I'd probably be working for my dad."

"Who knows where I would have been. Away from the fosters from Hell, for sure, but other than that, who knows. Probably working in fast food."

"Can you cook?"

She shook her head, remembering the event at the Chik'n Kitch'n... "I mean, I might be able to learn but no one ever taught me anything."

"My mom, she cooks well. I can teach you some stuff, if you want, sometime."

"Sure. I'd like that."

"Yeah? She makes some great chili."

"I do love a good chili."

"Maybe I can make it tomorrow."

"Go for it. I'll watch and learn."

Tyrus approached them. "Sparring time, Julius."

"See ya, Fenix." He stood, walking away while she moved into the cabin. She was ready with an Ice pack for the two when they came inside again. "You feel better?" Julius nodded.

"How about you?" She handed Tyrus one. He placed it on his knee. "I'm great. Never better."

"Will we always get injured like that?"

Tyrus looked her in the eye. "No. No, you just are new at this. Eventually, you'll be able to defend against the most common attacks. Just takes practice and repetition, so it's in your muscle memory. Anything you do in life worth doing, is worth doing well."

"Understood."

"I'm heading to bed for the night. See ya, Honor."

"Night, Julius."

Tyrus and Honor sat alone as the fireplace blazed in front of them. Both were quiet for a long while, enjoying the silence. Tyrus spoke first.

"I don't even know your favorite color."

Where had that come from? "What do you mean?"

"You're aloof. I get it, because I am too."

"Not trying to be."

"I know. So, what is it?"

"What's what?"

"Your favorite color?"

"I like all colors. Never really had a favorite. I have color combos that I like."

"Okay. What about favorite food?"

"Again, I love food too much to have a favorite."

He laughed. "I'm beginning to see a pattern here. One more.

Favorite time of the day."

She smiled. "At night, right after the sun goes down, but before the sky goes dark."

"And the blue crosses the sky."

"It's dark, but not so dark that the blue doesn't shine. It's peaceful. The day has passed, it has begun cooling off. That is my favorite time of day."

"Nice."

"Why do you ask?"

"Conversation starter."

"That's it?"

"I feel like you and I haven't gotten to know each other like I know everyone else. I know Connor loves football. I've played with the guys."

"I've seen you play."

"I know that Joy loves everybody and we are her favorite toys."

Honor laughed. "Sounds like Joy."

"I know that Julius misses his mom."

"Aww!" She made a sad face. "Oh, no."

"I know that Seth is obsessed with history."

"Right? He knows so much."

"I know Nix has a soft spot for puppies. Don't tell anyone. And I know that Levi is old. I'm talking, ancient old."

"You know a lot."

"I do. Just not about you."

"Well, ask me then."

"What was it like growing up in foster care?"

She wasn't ready for that one. "Wow. We're starting with the *easy* stuff, huh?"

"Just thought I'd get it out of the way."

"I never knew my parents. I was one of the unlucky kids that didn't get picked for a home. After a certain age, you stop hoping to find one. As much as we want to belong, we learn to belong nowhere. We don't let people in because people have let us down. What else do you want to know?"

He didn't speak for a short time, then he asked, "Have you ever thought of looking for them?"

"My birth parents?"

"Yes."

"What for?"

"Closure?"

She thought about that for a moment. "I suppose it wouldn't hurt to find out who gave me up and why. Then at least I would know, you know. Where I came from."

"It's something to think about. If you ever want me to help you find them, I can."

"You don't look like a social worker."

"I'm not. What I am is a man with contacts that you could utilize if you ever want that question answered. Believe me, you may want to think about it."

"I've been hurt so much, it just seems scary. What if they're drug addicts or dead or just mean people?"

"Then you would be thankful you got out."

"I guess. I don't know. Let me think about it."

"Got it." He moved the ice pack from his knee to his eye. Honor noticed.

"He got you there too, huh?" Tyrus nodded slowly. "What about you?"

"What about me?"

"What's your favorite color/food/time of day?"

He sighed. "Blue, apples and right before the sun comes up in the morning." He stood, balancing on his good knee. "I'm turning in, Honor."

"Good night." She watched him go and wondered about her parents. Could she really find them, and if she did, what would be the result? Getting nowhere, she called it quits after a few minutes. She decided she didn't care. It was kind of Tyrus to think she should, but she didn't. They gave her up for a reason, and she couldn't go back.

Why should she care who they are when they didn't care about her?

Chapter 11

"How are you feeling?" Nix asked, next to her bed.

"Good."

"Then get up. We've got work to do. Meet me in ten."

Nix waited outside for her. The group sat around the campfire, talking. "When the woman wakes, we'll help her find her way back home. She isn't up yet. Most likely a lost hiker who just needs help back to civilization."

Honor sat between Nix and Tyrus. Nix grabbed her hand for a quick squeeze.

"We also need someone on Maiden's news about the hidden coin." Tyrus sounded concerned. "I don't like not knowing my enemies."

"You don't have any idea?" Julius asked.

"That's why we call it the *hidden* coin, but yes, we don't know what he was talking about. Something big is going down. We need information."

"How do we get that?"

"We send someone to talk to the Mer King."

Honor looked at her friends. "We're out of water signs."

Maiden chimed in. "We don't need one. I can take someone through the portal and talk to my father on the beach."

"Who do we send?" Nix folded her hands and placed them on her knees.

"The leader of the Five most interests my father."

"That person would be Connor."

"Yes. I think he'd like to meet the Griffin."

"Are we sure this is safe? No offense, but how do we know you're telling the truth?"

"I was instructed to tell Tyrus a story if you needed proof."

"Ooh, story time!" Joy clapped her hands, then slumped her shoulders. "Oh, she's only going to tell Tyrus." She kicked the dirt in front of her.

Maiden took his hands, her eyes glowing blue. Nothing happened, as they stared at each other for a few moments before she released his hands. Her eyes stopped glowing and Tyrus said, "she's telling the truth." He wiped a tear away from his eyes.

"What just happened?" Connor was confused.

"She shared a memory with him."

Connor turned to Honor. "How do you know that?"

"Because he's shared one with me."

Nix glared at him. "Really?"

He shrugged his shoulders. "You weren't here."

"What's the problem?" Connor seemed confused.

Nix shook her head. "Nothing. So she's telling the truth then. Connor, go with her and then report back after you've learned something helpful."

He nodded. Honor watched as they walked toward the lake. A whirlpool, much like Levi's appeared and then they were gone. Turning back to the group, she debated bringing up the figure in her dream.

"What is it Honor?" Joy asked.

"Nothing."

"No, it's something, but for some reason, I can't see it. There's a cloud around you. That's strange."

Nix stood and walked behind Honor. "What do you mean, a cloud, Joy?" Tyrus seemed alert too.

"It's dark around Honor. I don't know why. I can't see her path."

"Tyrus…" Nix started looking around the area.

"I'll check it out. Everyone stay put." His wings unfolded and he flew away.

Honor turned to Nix, who had knives drawn. "What's wrong?"

"You've been marked." She was constantly vigilant, refusing to meet Honor's eyes.

"What does that mean?" Joy wondered.

"We don't know, but we need to secure the area."

"What's so dangerous about it?"

Nix looked at the four of them and said, "That was the first sign. Our leprechaun was marked, and a week later, she was dead."

"And you never found out what had marked her?"

"No. It was like a curse. Everyone got angry, we splintered and half of us died. We can't let that happen to you."

Connor's vision blurred for a small moment, before the world became clear again. He was standing on a beach amid the most colorful hills he'd ever seen.

"Ireland."

Maiden nodded. "One of the lands of my people. We love the northern islands. Our history is here. Thousands of years of it, hidden under the water."

"How does it survive?"

"In its people." She walked to the water's edge and placed both feet where the waves could wash over them. As Connor listened, she sounded out a soft, steady tune, beautiful and haunting. Stepping away from the water, she turned to him. "Now we wait."

"What did you just do?"

"I called to my father. Every merfolk has a song. I sang his."

She sat down on the beach, motioning for him to follow. "It may take a while. He's a busy man."

Connor joined her, folding his hands in front of him, awaiting the arrival of the Merking.

Minutes later, she stood. "Get ready. Greet him standing."

Connor obliged and the water began to change. Swirls and waves, beautiful chaos began to overtake the coast. From the center came a man of water, whose shape changed gradually to a more human form, but his eyes retained the chaos of the sea. His hair was long, white, but in the sun, shone with a hint of gold. He stood taller than Connor by at least a few inches.

"Connor Owsen." A loud, booming voice hailed him, while stretching out a hand. He shook it, noting a strange strength that was fluid as well. "I've been waiting to meet the young leader of the group that survived the bombing of Jackson Genetics."

"I was sent by Tyrus to- "

"Yes, well, I'm afraid that will have to wait. We have an urgent matter that requires our attention, and your help." He pointed out to the ocean.

"Uh, I can't breathe underwater…"

Maiden chuckled. "You can with my father's magic. It is great."

Placing two hands on his shoulders, the Merking closed his eyes and Connor felt a wave of…some magic pass over him. It was as if every organ was suddenly pure water. Opening his eyes, he stared at his host.

"What did you do?"

"For the next forty-eight hours, you are no longer a Griffin. You are Mer. Now come. We have need of you."

He descended into the ocean, and out of sight. Maiden grabbed his hand. He hesitated.

"I promise, my friend, the change does not hurt. Come feel how free the ocean is, with me." She smiled up at him and he was no longer afraid. Taking her hand, they followed her father, slowly disappearing into the water.

A rush of cold, around and inside him, then he could see, breathe. He touched his neck, noting gills had formed. Looking beside him, he saw Maiden in her true form, from the large tail to the webbed hands, to her hair, lit with fire from the tendrils of sunlight that penetrated the surface of the water. Looking down, he saw that he had changed as well. While Maiden's fin was green and yellow, his fins were blue and purple. Amazed, he stared at her for a moment.

Never letting go of his hand, she began to swim, slowly at first. He mimicked her movements until he thought he had the hang of it, but then she dove. Down into the dark. He followed, his eyes adjusting quickly. Following the two of them, they traveled for some time before coming to an underwater mountain chain, hidden beneath the sea. Entering a small cave, he was surprised to find air. They reverted back to human form, walking up stone stairs to a huge cavern, alive with plants and glowing lights.

Robes were placed over them. He had no clue what material this was. It was unlike anything he'd seen or felt before. It shimmered in different colors and was strong and warm as wool but smooth as silk. A belt was cinched around his waist, of another strange material, scaly but the consistency of leather. Finally, shoes were brought that though thin made him feel as if he were walking on clouds.

"Wow." He turned to Maiden. She held a hand to her lips, asking for his silence. He smiled.

The Merking turned and held out both hands. "Greetings, Connor Owsen. You are the first landwalker to see Oceana, our sacred city, in a thousand years. May you learn much while you are here. I am Daileass, Merking of Oceana. I welcome you to our home." The king grabbed his elbows and finished with, "May the waters of fate deliver you."

Maiden nudged him and whispered, "Say it back."

"May the waters of fate deliver you." Daileass smiled at that, and turned away, walking into the tunnel ahead. Maiden grabbed his hand and walked after her father. As they entered, the flora lit the tunnel, a blue hue guiding their way. He turned to Maiden.

"It reacts to our electromagnetic fields. Cool, isn't it?"

"What do you call it?"

"Its real name is *solas agus dubhar* . It's direct translation is light and shade, but we call it lightshade in English."

"it's beautiful."

"It covers every inch of the walls of the city. It's the reason air exists down here. It's older than our history. It never grows, but never dies." She reached a hand out and touching it, the blue hue changed to purple. "It reacts to everyone differently when you touch it. Try it."

He did, noting his color was golden. "This is awesome." He turned back to Maiden who was looking at him strangely. "What is it?"

"The only other person with golden hue is my father. Strange." She walked on, his hand in hers.

A hundred steps and the tunnel widened into a gigantic open city. What he assumed were homes were carved out of the rock of the mountain. Stairs were everywhere going up and down. A road led through the bottom of the city, where strange plants and trees flourished. Farther down, a large structure appeared in the distance.

"That is my home." Maiden whispered.

Daileass turned. "You have much to see, much to learn and much to report back to your dragon. First, I would have you understand us. To do so, we must visit the city center. Come."

They walked, passing people dressed in similar robes, all of whom stared after the newcomer with curious smiles. Some of the younger girls giggled as he walked by. One small child touched his hand quickly and ran away. Every skin tone was represented, even some he'd never seen, with colors of blue, purple, and green.

"They haven't seen an outsider their entire lives. Neither had I, until I went to find you."

He nodded. The trees and plants gave way to a circular clearing, at the center of which stood a magnificent green tree that reached from the floor to the ceiling of the cavern. A small moat of clear water surrounded it. They carefully sidestepped the moat, reaching the very center of the city.

"This is the Fate Tree." Walking around to the other side, Connor gasped to see a small waterfall springing forth from its trunk.

"And this is the Water of Fate. Along with Lightshade and the Fate Tree, these three phenomena are what keep our city alive."

A cup of silver stood on a pedestal to the left of the tree. The Merking took it and filled it with the water of fate. He presented it to Connor, saying, "May the Water of Fate deliver you."

Maiden nudged him and he repeated the phrase. Taking the cup, the king motioned for him to drink it. He took a sip. The water was clear, crisp and a little sweet. The king motioned again, and Connor emptied the cup. Handing it back to the king, he smiled. "Refreshing."

Several young people giggled. A look from the king and they

were silent again.

"You are now tied to us by the bonds of fate. May we prosper together in friendship."

He reached out a hand and Connor took it. Maiden nudged him again. "May we prosper in friendship."

The people in the city center cheered at that, and he was quickly embraced by the king. "Now that the formality is over, I'd like to welcome you to my home." Placing an arm around him, Daileass walked forward, dragging the young man with him. "We have much to show you, and very little time to do it in. You're about to get a crash course, not just in our history, but your own. First, though, we eat. I hope you like seafood."

Ahead of them stood Maiden's home, a fortress among the small homes that were carved out of the rock. "It was made from a small mountain near the center of the city. We live there, as well as housing advisers, their families and the orphaned."

Walking up to a large two-story door made of green wood, the king let go of his shoulder and said, "welcome to our home." The doors opened and he stepped into his first castle.

A large room housed a throne in its center, with tables and chairs throughout, all made of green wood. Doors stood on either side of the great room, six in total. A large staircase to the left lead to a second story, where many small doors lined the balcony.

"Nice home you have here," he whispered to Maiden. She smiled. The king sat on his throne and motioned for Connor to sit at the nearest table. "We eat, then we will talk." Everyone in the hall waited until their visitor was seated, even Maiden, then they sat all at once, beginning to chat amongst themselves. The first door to the right opened and more merfolk with plates of food came pouring out.

Before he knew it, Maiden had piled his plate high with several different types of seafood, as well as what looked like vegetables and fruit from the strange trees that grew here. A full plate, she poured him some water and said, "enjoy."

Connor never did like seafood, so he slowly took the first bite.

His taste buds must have been changed, because when he would normally gag at the taste, he now found it pleasant and comforting. Digging in, he enjoyed everything she had given him.

Looking around, he was amazed at the people here. They'd survived for thousands of years, underground, away from the world. How were they connected to him? What could they possibly need him for? Maiden touched his arm, and he looked to see what he thought was dessert being shoved at him. He smiled and took it happily. Whatever it was, he was grateful to be of help.

He stared after his companion for a moment, savoring the way she shook her hair, the way she smiled at him, the warmth in her eyes. She was so pretty. He caught himself staring and looked down at his dessert, digging in. Not the time to think of a gorgeous mermaid princess.

While Connor ate his first royal meal, the camp wasn't faring well. Honor was the only person sitting, practicing her meditation. Around her, as she tried to ignore it, was movement.

Joy and Seth were scouting the camp, looking for anything unusual that could be causing a dark aura. They were told to look for strange trinkets or symbols. So far, the two of them couldn't find anything.

Julius was looking for people. For anyone else hidden around the camp that may have an ulterior motive. He ran through the trees, faster than a normal human could, jumping over and rolling under logs with ease.

Tyrus and Nix had summoned Levi again, who was using his own meditation to "connect to the water." Whatever that meant. Nix was searching her cabin, and Tyrus was…thinking? She wasn't sure but the look on his face was quite intense.

And she sat in the middle of it all, meditating near the fire. Her flame came easily now, and her skill and control were immensely better than only a few days prior. She changed the size and shape of the flame that flew from her fingertips to the circle of stones and wood.

Eventually, she got bored of that, and began to envision swirls, patterns, shapes, then eventually animals. When she'd made a flame giraffe launch itself into the fire, she chuckled.

"Honor…" She wasn't sure if she'd heard that correctly. Was that her name, or just the wind? Looking around, she saw no one. Deciding she had imagined it, she went back to her meditation.

Moments later, she heard her name again. "Honor…come to me." She couldn't tell if the whisper was male or female, but it was a strange and twisted sound. She looked around again. Levi opened his eyes.

"What is it, firebird?"

"I keep hearing…something."

"The wind?"

"Maybe. Never mind." He closed his eyes.

She again started to meditate, making intricate patterns in the flame. It rushed at the fire, surrounding it before it dissipated, making waves and circles around the stone. Nix came out, finished searching her room. She walked next to Levi and placed a hand on his shoulder. "Anything?"

"Not yet."

"HONOR!" The sound from the voice scared her, and her control was lost. Her flame went wide, hitting Levi and Nix in its wake. She stood, and said, "sorry."

Her mentor sighed, then locked eyes with Levi, whose gaze held an intense longing. Levi moved to Nix and the water swirled around the both of them until they'd teleported away and only a few droplets remained, soaking into the earth.

Tyrus ran to her. "What happened?"

"Nix and Levi…" She realized that she didn't even want to try to explain. Looking at Tyrus, it turned out she didn't need to.

"I get it." He rubbed his head, clearly getting lost in his thoughts again. He mumbled something to himself as Joy and Seth bounced to the campfire.

"Honor, come to me. Leave them. You will only destroy the

ones you love." The voice no longer whispered to her. It was as if the voice was next to her ear, shouting. She covered them, trying to escape the pain.

"Honor, what is it?" Tyrus rushed to her, placing two hands over hers. "Are you okay?"

She couldn't answer through the continuous voice clouding her mind. She heard Joy mumble something, saw her produce something from her pocket. She placed it on the stone seat and Tyrus smashed it under his foot. The voice immediately receded. She could think again.

She opened her eyes to Joy's smile. "The cloud is gone." She gave Honor a hug. "You're saved, my friend."

"What was that?"

Tyrus turned to her. "A black crystal, with dark flame swirling in its center. I've never seen anything like it. It's like someone bottled Omega Flame. What was it doing to you?"

"I kept hearing voices."

"A method of communication, maybe?" He swept the shards up with his hand and walked away with them.

"When you smashed it, the voices vanished."

"The cloud too. They must be connected."

"But how?"

Julius returned shortly after, his chest heaving with exhaustion. Honor went inside the cabin to get him a bottle of water. Even their endurance had its limits. She tossed the bottle to him, and he drank it down, whispering his thanks when he was finished. Still sweating, he took off his shirt.

"The things I do for pretty girls…" He winked at Honor then headed to the lake. "I'm going to cool down." He proceeded down the path without a backward glance. A few moments later, Tyrus came back out of the main cabin.

"I placed the shards in the safe, just in case we could find someone to analyze them. Maybe Dr. Jackson can make something of it eventually. Nix can contact him…when they get back."

He sat down and rubbed his face with his hand. "Well, Honor, someone's definitely got an eye on you."

She shivered despite the sunny day. Looking at the tree line, she wondered who it was, and why they'd be interested in her. What had she ever accomplished?

Connor sat back, satisfied and full. He'd never eaten so well in all his life. "Wow."

"A feast fit for a king, yes?"

He laughed. "I'm no king."

"Not yet, anyway." She smiled as he gave her a quizzical expression.

"Where we live, there are no kings. Everyone is equal."

She laughed. "Landwalker, we've watched your kind for a thousand years. Man is greed. How can you be equal with someone who thinks, at their heart, they are better than you?"

"You can't, but we at least make the effort to *believe* we are."

She smiled and touched his hand. "It's a start I guess." She squeezed gently before letting go. From his seat on the throne, the king bellowed. "Silence!"

The entire hall immediately looked to their monarch. "We have a guest here today. The first of his kind to visit us in our home in over a thousand years. Connor Owsen, Leader of the Five, and Ambassador of the Landwalkers, welcome to my hall. May the Waters of Fate deliver you safely home, always."

Seeing that everyone raised their goblets, Connor raised his as well. Drinking a single sip, they sat their glasses down. Then the cheering began. Maiden elbowed him, but he was unsure what she wished him to do. Standing, she grabbed his hand and walked him to her father.

She didn't bow. "Dear father, may I present to you the person you've honored in your hall." She practically shoved him forward. He tilted his head at the king. He thought a moment, as silence greeted him. Everyone was waiting for his response, and for a second, he was frozen, unsure of what he should say.

But the king was wise and had changed his fate for the next two days. He relaxed as the answer seemed to come from his very bones, words he didn't understand, of an age he didn't belong came from his lips.

"Mhà uisgeachan thachair lìbhrigeadh dhachaidh mi thu, an-còmhnaidh." The words echoed with weight as if they were old and powerful. He thought he felt the hall rumble beneath him for a moment.

Applause erupted again behind him. The king came down from his throne, and linked arms with him, facing his people. "May this be the start of a new era, where we and the landwalkers live in peace."

Everyone stood and more applause followed. Connor didn't realize this was such a big deal. When everyone had quieted, they left the hall, walking into a room to the left filled with ancient scrolls, books and tablets of stone.

"This may not look like much, but you're in the presence of the greatest library left on the planet, full of carefully preserved parchments from ancient times dating back ten thousand years. Though some volumes were lost when the Library of Alexandria sank, we had copies here. Many of the information some of you still lament is safe within our walls."

"How do you preserve the scrolls? Why are they not just dust?"

"Once a generation, we rewrite them, leaving the original meanings intact, unlike your modern historians who seem to color everything with your cultural preferences at the time."

"I thought you said you'd lived in isolation for a thousand years?"

"No, I said that you were the first landwalker to come *here* in a thousand years. Our scouts walk among your people to keep an eye on humanity."

"That's how you knew about us?"

"Your news and technology make it easier than ever to find the information we need."

"To what end?"

"To help where we can, to steer the course of this world to a better fate."

"And for a thousand years, you've kept watch. What's changing now to bring you out of hiding?"

Daileass turned and reached out a hand toward a wall of lightshade. A screen of water appeared, through which he could see his companions.

"What you are seeing is the present. Your friends, at their camp, who just finished finding an Omega Crystal. It was tormenting your phoenix."

"Did we cause some sort of galactic disturbance?"

He laughed. "No. You are but fibers in the thread of this life, although you are more vibrant than most." He waved his hand again. This time, Connor saw Nix, Levi and Tyrus locked in battle.

"This is the past. Nix was not supposed to lose her firebird, and yet, it was so. For Nix, this saved her life. For another, it will destroy it."

Connor watched the scene unfold, saw the two beasts sever her connection to her bird, who instantly vanished. It happened so quickly. Sadness filled him. "Why did they do it?"

"Do you blame the hands for the actions of the mind?"

"No, the mind controls the hands."

"Your friends were but the hands. The minds behind the chaos, the hidden coins, these are your true enemy."

He waved his hand one last time. This image was hard to describe. Black flame covered the entire world. You could see it from space. It swept across continents, in an instant, and everything became ash.

"This, unfortunately, is the future if we don't intercede. We must help you five survive, so that this future does not come to pass. Long have we sat, vigilant, waiting to be called to our fate. It rests with the five of you." He paused a moment, while Connor looked at the flame. It was almost…beautiful, in its destruction.

Another wave of his hand and the screen went dark. Connor snapped out of his trance. "What was that?"

"Many have died while mesmerized by the Omega Flame. Don't be its next victim. Look away."

Connor shook his head, attempting to clear it. "Got it. Don't look at the pretty…dark…painful…light."

"Indeed." Daileass walked toward the door and said, "but enough of omens. Come, I would show you the rest of my home. Tomorrow, your work begins."

They walked out of the room, but Connor had a sinking feeling in his gut. Whatever they needed to show him, whatever he needed to see, this wasn't all of it. There was more dread to come.

The dark figure tilted their head, amused. So, she's found the curse, and managed to break it. How…cute. Yes, that was the word. This little pet would be harder to tame than the last.

For now, pets would have to wait. There were other, more important matters to attend to. Leaving the beach, they walked into an old, abandoned factory made of metal. The windows had long since been broken, much like the workers within. Thousands of people walked about, hauling coal, metal and working the furnaces. Thousands, doing their bidding. As it should be.

They walked upstairs, following a worker. The floor creaked as the worker trudged on, but their own footsteps were silent. One of the benefits of being…well, singular. Inside a room at the top was a very sophisticated laboratory. To the right stood the mind raised to do important work.

"Well?" It was a harsh whisper. They'd long forgotten what their real voice sounded like. "What have you got?"

"The projected numbers aren't moving fast enough. If you want your timetable to play out at the exact right moment, we need to speed things up."

"You need more workers?"

"No, no, that won't work. We need a better delivery system. Even at my best calculations, we won't make your deadline this way."

"So, what do you intend to do?"

A smile lit the man's face. Turning, he held a hand to a microscope. "Look."

The figure did so. It looked like a small, microscopic bug. "What is it?"

"Our new delivery system, courtesy of the innovative Japanese."

"Will this allow us to proceed on my timetable?"

"With this, we can complete the project in a matter of years, not decades, as we had originally planned."

Their mind drifted to the defiant pet. "What do you need?"

"Only funding. I'll need a small team of tech experts, but there's always someone looking for work. And the tech from the Japanese. I thought one of your operatives could do that?"

"Money and information."

"Yes."

"I'll make the arrangements."

The scientist smiled like a child with his favorite Christmas toy, returning to work. The figure began walking out. "Oh, and this group? They've done their jobs. I won't be needing them anymore."

A wave of the hand, and everyone stopped what they were doing. With blank looks on their faces, they turned toward the ocean and began to walk stiffly toward the water…

Julius rose out of the water, lifting himself onto the dock. The swim had been good for him. Taking the towel he'd left there, he dried his hair, then his chest. Walking toward the main cabin, he waved at Honor and Joy. They smiled back at him, and his heart took a small tumble. He was a lucky man.

Thinking of beautiful women, he walked into the main cabin and checked on their still unconscious female visitor. There was absolutely no reason for her to still be asleep. She should be waking any day, and they all took turns checking on her. Today was his, so he placed a hand on her forehead, checking her temperature.

Something whispered to him, gently pulling at the back of his mind like a breeze. He quickly took his hand away. The pull remained. He touched her again and the sensation intensified, until it became a voice singing his name. It was a sensation unlike any he'd felt before. His eyes glazed over, and an image of calm ocean stretched out before him like a dream.

"Julius?" Honor brought him back to the cabin. "Are you okay?" He quickly removed his hand from the woman's body and backed away. The sensation finally faded from his mind.

"You look like you've seen a ghost. What happened?"

"I…I don't know. Be careful when you touch her. I don't think she's just a person. I think she's a Mythic."

"You think she's on our side?"

"I don't know."

"Okay. Tyrus wants us outside. Always work to be done."

"I'm coming." He wiped his hands off on his jeans, trying to rid his mind of the feeling he'd encountered. Pushing the strange event away, he walked outside, the smell of Honor's hair reaching his sensitive nose. He inhaled deeply. Vanilla and berries...

Nix sat on the beach, gazing at the gentle waves that lapped at the shore. The sun had just set below the water on the horizon and a purple hue was visible. It was beautiful. She heard footsteps behind her. A moment later, Levi was sitting next to her.

"It's been a while since we've done that."

She laughed. "Don't get used to it." He handed her a bottle of water. She took it and drank gladly. She was so thirsty. "I understand, being here, why you chose this spot. It's lovely."

He ran his hand down her cheek, gently. It felt like a butterfly's tickle. "Doesn't compare."

She looked down. "I'm still angry with you."

"I know."

"You aren't forgiven."

"I know." He wrapped his arm around her, and she leaned her head on his shoulder. "I don't expect forgiveness."

The silence drifted between them, the gentle rhythm of the ocean and the soft breeze creating a feeling of contentment. She sighed. "How did we get here?"

"What do you mean? I brought us here."

"No, I mean, how did we let our lives get so twisted? How did we go from idealistic heroes to…to this?"

He squeezed her shoulder. "I don't know."

"I mean, I can sit and blame the hidden coin, but…"

"But we made our choices."

"We did. And here we are. Is something so complex really that simple?"

"You don't always have the best choices. You just make the best choice with what you're given. We did what we could with what we knew."

"It sucks we can't go back. Fix it."

"Yeah, there's a couple things I wouldn't have done."

"But we can't."

"No, can't go back, but we can move forward."

She laughed. "To where?"

He gazed down at her, his blue eyes quiet and calm, mirroring the sea. As they locked eyes, the ocean created a huge wave, large enough to deposit something at her feet. A small clam opened as her gaze turned, revealing a pearl ring.

"Levi…" Her voice was a warning, but he squeezed her shoulder again.

"For moving forward, if you ever decide you want to… with me."

She leaned down and took the ring. The shell closed and the pearl glistened in the faint light. The moon began to rise. "It's gorgeous, but I'm not ready."

"I know, but I wanted you to know where I stood."

She watched the light reflect off the pearl. "Why a pearl?"

"Diamond of the sea."

She laughed. "That *is* something you would like. Okay, well, hang on to this." She handed it back to him, "and I'd say it's about time to get back to the others."

"If you insist."

A whirl of water and they returned to the campground. The lack of activity made her curious. Joy came to greet them.

"Has Connor returned?"

"No. He's swimming."

Nix walked around, looking for the others. She was beginning to think that they wouldn't get him back without a fight.

He took a chance and opened his right eye. Around him, the king and Maiden, along with members of the court, were meditating silently. They sure loved their rituals. He wondered when he would get to the information part of his underwater tour. Closing his eyes, he tried his best to participate.

After a few more moments of silence, the king startled him by making a long, low sound with his voice, as if he were singing, but the syllable was not one Connor had heard before. Then Maiden and the court joined in, and Connor was amazed by the sound.

It wasn't any music he'd ever heard before. There were no lyrics, no drumbeats, just waves of sound, coming and going. The tones almost seemed in conflict with one another, then they would resolve into these beautiful, blissful chords of pure magic. He didn't participate, but he did enjoy it.

When they finished, a strange sensation hung in the air, as if the sound wasn't done, and was carried slowly away to somewhere else. When he opened his eyes again, they were standing.

"What was that?"

"A tradition. A cleansing ritual to wash away the sadness of your former life, so the Waters of Fate may guide you home, always."

"It was beautiful."

Maiden chuckled. "It's Mer. We are a beautiful people."

"I'm beginning to see that." He desperately wanted to know why they had all these rituals, but something inside him was saying that it was the wrong time to ask. He could always talk to Maiden, later.

A young boy came running into the garden. "My King! Something has happened off the coast of Cameroon, in Africa!"

The court whispered, quietly. "Silence." The word rang out with such weight that Connor couldn't have talked if he wanted to. "Come, tell me what you know."

The boy rushed forward and kneeled. "Ten thousand corpses line the shore of Cameroon." He had tears in his eyes.

The court suddenly kneeled as well. The king turned to Maiden, and said, "Lead the court in our grief song. Connor, with me." He held out his hand to his guest, who took it. A moment of disorientation and he was suddenly surrounded by hot sand on his feet.

He danced away until his feet touched the water, but when his vision cleared, his feet were stained with blood.

"What happened here?"

The king said nothing. Instead, he walked to a corpse of a woman, and touched a hand to her forehead. Connor watched as the king's psychic creature lowered its head to hers. After a few moments, the creature returned to its owner and he stood.

"I have seen their fate. We can do no more here. We must leave the bodies for the authorities to find. Come, and I will explain what happened at home."

A few minutes later, they were back in the garden, surrounded by the court, who were singing the saddest song he ever heard. It was as if the music itself was crying out with grief.

"They lament the landwalkers who died at the hands of a madman."

"I didn't know you had so much empathy for us."

The king gave him a strange look. "We are all connected to this earth. What you do up there affects us down here. We are the keepers that guide you, so we care that you are well and safe. Landwalkers are our distant cousins. The decision to separate ourselves from you was greatly debated, and ultimately, it was only done to protect ourselves. As you have grown, so have we. We care very deeply for all of you."

Connor felt guilty for opening his mouth. "Who do you think is responsible?"

"An ancient evil." Maiden approached. "What is your plan, father?"

"It is time for Connor to learn of his fate. Come with me." They walked into a small room at the back of the garden. A slab of stone lay beneath the statue of a mermaid, her hands reaching down to the ground. "I'll leave Maiden to prepare you."

He left, and Connor looked at the young woman. She motioned to the slab. "Lie down."

He gave her a look but complied. As he rested, she rubbed his temples and began to sing. The song was different than the others, gentle, peaceful. He found himself drifting off to sleep. Raising his head, he tried to remain awake, but she said, "don't fight it. Sleep, Ambassador Connor. We will keep watch."

A few minutes later, the dark took him.

Miles away, another darkness surrounded a man tied to their fate. Dr. Jackson sat in his new office, as the moon rose, and listened as the head of security cleared the new staff. He didn't want anyone slipping through the cracks like they had last time.

When it was over, he looked out at his estate. A little over 100 acres of land, secured at the western edge of the city, outside the suburbs and the chaos that people created. It was idyllic, charming, and quiet. He'd chosen the perfect spot for his refuge.

He was going crazy. He was used to the city, the hustle and bustle of its noises. This estate was a huge adjustment for him.

Thinking on what he could do to improve, he debated a few options before picking up the phone. If he could work out a deal with a telecom company, at least then he'd have access to the internet here. The recluse who owned the place prior to him had been quite the hermit, not permitting anything but nature to surround him. Boring….

"Yes, Hello, Director, I was wondering if you had a few moments?" Of course, he did. The Jackson legacy gave him access to people that would otherwise be beyond his reach. It was time he started using those people to his advantage.

As he waited, he looked at the photos on his desk. The best private investigator in the country was working for him, and had brought him an interesting one, taken by a vacationing couple who'd returned today from Africa. It was a picture of the two, happily laughing on the beach.

He wasn't concerned about them. What concerned him was the top right corner of the photo, which showed an amazing stretch of beach. You couldn't tell in this picture, but technology was so helpful in that the next photo, a blown-up image of that section, showed the same shadowy figure he'd seen in countless other photos of Mythics being born.

"Who are you?" It was a whisper, more for himself than anyone else. One thing was for sure, this was the hidden coin he sought.

Chapter 12

Honor watched as Nix walked into the main cabin, looking around. She smiled as their eyes met, but her look was anxious. "Have you seen Tyrus?"

Honor shrugged her shoulders. "No. Is something wrong?"

"It's been a day since Connor left. How long does it take for them to deliver a message?"

Honor had been silently wondering that herself. Standing, she said, "let's go find Tyrus and see if he's worried. He's the one with the connection."

Levi cleared his throat. The two turned to him. "Actually, he's not the only one with a connection to the water people."

Reaching out his hand, Levi let water swirl from his fingertips. It flowed in the air, circling in on itself until a mirror formed at its center. "Let's see what Connor is up to…" He said it more to himself than to her. As she watched, the reflection disappeared, and she saw Connor lying down, in some sort of building.

Next to him sat Maiden, who was singing and rubbing his temples. Nix snorted. "Well, then, I guess there's no need to worry. Prince Connor is doing fine."

Levi chuckled and the image faded. Honor sat and began to practice her meditation exercises again. She didn't get far though, as Tyrus came bursting from the back room. "Everyone outside in five."

She walked to the campfire in the center of the complex and sat, waiting. Nix and Levi joined her. When the other three had been rounded up, Tyrus began to speak.

"I just got off the phone with Agent Ryan. Nix, we may have another Mythic to find."

"What?"

"Reports of Omega Flame being sighted in the middle of nowhere in the Midwest."

"When did this happen?"

"Not sure, it just hit the news. One survivor."

Nix was silent for a moment. "Five last year, one this year, six Mythics created after a twenty-year gap? What the hell?"

"Your guess is as good as mine, but if another victim has been found, we should be the ones to help them through this. I have no clue on the details. We have to send a team to Iowa."

"Levi should go with them. He can get them there and back quickly." Nix looked at him and a strange soft light shone from her eyes. Honor had a feeling they'd made up, somehow. Her anger at the loss of her friend's bird began to return, but she hid it. Now was not the best time for revenge, and if Nix wasn't mad, was it her place?

"Agreed, if you're willing?" Tyrus looked at him.

Levi waited a moment. Honor almost thought he'd refuse. "Burning moonlight. Who's going with me?"

"We need to stack the deck. More luck than physical ability." Tyrus looked to the younger Mythics.

"That means…" Joy thought a second. "I'm going, with Seth and Julius."

"Yes. You need to make contact with this Mythic and bring them back here, peacefully. We don't know anything about them, but you remember how you felt when this happened. Assume they won't know how to control their power, and unlike me," he looked to Honor, "don't underestimate their abilities."

"Right. Let's go."

Honor watched their friends depart through a water portal, leaving her alone with Tyrus and Nix. "Honor…"

"I know, I know." She reached out her hands and pushed flame into the campfire. It was a good thing she knew what discipline was, or this would be getting boring. She thought back on her life before all this started. It was all social media and technology. Posting selfies and worrying about school. Now, just two years later, she was surrounded by trees, hadn't looked at social media in days and couldn't care less. Just two years, and yet, how her life had changed….

◆ ◆ ◆

Miles away, the portal opened into a corn field, and the four Mythics stepped out into a large, open area surrounded in smoke. Coughing, they were quickly reminded of the devastation the black flame could cause.

"Look," Levi pointed toward the center of the field. "That's the scene. We'll check that out first, then find the Mythic. Probably at the hospital. Remember, no contact with police."

Moving as a unit, the three followed instructions. Julius dove into the middle, moving more like dog than man. Joy glowed momentarily, then seemed to vanish from sight. Seth stayed toward the tree line, his momentum leaving no footprints. Levi watched as they worked, impressed by their ability to communicate without talking. They just knew where to be and what to do. He watched Seth distract the police so Julius could slip through, then when he'd done his sniffing job, Joy got him back out. It was perfect. They made a great team.

When they'd finished, they met him at the edge of the trees. "What did you find out?"

"It's definitely Omega Fire. The smell has soaked into the very earth. The survivor is female." Julius sneezed.

"Bless you." Joy turned and talked to Levi. "She's scared. They took her to the hospital, two hours away in Des Moines."

"Anything else, Seth?"

"The police are actively looking for suspects. We need to be careful. We wait until sunrise to visit her. She has parents."

"What age are we talking, Julius?"

"Maybe twelve, thirteen years old."

"So young…but then, Omega Fire doesn't care."

He looked out toward the big crater of flame in the center of the field, wondering what strategy they could use to help this girl, whose life had just changed forever.

Connor woke, hours later, with a vague feeling of urgency

about him. Sitting up, he said, "what was that?"

"It was what you needed to see."

"It's a bunch of random images. I can't make sense of it."

She nodded, her brown eyes big in the dim light. "That's the way. You'll spend the next couple of weeks figuring out what it all means."

Connor sighed. "I have a headache."

"Most do, the first time."

"You've done this too?"

"Yes."

"What did it show you?"

She averted her eyes, looking at the ground. "It's personal."

"I'm sorry. I didn't mean to overstep."

She smiled and met his gaze. "It showed me what I needed to know."

He nodded, forcing himself to be satisfied with the explanation for now. "Got anything to make a splitting headache go away?"

She reached a hand up to his forehead and a moment later, his head felt better. As he watched, she grabbed her head. "Wow. You did have a bad one."

"What did you do?"

"I took your pain." She composed herself, and a moment later, looked back at him.

"Why would you do that?"

Her look softened. "Let's just say I'm safeguarding my future."

He tilted his head, confused. "What does that mean?"

"It means, it's time for us to leave here. My father is waiting to show you to your room. It is time to sleep."

They stood and walked back inside the great hall, where the king waited for them. "You are truly one of us now, Connor. I hope that tomorrow, as we talk about the future, you remember that you always have a home with us."

Connor nodded and the king turned. "Follow me. Goodnight, Maiden."

"Good night, Father."

Connor followed the king upstairs and to the back of the great hall. Opening a door, he said, "This suite hasn't been used for some time. It sits over the royal quarters and is reserved for visiting guests. I hope you enjoy our hospitality." He opened the door but did not follow Connor inside.

The door shut and Connor was surrounded by…wonder. The room was large. Green wood adorned the floor and walls. The ceiling was made up entirely of lightshade, and it glowed as if the plant were a starry night sky. A large bed stood in the center of the room, of the same material as his clothing. On the wall, were orbs that glowed with a blue light, that moved as if it was water.

Another room connected to the right. It housed what he thought was a bathroom. He stepped into a closet, and regretted it instantly, as hot water began pouring over him. Stepping out quickly, he backed into a counter, where more water came out of the wood in the middle. *Sink and shower, check.* Where was the toilet?

He looked toward the back of the room, and eyed a separate, circular cove made of some kind of blue stone. Maybe a bathtub? He reached his hand in, and water instantly started to flow. Across from it was a stump. It looked like a tree stump. He looked at it, wondering. Then he sat down.

It was definitely a tree stump. Nothing was happening. He reached for a branch to the side to stand up, and as he did so, the top of the stump disappeared. Trying to catch his balance, he barely avoided falling in.

Catching his breath, he walked back into the other room and folded back the covers. It had been an incredible collection of firsts for him. He wasn't even sure the others would believe him when he got back. Thinking of them, he lay back and wondered what his friends were doing while he was playing diplomat.

Everything was in place. She was sitting in a room, bored out of her mind, waiting for her moment to strike, but everything was ready. She could wait, bide her time, until the opportune moment.

She jumped as her cell rang. Answering it, she said, "Yes."

"Daughter."

"Papa. It's lovely to hear from you."

"I'm calling on behalf of a client. While you sit twitting your thumbs you can look up and hire some tech experts for me."

"How did you…"

"I know everything dear. The client needs experts in Nano tech, biology and chemistry. Try to avoid anyone too brilliant or idealistic."

"What package am I offering?"

"Let's do the standard silver package. Should be enough to entice some rather unsavory masterminds to come out of hiding. If they don't go for silver, offer them gold."

"And what do you wish me to put for the job description?"

"Private donor seeks research and development team to work off the coast of Cameroon. Make history on the beautiful beaches of Africa." Something witty but exclusive."

"And how long is the contract for?"

"Two months."

"That seems short for a research project."

"Yes, it does." He chose not to elaborate, and she knew better than to push him. "Is there anything else I need to know?"

There was a long pause before he said, "When you purchase the airfare, you only need to worry about one-way tickets."

She swallowed. That meant they wouldn't be returning. "I'll also start on a cover story then."

"You're thorough, as I taught you to be." He hung up.

She opened her laptop, and as she began her search, a smile played on her lips. Feeling hungry, she picked up the phone and ordered room service. Tonight would be a long one, but oh, how much fun it would be.

Thirty minutes later, a knock sounded from her door. She

opened it to room service. “Set it down over here, please.” She turned her back, closing her laptop. A sharp pain to her head and she was no longer conscious.

When she awoke, she was in a dark room, surrounded by four very small walls. She touched her head, coming away with blood. *How could you be so stupid? Never turn on the help!* She tried to stand, but the pain was too great. She sat and breathed slowly and centered herself.

The door opened, and her heart sank. Two figures entered the room.

“Miss Wills.” One walked across the room while the other shut the door. Turning on the light, she shielded her eyes from its harsh rays. “I believe you and I have something to discuss.”

When she could see again, she turned her face toward them and spat at their feet. “If you hurt me, in any way, my father will see you destroyed.”

A feminine laugh filled the building. Guards down the hall who could barely hear it shuddered, wondering who was unlucky enough to be the center of their mistress’s affections tonight.

The figure leaned down, and the smell of jasmine wafted from her. “Oh, child, did your father not raise you better?” She lifted her hood, and medium toned skin, thick black hair and tilted eyes stared back at Wills. Her breath caught in her throat, and the name of her enemy came unbidden from her lips.

“Chimera…”

As the sun began to rise, the four figures walked into the hospital in Des Moines, Iowa. Avoiding cameras and security, they infiltrated their way upstairs, to the room of the newly created Mythic. Parents and doctors were active on the floor, so they watched from a distance as progress was made around them, waiting for their chance to assess the situation.

Finding an opening, Joy, dressed as a nurse, sauntered into the teen’s room. She was awake and alert. Big brown eyes looked up at Joy, her face collected but frightened. Joy smiled at the teen, and reached a hand out to touch near her wrist, getting a pulse.

"How are you doing?" she asked.

The girl looked out to her parents, then back at Joy. "I just want to go home."

Joy noted the environment around her. Several flowers had been brought in, and stuffed animals lined the bed and countertops. This girl was definitely cared for.

"I'm sure the doctors will allow that soon." Picking up her chart, she noted her name. "Jayde…"

"Jayde Liana Fletcher."

"Right. I'm just marking your pulse…" she pretended to write while looking over the information quickly. "There. Anything you want me to add on the chart?"

She shook her head.

"Anything you'd like to talk about?"

She looked around, nervously.

"Are you experiencing some unusual symptoms?"

"You promise not to write it down?"

She put her pen away. "Sure. I can do that. What's wrong?" She sat next to the girl on the bed.

"Can I ask you a question?"

"Anything."

"Are flowers supposed to…. grow once they've been cut?"

"What do you mean?"

"The roses. They weren't that big yesterday."

"Huh." Joy looked dumbfounded. "Well, I suppose anything's possible." She smiled again at the girl, who smiled back.

"Oh, good." The look of relief shone on her face. Joy looked over, and as she watched, the roses grew before her eyes, blossoming in front of her. Strange.

"Can I get you anything?"

"No, I'm fine. I just want to get out of this bed."

Joy thought of her time after the fire, how long she lay

unconscious in a hospital bed. "I hear you. Just be patient."

Her parents walked into the room as Joy turned to leave. "Who are you?"

Joy said, "Just covering for her regular nurse, checking vitals." She turned and continued out of the room. As she approached the group, they surrounded her, following out of the hospital, as stealthily as they came.

When they were back in their vehicle, she turned to Levi. "She can grow plants." He tilted his head. "What?"

"I watched the roses bloom next to her."

"Some sort of earth sign. Makes sense."

"Why?"

"Because none of you are one. Somehow, Omega Fire keeps the balance. You'll never find an overabundance of any one type of mythic. We don't know why. I guess this is evidence that it accounts for Synthetics. We'll have to keep track of any new Mythics, to see if we are correct."

"Her parents are very active. I think we need to consider a different approach. Reaching her is going to be a long-term op."

"Agreed. We can't alienate a child from her parents. We need a better plan. Joy, we're leaving you here to keep an eye on her for now. I think the rest of us need to get back to the camp and report what we know."

"Got it." She exited the vehicle, walking back into the hospital. Seth looked anxiously after her.

"Don't worry. Unicorns have multiple strategies for avoiding trouble."

"Still, she's on her own…"

"Simmer, lover boy, we have our own work to do. You can always come back when we're finished if you want to check on her."

"Right." Stepping out of the car, they walked to the middle of the garage and summoned a portal to the camp. Upon arriving, everyone was still asleep, and the sun had not yet cleared the mountains in the distance.

"Take a nap. I'll stand watch."

They walked away. Levi sat down, waiting for the sun to show its face. Nix walked out a few moments later, sat down with him. "Well?"

He filled her in. "Sounds like she may be Gaian."

"Like the goddess."

"Exactly. She'd be able to grow anything at will, as long as it's plant life. Definitely dangerous in the wrong company."

"How could that be dangerous? Aren't plants nature?"

He gave her a cold stare. "I was around for the last Gaian, a woman of tremendous power. She safeguarded the land now called the Amazon Rainforest. Beautiful, vibrant. She was its keeper, in tune with any threat. She was taken out eventually, but it took a very powerful air elemental to even find her. It was a loss, deeply felt, not just for those that knew her, but for the world as well.

"Anything can be weaponized. Imagine a world in which plants were all poisonous. How many people would die? This girl has been given a tremendous gift of power. We must help her safeguard it."

"Joy's absence…"

He nodded silently.

"Could you tell if it was Synthetic? Like the Five? Or natural?"

"Seems natural. One survivor, wide area of destruction to nature. The synthetic fire only affected the immediate vehicle, not the desert. My best guess, without any scientific inquiry, would be natural."

"Good. Tyrus wants us to go find Connor." When he laughed at that, she added, "what's so funny?"

"Fire signs are not welcome among the Waters of Fate. I'll take Julius with me, maybe Seth. You three need to stay away from the water people."

"How well do you know these Merfolk?"

"Let's just say that there was a time in my life where I needed to be set on a different path, and they…forced me in the right direction."

"Levi…"

"Nix?"

"What did you do?"

He shrugged his shoulders. "It's faded into history, but if you think I'm a bastard *now*...you'd have killed me then."

"How old are you, anyway? I don't think you've ever told me."

He looked at her, confused. "I haven't? I thought I had."

"No."

"Interesting. Let's get your Griffin back."

She sighed, frustrated with his lack of transparency. "Fine." Standing, they walked to Julius and Seth, who were debating fishing tactics.

Seth looked at the two adults approaching. He had a bad feeling about what was coming next, but no matter what he chose to do, someone he loved and cared about would suffer. He didn't dare say anything, though. He didn't want to change the balance, somehow make things worse.

"We are going after Connor." It was a statement, not a question.

Levi nodded. "We are going to see the Merfolk. Under the ocean. It should be fun for *you* two."

Julius hopped up and down. "I'm ready."

Seth looked at him, wishing for his enthusiasm. Grabbing Nix's hand, Seth looked her in the eye. "Something bad is coming, but I can't tell what."

Nix smiled. "We'll stay vigilant."

The feeling in his gut did not recede. "Just...stay together."

"Will do." Nix walked away, and Seth waited for the portal to float around him. The swirls of water moving them through space to another location were disarming, not as smooth as his own portals, but alas, he could only bounce them when he knew where they were going. After a few seconds, they stood next to a giant tree. Water flowed from its middle.

As Seth watched, a high-pitched song began to echo through the courtyard. Armed guards came running out with spears and surrounded them. They put their hands up, showing they meant no harm. This was the bad feeling he had in his gut.

He leaned into Levi and said, “I thought they were your friends?”

Levi, smiling the whole time, said, “I never said that, only that they helped me change.”

Julius elbowed him. “What the *hell* man? What did you just get us into?”

Levi laughed. “Come on, you’re more than ready for a little trouble.”

Seth felt his gut wrench and turn. The feeling he had kept getting worse. One thing was for sure, they would need a miracle to get out of this in one piece.

Images flashed through his mind, though he couldn’t place their meaning. A set of wings, high on a mantle sat while old men laughed, bars of gold at their feet. A moment of blurriness, then another image, of war, young women and men dying at his feet. His vision blurred a final time, and he was in water, floating, while Maiden looked down on him, laughing, swimming around him in the water. He chased her, and she splashed at him. Grabbing her, playfully, he turned her close to him. “Wake up.” It was a whisper, but it reminded him that this was a dream.

Connor woke to her, standing over him, a slight smile on her face. He stretched before he realized he wasn’t underneath the sheets. Grabbing them, he quickly covered himself. She chuckled.

“Landwalkers are not comfortable with nudity?”

He shook his head.

“Well, I wouldn’t want to offend you, Ambassador. My father is waiting for you in the great hall. You slept for a long time.” She winked and let him be. He woke and got dressed, before following her out.

As he approached the large room, he could tell that some

commotion was occurring below. He saw the hall crowded with guards, and the king was chastising…someone.

"You swore!" Daileass' voice wrung through the halls, so loud he had to cover his ears. "You swore to leave and never return!"

He rounded the stairs, descending at an angle. Slowly, as he did so, he could see the object of the king's ire. Why was he not surprised to see the Leviathan?

Levi looked at him. "Oh, hey! You're alive." He got out that much before a guard shoved the broad end of a spear into his stomach. He groaned loudly.

The king turned to Connor. "You have dealings with this water snake?"

Connor walked to the king, tilting his head and addressing him softly. "King of the Merfolk, I beg for forgiveness if I've offended you."

The king's angry eyes softened. "Take them away. I will deal with the traitor tonight."

The three were led away, while Connor watched, wondering what he could do to help his friends. Thinking quickly, he began, "what did he do?"

"Other than trespassing? Let's see…" A scroll was brought out and handed to the king. He unwrapped it, and it went to his feet. "Larceny…looks like...twenty counts. Breaking and entering…. five counts. Lying to the court…ten counts. Twenty counts of dowry stealing…"

"How did he steal a dowry?"

Maiden whispered, "If you take a woman's dowry and refuse to marry her."

"Oh." Connor's face turned red. "Continue."

"Nine counts of public nudity…while intoxicated…holding a" he coughed, "weapon." He cleared his throat. Maiden chuckled, but the king gave her a stern look, and she quieted.

"Moving on. Fourteen counts of bribing state officials. Three charges for being found in restricted zones of the palace, most notably in the women's bathhouse. Two counts of possession of illegal substances…oh, and one count of operating heavy machinery without a license."

Connor cleared his own throat. "That's…quite a list. Is there any way I can take him off your hands?"

The king laughed. "I've been trying to be rid of that fool for generations. He is a curse on my kind." He handed the scroll back. "I thought we had an understanding last time. He was told simply to never return."

"I'm sure the only reason he did return was to ensure my welfare. Please, he is my ally." At the king's stern look, he added, "may he be released to my custody?"

The king paced back and forth for a time, thinking on what to do. "I do not wish to alienate you, young Ambassador. I didn't go through the trouble of bringing you here to destroy our people's relationship with each other. However, he is a menace. He will remain in chains, in the dungeon, until you leave us. Then, he must swear an oath to leave my people in peace."

"Of course. What of the other two?"

"They are trespassers."

"Yes, but they were only trying to find me. They may have need of me, or a message from Tyrus for you."

The king thought on that. "I cannot delay a messenger… Very well. Release the other two, but the water snake stays in his cage."

"As you wish, your Majesty."

He backed away, and Maiden walked with him to the side. "The dungeon is below us."

"You don't have to follow me."

She placed a hand on his arm. "I am bound to accompany you while you are in the city."

"Why?"

"It is our tradition. In a way, you're my responsibility."

"So you go where I go."

"Yes. Even to a nasty, creepy dungeon."

"I'll protect you." He grabbed her hand, locking her fingers in his, his heart beating wildly in his chest. It was a bold move, not one he was sure of. What would she do?

She allowed it, and said, "oh, landwalker, it is I who am protecting you." She touched a hand to his nose, and he smiled. Walking hand in hand, they made their way down the stairs to the dungeon, a series of basement cages and rooms with small, uncomfortable furniture. Unlike the upper level that was all blue and green, this level was dark, dank and black.

"I wouldn't want to be locked up in here." His eyes quickly adjusted to the light, and they walked toward a guard at the center of the structure. It seemed rows of cages connected in the middle, like spokes in a wheel.

"Hello." Maiden spoke first.

"Princess Maiden. How may we help you?"

"Two prisoners are ordered released by the king's decree."

"Name them?"

She turned to Connor. "Seth and Julius."

"Ah. The other land walkers. I had a feeling they wouldn't be down here long. The one has an air of luck on his side, after all." He signaled to another guard, who left, walking downward and into the shadows.

"What earns someone the unfortunate fate to be locked down here?" He asked it more to himself than out loud, but Maiden heard.

"Anyone that breaks the law is punished with varying sentences. Some only spend a few weeks down here, some are permanent residents."

"It surprises me in a city as idyllic as this that you would have need of prisons."

Maiden's face was cloudy, like a dark thought weighed on her soul. "Well, there are those that are just…destined to be…rogues."

Connor sensed there was more to the story, but the guard was already returning. Julius and Seth followed behind him. "What the hell, Connor?"

"Julius. How did you two manage to get into trouble just by dropping in here?"

Seth sighed. "Wrong place, wrong company, I guess."

"Well, Nix never said Levi was a good guy."

"You'd think he'd give us a heads up or something."

"We get out of here, now? It gives me the creeps. I don't like to be caged."

Maiden turned and they walked back out. "For the remainder of your short stay here, you are confined to your rooms, unless you are accompanied by guards, Connor or myself. Please respect our rules."

"What are their rules?" Julius whispered, but Connor elbowed him to be quiet.

"We will feed you, clothe you and" she sniffed, "bathe you…" She looked at back at Julius briefly, "and make sure you are safe. In return, you promise not to steal, cheat or dishonor the Merfolk in any way. Those are our rules, Hell Hound."

Julius sniffed his armpits. "Hey, I don't stink."

"You smell like wet dog."

He growled. Connor placed a hand on his shoulder as they finished climbing the stairs, entering the grand hall. "We are surrounded by guards. Be smart."

Julius calmed, and said, "dogs are loyal, to those who earn it. I know my heart. I don't need assurance from you."

Maiden stopped and turned. "Of course, you don't. Here is the guest room. You will both be staying here." She opened the double doors on the bottom level to a small suite, with an attached bath. "Enjoy your stay."

Seth and Julius walked in, and she began to close the doors. "Connor! We need to-" The doors shut before he could hear the rest.

"Don't you think you were a bit judgmental?"

Maiden smiled. "I am still young, and like you and the Cerberus were rivals, so are Merfolk. Surely when you met you couldn't stand the sight of each other."

He thought back to their first big fight at the motel. "Oh,

yeah."

"I'm sure I'll grow accustomed to him in time. The leprechaun on the other hand…they used to visit us all the time, a thousand years ago. When people in the isles were…free."

"Interesting."

"Yes. I should ask father to have him bless the fate tree. While he's here. It would be nice to have luck flow for us once again."

"I'm sure he'd be willing to help."

"Come, before all of this started, my father wished to speak with you in private. Walk with me to the library."

They walked the distance, and the king met them at its entrance. "Today, you will learn what we have to offer here. You've already been given your prophecy. It will guide you, but you also need context. These texts are steeped in history."

"What does that tell me about the future?"

Daileass tilted his head. "Have you not learned that life is cyclic? That history has a tendency to repeat itself?"

"So knowing what happened before will help me know what to expect."

"And will give you ways that others approached problems of their time, some with success, others failure. Either way, you learn." They entered and the king motioned to a bath in the center of the room. "Please, enter the bath."

Connor looked to Maiden, confused. "We don't have time to allow you to read all these scrolls, so my father intends for you to learn through…the water. You will gain all his knowledge, all at once. You will be unconscious for a short time afterward, but I will protect you."

Connor nodded and placed his foot into the tub. "You must remove your clothing. Maiden, give the nervous land walker some privacy." They both showed their backs and Connor quickly lost the robe and sank into the cold water. He shivered. "Couldn't it at least be warm?"

She chuckled. The king turned and walked toward him, placing a hand on the surface of the water, another to his forehead.

"A h-uile fios agam, bheir mi dhuibh. Gliocas stiùireadh thu dhachaigh." Connor felt the words reach deep into his being, touching his heart, mind and soul. A rush of images and words came flooding over him like water. It lasted forever, yet seconds. He saw their history. He saw the destruction of Atlantis, their grand capital. He saw the Romans conquer the Gales. He witnessed a free people destroyed by greed and corruption. He couldn't feel it, but tears streamed down his face. When it was over, when he'd seen it all, everything turned to darkness.

Chapter 13

When he woke, he was on the floor of the library, covered in cold water. His two companions kneeled next to him, waiting for him to wake.

"What was that?"

"That was the history of us, and the key to the future."

"I don't really understand what it was."

"Your brain requires time to sort through the information it was given. After a few weeks, it will become clear to you."

"Thank you for this…gift."

"It is more a responsibility than a blessing. The time that we remain hidden is drawing to a close. I fear the next time we meet, it will be under much different circumstances. You have the rest of the day to stay here, then you'll be released with your friends. Since you have access to the snake's portals, I won't worry about getting you back to the surface myself. Just make sure he doesn't return."

"I will do everything that I can."

"I leave the two of you to enjoy your day."

When the king had gone, Maiden hugged him, tightly. "Oh, I was worried. I've never seen this ritual performed before."

"How…old are you?"

She smiled. "I'm still young by our standards, but in your years…" She counted to herself in her head. "Three hundred and sixty-two. And a half."

His eyes popped out of his head. "How old is your father?"

"Over a thousand. He's one of the few left here that remember life on the surface. Only five remain."

"Well…you both look good for your age."

She laughed. "I hope so. Come with me. I wish to show you some of my favorite places here."

She grabbed his hand and he stood, wobbling a little before he found his footing. "This is going to be the best day ever."

He smiled, but his head was still foggy. The only thing that was clear to him was the desperate sadness that lingered through the memories. It threatened to overwhelm him, and he was having a hard time separating that emotion from his own. Still, he faked the smile. No reason Maiden needed to be upset. They had one day to be together. He was going to make that day count.

Levi was bound in chains. He knew he should have just left when he had the chance. They had discovered a way to magically restrain him. For one of the first times in his life, he was helpless and at the mercy of another. He didn't like it.

His eyes had long since adjusted to the dark, his nose no longer aware of the dank, moldy cell. His hair was draped over his face, and his shirt had been removed. The scars on his back were crossed, as if a whip had long ago been put to his flesh. Above him, water fell into the middle of his back, slowly dripping every few minutes. It was driving him nuts. They'd bound him so he couldn't stand, but kneeling was equally uncomfortable.

A commotion down the hallway drew his attention, and he lifted his head as his cell door was opened. The king walked in, alone, and the door shut behind him. He sat on a stool, regal amid the decaying dungeon around him. For a long moment, he simply looked at Levi, a stern expression on his face.

Levi smiled, refusing to allow his surroundings to get him down. As he met the king's face, a slow smile spread. Levi laughed, the king laughed.

"Do you think they bought it?" Levi inquired.

"Yes, you're very scary when you wish to be old friend."

"How long will I be here this time?"

"Only a day. I hope the atmosphere isn't driving you too insane."

"No, not at all. Just a bit cramped in here."

"How is our young friend Tyrus?"

"He is…noble as always."

"Nix?"

"She's the same as she's always been. Any word you want me to send back to them?"

The king stood, placing a coin in his pocket. "I gave the boy the information he needed. The coin is charmed to show the first fingers who touch it the answer to the question you need to know."

"Why didn't you just give this to Connor?"

"There are some evils, some ancient demons that they aren't ready for. Someday, it will be up to people like my daughter and your five to save the world. Today, however, is not that day. Show this to Tyrus, and he may tell them what he wishes."

"The Five are quite capable."

"Yes. I believe that. Connor shows an excellent ability to adapt to new cultures. As I would expect from a Griffin. However, this is…bad, old friend. Not all of us old people will survive this cycle. Let them have what remains of their joy while they still can."

"So…dowry stealing, huh?"

The king laughed. "I think my favorite was the public nudity while holding a weapon."

Levi burst into laughter. "I can't believe that came out of your mouth."

"It was hard for me to keep a straight face."

"I'll bet." The two friends laughed, until a knock sounded on the door. The king leaned in and whispered. "My daughter doesn't know who her mother is. Keep it that way, even if I perish. The vial woman must never know Maiden survived."

"I swore an oath to you, and I am forever bound to keep it."

"As did I to you, Levi, Keeper of Secrets."

"May the Waters of Fate guide you home, always."

"May the darkness never shine brighter than your light."

The king left, and Levi chuckled again. "Holding a weapon…"

Connor struggled to keep up with Maiden who walked quickly

from the castle. She had a vise grip on his hand and wasn't letting go. Picking up their pace, they turned the corner at the fate tree and walked up a stone path to a little cave set to the side of the village.

"This was one of my favorite places to hide from my chores as a child. Not many people know about it."

She let go of his hand and walked inside. He followed slowly, allowing his eyes to adjust to the dim glow of the lightshade around them. The path lowered, slowly, until they came to an underground pool. The lightshade reflected off the water, creating a glow that spread throughout the cavern.

Maiden sat by the edge of the water and patted a stone next to her. He complied and she turned to him smiling.

"Watch this." A song came from her lips, and the cavern echoed back a response, but it was not a true echo. Some of the notes were different.

"Huh."

"You try."

"I don't sing."

"Everyone sings, besides, it's only me that will hear you."

He wanted to say no, but her smile softened his resolve. Clearing his throat, he let out a series of tones as best he could. The cavern echoed him, the tones rising where his had fallen. "What is that?"

"No one knows why the cavern does this. It's just…interesting to come here and envelope yourself in the peace and quiet."

He looked at the water. "You ever go swimming in this?"

Her eyes lit up. "Yes." She stood and removed her robe before he could stop her. He looked away respectfully until she was surrounded by it. "Join me."

He stuck a toe in, shivering from the cold. Standing, he slowly took off his robe and followed her. She swam in circles around him. He noted her tail was back. So was his. He chased after her, splashing water in her face.

They played for some time before heading back out of the

cave. "There's one other place I want to show you." Taking his hand, she walked expertly through the city's center, in and out of the foliage. They came to a large tree on the side of the city, as tall as the fate tree, but whose trunk had long since entangled itself in the rock next to it.

"We climb up."

Without waiting, she did so, leaving Connor to follow her. She was adept at climbing, and soon she was well out of sight. Connor continued, wondering where this would lead, refusing to look down.

Eventually, he found a ledge. Climbing onto it, he walked some short distance to another cavern. This was separate from the city, yet part of their world. Strange creatures flew and walked in a large forest. He could see from his point of view to the other side, where mountains rose up. Lightshade surrounded everything.

"This is a sanctuary for animals that we built."

"How…did you get them under the water?"

"Magic."

"I'll bet."

"We aren't allowed to enter, only hunters or caregivers, but I like to look at all the animals."

"I don't even know what half of these are called."

"They are the forgotten breeds and species of animals on the surface. Those that were endangered a thousand years ago. We brought them here to safeguard them."

"I'm speechless."

"I know." She smiled at him and sat, watching animals move below them. He placed a hand on her shoulder and drew her close to him. She allowed it. "I hope you have a good impression of us now."

"I do. Mostly thanks to you."

"I did my best."

"Your best made me feel at home."

"It's true, you know, now that you've gone through all the rituals, you always have a home here with us. With me."

Before he could question it, she reached in and placed her lips next to his. She tasted like the sea, but sweet like candy as well. He tightened his grip around her, drawing her closer to him, prolonging the kiss. When she finally backed away, they looked at each other for a few moments in silence.

"What was that for?" he whispered.

"For my heart."

"So…are we like…together now?"

She laughed. "No, we didn't perform any mating rituals or anything, if that's what you're asking. It was just a kiss."

He laughed, awkwardly. "Okay, just checking."

She stood and motioned to him. "We should be getting back to my father."

He just remembered who that was, and a wave of fear swept over him. Hopefully he hadn't offended the king by kissing his daughter.

"Is he going to care that we…"

"I'm not going to tell him. You can risk it if you don't value your life."

He gulped hard. "No, no I think I want to live."

She laughed and they headed out, but he didn't think it was funny.

He paced back and forth, worried about the latest phone call he'd received from Ryan. Sitting at his desk, he scanned the document again, just to be sure he read that right. Not finding any comfort, he stood again, pacing. Why?

His phone rang and he picked it up. "Dr. Jackson."

A moment of silence followed. "Good evening, Director."

Chills ran down his spine. "To what do I owe this pleasure, Director?"

"I assure you that I come on peaceful terms. My trip to the states will be as short as possible. I am not coming on business but a personal matter."

"What matter would that be?"

"I feel it's more appropriate to discuss this in person, at a neutral location. Meet me at Pier Side Park in the morning."

"Why are you reaching out to me?"

Silence. "Because it involves someone with whom you are acquainted. A Dr. Wills."

"I'll be there with ten security guards."

"As will I." the phone call ended, and Jackson paced again. Dr. Blanc had not stepped foot outside of Europe in ages. Why would he go through all the trouble of doing this for an operative? Unless, of course, Wills was more than that.

Picking up the phone again, he made another call. "Ryan. Dr. Jackson. Yes. I need a favor of you."

No way was he going into that meeting blind. He may be young, but he was gifted with an intelligence most dreamed of having. He would come out of this meeting, safe and sound, and Dr. Blanc would gain nothing from him he didn't wish him to. After he hung up with Ryan, he called his aunt.

"Nix."

"Aunt."

"What do you need, Gregory?"

"I need you to accompany me to a meeting in the morning."

"With whom?"

"Dr. Blanc."

Silence. "Why the hell is he in the states?"

"I thought Tyrus and Ryan could find that out while we meet him face to face, see what he wants. Are you in?"

"Am I allowed to torch him?"

"I'd prefer not."

Silence. "*Fine*, I guess."

"Will you be coming in tonight?"

"Yes. I'll be there late. How is your driver?"

"Fully recovered."

"Glad to hear it. And yourself?"

"I've been better."

"See you soon, Greg."

She hung up. He paced back and forth, before an email grabbed his attention. Ryan had been keeping tabs on Wills for him. Opening the email, his blood ran cold. Wills was missing. Last seen twelve hours ago being dragged out of her hotel room by masked men. He thought quickly. Did Dr. Blanc stage this? No doubt he would have counted on the security being in place… Or was this some other party come to interfere? Would Dr. Blanc think he'd done this?

Sitting down, his head went a mile a minute, preparing for every contingency. They'd go in there tomorrow prepared. Making one more phone call, he waited for the person to answer.

"Hello, Dr. Jackson."

"Good evening, Director Li. Or should I call you Chimera." He'd go forward with as much information as possible.

"Ah. I was expecting your call. Did a messenger pigeon give you something from me?"

"In a way."

"We will discuss this after your meeting with Dr. Blanc." The phone went dead. Noting that she must be involved, he sat down again, debating, calling for more help than just his aunt. Giving in, he dialed.

"Nix."

"Bring an enforcer."

"We're low on manpower. I can bring Tyrus."

"Alright."

"Will do."

Now that they had someone who could take a punch, he was more confident the meeting tomorrow would go smoothly. Sitting down, he allowed himself to relax, although his body wasn't quite working with him. His shoulders wouldn't cooperate. Dialing the number for his private masseuse, he thought again about this predicament.

Walking toward a bookcase, he merely waved a hand over a paperweight, and it gave way to a secret storage room. His father, the smart man that he was, had taught him to prepare for…every eventuality. Opening a case, he found rows of sunglasses. Taking out three, he smiled. If Dr. Blanc intended to neutralize him with his power, he was in for a surprise.

◆ ◆ ◆

"You're leaving me…alone."

"Yes." Nix looked at Honor. "You'll be fine."

"Sure, if I don't burn the camp down."

"Look, the only person who you can damage is yourself."

"We still have the sleeping woman."

"Right. Well, hopefully she wakes up before you burn the cabins to the ground."

"Not funny."

Tyrus walked up with a bag. "Honor, sooner or later we needed to test you, anyway. Looks like the universe has decided to make that time now. You're more than capable."

"I still feel like I don't quite have a handle on my flame."

"You've grown since the change. You didn't have one episode yesterday. The good thing about having time by yourself is you can let loose a little. Just…meditate and swim and enjoy your time alone."

She hadn't been alone since the tower. "You realize if I burn everything down to the ground or start a forest fire it's your fault, for leaving me to destroy everything."

He laughed. "I'll take full responsibility." Grabbing her hands, his eyes grew somber. "Honor, never apologize for being who you are. You are a phoenix, not a monster."

She lowered her eyes, unable to meet his gaze for a moment. "I know, it's just…"

"Your nature to self-deprecate with humor? I know. It's important to me that you understand how special you are, in spite of the setbacks you've had."

"I understand."

"Don't apologize for your power again. We will handle it as we always have, as a team." He gave her a quick hug as Nix hopped into the driver seat. "Be as safe as you can be. It's only for twenty-four hours."

She hugged him tightly, suddenly afraid of being alone. He allowed her to take as long as she needed. Nix honked and Tyrus whispered. "You're not a kid anymore. It's time for you to be independent, like us old people."

"I am an adult."

"I know."

"I'm nineteen."

"I know."

She punched him in the arm after she released him. "Fine. I'll be ok. Leave already."

He punched her back lightly and got into the car. They drove away in silence, but he couldn't help looking back. Honor stood with huge eyes, watching them depart sadly. It pulled at his heartstrings. Luckily, he had surveillance on the outside of the camp, wirelessly connected to his phone. If anything did go wrong, he could be back quickly. It'd be fine. She'd be fine. Why he felt so connected to her was beyond him.

"You're smitten."

"What are you talking about?"

"I think you've been around her flames too much. You should let me take watch more often."

"Maybe. Maybe the time away will do me some good."

"So…you have a type."

"Nix…"

"I'm just saying, you like firebirds."

"Shut up."

"I think it's cute."

"I think you and Levi are much more interesting."

She glared at him as if she were looking for soft spots to stab.

He smiled widely. "You want to talk about our love lives, fine, how was your trip to the beach? You like the motion of the ocean?"

She punched him, swerving on the road. He laughed. "Let's just focus on the road."

"Fine." She didn't say another word, but she did whistle a romantic tune. He blushed, looking away. "It's just the flame."

"Keep telling yourself that."

He did, over and over. Just the flame. He looked back in the mirror, but Honor had long since faded from view. A twinge of sadness flowed through him. Shaking it off, he returned to the mission at hand. Just the flame.

Connor and Maiden spent the rest of their day in merriment. By the time dinner arrived, he felt as if they'd been best friends forever. He couldn't help but smile as they walked into the great hall. His smile fell only as her father gazed back at him. He swallowed hard and sat down to eat.

After the ceremony was over, they brought out another feast of food. He was ravenous and ate everything in sight. Maiden watched him, as did her father. When they'd finished, he sat back and relaxed in his chair.

"How was your day, my princess?" Daileass asked, gently.

"Wonderful, father."

"And yours Connor? Was my daughter a good host?"

He fought the urge to blush. "Yes. She showed me many interesting places around the city."

"I am glad you've enjoyed our hospitality. Tomorrow you'll return to your world. The night is yours. Do with it what you please."

Maiden stood, motioning him to stand as well. They walked out to the gardens and sat down. "Will my friends be fed?"

"Yes. They'll receive dinner in their room."

"What about Levi?"

"The prisoner will receive bread and water."

"So, I leave tomorrow."

"I'm aware."

"Will I see you again? Or are you going to stay below ground?"

"I must follow the king's wishes. For now, I will stay here. But hopefully, in the near future, we will have a better relationship with the landwalkers. I would very much like to continue to see you."

He did blush, then. "And I you." He took her hand in his and she pulled him down to sit next to her. The lightshade around them glowed, but it was fairly dark in the garden. He smiled at her and she at him. Leaning down, he placed a kiss on her lips. Hopefully this would be a night to remember…

Honor sat down at the fire pit, meditating, *again*. She felt like this was all she did anymore. She listened to everything around her, drawing strength from the silence. She poured her flame into the fire, which rose to the top of the trees.

A sound from behind her had her turning quickly, her eyes alight with an amber glow. Seeing nothing, she returned to her meditation. It must have been the wind. Another sound a few moments later caused her to jump again. Standing, she investigated the camp. Walking around, she heard a twig snap. That couldn't be the wind, could it? She carefully looked backward.

A woman sat at the fire. She was dressed all in red, wearing a dark red robe with a hood. Walking to her cautiously, she summoned her flame to her hand, ready to fight if she had to.

"No need for your flame, Phoenix Honor. I'd be able to counter it anyway." Her voice was strange to American ears. A strange mix of Indian and other Asia accents. "Sit down. We must speak."

"I don't think I want to speak to you."

The woman laughed. "No, no you don't. But it is to your benefit to listen to my message. I can leave, but doing so will result in your death. Wouldn't you rather stay alive?"

"Why would I die?"

The woman turned and lowered her hood. "Because someone is trying to kill you. And she will not attack, as long as I am here."

"What makes you so special?"

A wide smile lit her lips. "My age. My abilities. The fact that I have for generations kept the secrets of nations. Take your pick, fire child."

"Who are you?"

As she watched, the figure changed. A snake came from her back and hissed at Honor. Horns formed on her head. As Honor watched, she held out a hand, and her psychic beast was released, pouncing at her, stopping a few feet from Honor's face. Her phoenix reacted, protecting her, hovering in front of her, her flames fanning the creature back.

"Easy…I mean you no harm, Honor."

Calming herself, her firebird disappeared, leaving the woman's beast. It had the body of a lion, tail with a snake head at the end, and a goat head in the middle of its back. As Honor watched, it lay down, cleaning itself like a house cat.

"What are you?"

"Do you not know your Greek myths?"

Honor shook her head. "Foster care didn't provide me the best education."

"Foster care. I see. Well, allow me to educate you. I am Chimera." She bowed, her head falling low to the ground. Long, dark black hair flowed from her head. "And you, are a newly risen, orange phoenix."

"How did you know my chosen name?"

"I visited the mural before coming to see you."

"You know where the mural is? Are you friends with Nix and Tyrus?"

She turned and sat. "I will say no more until you join me at the fire."

Walking carefully, Honor sat across from her. After a moment of silence, the woman answered. "I do not know your companions, other than by reputation. Tyrus is…over a hundred now? He has made a name for himself. Helping people, of all things. Word that a firebird was severed from its owner reached my ears as well. But friends? Honor, if you are as powerful as I think you are, there will come a time when you have to come to terms with the fact that the world is not forgiving to powerful women. When you do, you will understand when I say that I have no friends, save my beast and my power. What I do have are lackeys, and enemies."

"Then why warn me?"

"It serves my purposes for you to continue to exist. Is that not enough?"

"Why do you need me?"

"I don't. I need no one. The world, on the other hand, is changing. I feel it in the very earth. Something is coming, and you and your other companions are tied to that change, somehow."

"So, you came to preserve the world? I thought you didn't have any friends?"

She laughed. "You are clever but mistaken. I have interests. Business interests, money, and reasons to live that involve the world continuing to turn as it has been. You and your friends can see to it that comes to pass."

"Who is trying to kill me, then?"

She gave her a strange, hard smile. Standing, she looked toward the main cabin, and released her beast. It went through the walls and a scream followed some moments later. The unconscious woman came out of the cabin, chased by the beast.

"Leave her alone. She's just a hiker." Honor readied her flame.

"Really?" Chimera didn't move a muscle to stop her beast. As it approached the woman, she let out a screeching sound, and the beast ran from the power of it. Honor covered her ears and ducked as the wind around the camp suddenly picked up.

"Damn, you, Chimera!"

"Be gone, Siren. You have no power here, any longer."

The woman crossed her arms in front of her, and the wind condensed on her, flowing her hair wildly around. After a few moments, she was completely enveloped by it, and it swept her away as if she'd been made of dust.

Chimera waited for the wind to return to normal, then turned back and sat down near the fire, warming her hands. Honor sat too, breathing quickly.

"What the hell…"

"A siren. A wind elemental that can control men, lure them to their death. Luckily, her job was not only to kill, but to collect information, or she could have long ago used your Tyrus to kill you."

"He's not *my* Tyrus."

She gave Honor a strange look. "Do they not teach you Mythics anything about history anymore?"

"What does history have to do with me, and my-I mean, *not* my Tyrus?"

She smiled knowingly. "It repeats itself."

"So?"

Chimera sighed. "Have you heard the expression, fight fire with fire? Like attracts like?"

"What does that mean?"

"Most assume it has something to do with controlled burns and forest fires. And it can, but its meaning changes when you apply it to Mythics. Certain fates are intertwined. Something for you to think on, I wager."

"What is that meaning?"

"You'll discover it in due time. As for me, I will stay with you tonight until I am sure the Siren moves on. It is less time than we think we have. You are a very lucky young woman, Honored Phoenix. There are people in this world that would pay millions for five minutes of my time, and I'm giving you a night for free."

Honor didn't feel very comforted by that thought. Whoever this woman was, she was no saint, and dangerous. "So, what do I owe you in exchange for saving my life?"

The twisted, sadistic smile returned. "I'm sure, when I call on you in the future, you won't mind doing me a favor."

"I'll not harm my family."

"I'll not ask you to. Now, about your flame. I see they've taught you some rudimentary meditation. How about I give you a few more examples? Help you learn more quickly?"

"How will you do that?"

A challenge lingered in her gaze. "Until now you've been kept cocooned from your greatness. They…control your power, instead of giving it an outlet. I am not interested in your control." She stood, her beast at her back. "I want only one thing out of you." Her eyes changed from human to snake. "Your power."

Honor had a moment to stand, before her beast attacked. She rolled out of the way only to see the beast approaching her again. Still awkward, she managed to avoid a second strike, but on the third, the beast pinned her, so she summoned her phoenix to her. This would be a long night, indeed.

Chapter 14

The sun began to crest over the mountains. The world was waking up, but for her, the night had been exhausting. Honor's back dripped with sweat. Chimera looked like she was unaffected by the exercises they'd been working on for the last eight hours. She walked around in her robe, her hair perfectly in place.

"Again."

Honor stood, slowly, taking much effort. Chimera unleashed her beast, which ran for her. She summoned her firebird, who grabbed her by the shoulders, and picked her up, tossing her to the other side of the battle. She hurled flame as she fell, but it didn't affect the woman at all. The beast lunged again, and her firebird grabbed it, rolling it away from Honor.

The beast shook itself off and sat down. "You're beginning to understand, beginning to get creative with your bird. Excellent. It only took you eight hours. My, what a disservice your fellow Mythics are doing you. Your education is severely lacking in fundamentals of war."

Honor looked at her, the fire coming to her eyes, despite her aching muscles. Chimera acknowledged the look. "Good. You haven't given up. There are three things that determine success in battle. One of them, is willpower. You have that in spades. It serves you well, when everything else fails."

"What are the other two?"

"Preparation. That involves knowing yourself and your enemy, knowing how to fight, when to fight. When to run."

"I doubt you've ever had to run."

"Even I was a young Chimera, once."

"You mean there's someone out there who can kick your ass? Got their phone number?"

"Not anymore."

Honor breathed in and out, the air hurting her lungs. "What's the third?"

"You'll find that out on the day of your first real retreat. It is not a lesson one can teach. It must be learned by circumstance."

"You can't tell me?"

"No." She turned her back and Honor took the opportunity to try one more fireball. It fell off her cape like water. "Did I forget to mention that this cape is magical and element-proof? Built by the last Maji. A weaver, if I remember correctly."

"What killed him?"

"She…was killed. By…friendly fire."

"By you?"

"What is the advantage of having a magic cape if everyone else can just get their hands on one?"

Honor shivered, despite being overheated from exercise. Chimera again summoned her beast, its form fading into her flesh. She turned and looked at the firebird. "You will do well to remember who you are."

"What does that mean?"

"Your bonds to this earth. They are strange." She tiled her head, looking at something near Honor that she couldn't see herself. "There are many forces…pulling at your spirit. You will have to decide, eventually, who you are, and that decision will cause ripples. Giant ones. Choose wisely, Phoenix Honor."

Summoning her beast, she sat on its back and said, "until the next lesson." She bowed low again, and her beast ran off into the woods, jumping the fence easily. Honor, heaving and covered in sweat, sat down by the fire. She was certainly grateful for one thing. She was still breathing.

Connor woke suddenly, as if he'd fallen asleep somewhere he shouldn't. And he had. Looking around him, the flowers of the garden stared back at him. He glanced at Maiden lying next to him, sleeping soundly. He grabbed his robe, dressing quickly, then laid hers over her form.

"Maiden. Wake up, princess."

She stretched and opened her eyes. A smile lit her features. "Good morning."

"Good morning. Let's get out of here before your father sees us."

She gave him a confused look. "He won't know. He never comes to the garden in the morning."

"We just…" Now he was confused.

"Is it not normal for landwalkers to make love?" She laughed. "Well, do you intend to steal my dowry?"

"Uh, no? I don't even really understand that…custom."

"Then you're safe. Merfolk are very open people by nature. While this is still special, it's not forbidden. I should have remembered that from my studies. Landwalkers are very…repressed. In this sense. Be at ease, no one will tell my father because it isn't their business, and he won't be coming to the garden. We are absolved and you are safe."

He laughed nervously. "As you say, Princess."

"Well, I don't know about you, but I had a great night. I will definitely petition my father to see you again."

He blushed. "You're welcome. Let's go."

They walked into the great hall, where the king was gathered with the prisoners. Daileass turned toward Connor with a strange look. He definitely knew what had gone on.

"Ambassador. You are awake. Your charges are to be released to your custody."

Seth and Julius were standing there, as was Levi, who was still in chains. "Thank you, King Daileass."

"I am glad to have met you, Connor of the Five, Ambassador of the Land Walkers. May the waters of Fate keep you."

"May the Waters of Fate guide me home, always."

Maiden took his hand, and he gazed at her. "May the darkness never shine brighter than your light." She placed a chaste kiss on his cheek.

He walked to his companions, as Levi was released from his bondage. The four men stood close together, and the water swirled around them. A moment of confusion, and they stood in the center of the camp, staring at a very sweaty Honor.

"Yeah, *now* you come back." She dropped to the ground, clearly exhausted.

"How's life been the past couple of days?" Connor walked to her, patting her on the back.

"Swell. Yours?"

Julius chuckled.

Connor glared. "What?"

She looked at them, confused.

"Well, I think one of us had a pleasant experience." Seth looked at Connor, who gave him a dirty look back. "Ambassador." Seth bowed to his friend.

Connor sighed. "It's not like I didn't stick up for you."

"No, no. being locked in a room is totally the same thing as getting a one-on-one escort around the city with the princess." Julius said it menacingly.

Connor felt rage bubbling up inside him. "Don't say another word..."

"Like what? Like she's your whole world?" Julius batted his eyes.

Connor's hands became fists. Levi stepped between the two. "Not the time, you two. Honor, what happened here? I sense…someone strange."

"You want to sit down for this. Seth, can you grab me a water?"

"Sure."

He left, and Honor waited until he'd returned and she'd downed the bottle before she filled in her companions on the events of that night. "Ever heard of a woman called Chimera, Levi?"

With a fearful expression on his face, he asked, "have you?"

Honor laughed and started at the beginning.

◆ ◆ ◆

Joy walked into the hospital as she'd done for the past few days, stopping at the desk to wish the receptionist a good day, and give her a coffee. The more she looked like she fit in, the less she'd be questioned.

She walked to the elevator, riding it up to Jayde's floor. It opened to reveal a level surrounded by green. This was the girl's power, and it was growing. The nurses and doctors didn't know what to make of it, murmuring about hiring a gardener as she walked by. She chuckled.

Jayde greeted Joy with a smile. "Hey! I was hoping I'd get to see you."

"Well, here I am. Nurse Joy reporting as ordered."

The younger girl giggled. "Can I ask you something, Joy?"

"Anything."

"Do you believe in magic?"

Joy looked behind her, like someone could be listening. "Want to see something cool, Jayde?"

"Sure!"

Joy turned and pointed out the door toward the nurse's station. "Watch the one on the left."

"Okay."

As they watched, Joy sent out a small vibration, a wave which hit the nurse, who turned the music up and suddenly began to dance. After a few moments, she got onto the counter and continued her fun. The two conspirators giggled wickedly.

"Do you mean magic like that?"

"Sort of. I think," Jayde hesitated, unsure, "I think I may have some magic of my own."

This was good. She was coming to terms with her power, finally. "Really? Why do you think that?"

"Do you want to see something cool?"

"Always."

Jayde looked at the roses next to her bed. She held out a hand toward them. The roses grew, doubling in size. Joy looked back at her, a look of surprise on her face. “Maybe you are magic.”

“That’s why you’re my favorite nurse.”

“Why is that?”

“Because you don’t look at me like I’m a freak.”

“Do the other nurses think you’re a freak?” Joy sat on the bed next to her.

“They don’t say it, but I can see it in their eyes. They’re afraid of me.”

“Well, the difference between me and them, is I understand magic. It’s everywhere and all around us. I believe. Do you believe?”

“Yes.”

“See, they don’t. And they don’t understand because they don’t believe. People fear what they don’t understand.”

“Why can’t they?”

Joy shrugged her shoulders. “Because some people are special. Some people see magic more easily than others.”

“Like you and me?”

“Exactly.”

Jayde relaxed, accepting that explanation. “Can you bring me some Jell-O?”

“Sure, I can. What kind?”

“The green.”

“Be right back, Jayde.”

Joy walked out of the room, listening to the conversations around her. The nurse got down off the counter and said, “I’m so sorry. I don’t know what came over me.” Joy chuckled.

Joy was in the elevator when it stopped on the second floor, two agents stepping inside. She waited until the doors were closed, then the agent’s walkie went off. “Warning, security breech on floor four. Unauthorized person with blonde hair, seen leaving restricted area. Be on alert.”

The two men turned to Joy, looking her in the eye. “Gentlemen. Can I help you?”

The doors opened on floor 1, the agents dancing into the

hallway. Joy walked around them, chuckling. Good news was she wouldn't get caught. Bad news, Jayde wouldn't be getting her Jell-O, and Joy had been made. Someone wanted this kid bad enough to go to war. She couldn't fight one alone.

Turning into the parking structure, Joy walked until she found a shadowy corner, then she opened a portal and moved through to the camp.

Honor and the others sat by the fire pit. Joy approached, a concerned look on her face. Something had happened here, but she was confused. She saw multiple Mythic signatures, and she couldn't distinguish what had come through here. It was like one was hidden partially from her view.

Honor looked at her friend as she approached. "I was just about to tell a story. Want to listen?" Joy sat and looked at her friend to begin.

The others stood waiting in Pier Side Park for the notorious Dr. Blanc to arrive. Nix and Tyrus were to either side, and Dr. Jackson was in the middle, surrounded by twenty bodyguards. They waited as a series of limos pulled up to the park, and figures looking like agents stepped out, followed by a man wearing sunglasses, even though the day was overcast.

The man walked toward them, hobbling on a cane, but Dr. Jackson wasn't fooled. *Look feeble all you want. I know what you are.*

Nix stepped toward her nephew slowly as the man approached. When he reached Dr. Jackson, the man sat on a nearby bench, motioning that he should follow. Nix at his back, Tyrus watching the perimeter, he sat next to the founder.

"Are we finally going to discuss this personal matter?"

"Yes." He motioned to one of his men, who brought a suitcase forward, placing it in front of Dr. Jackson. "I believe, whatever price you name, this shall be enough for you."

"I'm confused. Why are you offering me money?"

"Come now, you think I don't know. You think I'm *blind?* Do not play with me boy. Tell me where she is. *Now.*"

"You mean Wills. You don't know where she is."

"You have a briefcase full of bonds, worth *billions* of dollars. Give her back to me and I will leave you in peace."

"Unfortunately, Dr. Blanc, I cannot take credit for the capture of your daughter."

He hissed out a breath. "How did you know?"

"I knew the instant Chimera's voice echoed through the phone."

The man looked out at the water. "Chimera. A name I have not heard in ages. Your father was one of the few who could reach that woman."

"While I realize we're discussing family, I'd prefer to keep it professional, to bring as little personal anecdotes as possible to light."

"Of course. Of course. I must be getting soft in my old age to not have seen this coming from her."

"Well, I have sources close by."

"Right. So, do I, they just apparently aren't as good as they used to be."

"So, are we done here?"

"Unfortunately, no. You will need to help me recover my daughter."

Gregory laughed. "And why would I do that?"

Dr. Blanc leaned back, but the move drew him closer. "Because Chimera, active, is a threat to all of us. I'll still give you the bonds. Still agree to call off all contracts. Do this favor for me, and I will…owe you one."

"Favor trading. One thing my father told me to avoid."

"I guarantee that owing you a favor is not on my bucket list, but alas, here we are."

"Yes, gentlemen," a voice in front of them said, "here we are."

He looked up to see a woman wearing a red robe standing before him. Dr. Blanc stood, hobbling on his cane. "What the hell- "

Before he could make sense of what was occurring, the world around him grew blurry, as if he was moving through time and space. He blinked, but it was slow, as if it took incredible effort. When he opened his eyes again, the Park was…different. Everyone except the Mythics were frozen in place, guards halfway done drawing their weapons.

Nix and Tyrus came toward him. "Not so fast." Chimera waved her hand, and Nix and Tyrus were blasted back. "You are not part of this discussion."

"What have you done with her?"

"Oh, we will talk of your daughter, but first, my old friend, we must talk of other things. The three of us have a problem, and it's bigger than anything Mythics have faced before. We must put aside our differences to deal with this threat."

"I will listen *after* my daughter is returned."

Chimera smiled sadistically at him. "You will do whatever I say you will do, and upon successful completion of your tasks, you will be rewarded by a reunion with your darling daughter."

"If you harm a hair on her head…"

"Threats?" Chimera rose up, her beast coming to call. It stood as tall as the trees. "You really want to test me, Gorgon?"

"All it would take is me removing my glasses."

"Yes, but we know this hood makes me immune to your charms. The most you could do is give me a headache. I, on the other hand," her beast growled, licking its chops, "could just kill you and take your empire for my own."

"So why don't you?" It was the first thing Dr. Jackson had said. She turned to him, her gaze assessing him. "Hello, Gregory, son of James. You bide your time, waiting to speak. Good. I have need of all of our contacts. It will take a massive, worldwide collusion for us to combat this coming threat. Every Mythic has a stake in this. I expect all your resources to help, equally."

"Why have you not kidnapped one of my people?"

She smiled. "You are at your heart, a hero. Unlike some who

would let the world burn for another dollar, you want what is best for mankind. I could take what I wanted, but you seem to be motivated all on your own. Which is good, for your people, this time."

Dr. Blanc sat down. "When will you release my daughter?"

"After your part has been played."

"What is this threat we face?"

Her eyes changed, then, turning into a vibrant green. "He who walks in shadow seeks bountiful light."

"What does that mean?"

"I don't know. Yet. I cannot see. His connections with the earth…they are shadow themselves. I cannot see where they lead. Only that they surround us all, changing our fate for the worse. A visit to your newest phoenix…Honor? She was surrounded by it. Whatever the shadow is doing, it involves the young ones, the five, the synthetically crafted Mythics."

"What are we supposed to do then?"

"Dr. Blanc will use his influence with the top governments in the world to fund a special taskforce. These agents will be given some of our secrets on Mythics, only enough for them to do their job. We will give up some of what we are to save what we have left. This force will globally patrol, faster than we could.

"When they have located the shadow, then, Dr. Jackson, you and I will lead your mythic force to do battle and confront it. This may or may not be conventional. You can't kill darkness, after all."

"You have no other information on this threat?"

"Only that he is older than me, and I am the oldest Mythic I know."

"Yes, I saw what you did to those that came before you."

"You've read my dossier? How informed you are." She seemed impressed. "Yes, I did what I had to do. It was a different time then, with a different set of rules. Gentlemen, if we are to begin, it must be now. Train your soldiers, ready your watchers. We go to war."

Honor finished her tale, and Levi grasped her shoulder encouragingly. "Well. I've met Chimera. You are indeed lucky to be alive."

She didn't feel lucky, just afraid. "It was strange. And the fact that the Siren had been here the whole time… Scary. How does someone gather information while asleep?"

"Wind signs can carry voices to them."

"Oh."

"Very useful, if you ask me. I wonder why she didn't attack though. *I'm* her target."

"Gathering information requires being unknown. Maybe that was why. Most of the time you were around you spent with Nix anyway."

Levi looked down. Connor coughed. "Well, I guess I should report to you guys as well."

Honor was distracted by something small in the distance rapidly drawing closer. Seeing her gaze, everyone turned. "What is that?" She squinted, trying to make it out.

Levi turned around. "Looks like Nix and Tyrus needed a quick way back."

Moments later, the two were on the ground. "Whatever you are doing, you need to stop. We need to talk to you, now."

"I think you should hear what they have to say, Nix."

"We don't have time. Elementals, with me. Enforcers with Tyrus. Your war training starts now. We'll talk tonight. Connor, welcome back. Honor, glad you survived the night."

"Barely…" Nix gave her sarcastic comment a quizzical look but said nothing. "Levi, go with Tyrus for now."

Connor and Julius walked off, leaving Seth, Joy and Honor with Nix. "We have some work to do. Up until now, we've been taking a hands-off approach in your training. We've allowed you a freedom that…wasn't given to us. We pride ourselves on being able to do that for you, but a bigger concern has reared its head, and we are needed as soldiers. For the next six weeks, you will be trained to hone your powers, your skills. You will test each other to the limit, and you will learn not only to be controlled, but to be powerful."

"Does this have anything to do with Chimera?"

Nix looked at Honor. "What happened while I was gone? No! Tell me later."

"Seth and Joy, you'll spar first. Honor, you're with me."

"What do we do?"

"Use your abilities to try to gain an advantage over your opponent."

"So…like this?" Joy jumped up and surrounded herself in sunshine, so much that she blinded everyone around her. When the light faded, Seth was on the ground, a hand at his face. "Hey. No fair."

Nix helped him up. "Fighting is never fair. Get used to it. Do whatever you have to. Win!"

She turned to Honor and hurled a fireball in her direction. After the long night she'd had, Honor did not want to go another eight hours in the ring, but it appeared she had no choice. She called her bird to fly her to safety, then came down on Nix's shoulder with a knee.

Nix dodged, but surprise widened her gaze. "Whatever happened last night, you learned some useful tricks. Did you see what she did Joy? You don't have wings, but you can use your power to fly, if you try."

"Great. Keep giving her ways to kick my ass." Seth wasn't amused.

"Leprechauns have portals, remember? Use everything you can think of." As Honor watched, Joy launched into the air, her bright light launching her behind Seth, who then bounced away. They continued to evade in this fashion as Honor and Nix grappled with their flame.

An hour later, they took a break. Apparently, Nix was not as cruel a taskmaster as Chimera. She cared that they didn't go too far, or too hard. Sitting down, they watched as the others returned, dripping in sweat. Connor and Julius both had scratches and were bleeding. Tyrus had a black eye.

"What happened to you?" Honor asked.

The men laughed. “Nothing much, just training.”

Tyrus tried to laugh, but it hurt his face. “Yeah, let me tell you what, Connor knows how to punch.”

“Well, you let your guard down.”

“On purpose.”

“Sure, it was.”

Tyrus looked at Honor strangely. “You know, it’s been two days since an event now. I think you’re finally getting the hang of your power.”

“Agreed... Considering the lack of control you had at the beginning, you’ve made miraculous progress. I have never seen ANY mythic do what you do so naturally.”

Honor turned red, unsure what to do with the praise. She never received words of encouragement like that in the foster system, and she didn’t know what to say or how to act.

Nix bumped her elbow, not waiting for a response. “Now, while we’re on break, why don’t you share your Chimera story?”

Honor launched into her story again, sharing what she remembered. “So, you already had eight hours of training, and were able to go one on one with me anyway? Wow.” Nix rubbed her forehead. “Maybe I’ve been underestimating you.”

“Maybe.” About to blush again, she ignored the urge. She wasn’t going to downplay herself. “It was hard. She didn’t give me any breaks.”

“From what I’ve seen, you’re lucky to be standing.”

“I’m aware.”

Connor cleared his throat, again. “I also have a lot to report, if you’re ready.”

“Yeah, what took you so long?” Nix looked at him, curiously.

“The princess, apparently…” Julius teased. Connor punched him in his already weak shoulder. “I just got that back into place. I’m just kidding.”

“I don’t get it.” Nix was confused.

“The king graciously accepted me as one of their own. I was

shown a prophecy of the future which I don't understand and was given access to their past, which I don't understand."

"And given access to- "

"If you say it, I'll hit you again."

"Sorry. I'll shut up. I just wonder, you know, Honor, Connor's got Maiden, when are you and I gonna hook up?"

Honor tilted her head at him. "Not funny."

Tyrus coughed loudly, ignoring the urge to throw something at Julius. Jealousy wasn't like him. "Now is not the time for…romance, or whatever. It's about time for us to get back to training. You'll spend the rest of the day this way, battling by ability. Tomorrow, you will all be battling each other. Then, you'll battle the three of us. It's the best process we can give you. Be prepared. Remember, fight smart, then hard."

Over the course of the day, they continued in this pattern. They didn't stop until the sun had set, resting for five minutes once an hour. By the time the five walked to their respective beds, they were dragging their feet, more exhausted than they'd ever been.

Tyrus watched them enter the main cabin. He knew that they were doing the right thing, but he also knew it wasn't right *for them*. How would their memories be affected if they transformed from this activity? Who would they start to forget?

Levi walked up to him. "I have a gift for you, in my pocket. Compliments of the Mer King."

"You expect me to reach into your pocket?"

"My *shirt* pocket. It's enchanted. I can't touch it."

Tyrus reached in, gripping the coin. As he did so, his vision grew cloudy. The image came unbidden to his mind.

He was surrounded by beach, the sun setting on the horizon. He turned and walked, where, he didn't know. After some moments, he came upon what could only be described as darkness. It looked at him, hissing. "How did you get here? How can you see me?"

"What are you doing?" The darkness was watching bodies drift onto the shore. "What happened to these people?"

The darkness let out a growl, low in its throat. "Be gone, Red Dragon. I have much to do. You are not wanted here." A wave of darkness drifted toward Tyrus, rocking him backward.

Levi couldn't catch him, and his body was sent flying backward into the fence. Wood splintered as he was forced through it, and two tree trunks before he lay unconscious.

"Nix!"

They all came running out. "What happened?"

"Something broke Tyrus." He pointed. Nix looked at him accusingly. "What? I didn't do it. The coin did."

"Joy, check him."

She walked to the still figure, a glow appearing and after a few minutes, fading again. "He's wrapped in darkness, much like Honor was. What happened?"

They all looked at Levi. "He got a coin from the Mer King. He touched it, then a few minutes later, flew away."

"Connor, Julius, get him inside. Carefully." They leaned down to obey, walking slowly into the main cabin. Joy looked at Levi, curiously. "What?"

She poked him. "Ouch. What was that for?"

"You're running out of time. You should be spending it with Nix."

He sighed. "I am an old man. If my time has come, Joy, I accept it."

"I warned you before, you need to be spending time with her. She is your salvation."

"I will, but the world comes before Nix."

"Nothing should come before her as far as you're concerned. That is, if you want her forgiveness."

"More than anything, but I just don't see the same future as you do."

She tilted her head. "My future's better than yours."

"Obviously."

"Well, all the more reason for you to listen to me, Kraken."

"Tell me again what you see."

"Not here. Not now. She comes."

Joy skipped toward the cabin, away from Levi. Nix walked toward him as she did so. "Listen, Levi," she wrung her hands, "the contract has been absolved, but I wouldn't bet on the operative backing down. They still may want the trophy kill of taking your head. Don't feel you have to stay here…"

Levi leaned in close to her. "I'm not leaving you, Nix, not now, not ever."

"I'm fine. I don't need a bodyguard."

"No, no you don't. You're very capable. I don't want to be your bodyguard."

"I told you, I'm not ready for more than that."

"And I told you I'm not leaving."

"Well, we can't protect you here."

"No matter where I am, my time will come when it does. Until that moment, I can't think of anything but you." He drew her close to him. "I'm not going anywhere."

She was tempted to stay in his arms, but she drew away, nonetheless. "I have to go check on Tyrus."

"Go ahead. I'll take first watch."

"See you in the morning."

"See you."

She walked away, and he watched her go.

Honor was trying hard not to go to sleep. For the next two hours, she was supposed to watch Tyrus. He wasn't to be left alone. The hard part was she'd already pulled one all-nighter. She didn't want to do two.

She tried to keep herself awake and aware, but the urge to sleep couldn't be fought off. After a half hour of fighting it, she slumped forward, her head resting on his chest.

Though he was asleep, his arm came around to snuggle her

anyway…

She was standing in the damn meadow again. Used to the routine, she called out for Joy. Finding no answer, she turned and walked to their usual meeting spot, where a maypole had been decorated in the middle of a bright, sunny field of flowers.

When she reached it, she called again, but Joy didn't come. What the hell was she doing here if Joy hadn't brought her? She looked out at the distance, almost forcing Joy to come into view, but she was nowhere. A shadow crossed over her and she turned, ready to battle.

Tyrus's dragon stood behind her, eying her sideways. He was gorgeous in this plane, much larger than he was when he melded with Tyrus. Red wings lined with gold and turquoise eyes similar to his master. His muscles showed beneath his scales as he moved, revealing his strength.

Strange. Why was his dragon here, but not Tyrus? As she thought it, the dragon leaned its head down to her, as if to show submissive behavior. She reached out, touching its forehead, and its thoughts came to her mind.

Firebird. My master…he is gone.

Where did he go?

I do not know. Will you help me find him?

Where should we look?

To the sky. I can take you.

Before she could say no, he was gripping her in his claws, and they were flying. They flew up until the trees were the size of cookies. She looked down, but the heights didn't bother her. This was a dream, after all.

They flew until they spotted a small dark forest

below. The trees were twisted, their leaves barren. They flew to just outside the darkness, then landed swiftly. She touched the forehead again.

I cannot go any further. You are the only one with the light to traverse this perverse madness. Please, find my master. I await you here. I look to the sky for your coming.

The dragon flew away, leaving Honor alone in front of twisted branches and gnarled roots. She stepped softly at first, afraid of the trees themselves. They hissed, as if to taunt, but didn't reach out to block her. She walked until she found a path, hidden by the cropping of tall trees. She lit a flame ball in her hand, and sent it to hover forward, ten steps in front. As the flame preceded her, she could see. Tensely, she began to walk.

It seemed ages before she came across any significant structure. A wall of stone surrounded a decaying castle. No gates were in sight, the wall solid. She tried to fly over, but the tree branches lashed out at her, forcing her down. She would have to find another way in.

She walked to the right, touching the wall as she went. Her flame danced in front of her, like some strange pixie guiding her way. A light up ahead signaled to her, blinking three times fast, three times slow. She knew that message. Someone she knew was up there. She quickened her pace, ignoring the groaning sounds of the forest.

Though the light shone more brightly, she couldn't make out who it was until she was touching skin. Then the light faded. Joy smiled at her. "You made it."

"I did. Where are we?"

"Tyrus's consciousness is trapped in here. We

have to help get him free."

"Why can't we just wake him up?"

"It's hard to explain. It's like he wants to wake up, knows he should, but he can't, because his own demons are keeping him asleep. We need to free him from those demons for him to wake. Come. I found a way inside, but I didn't have the courage to go in alone. Let's get your Tyrus back."

"He's *not*…" Honor sighed, letting it go. Just a dream.

The two walked toward a small opening in the gate. "This leads into the lower levels. We can get to him from there. Are you ready?"

Honor wasn't going down there until she knew it was safe. Casting a fireball, she waited several seconds, listening. "Nothing there? Good. Let's go."

Honor sat on the ground, placing her feet into the hole first. She scooted until she was at the edge, then let herself drop. She fell only a few feet before splashing into some water. Quickly creating another flame ball, she split it and launched it in both directions. Nothing for ten feet on either side.

"It's safe Joy, come down." Her friend did and they looked down each corridor, wondering which way to proceed.

"Let's go…" Joy thought a moment, walked five feet to the left, turned around, said, "hmmm…" then walked toward the right. "Right."

Honor followed her friend, her flames protecting them front and back. They walked until a crossroad was reached, cells lining either side. "Which way, Joy?"

"Uh. Left." Joy began walking down. The cells here were empty, save the occasional decayed corpse staring out at them. Honor wanted to puke but couldn't because it was a dream world.

"Where are we?"

"His worst nightmare."

"Oh."

"I brought you here to help him. Only you can breech this."

"Why do you think I'll do any better than you?"

"Not better than me. Different than me. Unicorns can't kill. If we do, we go evil. You don't want to see me go evil."

"I'm going to need to *kill* something."

"Yes."

"What is it I'm killing today?"

They reached another hallway. "Right." They turned and Joy said, "The demon that's holding Tyrus here. You'll have to destroy it."

"Well, that doesn't sound too hard."

Joy laughed ominously. "Right." They turned again, a staircase in front of them. "It will be hard. You'll have to make a choice. A hard choice. I can guide you, but in the end, you'll have to choose who you save."

"I don't understand."

Joy looked at her, a sad expression on her face. "You will." Her friend continued up the stairs at a slower pace, as if she feared what might be up there. Honor followed, confused, but ready to do the right thing. The question was, what was the right thing, and if she saw it, would she know it?

Chapter 15

The climb up the stairs seemed to take forever. As they progressed, the darkness grew thicker. The light was harder to create, harder to keep going. Several times her flame balls disintegrated and recalling them took more effort each time.

Finally, they reached the top, which opened to a ritualistic looking area, wide and windy, from its height above the forest. How had she not seen this from the dragon?

Tyrus stood in the middle of the structure, huge chains binding him to two huge walls, made of stone. He was surrounded by darkness, thick and twisted, whirling and churning about him. As Honor got closer, Joy got farther away. "Are you coming?"

"No. You have to do this by yourself. I'll be here, though." With that, Joy shone bright again, a blinding light that covered the top of the tower, but the darkness around Tyrus refused to give way.

Honor approached him, casting flame balls at the dark. They were absorbed, and the darkness continued to wreak havoc on Tyrus, who writhed in pain, screaming out loud. Honor didn't know what she could do, if the darkness absorbed her flame. How else could she help him.

Thinking quickly, she walked closer, allowing herself to be surrounded by the dark. It was cold, confusing her mind, showing her glimpses of her past and future, but twisted, and mean. Each step she took, the voices of the dark, the images in her mind, became more real.

She was three and being taken away again. She cried, not wanting to leave her family. The social worker looked down at her and said, "Why would they want you when they can have someone special in their home."

Another image, one of children surrounding her on the school playground. Another girl was ready to fight her. "I don't want to fight," Honor tried to explain. The other children teased and mocked her, calling her a sissy and weak. She felt tears welling in her eyes.

Another image, another step. She was inside the tower, the flames burning around her. Joy was there, but instead of saving her, the image merely said, "It'd have been better if you'd died here."

A tear fell unbidden from her cheek. If she was experiencing this, what was Tyrus going through? The tear fell and hit a swirl of darkness. It steamed, and the spot of darkness screamed before fading to nothing.

Was that it? Her tears.. Another step, another image. This time, she allowed herself to feel the image as if it was real. She was on a beach, Nix standing beside her. "Whatever happens, don't interfere."

"What do you mean, Nix?"

She tried to walk forward with her, but she found she couldn't move. Nix walked toward a swirl of wind. Blasting it with her fire, she fought as hard as she could, to no avail. The wind overcame her mentor's power. As Honor stood frozen, the wind hit Nix, sending her flying. Her friend lay on the ground, motionless and dead. The wind hissed at her, "You couldn't save her. How does it feel? Knowing how perfectly ordinary you are?"

Another tear, another piece of the darkness gone. She was close enough to touch him now, and she reached out with both hands, doing so.

This image was different than the others. She was not in her memory, but his. He stood, chained in a dungeon, watching as a hooded figure killed soldiers, shooting them in the head. They were lined up for miles.

"Stop!" It was from Tyrus. "Stop killing my boys. I'll tell you whatever you want."

"There is nothing we need from you but to watch the death before you and despair."

Honor walked forward, a specter in this universe. She was unsure what to do. Summoning a flame ball, she tried to launch it at the hooded figure, but it turned, looking at her and said, "A visitor? Or a volunteer?"

Suddenly she was no longer a shapeless ghost, but a soldier herself, lined up and waiting to be shot. She struggled against her chains, the figure five people down from her. Tyrus saw her. "No. Not her!"

"Yes, her. She will die, and the despair you feel will haunt you forever. We will drink it like thick blood wine."

Honor thought quickly. She couldn't get through her bonds, but maybe she could still reach him.

"Snap out of it, Tyrus. This isn't real. You're dreaming. Fight it."

He just kept saying, "no…no…no" as he looked at her and cried.

"Tyrus, listen to me, you don't have to be locked up. You can break free of this any time you want. Listen to me dammit!"

She screamed and pleaded with him, but to no avail. Whatever the darkness was doing, he was stuck, more strongly than she was. The figure executed the next victim in line, then turned, placing the gun against her left temple. "Say goodbye, Honor."

Like hell. Her rage lit her like a Christmas tree. Her bird sprang forth, knocking the figure to the ground. As the darkness struggled against her flame, she was able to free her bonds, become a specter again.

"Now you can pick on someone your own size." She walked toward the figure and threw the hood back. Then she gasped, her breath leaving her. Tyrus stared back at her, a look of hate and revulsion on his face.

"What do you know anyway? What are you, like, a baby bird?" He stood, and she was momentarily confused. "I'm the reason he's still alive. You can't kill me. If you do, he dies with me."

"What are you talking about? I'm fighting his demons."

The figure laughed coldly. "I *am* his demons. He fights himself. Do you get anything? Do you have any intelligence at all? Maybe that's why the foster system kept spitting you out."

Hearing the harsh words come from a face she trusted caused tears to fall again. Although she couldn't see it, they were erasing the darkness.

"Why would you say those things? I thought we were friends?"

"Friends? What could you and I possibly have in common? What would a twenty something little girl have to teach me? A seasoned soldier who's survived more days in battle than you've been alive? Tell me little girl, what could you possibly have that I don't?"

Obviously, the choice was to destroy the strong but dangerous side of Tyrus, or the weak but kind side. She was getting that, but she didn't think she could make that choice. With the world in danger, they needed his strength, but that was useless without a good heart. If only there were a way to meld the two and get rid of the bad.

"Nothing? You have *nothing*?" She heard the words but ignored him for now. Walking over to Tyrus, she touched his shoulders, and tried one more time to get him to snap out of it.

"Tyrus, come on. We need you whole, not half of you. Wake the hell up!"

She slapped him, shook him, and cried for him, but it was useless. He was unable to awaken from the image. That's right, she thought, because this version of Tyrus is weak. If she wanted him to break free, the strong part of him had to do it.

She turned back to the evil Tyrus. "What? You ready to fight me yet?" Black wings sprouted from him, and he lunged at her. Her firebird came to her rescue, hitting him and knocking him out of the way. He flew into a wall as more tears streamed down her face. "If I have to, I will destroy this evil. No matter what."

He laughed, standing back up. "As if you could destroy tissue paper. You're weak."

"No, I'm aware. *You're* weak."

"Stupid girl!" He lunged at her again, but her bird was ready, grabbing his neck with her talons and flinging him down again.

"You're weak, because you allowed yourself to get trapped in here."

"I am not trapped. I am in control here."

"How long before this weak version of you ceases to exist? What will you do then?"

The figure thought for a moment. "I will tear you apart!"

"I won't be here. Face it, without him, you have

nothing, are nothing. You'll be trapped here forever, with no one to torment but yourself."

"Shut up! Shut up! I don't have to listen to you." Instead of attacking her, the figure covered its ears. Good. It was working.

"You can eat away at him all you want, but at some point, when you win, you'll grow bored and tired of this castle. What will you do? Smell the flowers? Decorate a maypole?"

"Oh, the horror…"

"If you allow him to die, you'll be trapped in death as well. So much for you being the *smart* one. I think it's pretty stupid to want to be stuck in here, instead of wreaking havoc in the real world."

"We did have fun, him and I. But no…I won't…let…you…"

Her tears were doing the trick, and the darkness around him was fading, but the image was holding on to its life.

"You're growing weaker, dimmer. Soon, you'll be nothing but a faded nightmare. Unless, you release him."

"You're right. The darkness leaves me already. We must hurry, before I am trapped here." Dark Tyrus walked over to Light Tyrus and removed his bonds. "No, no, no," he murmured.

"It's the only way. I won't let you die and condemn me to death. We must again become one, my oldest friend."

Placing two hands on his temple, the two Tyrus figures blurred to one.

Honor's tears had almost disrupted the darkness, but they were no longer falling, as hope surged through her. The rest would be up to him.

He looked at her, confused. "Honor?"

"You need to wake up."

"What…happened?"

"It's not important. Listen to me. We're in a dream, and you need to wake up. Now."

"I don't know if I can. The dark…"

"It pulls at me, too, but you have to find a way, before the darkness consumes you."

Tyrus stood, nodding. He walked over to the last dead soldier, picking up the gun on the ground. Honor watched, scared for him. "What are you doing?"

"This is the only way." He raised the gun to his temple, and before she could tell him not to, before she could talk him down, he fired a shot right into his skull.

He slumped forward, her tears flowing again.

The darkness vanished as she sat, convinced he was dead. She sobbed as he lay chained, unconscious but no longer in torment. Joy's glow chased away any remaining shadows. Her friend rushed to her, as she opened the locks and tried to get him to the ground.

"Joy, help!"

"I'm here. I'm helping."

"He shot himself."

"I felt it, yes. Why would he do that?"

"Only way to get himself out of the nightmare. Can you heal him?"

"I can try. Keep crying on him. Your tears will help."

The two kneeled in front of his limp body, and Joy's glow surrounded him from head to toe. The tears continued to fall, until the glow faded again, and he took a breath.

His eyes opened a second later. "Honor." He raised his hand to touch her face. "What happened?"

"I saved your ass, that's what. We still need to get you out of here." Tyrus stood slowly, as if all his muscles ached. "Joy. Hello."

"Thank me and my brilliant plan later. Call your dragon."

He closed his eyes and reached out with his mind. The dragon appeared a moment later, landing on top of the tower. Tyrus placed a hand on his forehead, much as Honor had done, and whispered, "Hello, oldest friend." The dragon let out a roar, fierce and loud, powerful enough to shake the stone beneath them. Tyrus grabbed Honor by the waist and lifted her onto the dragon's back. He followed, then held out a hand to Joy. "Let's get out of here and go home, ladies."

As they flew away, the castle and the forest fell apart, as if it was decaying before their eyes. The stone fell with a crash, the trees shrank from view, until only the flowers and the meadow remained. Reaching the maypole, they sat down and climbed off the dragon's back.

Tyrus approached his mythic, and the dragon bowed his head.

"Thank you for staying by my side."

The beast let out a low soft growl that almost sounded like a purr. It was clearly happy to be back with its master.

"Let's go home." The dragon touched his forehead to Tyrus, and a red light surrounded them both. As the girls watched, the dragon slowly faded back into Tyrus's body.

"Ready to tell me what happened?"

"You have to wake first." Joy hit him on the head, and he was suddenly gone. She turned to Honor and said, "you too." Honor felt a smack, and then she was awake.

Tyrus was breathing heavily, and she was in his arms. He was holding on tightly, and she lifted her head slowly to see him watching her. "You're awake."

She gulped, suddenly feeling her stomach flutter. "You are, too."

"Was that real?"

"No, it was just a dream, right?" Even as she said it, she didn't believe it for a second. She sat up, and his arm fell away. "Can you stand?"

He tried, touching his side as he did so. "No. It appears the pain at least was real."

"Don't move. I'll go get Joy."

She started to move but he said, "No. Wait." He grabbed for her hand, and she grasped it.

"What is it, Tyrus?"

He looked at her, and said, "I'm sorry I dragged you in with me."

"If you hadn't, I wouldn't have been able to save you."

"I know. I'd still be in that hell. Those dreams were laced in with my memories. I hope that you understand I don't want the others knowing my nightmares."

"I would never do anything to harm you."

He smiled softly at her. "Nor would I harm you." His thumb moved, caressing her hand.

"I'm here." She turned, watching Joy walk in. "It's your turn to sleep. I'll heal him, and hopefully, this darkness will be behind us. Great work by the way."

"What do you mean?"

"I was sure you'd have to kill part of him to get him out, but you didn't. You found a way to save him, demons and all."

"Wait, that was real?"

"In a sense, yes. Go to sleep. I got this."

Tyrus gave her a look, then released her hand. She walked out of the cabin and didn't look back. She thought about something Joy had said in the dream. If she were to kill someone, she would go evil. Seeing her powers used for good, Honor shivered as she imagined the myriad of ways Joy could screw with people for fun if she did go bad. That must never happen. Ever!

Honor woke before the sun had begun its daily journey. She stretched, feeling rested, even though she'd only managed to get a few hours of sleep. She got up, hoping she could go for a run before training. Something about this flame was different. As she did more, she got more energy, not less. Chimera had been on to something when she said she wanted her to be powerful.

Tyrus had said the same thing. Were they really that special? She didn't feel special. Yet she'd managed to save the Red Dragon from his nightmare, when he couldn't. She wondered what the hand meant, why his smile changed last night.

Stopping herself from continuing that line of thought, she began a run around the lake, hoping it would settle her. Unfortunately, Tyrus was using the lake for a swim. She saw him expertly dip into the water, swimming from one side to the other. The lake was large, larger than a football field. He must be very strong to be able to swim for hours like he did.

She stretched and readied herself for the run. Starting at a slow pace, she set out, coming to the other side as he finished his second lap. He walked out of the lake, in front of her.

"You're up early."

"You as well. How are you feeling?"

"Better." He nodded as he said it. "How about yourself?"

"Like a run is a good idea."

"I hear you. Can we…take a break and maybe walk back together? I'd like to talk with you about something."

"What's on your mind?" She began to walk with him. Although he was only in swim shorts, he didn't seem cold.

"You and I shared quite the experience. I just wanted to make sure you understood where that came from."

"You were a soldier. You served in wartime. You had to lose people. I assumed that's where it came from."

"Yes, and no. A soldier fights for the guy to his right and his left. It's a brotherhood. We spent an enormous amount of time making sure our brothers made it back home. When you're done, though, when you're out, that's when it gets tough.

"See, no one tells you that, as a soldier, you also have to fight for yourself."

"What does that mean?"

"It means that once you're back in the civilian world, it's so hard to adjust. Your battle isn't with the enemy anymore. It's with yourself. And your guilt."

"Is that what I fought in there? Your guilt?"

"You fought to *save* my guilt."

She thought about that. "The chained side of you carried that piece of you."

"Yes. The dark side, the strength in me, was fighting to release it."

"And I kept the guilt inside you? That's awful!"

"No, Honor," he stopped, taking her hands, "it's not awful. Guilt is necessary. For what I've done and what I've been through, guilt keeps me sane."

"I'm not sure…I mean I understand what the words mean, but I don't get it."

"I just wanted to thank you for returning me whole. It would have been easier to kill off part of me than to save me."

"You already thanked me."

"Yes, but now you have a better idea of why I won't *stop* thanking you."

"Because you need your guilt."

"Yes."

"I don't get it."

He laughed. "Not yet, but maybe someday after you make the huge mistakes that we tend to make, hopefully then you will understand. And you'll look back and realize that I was right."

He still held her hands, his thumbs sliding along her knuckles.

"Is this because of my current flame?" She asked it without looking, wondering exactly what was happening between them.

He leaned in but didn't touch her. In her ear he whispered, "this is because you are power, personified. And it's gorgeous, and scary, and alluring."

He released her hands, walking away. She turned to continue her run, thinking that she needed to add a couple more laps around the lake. She needed to work off some steam.

Later that morning, the training continued. Honor stood surrounded by an old forest, awaiting instruction from Tyrus and Levi, who were talking quietly, between the two of them.

"You know what they're discussing?" Honor asked.

Joy shook her head. "No, not really. Something about the hidden coin."

"Don't you think that's important enough to listen in?"

"No. Not right now."

She sighed, frustrated with her friend. For all her abilities, their unicorn was very fickle.

They turned at long last, walking toward the girls. "Today, we will be teaching you how to fight assailants that are not built as you, or magical. There may come a time where you have to rely on your wit, your strength and your natural abilities to be able to survive. We are using those tools today."

"For the purposes of this exercise, we are going to ask that you not use your powers."

"How do you intend to stop us from using them?" Honor was

curious and a little angry.

"We won't force you to stop, no. We are just asking that you take this exercise seriously and focus on training based on your natural abilities."

"Okay."

"Joy?"

"Sure." Although she let out a twisted, maniacal giggle.

"Good. When fighting male enforcers, you will almost always have to rely on your powers to win. What happens, though, if you have none? There are dark ways to keep people separated from their abilities, and if you can't use those, you could find yourself in a situation where you feel powerless."

"This exercise asserts that you are in that situation. We'll be teaching you self-defense moves to counter someone who is stronger and faster than you. That doesn't make them smarter. Remember that your intelligence is your greatest strength."

"We are going to practice some basics first. Joy, with me, Honor, with Levi."

The girls walked forward and the training began…

An hour later, Honor picked herself up from the ground, her nose bleeding, her jaw sore. "Damn." She wiped the blood away from her mouth.

"What did I tell you? Intelligence, not strength. You will not always be the strongest. Try again."

Taking a quick breath, she rushed him again. She countered his strikes but couldn't find an opening. "What do you do when you can't find a way to neutralize your opponent?"

She backed away, holding up her hand for a breath. "You…"

"Come on. This is essential. What do you do when you can't neutralize your opponent?"

"Change the environment, conditions or momentum of the battle." It was Joy who said it, not Honor, who gave her friend a look. Joy didn't have a single hair out of place. Who would have thought someone so perky would be so adept in hand-to-hand combat?

"How would you change this environment?"

She backed up, retreating. He followed, and she used a tree branch to kick him in the chest. "Good." He said it through a tight jaw.

"Change the conditions."

She grabbed a rock, and threw it toward him, hitting his shoulder. "Good. Change the momentum."

She looked around, wondering just how to do that one. This was the hard one. Before she could, Joy kicked his feet out from under him. "There you go."

Honor helped Levi stand up. "What about a fair fight, Joy?"

Levi laughed. "I've lived a long time, Honor. If someone fights you at all, they believe they can win. There will never be a time in your life where a fight you must engage in, is considered fair."

Tyrus stood from his spot on a tree stump and walked toward them. "Time for a break. Go grab water."

The two girls walked off, Joy touching her hand to her friend's nose. "There."

"Thanks." She felt so tired. This was definitely a portion of their training they'd been neglecting. Though she was sore and aching, she was grateful for the lesson.

The boys were sitting around the fire pit when they walked into the main camp a few minutes later. Seth smiled at them. "How did yours go?"

Honor gave him a dirty look. "Oh, hush."

Julius handed them some water. "Thanks."

"No problem. Nix…didn't go easy on us."

"Good to know we weren't the only ones."

"Did they make you not use your powers, too?"

Honor nodded, then drank the water down in several gulps.

"Why would they do that?" Connor asked out loud to no one in particular.

"After the night I had, I'd say it's a good thing to be physically prepared. You never know when someone might…get the upper hand."

"There's so much about this world we don't know. Don't assume you'll always be on top." Joy sounded cheerful while she spoke, but the warning was still ominous. "That's when you fall the hardest." Honor shivered again, thinking about last night.

Their instructors were talking at the main cabin, some thirty feet away from them. "What do you think they'll make us do next?"

Honor shrugged. "No clue."

"Whatever is going to happen, it's not pleasant." Seth grabbed another water, then put it back. "We don't have time."

"Did your gut tell you that?" Seth nodded.

Tyrus walked up to them and sat down. "The rest of the training today, you'll be facing each other. Joy and Julius, Connor and Honor. Since you're the odd one out, Seth, you'll be training with Nix again."

They all sighed. Tyrus responded. "Take an hour. Meet us in the forest to train."

The hour passed quickly, and they walked toward their training ground. Tyrus, Nix and Levi stood together, whispering. Again.

"Wish I was part of that team…" Connor said it low, and only to her.

"We are. I think."

"Listen up. We will be watching the matches. We are only here to make sure that one, you don't activate your powers while training and two, you don't go too easy or too hard on each other. We don't want anyone to get seriously hurt. This is just day one, after all."

They paired off and began to circle each other. Honor focused on Connor, who stood in front of her, a sympathetic look in his eyes. For some reason, that made her angry. She waited for him to attack, a slow punch with no heart in it, and easily evaded, hitting him directly in his kidneys, like they'd shown her. Three strikes and she drew away.

The look of surprise on his face made her feel better. The next strike wasn't slow, and she had a harder time evading it, but she didn't have the leisure of thinking past the next blow to get worried about it. She merely countered, changing her stance and position as necessary. She let him back her toward the trees, and suddenly ran away.

He followed and she used the same technique, on the same branch, as she had with Levi. Connor went flying, unprepared. Standing back up, he turned toward her with a different look. She kept her face blank and stern.

She was about to strike again, when a yell from Nix had her turning. Julius was attacking Tyrus. Joy lay on the ground, unconscious.

"What the hell, bro?" Connor ran to the two men. Levi was already stepping between them, but Julius didn't stop. Instead, he focused on Levi. It was as if all his moves were lightning fast. He was not responding to reason.

Honor ran to Joy, who lay on the ground, unmoving. Nix was unleashing flame balls on the young man. Seth made it to Joy and the three of them were bounced away.

"Is it safe to move her?" Honor inquired as their senses came back, the camp surrounding them.

Seth shook his head. "Not yet. Stay here with her, please." He grabbed her arm, tight. "Please." She nodded and sat down on the ground. "I'll make sure nothing can touch her."

Seth was gone a second later. Honor sat, and focused her flame in a circle around the two of them. She didn't know enough to fight, yet, but she could protect. She sent a silent thought to the others, hoping they would figure out what was going on…

Connor felt the punch of his friend's fist connect with his jaw. Pain radiated from his mouth to the top of his head and down into his shoulder. Whatever was happening, his friend was not in his right mind.

He didn't know how, but it was as if Julius had been gifted with speed he didn't have before. Connor hadn't even had time to see the punch, let alone defend and counter. He stood anyway, refusing to give up.

Tyrus and Levi looked at each other a moment, and said, "Connor and Seth, stay back." The two listened, although they were clearly ready to help wherever they could. As they watched, the three Mythics became a unit.

It was like something out of a movie. As if someone had choreographed a flawless fight scene, and it was playing out before them. The three moved as one, anticipating each other's moves and filling in the negative space. Julius was able to counter, but at least the three attacking together stood a better chance at victory.

"What's going on?" Connor asked Seth.

He shook his head. "I should have said something, but I didn't know what to say."

"Always listen to your gut, man, but this isn't your fault."

"I know. What has gotten into him?"

Connor shrugged and turned back to the fight. Julius was still going strong. Connor had watched him fight before, and it was nothing like this. This superfast, untiring Julius was new. It was as if he were suddenly given access to an unending well of power.

The wind picked up around them. It made the hair on the back of his neck stand on edge. He watched as Nix managed to grab a foot, twisting it so the boy fell to the ground. At the same time, Levi and Tyrus grabbed both his arms, pinning him as he fell.

Thinking that was it, Connor started forward, but a gust of wind picked up, throwing him and Seth to the ground. The same gust impacted the three, lifting them off of Julius. Connor turned to Seth, who seemed to have the same thought. *Someone else is here.*

They backed away, and Connor touched Seth's shoulder. They bounced, further from the scene, so they couldn't hear the battle anymore. Without speaking, they searched the area. When they found nothing, Connor tapped Seth's shoulder and they moved again.

It took four times before they found her. She was hiding in a tree, her eyes closed, meditating and holding out her hands toward Julius in the distance. Connor crouched, and signaled to Seth, who bounced to Nix, and brought her back. They had seconds before she opened her eyes. Connor picked up a smooth rock lying nearby and flung it, using his strength and eagle vision to hit the woman at the base of her spine.

She fell from the tree, unconscious. Nix saw what was happening, but no one had time to react. Julius rushed from his spot to theirs in seconds, grabbing the woman and fleeing with her.

He was gone before they could stop him. Seth took the three back to Tyrus and Levi, who were bloodied from fighting, wolf-like scratches dotting their legs, arms and chest.

"What was that?"

Levi looked at him, and through labored breathing, replied, "someone who has a contract out on me. Apparently, she decided on going for the trophy kill, despite the contract being null now. I wonder if Dr. Blanc knows."

"Why would he risk this failing, risk the anger of Chimera?"

Levi looked at Nix. "There are worse things in the world than Chimera. Ancient, horrible beings that lurk, waiting for their chance to strike. It's very simple. This assassin is more afraid of the lurkers than she is of Chimera or Dr. Blanc."

"What kind of Mythic can do that to someone? She was unconscious and he was still under her control."

Levi looked at Nix, walked to her, and wrapped her in his arms. The others stood confused. "A siren." Nix pushed him away and walked backward. Her eyes filled with tears, and before anyone could stop her, she turned, walking toward the camp.

"What was that about?" Connor asked.

Tyrus placed a hand on Levi's shoulder. "That makes sense. Sirens are air elementals, which means she can communicate with her victims through the wind, even when unconscious. She also can control men, leading them to their death."

"No, I mean Nix."

Levi looked at the younger two. "Nix is fine."

"She was crying…"

"Leave her be. Whatever is in her heart, if she wanted us to know, she'd tell us. Don't spend years trying to figure her out like I did."

Levi and Tyrus began to walk back, Connor and Seth following. They were one man down for now, and that placed a weight on his heart. He was off playing Ambassador while his friend was taken over. If he'd been here, maybe things would have ended differently.

When they arrived, Nix had reached Honor, the flame dissipating. "You're gaining quite a lot of control. That's good." Honor smiled at the compliment.

"Where's Julius?"

"He's beyond our reach, for now. Let's get Joy inside."

Connor watched Levi do just that, walking inside, followed by the others, except Honor and Tyrus. They glanced at each other, a strange look passing between them. Confused, he didn't know what it meant, so he went inside. Maybe it would be better to give them their space.

Chapter 16

Honor stood, awkward and silent. Her hands in her pockets, she wanted to be the type of person who could just understand and admit what she was feeling. She found this particular situation so far outside her comfort zone that she wasn't sure what was in her heart. She kicked at the ground before she spoke.

"How…are you feeling?"

Tyrus smiled at her, but it didn't quite meet his eyes. "I'm okay, in large part thanks to you falling asleep on watch."

She kicked her feet in the dirt, again. "I was so tired."

"I keep wanting to view you as victims, due to the circumstances of your changing, but the more you learn and grow, the more I see you for who you are."

"Who am I?"

He tilted his head, looking at her with admiration. "Powerful. You managed to save me from something I thought I'd conquered fifty years ago. You, at twenty, did something even I couldn't do. The five of you are special."

"That's what Chimera said."

"Be wary of drawing too many celebrity Mythics to you. You never know their true intentions until they want you to, and then, it's often too late."

"How old do you think she is?"

"Thousands of years, I'd imagine. One of the oldest, and most powerful."

"I guess I'm lucky to be alive then."

"You are." He smiled gently at her.

"How do we get Julius back?"

"How indeed. We'll need a plan, and we won't be able to come up with it on our own." He held out a hand to her. She took it, and they walked inside the cabin, where Seth was lying next to a still unresponsive Joy.

"She's okay, she's just not waking up."

"Give her time." Nix sat down in front of Seth. "She's strong."

He nodded, and she placed a hand on his shoulder. Levi cleared his throat and said, "We need a plan."

"I agree." Tyrus let Honor's hand go and walked toward the group. "Any ideas?"

Levi tilted his head. "There's the obvious."

Nix stood. "No!"

"A trade would ensure the five remain intact."

"We aren't letting you sacrifice yourself for Julius, for *anybody.*"

Levi sighed. "Well, then what do we do, Nix?"

She turned. "We wait. If it's a trade she's after, she'll contact us. She won't turn Julius loose. We need a way to combat the power she has on men."

Levi held out his hand from his pocket. "I have an extra pair of these."

"What are they?"

"Noise cancelling earphones. Technology is great."

"We have to get those into his ears, though."

"Or…" Tyrus said it quietly, but everyone looked toward him. "Or…we take her out, avoid Julius and gain him back with her death."

Honor shivered, the memory of the dark forest still recent in her mind.

"How do we do that? She'll use him as bait, or a shield."

"True. She can use him however she wants, but even an air sign can't be everywhere at once. We need to think of this as an unconventional battlefield."

"What do you propose, Major?"

He looked at her. "I think we need to consider what Levi said."

She backed away as if he had slapped her. "No!"

"Hear me out. We are a group of seven vs a group of two, and we know Julius's strengths and weaknesses."

"He has *no* weaknesses."

"Okay, well, maybe his friends would be one."

"What are you talking about? He left Joy unconscious."

"He could have left her dead."

"You're saying he's able to resist her."

"I think so. He went after us, but he pushed the others away. I think the four are the key to getting him back."

"So, Levi is bait, we take out the siren and they corral him."

"Yes. We won't be able to control the environment. She'll have us meet where she desires, but the conditions, the momentum, there are always ways to turn the advantage. We need to look for those. We need Joy awake, and we need more of those earbuds.

"Connor, where exactly did you hit Siren with that rock?"

"Between the head and the top of the neck."

"We've got at least a day or two before she recovers then. Let's work on helping Joy heal."

"How do we do that?" Honor was confused. "She's our healer."

Tyrus gave her half a smile. "There are other ways to help the healing process. You talk to her, sing to her, even snuggling will help. You are the two that are closest to her, so you're on duty tonight."

The others left, and Seth sat with Honor watching over their best friend. For a while, the two didn't speak, just watched Joy, willing her to wake. It was Honor who broke the silence.

"Do you remember the first day the three of us met?"

"How could I forget?" Seth didn't look in her direction, but he did smile. "You walked into our seventh-grade class dressed all in black."

"It was January. Cold. I remember thinking it matched my heart. I was going to write a bad poem about it later."

"Marie was your partner for classwork. She was the polar opposite of you, all color. I can still remember the two of you looking at each other in horror."

Honor chuckled as the sadness pierced her heart. "We were friends by the end of the day."

"We got to lunch and Marie had you sit with us. You wouldn't eat meat. Remember?"

"I love chicken, now."

"You were taking a stand."

"I was."

"I was proud."

"Thank you."

"Do you remember lecturing us on why we don't need meat?"

She chuckled. "Yes. I was going through both a goth and a vegetarian stage."

"You also loved heavy metal."

"Well, that goes with the whole, black as my soul metaphor, right?"

"Why did you change?"

"I don't know. Over time, as we got close, as I realized I would get to stay in the same place for more than six months, I guess my outlook changed."

"That's a good thing."

"Oh, yeah. Black washed me out big time."

The silence stretched between them. "I miss Marie." Honor said it out loud, not expecting a response. Had she looked down, she would have seen a tear flow from Joy's eyes.

"I miss her too." Seth placed a hand on Honor's shoulder. When all three were connected, a bright light engulfed them. When Connor came to check on them an hour later, they were all unconscious…

"What happened?" Tyrus demanded as he entered.

"I don't know." Connor looked back at him. "I just came in to see how they were doing, and they were asleep."

Nix walked in and took a moment to assess. "You think she drew them in to the dream world?"

"She seems to like it there."

"Connor, do me a favor."

"What, Nix?"

"Go… touch them."

He looked at her like she was crazy. "Why?"

"I'm just testing a theory. Go tap Honor on the shoulder."

Connor walked over to the others who slept soundly. Reaching down, he hesitated a moment before touching Honor's shoulder. Nothing happened.

"Okay, so it's not a five thing. Must be a friend thing. We'll have to switch watch every two hours. Not many of us left." Nix walked back out. Connor looked at Tyrus, who shrugged.

"If she's not concerned, I'm not. Maybe this will help Joy wake more quickly."

"You two need to take care of your wounds."

He looked down as if he forgot he was bleeding, slowly. "Don't worry. Levi already healed himself. One of the benefits of being one hundred percent in tune with your beast is that they heal you during the change. Keep an eye on them." He walked out. A few moments later, the sound of a dragon's roar shook the cabin. Connor hovered over them, touching all three at the same time, and fell asleep....

They awoke together as well, hours later. Looking at each other stretch and wake, they felt refreshed, whole, as if they'd slept deeply for days.

Joy spoke first. "Do you think Jayde will be okay?"

Honor's eyes filled with tears. "There aren't enough of us to go after her. She has to be okay."

Joy felt a tear trail down her cheek. "She was so scared in the dream."

"I know. What can we do? We don't have enough people to go enough places."

"We can't help her until the five of us are a unit again. We need Julius to find her."

Tyrus walked in. "Good. You're all awake. How was the dream world? Any dark trees this time?"

Honor shivered. He saw it, but she didn't say anything else. Joy spoke up. "We were in the hospital with the newbie."

"How is she?"

The four looked at each other, not quite knowing how to

explain what had happened. “Not good. Put it on our list of things to do today.”

“We’ll find a way when we have Julius back. Here, boys. Wireless noise cancelling headphones for all of us.”

He tossed them to the others and walked out, saying, “ready in ten.”

The others looked at Honor. “Should we have told him the rest?”

Honor blushed. “No, no I guess that’s my job.”

Seth placed a hand on her shoulder, not speaking. Connor walked away, pulling the ear buds from the plastic harshly. “Let’s go.”

They stood, following their leader out of the cabin. They had a friend to find.

Nix stood with Levi, talking quietly as they waited for Tyrus to get the others. She turned to him and spoke softly.

“Are you sure you want to marry me?”

“Are you sure you can forgive me?”

“We’ve been through so much…”

“I know. I was there. I remember.”

She looked off into the forest, recalling a memory. “Do you remember the trip we took to Australia?”

“Yes. What about it?”

“You were different. The contract wasn’t for a kill, but a rescue.”

“Right. Rich girl needed saving.”

“We didn’t even know who she was.”

“No. It wasn’t our job. Everyone wanted her identity kept secret.”

“Should we have lifted her hood? Found out?”

“What are you getting at Nix?”

She sighed. “Something in my gut is pulling at me to recall that memory.”

Levi laughed. "Well, after we were done, your flame_"

She elbowed him in the stomach. "Stop it. I remember very well what my flame was doing that night."

"I was and always will be willing to help you with that."

"As we proved earlier this week. I know. Please stop bringing it up."

"I don't know why you're embarrassed. Makes me happy." He smiled, and she couldn't help but smile back. "See? I can still make you happy too."

Tyrus walked out, followed shortly by the others. Levi backed away. "We can talk about this later, right?"

"Right." All business, Nix turned away and walked to the four remaining. "Sit down. We need to talk strategy for when she contacts us next."

"I have a question." Joy added. Nix nodded for her to continue.

Joy smiled and asked, "when is the wedding?"

The others, shocked, looked at the two. Nix gave her a stare that would have turned anyone else into a frozen icicle. Joy, bouncy as always, didn't even care. The others began asking questions, and while Levi hammered out a stuttering answer, Nix placed her head in her hands. This would be a long meeting.

Tyrus found Honor after the meeting was over. She seemed upset. "What's wrong?" He wrapped an arm around her, the action making her feel both safe and warm. "I get to stay at the camp. *Again.*"

"I know it sounds like you're missing all the fun."

"I'm one of the most powerful Mythics here, yet you guys refuse to utilize me."

"While that's true, power without control is dangerous, not just to your enemies, but to yourself."

"I get that, it just seems like I haven't left camp in forever. It's boring. Look! See that? It's a tree growing." She even held out her hand to showcase its majesty beauty.

He laughed. "I get that its serene."

"It's getting old, keeping me here. I want to do something to help."

"Staying out of the way is helping." He stopped her and pulled her in front of him with his arm. "Do you think I want to have to worry about protecting you while I'm fighting?"

She searched his eyes. "Why would you worry? I can take care of myself."

Something haunted his eyes for a moment. "I've known three firebirds. Did you know that?"

"No. You never mentioned it. Who's the third?"

"The first phoenix was the woman who found me after my change."

"I take it she isn't around anymore?"

"No. She is not. Because of me."

"Why?"

"I was young and stupid."

"Are you calling me young and stupid?"

"You are not stupid, but you do lack experience with death."

"You're right. This closeness. Not just with you, but everyone. It's new to me. I didn't grow up with a caring family, so I wouldn't know what to do about losing you."

He hugged her then, bringing her close to him. In her ear, he whispered, "then understand that I don't want to lose *you*." He pulled away and walked on without looking back at her.

Honor waited. She wondered what had happened from his point of view in his nightmare. Since then, he'd been more at ease with her. She watched him walking away, and wondered how that made her feel.

She smiled slowly as he walked away, tilting her head slightly. Maybe it wasn't so bad to see him walk away. Her eyes narrowed for a moment.

"Am I interrupting something?" Joy had found her.

"No. What is it?"

"Tyrus talked to you."

"He did. Do you know everything?"

"No." She stated it as if it should be obvious.

"You sure?"

"If I did, there would be no point in continuing to exist."

"Okay. Did you need something?"

"I wanted to see how my best friend was doing."

"She's okay."

"Good. Because I have bad news."

"What is it?"

"I can't tell you."

"Then why did you bring it up."

"Oh, right." Then she walked away, leaving Honor wondering what was on her friend's mind.

They watched through the screen, careful this time, only using shadow. New pet was well connected. They would have to readjust their strategy. They weren't yet ready to come out.

The figure stood and used another shadow to watch another. A girl with the power of Gaia. Wonderful. Another earth sign. That meant that water was the next one up, then air.

Everything was cyclical. Everything that had happened before would happen again. The only thing that changed was the people. Except of course, for the dark and shadow.

Still, the girl could be of use. She knew of Joy and Joy knew new pet. They tapped shadow fingers in the darkness. Forming the plan, they walked out to the factory floor, where engineers were busy making prototypes. A sadistic smile crossed their face. She would be theirs, as would the world and everyone in it.

Chapter 17

Three days had passed since she'd attacked. Her thrall was looking quite famished. She needed to either feed or release her hold on him soon. Hopefully he would live long enough to finish her contract.

Sirena had spent a lifetime being groomed to handle hard to complete contracts like this. She'd taken out dozens of high priority targets, and this water monster would be no exception.

She swiveled in her office chair to look at the one she'd taken. His energy was wild, untamed. He was strong and had resisted her a couple of times already. She wasn't sure where his strength came from, but it was quite intriguing to be given a challenge after so many easy marks.

She sat on the couch next to him, his eyes vacant but his breathing heavy. Running a hand down his cheek, she watched him flinch. After three days of starving, no food, no water, he was still resisting her. She smiled and whispered, "All pets break eventually. You, puppy, are no different."

His breathing changed. She walked away, but a doubt trickled into her mind. She'd ordered him to kill and he'd only maimed. She'd ordered him to take her away and he had done so, but she had several bumps and bruises from the journey. She'd ordered him to sit, and he sat, but his energy smashed against hers, wearing her down.

She would hold on, of course. She would move the meet up to the next day, but she would win. It'd been her whole life. She'd used every advantage she had to survive, to grow, to punish men for their crimes. She would use this puppy to break the leviathan, and when that was done, she'd go after the others, just for the trouble they'd caused her. After all, less women, less competition.

Smiling, feeling better, she dialed her phone, ordering room service. She would eat, regain her strength, and then, she'd finish this contract. She looked down at her cell as it chimed, and the message below had her seething.

"Contract revoked. Please cease all activity. Payout will occur anyway."

She slammed the phone down, almost breaking the table it was on. She breathed calmly as Julius's breathing grew heavy. She sat contemplating a moment. She could walk away with the money, kill this pup, and live a long time on some quite beach resort. She could, but she wouldn't. The leviathan was more than a contract to her.

A memory began to form, of her waking, her first moment alive, and the Leviathan, standing over her…

She shook it off, staying in the present. She was not stopping. He'd evaded her attempts to kill him twice now. She would finish this for herself. This wasn't business. This was personal.

Tyrus received the call as the others heaved and sweated from exhaustion. He hung up with the info and walked toward them. Honor was the first one he came to. He placed a hand on her shoulder. She jumped but faced him.

"Sorry. I didn't mean to startle you."

Her eyes big, she said, "no, it's okay."

He sat next to her. "Do…we need to talk about this?"

"About what?"

"What happened in the forest? You look shaken. Is something on your mind?"

Yes, there was something on her mind, but it was jumbled, unclear, like if she thought about it her emotions would overwhelm her before she could determine exactly what it was that she felt. Taking a deep breath, she said, "I would like to talk about it, when I figure out what it is."

He nodded. "Okay." He gave her a soft look before standing. "Everyone, listen up!" He waited a moment. "We have received the call. Siren is asking for us to meet at the beach house, tomorrow, with Levi. She will initiate a trade, Julius for the water monster."

"But she won't get him." Joy placed her hands behind her back, kicking the dirt in front of her. "Duh, duh, duuuuh!"

"That's the plan. Everyone clear on their jobs and location?" Nodding heads were their reply. Honor didn't move. "Honor?"

She jumped again. "Sorry. What?"

"Are you clear on your job tomorrow?"

She laughed. "Uh, yeah, I have the easiest one."

He chuckled. "Well, you know."

"I know, my flame is too wild. I got it. I sit and am ready with the first aid kit."

"Remember what I taught you?"

"I'll make sure no one dies."

"A necessary job."

"Right." She resigned herself to her job, but no one said she had to like it.

"Everyone, you need to rest. Tomorrow will be…grueling to say the least. Spend your last night in camp taking time for self-care. Talk to those that matter. Nothing in our lives is guaranteed, especially a tomorrow."

He walked toward the water, obviously intent on meditation, or a swim. The others dispersed. Honor watched Nix and Levi walk away, as Joy and Seth moved in the opposite direction. Connor took something out of his pocket, placed it around his neck. It looked like a charm made of stone. Sitting near a bucket of water, he placed a hand in and was surrounded by blue magic.

Impressed, she surmised he must be communicating with his girl, Maiden. Rocking back and forth on her toes, she sighed. She didn't want to be alone, nor did she wish to be bored. Resolved, she walked toward the lake.

She waited while Tyrus meditated, until he'd swam for hours. She sat watching his progress. When he was finished with his routine, he saw her and smiled. He walked over and sat down next to her, towel drying his chest.

"What is it?"

She gazed at him uncomfortably. "Everyone else is…talking

with their S.O."

"Ah." He continued drying himself off. "Awkward for you."

"Very."

A small chuckle escaped him. "I get the feeling you aren't comfortable with affection."

She thought a moment. "It's not that."

"What is it, then? Everyone else is very hormone driven lately, and you seem to be above such things."

"I've…never really thought about it."

"Try. Knowing yourself is important."

She furrowed her brow, thinking back to any time she had a crush. "I think I have walls."

"They can be quite safe."

"I think that's why I have them, yes. Every time I had a crush, I just told myself I wouldn't be around long enough to see it through, so what point would there be in pursuing it?"

"Did you really move around that often?"

"I was considered a problem child."

"Your demeanor is so calm. I have a hard time seeing you as a troubled kid."

"I…developed that strength early."

"I imagine. Those walls must be difficult to let down."

She tilted her head at him. "Why would I let them down? They're there to protect me."

He nodded. "Of course, they are. You do an excellent job of protecting yourself, but there is a cost with walls."

"Such as?"

"They keep out…life as well as threats."

She thought about that for a moment. "You…think I'm missing the experience of being in love because my walls are up."

"Its…a possibility you should think about. Ultimately, who you are will always be your decision. No one should or could force those walls down. Speaking as a person who has had a similar experience, though," he moved his hands as if he were physically trying to locate the words. "Love comes with an…openness, a vulnerability that can break you, but it can also heal you.

"I only wonder if you've had the time to explore what you want, what you need, what you would like to see in a life partner. You can't do that with your walls up so high. You'll be safe, but you'll never…really be free."

He walked away and she thought for hours on that very subject, wondering about his query. She was so lost in her thoughts that she missed the sunset. Her brow furrowed; it wasn't until she heard Joy's giggle that she came out of her head. Looking at her friend, she smiled.

Joy jumped up and down, dancing in place. "You're growing, my friend."

"Am I?"

Eyes wide, Joy sat down. "Yes. It's amazing. Like watching a rose bloom." She looked around Honor as if she were seeing something her friend couldn't. "It changes…everything." When a squeak, she was enveloped in a bear hug. Struggling to breathe, she whispered, "Joy…"

"Oop." Joy released her. "Sorry. Time to sleep!" She skipped back to the cabins and Honor followed. She needed sleep.

Morning came too early for everyone. Honor rose with the sun and walked out to see the entire squad ready to depart.

Tyrus smiled at her briefly, Joy giggled, and Honor glared. Clearly his throat, he said, "are all teams ready?"

Everyone nodded. Honor sighed when he looked at her, but signaled she was as well. They would go their separate ways and finish this, now.

"Good. Team A. If you please."

Nix, Levi and Joy stepped close to each other. A flash of water and they vanished. Tyrus looked at her. "Be back soon."

Seth and Connor walked to him and the three were gone a moment later. Honor sat, feeling alone, and began to whistle. Her phone and supplies next to her, she stretched, and began to meditate yet again.

Siren watched from the distance. She knew they'd leave the young phoenix alone with the right motivation. She turned to her pet and whispered through the air, "*kill her.*"

Julius began walking toward his friend, and Siren vanished in a burst of wind. By the time she was done with the others, there would be one less fly to swat.

Seth stopped the bounce early, which caused a strange tear in the fabric of time. They leapt through, but as they reached the ground, they smashed ungracefully into a tree. He hurt all over from changing the location mid-jump. Tyrus and Connor lay on the ground moaning. Seth was not feeling much better. It was like his atoms wanted to rip apart.

"What the hell?" Tyrus regained his composure slowly.

Connor groaned, holding his stomach as if it would burst open. "Dammit, Seth!"

He caught his breath and tried to speak. He couldn't. Tyrus walked to him awkwardly. "Come on, catch your breath. You'll be okay. Just tell me why you changed the plan."

Seth tried again to speak, but his throat ached. He collapsed to the ground and wrote the first word he could think of that his gut was screaming for him to get out. "Honor!"

Tyrus looked at it, and back at Seth. "Shit." He turned away, each step aching. "Seth, Connor, get in position when you can. I'll go back for her."

"How can you…" He tried to speak again, but it was no use.

"It's not my first broken portal. Your body gets used to the pain. I'll make it, I'll help her, but we still need to go ahead with the plan for Siren. Can you handle it?"

Seth nodded. "Good." Tyrus turned, his eyes shifting from human to snake. His scales crawled over his body, changing his form. When the dragon was whole, he took off, flying back to the camp, but as he reached the air, he breathed fire, angry. They were so far, it would take several minutes for him to get back to her. He hoped she could hang on until he arrived.

Team A arrived at the coordinates given to them for the exchange. Joy was hidden, away from Nix and Levi. Her job was to be ready to heal them if they needed it. Nix and Levi stood, waiting on the small island, ready to do their part.

For a long silent moment, nothing happened. Nix looked around, but nothing save the ocean waves made a sound. Levi squeezed her hand once, quickly, before releasing it and walking forward.

The wind picked up, swirling around them both. Levi's platinum hair flew wildly around his face, blocking his view. Nix felt the wind around her pick up, before flinging her back, away from Levi, at the other end of the long beach. He turned in time to see her fall, and she didn't get back up. The wind had been knocked out of her.

Levi pulled his hair back, out of his face. His eyes shone blue, the water inside him churning like a storm. The wind formed a shape out of the sand. A woman's shape rose to greet him. He stared after the shape and smiled.

"Sirena."

"Leviathan."

They stared at each other, each mentally sizing up their opponent. Levi knew this would occur. Knew she couldn't be trusted to keep her word. There would be no exchange, only a battle, with one person walking away. The ocean waves began to churn, and the wind picked up. He placed his hands in fists in front of him, ready to meet this challenge, water and wind ready to wreak havoc on the small island.

Creating a shield, he protected Nix with water, cocooning her from the wind's force. He wouldn't allow Sirena to use his love against him. The sand figure grew denser, the particles compounding so it was more rock than sand. Levi took one slow, deep even breath. He shut his eyes for a moment, and when he opened them again, she attacked…

Joy felt it beginning from her vantage point. She sat on another island, surrounded by tropical plants, meditating on her friend's locations. She could see them all. If she opened her eyes, she would have seen the plants and animals on the island grow calm, coming into the open, near her. Her body began to glow as her energy grew, condensing inside her.

She smiled as she located Connor and Seth. She felt their pain as if it was her own, but she didn't fall back from it, merely embraced it, taking it away from them. They were the first priority. Without them, the plan would fail.

She focused all she had on their essence, their soul. Had she been next to them, she would have seen the same event unfolding, animals calming, revealing themselves, trees growing as if a year had passed in a moment. Seth and Connor stood, she felt it, felt the moment the pain absolved and left their beings.

She smiled and moved on.

Honor sat by the fire, bored out of her mind. It'd been seconds, yet it felt like ages since her friends left. She was beginning to meditate, when she heard a branch break behind her. She reacted quickly, and just in time, summoning her bird like instinct. The wings lifted her off the ground, and her firebird saved her from Julius's charge, which sent him ahead of her and into a tree, which broke clean through, falling with a crash.

She looked at him, and he growled back at her. His eyes, normally comical and alive, looked vacant and dead. No emotion flowed from his being. It was as if she was seeing a shell of the real person she'd come to know over the past two years. He picked up a large stone, and lifted it over his head, before throwing it in her direction. She was able to evade it easily.

"Julius," she began, hoping to reach him, "I know this isn't you. You have to fight it!"

For a second, she thought she saw hesitation on his face, before he turned to pick up another large stone. This time, instead of throwing it, he ran in her direction, jumping with all his might, as if to smash her with it. Again, she evaded him, continuing her attempt to free him. "Julius! Dammit, it's me. I'm your friend. You can do this."

Julius rounded, his fisted hands relaxing for a moment, before reaching again for a weapon. If he's still fighting, that means you're taking energy away from her. The longer she could keep him fighting, keep him resisting, the more she would weaken their enemy.

"Julius, I know you, and this isn't you. She isn't stronger than you." He threw another stone. "You are Cerberus! You're more loyal than anyone I've ever met. You need to break free of her." He threw a stone again, but his movements were slow. Honor knew he could move faster than this. That meant it was taking all of his willpower to fight her, but that he was trying.

"Try harder." She could evade like this for the entire day if she had to. As long as he didn't change his strategy, she would be okay.

Levi and the sand figure were locked in a battle on the beach. Nix, cocooned in water, was still unconscious, laying on the ground. Connor and Seth had not yet arrived, which was not part of the plan. Levi took the punches and hits from the sand creature, biding his time. No need to waste his energy prematurely.

Had he noticed anything around him, he would have seen the great storm brewing around the beach. Air fought with water, the waves forming circles, beginning to rise as if a hurricane was forming. On land, the air was swirling in the clouds, forming a tornado. The two would end up destroying everything around them, if no one intervened. The earth reacted to their fight, the forces of nature itself caught up in their momentum. Levi took another punch, wondering where his back up was…

Connor and Seth, arriving late, still made it to their location, another island farther from the battle. They looked at the storms brewing, and Connor said, "We had better hurry."

"I'll search with my portals, you use your wings. She has to be here somewhere."

They split up, hoping Seth's gut had made the right call. The sand creature was not the real threat. Somewhere, Sirena sat, safe and alone, summoning these forces. If they could find her, they could end this. The only question was, where on this island was she?

Tyrus flew, immune to the cold atmosphere of the clouds. He was almost there, the pain tearing through his body, threatening to slow him down. He just needed to make it back, and everything would be okay. Thinking of Honor lying on the ground, bleeding, he willed his mind to ignore the pain, flying faster. He had to get there in time…

Joy looked for the next person to heal. Her choices were Tyrus or Nix. She had to make a decision, and she did so quickly, as her energy could only go to one point on earth at a time. She was not yet powerful enough to heal more than that.

She made the decision based on danger and need. Sorry, Nix. Tyrus needs to make it to Honor first. Her decision made, her energy focused, she reached out to him and began to heal. She watched as his pain flowed away from him, his dragon form flying faster, now close to the camp. She smiled, but her head was starting to hurt from the effort. She had to keep going…

Connor and Seth both used their powers to surround the island quickly, check in every location from North to South, East to West. They covered their ground quickly, but it was a large island, and they each worried that she would be hidden in some hard-to-reach cave. Still, they quickly scoured the earth, looking for signs of Mythic activity. They had to find her…

Levi flew back, knocking into the sand. The wind left him for a brief second before he recovered, and he was able to cross his arms in front of him as the sand creature attacked, blocking the fist with his forearms. The creature grew in strength every second, and it was getting more difficult for him to casually take these punches. The power this Siren had was remarkable, but he wasn't ready yet to show his true strength. He had to hold on a little longer.

Honor evaded another attack by her friend. Julius was slowing, sweat dripping from his brow. If she could keep him occupied, she may end up helping the others. She readied a fire ball, changing the momentum of the battle. Let's make her work for it.

She hurled a slow ball at her friend, enough so that he could dodge it, but not slow enough for her to know. It was effective. Hurling additional flame balls, she forced the Siren to engage her, instead of Levi. *You aren't taking him without a fight.*

Julius turned, and she saw another emotion flash in his eyes, but this was anger. She didn't think it was his emotion. She smiled, and then she laughed. The anger grew.

Out loud, she said, "Am I pissing you off, Siren? Did you really think it'd be that easy?" Honor hurled another flame ball, and Julius leapt toward her. Here we go…

Levi stood, his water aiding his recovery, as the sand creature became less dense in front of him. Someone was draining her power. Good. It would give him the time he needed to recover. Calling his water, he commanded the ocean to swirl around the figure, crushing it underneath. Now was his chance to fight back.

◆ ◆ ◆

Connor and Seth met at the beach. They were both breathing heavily, sweating. "You done?"

"Yeah," Connor turned toward the caves. "We both kind of knew she was in there, right?"

"Right."

"You good?"

"I think so…"

"Let's go."

The two walked toward the large mountain in the center of the island, old and worn, with hundreds of large caves and tunnels carved out of it. "This could take a while…"

Joy sensed their energy was draining, and they were essential for the fight, so she focused once again on Connor and Seth. She watched them enter the cave and gave them endurance for the fight that was to come. Once again, she had to wait to help Nix, who was still lying unconscious on the beach. Her headache had turned into a full migraine, straining her concentration, but she continued. The foliage was growing around her, enveloping her now, the animals laying down near her energy. She didn't even notice. A small trail of blood left her nose. She didn't care.

Tyrus came to the camp and saw Honor battling Julius below. He watched as she expertly controlled the battlefield, taunting the Siren, evading her attacks. The downside to taking a thrall was the large amount of concentration required to do simple tasks. Obviously,

Honor knew what she was doing, but it was also going to cost her, too. She was calling an enormous amount of firepower she normally would control. He was impressed by the beauty of it, but also worried she would call too much, considering how much they had been pushing her, lately.

He smiled as his dragon set him down, several yards from the battle. He changed back into his human form and jogged to help her. They had to force her to give Julius up. With enough pressure, she would have to. No Mythic's power was boundless.

Seth and Connor raced through the caves, each taking a different path, Connor always turning right, Seth always turning left. When they reached a dead end, they turned back to the next point where they could make another decision. With this method, they were able to quickly cover the massive amount of ground inside the curvy caves, until at last they came to a large structure in the middle with a hole in the ceiling. Ancient writings littered the walls, with pictures of Mythics and names written down. They looked at each other, coming from opposite sides. This was another Mural…

"If this is all you've got, you must not be a real assassin. I'd think you'd have a better strategy than throwing *rocks*." Honor said this as she evaded another rock.

Julius stopped a moment, as if he were a robot with no power left, then as Honor waited in the air, his muscles gathered, and he moved with lightning speed in her direction. She flew above him and kicked his back into the trunk of a tree. "Oops. Sorry Julius."

He bounced off of the tree with his feet, and the force flung him back to her. She tried to evade, but this time he made contact, grabbing her around the waist and squeezing the air out of her lungs as they fell to the ground. *Dammit, I should know how durable he is.*

They fell to the earth, and as her lungs emptied, she summoned her bird to lash out for her. Her body hit the ground with a thud, Julius rolled off of her, but the flame around her healed her instantly, orange fire dancing around her body. She was up a second later, and her power, which she had tried so carefully to control, was let loose, to do what it did best.

Julius attacked again, but before she could use her moves, Tyrus was there, rushing the younger man to the ground. Honor waited as they fought, her flame dissipating. A frown lit her face, and she said, "hey! I was doing it!"

Tyrus tackled Julius, holding him by the waist and slamming him to the ground. "I know. Just…" Julius grabbed him by the shoulder, trying to get leverage to choke him. "Helping."

Honor rushed over to the two, ready to help. No way was she going to sit on the sidelines while Tyrus took all the damage.

Levi's breathing heaved, as the sand creature had been turned to water by the force of his element. For a few moments, he would have the time to rest. Turning, he walked to Nix, who was still not awake. He touched her cheek gently, and muttered, "Joy, where are you?"

She was just about to get to Nix when she saw Connor and Seth engage the Siren, herself. That was the plan after all, to get this bitch. Saying a silent prayer again, she focused on those two, granting them her energy, as they started their attack.

Connor and Seth saw her in the middle of the Mural, meditating silently. Her body was covered in sweat, the wind flowing fiercely around her. Connor and Seth looked at each other, their energy renewed, and silently signaled. Seth went low, Connor when high, and they ran into the center of the room, straight into the force of her wind.

Tyrus wrestled with Julius, Honor getting in her punches where she could. If Julius got a hold of her again, he could easily defeat her with his strength, but she had the greater mythical power. His pain gone, he was able to meet half-changed Cerberus punch for punch, blow for blow as they grappled on the ground. Getting the upper hand, he grabbed him by the neck, only to have Julius headbutt him. The world swam for a moment, but it was enough for Julius to get away, and focus his attack on the target opponent. Standing and chasing after him, Tyrus managed to tackle him before he made it to Honor. They just had to hold on a little longer, until Siren broke.

Connor and Seth both broke the barrier at the same time, and their steps slowed. They had to fight the strong wind, ending up walking more sideways to the middle than straight through. Siren had to know that they were here now, and she focused more of her energy on her barrier, slowly their progress to mere inches. Luckily, Joy's energy surrounded them, making them glow, protecting them from the worst of the wind's wrath.

They made slow steady progress toward the middle, and their enemy's power was diverted again.

Levi withdrew the water, as the sand creature was not yet back. He cradled Nix in his lap, waiting for her to open her eyes. She did soon after, looking up at him.

"Is it over?"

"This is the calm before the storm."

"Damn. Her power's strong."

"She's old."

"Older than you?"

He laughed. "There's only one Mythic I know that's older than me, and it's not Sirena."

"You know her?"

"A tale for another day, maybe."

"She seems to be very into your death."

"I'm not dead yet."

Nix laughed, but her side hurt. "Why am I still in pain? Where's Joy?"

"Helping someone else, I'm assuming."

"Well, that sucks for me."

"Don't worry," he kissed her forehead, "I got you."

She smiled. "I know. You've always had me."

A confused expression lit his face. "You aren't dying, are you?"

She laughed again, despite the pain. "No, just drained and tired."

"Good. I'm not ready to lose you yet."

"I'm okay. Don't worry about me."

"That's… asking me not to worry about breathing."

"Not going to happen?"

"Never."

Nix pointed in front of them. The sand was beginning to reform. "You need to worry about her."

Levi put her down, a wall of water hiding her from the battle. He turned and readied himself for the full force of the Siren's song. Now that she was no longer fighting fully on three fronts, he would be able to have a challenge. He laughed aloud. He was ready and waiting.

Chapter 18

Connor and Seth, with Joy's help, advanced halfway toward Siren's refuge. They trudged forward slowly, as the wind swirled around them, biting into their arms and faces. Joy's energy kept them going. Seth suddenly stopped, allowing the wind to take him, swinging him out towards the rock wall. He hit hard, and the air fled his lungs. When he had breath again, he shouted into the wind, but Connor could not hear.

"Get out of there. It's a trap! Connor!"

Seth bounced to him and tapped him on the shoulder, as Sirena smiled and opened her eyes, full of vibrant yellow light. Before Seth could bounce back out, the ceiling collapsed on top of them, as if being smashed by an outside force.

Sirena stood, slowly, her smiling growing. She shook the dust off her hands and her clothing and stretched slowly. Two down, a few more to go. It'd been a long time since she'd been so in touch with her power. It was invigorating.

Joy opened her eyes, her concentration momentarily interrupted. Tears fell as she struggled to control her breathing, as the knowledge that her friends may be death wrapped around her heart and squeezed tightly. She wiped the blood from her face, and stood, but the effort it took was tremendous. She needed to sit. She couldn't help them right now.

Sitting back down, slowly, she focused on healing herself, so she could save Seth and Connor, whose life forces were slowly fading away.

Levi watched as three new sand creatures rose in front of him. *Great, I finally get a real fight.* Around him, dark clouds overshadowed the island, as the hurricane formed at sea from the use of his power. Her wind matched it, and soon, the tornado would be ready to meet its cousin in a clash of water and air. When Joy healed Nix, everything would go according to plan. There were too many of them to fail. He just had to stay strong until she could.

"Come on, Joy." It was a whisper, but it reached her ears.

Honor and Tyrus stood, facing Julius, whose bond with Siren seemed stronger than ever. His speed had increased, as if he no longer had the strength to ignore her commands. Now, instead of controlling the field, Honor only sought to avoid his blows.

Tyrus took most of them, half in dragon form, half human. It gave him an edge over Julius, but he didn't want to hurt him, only stop him. He held back and was taking hits for doing so.

"Julius!" Honor tried again, moving out of the way just in time to avoid being kicked. Instead, the tree behind her shattered, and she found herself jumping out of the path of the falling wood.

Tyrus shouted, "Honor, it's no use. She's stronger than ever. We need to neutralize him, now."

"Wait!" She tried again. "Julius!" For her trouble, he attacked, and this time the kick landed in her chest, the force propelling her back against a tree. Luckily, through the pain, she summoned her firebird, and the flame cushioned the blow, healing her.

"Tyrus, do it!" She said back to him, and she watched as he fully transformed, his dragon coming into view. Joy could always heal Julius later, right? She drew his attention with balls of flame, as Tyrus became his dragon.

He lunged at the younger man, who scrambled to get back up, but the dragon was faster than he was. Tyrus almost had him pinned beneath his claws, and Honor could see the will of the Siren leaving his eyes. "Almost!"

Then, they felt it. A moment where the world seemed to shift, to change. A wave of air came from somewhere far away, sweeping over them, causing chaos in its wake. All three of them fell to the ground, and for a moment, no one moved. The Siren had…changed, unleashed some power she'd been holding back. Honor propped herself up on her elbow, and watched as Julius changed, his eyes becoming wolf, golden as he began to change. She had no clue what had just happened, but her friend was gone. This was all Siren. Fear gripped her for a small moment, but then he attacked, fully transformed for the second time.

Seth bounced out of the rubble, leaning next to a tree. He wished he had the strength to save Connor, but with the blood pouring from his side, he knew that was his last bounce. His breathing grew heavy, and he fell unconscious.

Not far from him, Connor awoke beneath the stone rubble, and panic gripped him. "Seth! Where are you?!"

When no one answered, he tried to remove the stone, but it was no use. Even for him, this was too heavy. With a last breath, he whispered, "soluis, a thoirt dhachaidh mi." Then he too, was gone.

Joy felt it, the moment they left. She wailed, opening her eyes, screaming to the heavens. She watched through her mind's eye as Connor whispered the ancient words, and though she didn't know the language, she knew in her heart it was a wish to come home.

She felt a change, a shift in the fate of the world. Her crying stopped as she glimpsed the future, and a small smile played across her features. She finished healing herself, and then she opened a portal, momentarily gone from the battle.

Levi breathed heavily, lying on the ground. as the force that propelled Honor and Tyrus down had also swept over him. He used the water to stand upright, the sand creatures now gone. Relief flooded him, as they'd gotten a few good blows in. He bled from his nose, his knuckles, and he knew he would have a black eye soon. In their stead, was the woman herself.

"Why, Sirena?" The name came from his lips, but it was just a whisper.

She smiled, deadly as he said it. "I woke from the abyss, alone and afraid. I knew nothing of who I was, or where I was. And the one thread that I had to hang on to, was you. And you walked away. Now, you pay for that."

Levi laughed loudly.

She tilted her head, confused. "You think this is funny?" A curious expression lit her features.

"Yes, irony is funny to me. You've indeed forgotten who you really are."

"I don't know what you're talking about." She paced back and forth, suddenly unsure of herself. "I've taken down all of your comrades. The wolf finishes with the dragon as we speak. The two you sent for me in the cave are dead. Your ally lies hurt and broken, and your unicorn has fled, leaving you alone. All those things are expected. How is this ironic?"

He laughed again, so much so that he grabbed his stomach to keep the pain at bay. She tilted her head, eyeing him oddly. He finally quieted enough to speak. "You are old. Ancient. I know for a fact that you've lived for over a millennium."

"How do you know this when even I don't know how old I am?"

"You forgot the rule."

"What rule?"

"The code of the Mythics. Family first."

"I have no family."

"That would be where you are mistaken, but I don't blame you for forgetting them." His eyes grew sad then.

"Don't you dare pity me. I came here to end you, to finish this, and I shall." The wind surrounded her form, building in intensity as her power collected around her. Levi allowed his water to do the same, collecting around him, the hurricane and tornado around them drawing closer to each other, until they were both one with the storm…

Tyrus launched at the three-headed dog, his dragon teeth snapping as the heads snapped back. Honor was flying nearby, waiting for her turn to take over the battle. They were wearing him down, but it was taking some time to do so.

He glanced at Honor for a moment, and that was all it took for Cerberus to grab his neck. The heads bit down, and the dragon let out a fierce roar.

Honor saw it, and her heart sank. Whatever this woman was, she was very powerful. She hoped the others wouldn't be much longer…

But why was she waiting for someone else? Indeed, that didn't make sense. Why should she wait for someone else to save her when she could end this now?

She dropped to the ground, suddenly strong and certain. Eyeing the dog, she threw rocks at him until he looked at her. "Hey! Stupid! I'm talking to you Siren! You got the dragon, now come and get me."

The dog let out a fierce growl, and bunched his body together, ready to pounce. A smile lit Honor's face. *Here we go.* Cerberus leapt toward her, and she sent her flame toward and away from her, as she'd done on the rooftop, splitting her flame and creating a shockwave of fire.

The dog hit the first blast, yelping as it burned. She kept the fluxuation going, let the flame wash over her. When she opened her eyes, the orange flame danced against her grey irises, no longer overtaking her. The fire pulsed out in a circle around her body. Cerberus was caught in the blasts, each shock throwing him further and further away. His front paws burnt from the flames, and he yipped loudly and withdrew.

It was enough to allow Tyrus to recover, and he did so,

smashing his dragon's body into the dog, knocking Julius instantly unconscious. As Honor stood, her flame enveloping her, Tyrus changed back to his human form, quickly. Rushing to her, as she tried to stop the waves. Fear was evident on his face.

She laughed at it. What in the world did he have to be afraid of? Julius was safe, far from where Sirena could hurt him. They were safe. He wasn't bleeding.

"Get the earplugs in."

He did so quickly while Julius moaned on the ground. When he stood again, he turned to her and approached her slowly. "Honor…"

"What?" She felt so alive. She felt like fire herself. Like it was coursing through her. She looked down, and her hands, instead of being surrounded by flame, had turned into flame.

This brought her out of the spell her power had given her, and she realized what Tyrus was worried about. "What's happening?" The waves wouldn't stop.

"What happens to Mythics who can't control their power!" He had to shout it over the roar of the flames.

"How do I stop it?"

"Try to control it. Now!"

She did, summoning all the strength she'd gained in meditation, and focused on controlling her flame. The fluctuations had grown stronger, until choosing to release or to pull in were both no longer an option. She tried calming herself but found that fear was more compelling. At a loss, she glanced at Tyrus, apologetically, and ran away.

She ran until her lungs hurt, through the forest, while Tyrus shouted at her to stop. The pulses slowed as she physically exhausted herself. She ran as if she could extinguish the flames if she was fast enough. She ran until her pounding heart couldn't take it anymore. She ran as if her life depended on it.

When she stopped, when she was so exhausted that she could barely walk, she was near his cave, where he had hidden to heal. She crawled into it and doused herself in the pool of water that lay inside it.

Still, it was no use. The flame burned so hot that the water in the pool vaporized in mere seconds, sending a cloud of steam out into the forest.

Tyrus found her easily then, in the hole left from the water that was no longer present. He glanced down at her, but the flame was still burning, her arms and legs pure fire. If it reached her torso, she'd combust. She looked up at him, and said, "I don't know how to stop it. I've tried everything."

He sighed, heavily, and sat next to her on the edge of the pool. "No, no you haven't tried *everything*, Honor." He reached for her then, and she backed away. "What are you doing? You know what will happen if the flame touches you."

"I'm only trying to help. Do you trust me?"

"I just don't think you can."

"Honor, you have to control this flame."

"I can't!"

"Do you *trust me* to help you?"

She felt those walls come down, just enough for her to say, "Yes."

His mouth grew tight, and he walked forward, into her flame.

"Stay back!" She tried to draw away from him, but he grabbed her by her shoulders.

"Honor, release your phoenix."

"What? Why?"

"This flame, this power you're calling, you're not ready for it. It's too powerful, even for you. We pushed you too hard, and your body and soul are burning through itself. Release your power into your phoenix, and she will deal with it. Just, set her free. Tell her to go."

"What will happen to me?"

"You'll probably fall asleep."

"What will she do to get rid of the power?"

His eyes changed then, growing soft and kind. It was look he hadn't given her before, and she was unsure what it meant. He brushed her flaming hair away from her face.

"She will..." he cleared his throat. "She will fly until someone strong enough can stop her."

Chimera's words echoed in her head. You do not know your destiny...Your Dragon.... Certain fates are intertwined ...

"Who is strong enough to stop all of this?"

He drew close and said, "my dragon can handle her. Just do it, before the flame consumes us both!"

She hesitated, and he drew close to her. "Release your firebird!" With that shout, his lips descended upon hers. When they touched, a spark flowed from his body through hers, the passion from the kiss directing the flame away from her and into her bird.

She felt it, then, a tension leaving her being, as she thought, *be free*. She felt her phoenix take her fire from her, felt her rise away, and saw Tyrus loose his dragon before the blackness consumed her. She lay motionless in his arms, breathing softly. Her head lay on his shoulder, and their heartbeats slowly crept back to normal.

She flew across the sky, free for the first time, free like a winged queen should be. She dipped and soared, leaving a trail of smoke in her wake. Her flames emboldened her, diving toward the earth to rise again at the last minute. She flew fast, in circles, painting the sky with her fire.

The dragon gave chase, and she increased her speed. Merrily, she avoided him, evading and circling the beast until he let out a roar, and then she fled, as instinct told her to, but this was not about fear. This was a test, her question a pattern of rhythm and movement, an intricate, beautiful melody of her own design. His answer, harmonic, complimentary to her pattern, adding power to her beauty.

They flew so fast, that slowly, their shapes faded, until only two comets lit the sky, one orange, one red, their flames trailing behind them. Intricately, they made a path, weaving a tapestry of warm color, ornate and delicate in its design. When she rose up, climbing straight toward the stars, he pursued her, using all his strength to match and overcome her speed.

As he reached her, their wings, visible for a moment, wrapped around each other, and they hovered in the air for a moment, entwined, before they began to fall back to earth.

The comet of their combined energy fell toward the camp, which lay underneath. Their speed increased as they approached, the fire from both of them propelling them faster toward the ground. With great and powerful force, they hit the earth, creating a crater where trees once stood. Smoke and dust rose, the earth shaking from the weight of it all. Trees broke and scattered, their roots uplifted, and steam from the earth rose to the sky.

When it was clear, when the dust had settled, the steam a memory, the two beasts lay in the crater, the dragon making a perfect circle from head to tail. The phoenix stretched her wings around his body, and as she touched him, his scales changed from red to orange. Safe within the circle of him, she shielded her mate from the rain.

Julius woke as if from a long, hurtful dream. He lay in the forest, surrounded by broken trees. His head felt heavy, his body aching, and he was starving. The last thing he remembered was…

Foggy. He really couldn't tell where his last memory was. Standing, slowly, he leaned against a tree trunk until his breathing became even. Then, he stretched each of his limbs, deciding how badly he was injured. Noting the earplugs, he started to remove them, but something made him hesitate.

Realizing he could walk, he looked around. A burning path, full of smoke, lay to the left. He followed it. It wound around the forest, past the lake and into a large cave. Stepping inside, he noted that Tyrus was kneeling on the ground, Honor in his arms, a small orange flame burning in her hand.

"Honor!" He vaguely remembered battling her. What had happened to him? "Honor, are you okay?"

When she didn't respond, he knelt down and pulled her body

into his arms, relieving Tyrus. Worried he had done this, he lowered his head, feeling her breath and pulse. She was alive. After checking with the dragon, he lifted Honor up and started back to the camp…

When she woke, she was on the couch at the main cabin. Her head clear, feeling well rested, she stretched before a voice startled her.

"Honor."

She turned to see Julius at her bedside. "You're you again." She smiled and hugged him. "That's good to see."

Tears filled his eyes. "I found the both of you in a cave. Did I…"

"Did you what?"

"Did I hurt you?"

"No, no, the Siren hurt you. How are you feeling?"

"Hurt, bruised, but I have my mind back again."

"Good." She looked out into the hall.

"Tyrus is okay, just resting."

She breathed a sigh of relief. "Good."

"What happened in that cave?"

Changing the subject, she said, "We have to find the others. Now."

They walked to his room, where Tyrus was rubbing his head. She sat next to him on the bed and touched his head. "You alright?"

He smiled. "Yeah. You?"

"I'm fine."

"Good."

Awkward. They're both acting awkward around each other. Out loud he said, "Look, I don't know what's wrong, but aren't we supposed to be helping the others?"

Tyrus stood, and said, "I'll change quickly then we can leave." He shut the door as they left.

Julius turned to Honor. "You aren't going to discuss that, are you?"

"No." She wouldn't even meet his gaze.

"Are you really okay?"

"Yes." She walked forward and stretched again. "In fact, I feel…in control. Like I finally have a handle on my power." Testing it, she let the flame coalesce in her hand. "See?" With a flick of her mind, it was gone again. "It's not overwhelming me anymore."

"That's great."

Tyrus came out, ready to leave, dressed in black from head to toe. Julius watched as Honor stared after him. Strange….

"Let's go," he said. "We need to check on the others. Julius, you hold down the camp."

They walked out like a unit, locking in step with each other. Julius tilted his head. *What had happened in that cave?*

"Which team are we starting with?" Honor asked as they left. Tyrus turned to her and said, "B. Seth and Connor."

"Great, let's fly."

"Honor…"

"What?"

"Are you sure you're okay after what happened?" He placed both hands on her shoulders.

"Yes. Now's not the time."

"I agree." He stepped back and summoned his wings, now a bright vibrant orange. Honor smiled at him, finding the change beautiful. He flew ahead of her and she summoned her own. Catching up, they flew in unison to the south.

Connor felt the weight of the stone being lifted off of him, but he had no strength left in his body. He couldn't even summon the will to open his eyes. He felt gentle hands carry him toward the shade, felt them lower him to the grass. Then a feeling of water rushed over him, and the abyss claimed him again…

◆ ◆ ◆

Honor and Tyrus landed at Team B's location some time later, too late to do anything but survey the scene. The large island was intact, but the cave structure in the middle was rubble. Tyrus turned to her, but she knew how she could help. "On it." With her flame, she began to shove the rocks away.

Moments later, they realized their futility. "They aren't here anymore, are they?"

Tyrus shook his head. "No. It appears that they got away. Team A?"

She nodded, and they left the island, traveling further south.

Nix woke, dizzy. It felt like she'd hit her head, but she used her flame expertly to heal it quickly. She remembered where they were and what they were doing. Standing, the water around her receding, she surveyed the beach. The wind threatened to knock her down, storms raging around her. The island was being torn apart by the power of the two Mythics.

She slowly walked toward Levi, her flame protecting her from most of the wind's force.

"Levi!"

He didn't respond, so she walked into the center of the hurricane that had formed around him. Breathing heavily, with exhaustion, she touched his shoulder.

His concentration didn't waver, but he did say, "You feel better?"

"Yes."

"Took Joy long enough to heal you."

"How long had it been?"

"A few hours of this."

"You've been at this for hours?" Shock filled her eyes.

He laughed. "She's old, but I'm older."

"You never did tell me how old you were."

He looked at her then. "Very."

"Very old?"

"Yes." He didn't say another word, just went back to controlling his storm.

"So, what are you thinking?" Her voice was all business.

"We need to wear her down. She'll give before I do, and she was fighting on three fronts. She'll give eventually, then we attack. Stay by me and you'll be safe."

She locked her hands with his, and said, "We got this."

He smiled. "Yes, we do."

Her flame surrounded him, and spread into the hurricane, the two powers mixing, sparks flying, and together, began to overcome the tornado. Just a little longer, and their opponent would be dust.

They saw the storm before they saw the island. A massive system of clouds and churning water lay ahead of the both of them. Sensing a question, Tyrus shouted to her.

"We need to find an opening."

"I agree. The wind will rip us apart."

"Can you keep flying?'

She laughed. "I've got this."

"Good. Stay with me. When we see our chance, we'll take it."

Flying around the edges of the storm, where the wind was not yet strong, they waited in the air for the part they would play.

Joy bounced back to her meditation spot, finally ready to get back to the battle. She sat, and the glow surrounded her quickly, even though she'd been using her powers heavily.

She searched for the island, for the storm, and finding it, honed in on the others. A small, slow smile spread on her lips, and calm settled around her. They had this…

Then, it hit. A large, sudden boom echoed through the storms. It stopped the storms, throwing the parties on the beach to the ground. The clouds cleared and the beach was still, only the water taking some moments to return to normalcy.

Tyrus and Honor saw it, moments before it flung them away, tossing them through the air high above the sea. The force was so great that when they controlled themselves again, they were a great distance from the island. Looking at each other, they rushed forward.

Joy severed the link. A smile on her face, she stood and shook the dirt off her clothes. Then she saw it, a glimpse of the future. It shocked her to her core, filled her eyes with fear and pain. Sadness washed over her, and realizing she was too late, she fell to the ground, in tears.

Seth arrived a moment later, touching her face gently. Joy looked at him and said, "I didn't know."

"We both missed it."

"How? How could we miss this?"

"I don't know." He wrapped her in his arms as tears fell from his eyes as well. They'd done all they could, yet the aftermath of the storm was about to play out, and they both stood helpless, waiting for the inevitable.

Chapter 19

Levi stood, slowly, aching. Nix beside him, they squared off, ready to finish Sirena. The wind had settled, only normal breezes drifting to the shoreline. Their foe rose slowly, her body clearly aching as well. Her strength was wavering.

Levi walked forward, slowly, as Sirena matched him step to step. As they approached each other, the wind started to pick up again, but it was not the harsh wind of the storm.

"You have a chance to walk away." Levi looked at her brown eyes, which shone in defiance. "We have you surrounded. Two firebirds, both a fire and water dragon, and others you don't know about. What could you possibly hope to gain from continuing this battle?"

Sirena smiled then, and it disturbed him. Her eyes danced, and she tilted her head at him. "You are so sure of yourself, but I've been watching your tribe. I know everything you've done. The dossier they have on you is very…" her head tilted in the other direction, "compelling."

Levi looked behind him, suddenly fearful. He was right to be so. Sirena's eyes danced with her power as she laughed, lashing out at Nix, who, without a firebird, had a limited supply of energy to fight with.

The wind surrounded her, before the water could touch her. How could you be so stupid? He watched as Nix locked eyes with him, for a long moment, staring at each other. No words were spoken, but they knew what was coming.

Nix flared her flame out, stronger than ever, but the wind was fierce, stifling her fire. She tried again, to no avail. The pressure of the wind had her dropping to her knees. If someone couldn't find a way to break this wind, she would die, being ripped apart limb from limb as her flame faded away.

Levi turned back to Sirena, and poured the water over her, but she was ready. He had no clue how she'd become so powerful, but she had found her second wind. She began to laugh, low at first, but the sound echoed, growing louder and higher. Her wind protected her, as she reached a hand out, and slowly began to close it.

Nix let out a scream, her body beginning to succumb to the force around her. Levi heard it and had only seconds to create a solution. The fear left him, as he realized the only option that could save Nix. He turned to Sirena, and sent her one last, soft, sad smile.

"What's that for?"

"When you remember, I hope you can forgive yourself."

"What are you talking about?"

He didn't answer though. He turned back to his beloved and released his Leviathan. The beast flew from his fingertips to the earth below Nix. It rose, encircling her with its water, starting at her feet and ending at the top of her head.

Nix felt a pressure, near her heart, as the water seeped into her being. Some sadness, some emptiness that had been inside her since the loss of her bird was filling. She looked to Levi as the Leviathan's spirit encircled her heart, as it kept her safe. She saw the smile on his face and she knew what he was doing, but with the change occurring, she could do nothing but let the Leviathan in. Strings that were cut were found and sewn together with water. The world went black, and she was gone for a long moment.

Tyrus and Honor were close enough to see it, as they landed on the end of the beach with Sirena. Rushing her, the wind propelled them back, as she didn't want to involve them. The wind created a wall through which they could see, but not pass through.

She waited for the Leviathan to be gifted, then she gave a last laugh. Her wind surrounded Levi, who looked at her with his sad eyes. They only emboldened her, for she thought it meant he'd given up. In a way, he had given up something precious to someone special.

The others arrived with enough time to watch, but no time to help. Sirena brought her wind around Levi, and with a sweep of her hands outward, the wind ripped through his body. They rushed forward as he convulsed, his body struggling to live.

Sirena, powerful and strong, threw her head back, ready to end him, to get what she so desperately wanted. The power rushed to her fingertips from her soul, her essence about to end this monster's life. A mere snap of her fingers, and her wind would see him perish.

A hand gripped hers, forcing her body up and around to face the intruder. She stood facing eyes that held the ocean. For a moment, everything was foggy, as if she were struggling to remember something important. A necklace was ripped from her being, then, the word came to her lips. She knew who this was.

"Daileass."

Connor woke to see a mirror image in another pair of eyes. He lay on the grass, surrounded by figures. He looked at her face and held a hand to her cheek. "Maiden."

"The Waters of Fate have not abandoned you. You are one of us, even if you're a griffin."

"You…" his voice was dry, "you saved me."

"We saved you, healed you. Your unicorn is too tired. Luckily, my father had the foresight to give you a drink of the Waters of Fate, and that necklace, or I would not have been able to sense you."

"I'm glad you're here."

"I'm glad you're safe. Get up. We must help you stand."

He smiled, pleased that she was there. As she helped him up, he caught a whiff of her scent. Familiar, now, she smelled of seashells and fresh ocean air.

Nix came back to herself, the Leviathan connected to her soul with a string that had been broken long ago. She looked down at her hands. One held her flame, the abilities she would always possess, the other held…water.

With the two, she easily cleared away the last of the remaining wind, in time to see Levi fall to the ground. Tyrus ran to her, and her rage made a scream come to her lips.

"LEVI!" She cursed the air, the sand, the world in two syllables. Tyrus grabbed her shoulders, holding her in place. She pushed against him, the water doing her bidding. Tyrus was flung back, and she walked on to the still figure lying on the beach.

Her face was ridden with tears by the time she reached him. He was on the ground, not breathing. She touched him and willed with every fiber of her being for the Leviathan to return to its master. She closed her eyes, concentrating her spirit on giving back what he'd given.

Honor stood near Sirena and Daileass, listening to their conversation.

"How do I know you?"

"You have been a disappointment, Sirena. I had hoped that isolation would have calmed your soul, and instead, it only made you forget."

"Forget what?"

"Exactly. In time, hopefully your memories will return to you. I'm taking you home to be with your people."

"I'm not going anywhere with you."

He smiled the same sad smile that Levi had given her. Something twitched at the back of her memory, but it remained veiled. "I'm not giving you a choice." Without another word, the Mer King summoned the water, and Sirena was engulfed by it.

Daileass turned to Honor. "It is done."

Honor nodded. "What about my friend?"

Daileass turned and began to walk to him. Joy and Seth followed behind. Connor and Maiden came out of the water, rushing to the scene, unsure what was unfolding. Tyrus stood and marched back to Nix, who still focused, concentrating on the still figure she touched.

When he arrived, Daileass leaned down, touching Levi's forehead. Joy touched his foot. Together, their powers merging, fire, water and light, they flowed over Levi's body. Wave after wave of power seeped into his being. They did not stop until they were all spent. Sitting back, weary, they opened their eyes.

His body lay still, his chest not moving. Nix felt the tears fall, before a scream ripped from her throat again. She grabbed him by the shoulders and held him close, her Leviathan swimming around them.

Daileass stood, walking toward his daughter. His head weary, he touched Connor's shoulder. "The Leviathan is no more."

The color left Connor's face as he stumbled back, as if the knowledge was a physical force. Maiden gasped, covering her mouth with her hand. She grabbed her father in an embrace, whispering, "I know he was your friend." Though he was King, he couldn't help but shed a few tears.

Pulling away he said, "go to your friends, Griffin."

Connor ran to them and dropped to his knees beside Honor and Joy. They watched silently as Nix rocked Levi's body back and forth. No one had anything to say.

Tyrus took his shoulders from Nix, laying him on the ground on his side. He grabbed Nix and held her, trying to console her. Seth held Joy, Connor placing an arm around Honor's shoulders. Their tears fell softly to the sand.

Joy reached out to Levi, one more time. She placed her hand on his back, and felt softly, no longer forcing her energy through his body. When she reached his lungs, she felt something…off. Something was stuck. This wasn't mythical. She got up, motivated now and began to pound on his back.

"Stop it!" Nix screamed at her, but she continued, nonetheless. "What are you doing to him?"

Still, Joy pounded on Levi's back, over and over until Tyrus caught on and grabbed his shoulders, helping her dislodge what didn't belong. From his mouth came a clump of rock. Levi's chest heaved, and the air rushed into his lungs. Joy's glow surrounded him as he recovered, coming back to them.

Nix ran to him, Tyrus moving out of her way. She held his head with her hands gently and waited for his eyes to open. When they did, she saw a calm blue.

"Hey." Softly, she bent her lips to his.

Levi was somewhere else. A meadow stood before him, overflowing with flowers, surrounded by trees so old they looked like skyscrapers. A figure stood, clothed in white, in the middle of the meadow. He walked toward it, wondering where he was and why he had been taken here.

He expected the afterlife to be different, but he'd assume he'd be someplace…hotter. The figure turned as he approached, long curly black hair framing a heart shaped face. Blue eyes gleefully looked at him.

"You made it! Good." She embraced him quickly. "You can deliver a message."

"Who are you? Where am I?"

"I'm Marie. You are in my meadow. Can you tell Honor something for me?"

"I'm not sure I'm going to see her anytime soon."

"Oh, stop being so dramatic. You're only dying, not dead. Now listen, you need to give Honor a message for me. Can you do that?"

"Sure."

"Great. Tell her this in her hour of defeat." She whispered in his ear. And a shiver ran down his spine as he contemplated what she said. "Tell no one else. Bye!"

Suddenly, he felt a force pushing him away from the meadow,

back into the abyss. He fought it, but fighting was useless. He was back on the beach, his chest heaving as if he had not breathed in weeks. His brain, getting the oxygen it needed, alerted him and his body to wake.

He opened his eyes, seeing brown eyes swimming with the sea. "Hey," Nix said, softly placing her lips on his. He grabbed her by both arms and rolled her into the sand, so she lay beneath him. Propping himself up on his elbows, he looked down at her, his long hair sheltering them from the others. He leaned close and whispered, "am I redeemed?"

Nix felt the Leviathan answer him within her. She understood in that moment something that no other Mythic ever would. The spirits of these creatures, they were not something completely separate from them. The Leviathan he'd gifted her, it had his memories, his thoughts, his humor. Even now, within her body, it recognized the other half of itself. Levi had not just given her his psychic beast. Somehow, he'd given her half of his very soul.

She touched her cheek to his, and the Leviathan swam through her hand to touch Levi's cheek. "Yes, Levi, you're redeemed."

He kissed her then, in front of everyone watching, until at long last the younger generation grew bored and wandered off. They lay there for hours, the others departing slowly, touching and sensing wonder in each other.

How long will they stay on the island do you think?" Honor asked Tyrus back at the camp, surrounded by the others.

"Yeah, how long?" Joy echoed.

"We probably shouldn't hold our breath." Tyrus turned away from them and cleared off dirt from a stump before sitting upon it. Julius had been filled in, and the five were whole again. There were just a few things he needed to make sure were heard.

"Listen up!" He used his Marine voice, silencing the others. "Sit down. I have some things to say after the events that lead us here."

He waited until they sat with him near the fire, before he began.

"Until now, you've been in training. You've had something special that no one else has had. You had people like us, on your side, helping you, pushing you.

"That's a great thing. Unfortunately, as you learned today, we are not immortal. Somewhere out there is someone who's your opposite, waiting for you. It is no longer good enough that you be protected. No longer good enough that you train.

"I made the mistake of assuming you were young, that you were victims, and I see none here. I see survivors who have been shown things, have donc things…" he hesitated and looked at Honor, "that victims or newbies couldn't do. Until now, we've been reacting to the world. It is stone and we are water, but we can do more. We should do more.

"I will no longer treat you as anything less than an equal. Julius has fully transformed. That means he'll stop aging soon. Honor did something incredible in the dream world, Joy was healing left and right. Connor, you're growing closer to needed allies that saved our asses today. And Seth's gut saved Honor again. You aren't victims." He stopped for a moment before he whispered, "you are Mythics. You are the Five."

When the others had left, Honor walked to Tyrus, intent on asking some questions. "Hey."

He turned and looked at her. "Hey."

"So, can we talk now?"

He sighed. "What do you need to know?"

"What exactly happened between my phoenix and your dragon?"

Nix and Levi arrived back at camp then, and Tyrus held out a finger as if to say, "one moment." He walked to his friends and shook Levi's hand, hugged Nix tight. The others rushed over to him, grateful to have him back.

He came back a moment later and said, "maybe we should sit

back down." When they'd done so, he rubbed his hands on his knees, momentarily at a loss for words. "Your phoenix and my dragon…" Before he could finish, Nix walked up to him and grabbed him by the shirt.

"What's this I hear about a comet crashing to earth near the farm?"

He tilted his head at her. She showed him her smartphone, with a news article opened. "Oh, uh, I was just about to explain that." The others were gathering around, and Honor was feeling very uncomfortable. This was supposed to be a private conversation.

"Look, her phoenix was about to implode."

"Right, so naturally you chose the *best* option." Sarcasm dripped in her voice.

Levi walked up to Honor, as if sniffing her. "Hmmm." Then he walked away.

Honor looked at them and said, "I don't understand."

Nix set Tyrus down and turned to her. "Mythics sometimes have a mind of their own. Even though they're pieces of us, they are also a different being with intelligence and…needs."

"What are you saying though?"

Seth walked over and whispered something in her ear. Tyrus watched her blush and said, "Okay, can we all just move on from this tense moment?"

Nix turned and punched him in the face. He fell to the ground. "Sure, now we can."

Honor stood and walked away, obviously looking to find some composure. He turned to Nix and said, "It was the only way."

"I've known you long enough to know you're the knight, not the knave. You don't have to convince me. It just…seemed like what I needed to do."

"Well, Honor's a phoenix. You looking out for your own?"

"Maybe," she said, as the Leviathan within her swam to the surface of her skin. "But now I'm barely a firebird anymore."

"Yeah," he turned to Levi, "is this reversable?"

Levi's sad smile returned. Nix lowered her gaze. "What?"

Joy turned to the adults and finished what they wouldn't. "Levi can't take back what was given to save another. It is the payment he made with his beast to ensure Nix didn't die. His beast is hers now."

Tyrus sat down again. "So, Nix is fire and water?"

"Yes."

"Isn't that not supposed to…be viable?"

"It's not."

"So why is she not being torn apart from the inside right now?"

Levi touched her cheek, the Leviathan swimming to the surface again. "I think…that's something Nix and I need to discuss in private, but I know for a fact, my Mythic loves her just as much as I do."

Nix laughed. "You think a lot of yourself."

"I think a lot of you." Joy giggled, and they walked away, leaving Tyrus with the others.

"Back to work."

"Doing what?"

"I feel the urge to start building another cabin. If this month has been any indication of change, we need to be prepared for more of us to immerge."

They groaned in unison. "More wood."

"That's right, we all help. More wood."

Two days passed as they returned to normalcy. Honor waited until Tyrus was on watch with her, the others sleeping, to speak her mind. Now that it was time, though, she found it difficult to start.

"What is it, Honor?"

"So, our psychic creatures…mated, pretty much."

He struggled with how much he should say, and what to keep to himself. "I think the term, bonded, works better."

"Right, that does make more sense. So.." she paused, uncertain in her words, "what is that supposed to make me feel?"

"I don't know, you feel, however you feel. How do you feel

right now?"

"Awkward."

"Okay. Me too."

She breathed a sigh of relief. "Oh, good. This is weird for both of us then."

"Yes."

"Okay. That makes me feel better."

"Good." He turned back to watch. A few moments later, another question popped into her mind. "They can't…make a baby or anything can they?"

Tyrus's body went stiff and he dropped his night vision binoculars. "No, no, I don't think that's how that happens." He fumbled to pick them back up.

"Good." Again, they went back to watch, and again another question popped into her head. "So, are they dating?"

"They're pair bonded. They'll look out for each other, put each other first."

"Okay."

"Our psychic creatures performed a melding ritual. They exchanged energy, then that energy was released when they slammed into the earth. My dragon and your phoenix are now linked. They will prioritize each other, though. Their energies recognize and protect each other.

"They will come to the other's aid from miles away. We will be closer, because they are, but I promise you, this will not always be so weird. I did it to save your life. There is a difference between ascension and combustion."

She waited for him to continue, but he didn't. "Is that it?"

"Yes. That's all I know about our Mythics." He turned away and brought the binoculars to his face again. She turned and looked through hers, but her mind wouldn't stop thinking. Eventually, she found another burning question. "Has your dragon melded with anyone before?"

He dropped them again. He took three even breaths before he

said, "a dragon mates for life. If mine was bonded with another phoenix, I wouldn't have been able to save you."

She swallowed hard, but for some reason, that brought her comfort. "Is the bond we have similar to what Nix and Levi share now?"

He laughed at that. "No, no their…situation is a whole other level of crazy." That made her laugh as well, and the awkwardness faded, replaced with familiarity, easiness.

"Do you remember sharing a memory with Maiden?"

"Yes. Why?"

"I have a memory I feel I should share with you. We haven't had time before now. Can you see my memory too?"

He turned to her then, and said, "what happened?"

"How do we share?"

He placed her hands on his temples, then his hands mirrored her. "Think of the memory and send it to me. It has to be very vivid. Relive it in your mind."

She did, recalling the dream she'd shared with Joy, Seth and Connor…

She was in the hospital in Nebraska. She had never been there, but it seemed she knew because her companions knew. She walked out of the elevator and turned to the left, sure of the way to go, yet never walking there before.

The hospital path slowly turned to forest as she walked, the trees growing thicker with each step. It wasn't long before she was no longer in a hospital but stood in a thick wood. Turning, the trees parted for her, creating a new path. She followed where they led.

She walked into an old, dark forest, where the sun could no longer make it through the trees. Animals darted around, unafraid of the strange humans. She knew she was dreaming, but she still didn't quite understand why she was here.

"Honor!" She turned at her name, receiving a hug from Joy. "This is different, huh?"

"I'll say. What adventure awaits us today?"

"I'm not sure."

"What do you mean you aren't sure. You walk here all the time."

"This isn't my dream."

"Whose is it then?"

"Jayde's."

"The newbie?"

"Yes."

"We're in her dream."

"Yes."

"Hmm." She didn't know what else to say. "Any clue lying around we can use?"

Joy twirled and pointed. The trees created a path that matched her finger. "I think we should go that way."

They walked on, eventually finding Seth and Connor. The four continued wandering the trees, until finally they sat down, confused.

"It's a big circle or something. Everything looks the same." Joy noticed a flower blooming next to her. "Ooh. Pretty." She bent and watched it grow.

"I'm not sure what our purpose is here. Any insight? Anyone?"

"Well," Seth chimed in, "I think we need to just stay where we are until something reveals itself." A flower was rising by him as well. He moved away, and it seemed to follow him.

Connor was also avoiding growing flowers. Honor looked down, and noted a rose bloomed near her, almost as tall as her head as she sat. "What is going on here?"

"I guess we'll find out soon." Joy didn't take her eyes off her flower. When they'd grown fairly large, they changed, becoming speakers. "Hello?"

Seth looked at Connor. "Did my flower just talk to me?"

Connor shrugged. Honor's flower was next. "Can anyone hear me?"

"Jayde!" Joy shouted it into her speaker rose.

"Not so loud!"

"Sorry, Jayde, is that you?" Joy's voice was more pleasant.

"Nurse Joy?"

"I'm here, Jayde. Are you asleep?"

"I guess so. It's a dream, but it's like I can control it. Is that weird?"

"Nothing about you is weird." Honor chimed in. "You are special, Jayde."

One of the trees in front of them changed, as if a figure were coming from the center of the trunk. A Jayde made of tree bark stood before them.

"I'm scared."

"Why?"

"They're taking me away."

"Who is they?"

"The men that took me from the hospital."

"Sunglasses?" Joy asked. "Suits?"

"Yeah. Are they friends of yours Nurse Joy?"

"Not exactly."

"They told my parents that I was special too."

"What else did they say?"

"That they were taking me to London."

The four looked at each other. Connor knelt in front of Jayde and took her bark hands. "Listen to us, carefully, Jayde... You have to go because your parents need you, but don't listen to anything the strange men say. Even if they say something about us, we need you to be strong."

"I can be strong. Will they hurt my parents?"

"As long as they think you're their friend, your parents will be safe."

"Are they bad guys?"

He sighed. "Yes."

"Thank you for not lying to me."

"We are your friends, Jayde. We know that you're different, and as soon as we can, we will come for you. I promise."

"Are you different like me?"

He laughed. "No, but I'm different like me."

"Oh. That makes sense."

"Will you promise to be strong?"

"I promise." She turned. "My mom is waking me up. See you guys later."

She melded back into the tree, and the forest slowly faded, leaving nothing but blackness. This was strange.

"Why aren't we waking up?" Seth asked.

"There must be more." Joy walked forward, but the darkness didn't move. "This is...odd."

Honor reached out to touch the darkness, but it slipped through her fingers like fog, even though it was thick like oil. "Very strange."

Bubbles formed, that looked like oil. They floated to the center of the dark, in between the four of them. Connor reached out to touch one, and it popped all the bubbles at once. Then, they were falling into the abyss.

Landing, somehow safe and unharmed, the four were surrounded by harsh light. When their eyes adjusted to the light, they saw themselves inside a city with high walls.

"Where are we?" Honor asked.

"Uh, oh. I don't think we're supposed to be here." Joy shook her hands. "This is the future."

"The future of what?"

Joy turned to her friend. "The future of us."

The memory ended suddenly. He opened his eyes, and Honor gave him a strange look. "What is it? Why did you stop the memory?"

She swallowed hard, and said, "let me try again." She placed her hands on his temples and concentrated, but her eyes remained open. Tyrus, his eyes closed, experienced what she had seen. She watched as confusion, curiosity, and finally, surprise lit his features.

When he opened his eyes again, they were his dragon's. Honor swallowed hard again and said, "that wasn't easy to show you." He grabbed her shoulders and pulled her to him. He placed his lips on hers and kissed her deeply. She had a moment to think of the lovely feeling, harsh yet soft. He pulled away just as suddenly.

"Okay."

"We need to go save Jayde, first."

Honor nodded. "I agree."

"Save that last bit for later, when we're ready." He winked at her, and she blushed. That was one moment she wouldn't be able to stop thinking about, and it hadn't even happened yet.

In a dark dungeon, with dripping water, she kneeled, her hands entwined with magical bonds that permitted no movement. She didn't know how long she'd been there, only that she'd lost track of time.

There was never any light down here.

The gate to her cell opened, and he stepped in to see her as he did every so often.

"Hello, Sirena."

"Hello, Mer King."

"Do you know why I'm here?"

She laughed at that. "You're here…" she hissed as her shoulders ached. "You're here to save me."

"I would like to, if you let me."

"By drinking your stupid water."

"The waters of fate cleanse and renew not just the mind but the spirit as well."

"I already told you, 'No.'"

"You have."

"Why do you keep coming to see me then? You know my answer."

He knelt down, then, something he hadn't done before. He lifted her face up to his and she saw eyes that reflected the ocean. His gaze softened, and he caressed her face.

Though she didn't remember touching him before, the gesture hinted of familiarity and comfort. She pulled away, confused. "The answer is no."

He didn't get up, but merely held the water close to her. "The choice, as it has always been, is yours."

Sirena thought quickly, then. If she drank it, maybe he'd let her go. She could convince him that she was reformed. She'd done it before. Then she could get out of here and get her revenge.

Cursing herself silently for not having thought of that sooner, she said, "I guess it wouldn't hurt to have a drink, right?"

She watched his eyes light up. Things were finally looking up for her. He placed the shell with the water of fate to her lips and said, "Till gu mi mo ghràdh."

The water quenched a thirst she didn't know she had. It seeped into her pores, her blood. She felt the waves of fate wash over her entire being. She drank deeply then, downing all the water in the shell. Whatever this was, whatever it was doing to her, she needed it.

When the water was gone, the feeling subsided, she looked up and spoke his name. "Daileass."

"Yes, that's my name."

"No," she shook her head, trying to clear it, as memories came flooding back to her. He took her face in his hands and said, "Look at me, Sirena."

She did then. His ocean eyes gleaming at her. She knew that look. She knew him.

"I mean, no, it's not just a name."

He bent to his knees in front of her, his hands around her face. "No, no it's not."

"It's the name of every Mer King, given when he marries."

He nodded. "Yes." His eyes shone with tears.

"They give a name to the queen too."

"They do."

"Their name carries fate on the wind. A mermaid, but one with spirit."

"To the hearts of the serene."

"Her name summons songs to the hearts of men."

"To protect, to guide, to help."

"The queen of the water people. Serena. My name."

He embraced her hard, her bonds dissolving as her anger fled her. She wrapped her arms around him and began to cry. "I remember." She felt tears leave her eyes. "I remember everything."

He held her and let her cry, his tears mingling with hers. He tilted her head back and kissed his wife, thoroughly, deeply. When the tears were gone, he said, "welcome home, my love. At long last, we are a family once more."

"Thank you for listening to me."

"I told you I would always protect our daughter."

"How did you reach me in that daze?"

"The Waters of Fate guide you home, always."

◆ ◆ ◆

Dr. Jackson paced back and forth in his study, worrying over something that was beyond his control. Why was she coming here? Before he had much time to contemplate the situation he was in, the doors flew open, revealing a woman in a scarlet robe, followed by silhouettes in black.

"Dr. Gregory Jackson." Chimera asked it politely.

"Yes. Hello, Chimera."

"Good evening."

"To what do I owe this pleasure?"

"I am making rounds. I wanted to stop by and see how my dear friend's son was running the family business." She swept a finger over the desk, as if she owned it. He fought off the urge to shiver.

"And how am I doing?" He sipped his whiskey with two ice cubes, seated in his chair now, as if he were relaxed and comfortable with the exchange.

"In truth, I was hoping you'd be a bit quicker on the hidden coin, but no matter." She sat down, her legs showing through her robe. They were bare. "I come to you bearing a gift. One most precious to your enemy. One that can ensure that Jackson Genetics is the leading Genetic Modification organization of this new century."

"I highly doubt that you can deliver on that promise, even if you are Chimera."

She smiled harshly at him, her eyes cold. "Every man in my life has made the tragic and fatal mistake of seeing me as a woman. I hope you are exceptional."

"Why is that?"

"Because if you squander this gift, it could have far reaching consequences." She snapped her fingers on her right hand, and a bag was brought forward. "This is my gift to you, Dr. Gregory Jackson."

He glanced at it only for a moment before he murmured, "What is it, a sack of potatoes?"

She snapped her fingers again and the black figures opened the bag, pulling out an unconscious woman from it. "What is this?"

Chimera laughed. "My dear one, this is the daughter of your enemy." She grabbed the blonde hair and lifted her up so he could see her face. "I believe you're acquainted with Dr. Rebecca Wills?"

He answered the phone call on the first ring. It'd been three days since he slept. She was out there, somewhere, and when he found her, he would kill anything that stood in his way. "Bonjour."

"Dr. Blanc." A chill ran up his spine. He stood, pacing back and forth.

"Why are you calling me?"

"They took her."

"I know."

"And they have Sirena."

"I know."

"Everything you've done has been a phenomenal failure."

"Not everything."

"What have you done correctly?"

"They may have my daughter, but I…" he turned to a fish tank next to him, where something swam in the water. "I have royalty."

"Nabbing a fish isn't going to be enough. I am sorry dear friend, but if we are to succeed then it is no longer convenient for me to sit and wait on the sidelines."

His body felt hot and cold all at once, as if a powerful force were changing him at a molecular level. "What are you doing?"

"I am sorry my friend, but if you are going to defeat them, you need me."

The phone dropped as his body convulsed, his eyes turning black…

Julius tossed and turned in his bed that night, unable to sleep. He thought about everything that had happened to them since they survived that bus crash. Thought about his family, who he missed terribly. Maybe now that things had died down, he could go see them again. Give them some money to help out.

A thought occurred to him then. Out loud, he said to a sleeping Seth, "Dude. Am I the only one not hooked up right now?"

Seth stopped snoring for a moment, rolled over and went back to sleep.

Julius shook his head laying it on the pillow. He turned away from Seth murmuring about his luck.

Joy woke in the other room, unaware of his plight. Still, she clapped her hands as she felt a change in fate. Someone has made a wish, and the universe is answering. She chuckled as she lay down to sleep again, singing,

"The seas will flail, the wind will fail,
When Urchin Queen draws nigh.
The dragon's breath has nothing left,
When Urchin Queen draws nigh.
And when at last the storm has passed,
When birds of prey do die,
The shadow will have breathed it's last,
When Urchin Queen draws nigh.
When Urchin Queen draws nigh."

Chapter 20

Honor stood waiting for Nix to get out of the powder room. She tapped her foot impatiently. "If we don't hurry, we're going to be late."

"I know." Nix apparently didn't feel any urgency at all. Picking up her cell, she texted Joy to let her know they'd be late.

Nix opened the door a moment later, her makeup done, her hair in place. "Okay, let's get there."

It was only nine in the morning, but still, they felt the need to run out of the hotel. Finding their driver, courtesy of Dr. Gregory Jackson, they stepped into the limo and Nix gave him directions to their next destination.

Nix sat back and breathed a sigh of relief. "Well, first part of the day is done."

"Do you think we'll be able to pull this off?"

"I hope so. If we don't, God help us."

Honor felt anxious and nervous in a way she hadn't since before her accident. If everything didn't go exactly as planned, they were all doomed.

In another hotel room, with the shades drawn, a group of men lay about on couches, beds and some even on the floor. Something around them was beeping, hideously. Levi reached for the offending electronic and swatted it until it shut up. He stretched and started to drift back off to sleep, thinking of Nix.

Nix.

Shit. He was suddenly awake. He rose, walking to the window and opening the shades. The others groaned aloud.

"What's your problem?" Julius rubbed his aching forehead.

"Get up. All of you. Now. It's already ten in the morning. Today is operation day. Let's go."

They sprung into action, quickly composing themselves.

Moments later, the group of men left the hotel room, striding on a mission to the elevator doors. They were dressed all in black, ready for their day.

Tyrus turned to Levi as the doors closed. "Do you think we can still make the deadline?"

Levi looked at his friend. "If we don't, we're all dead."

Tyrus swallowed hard. He definitely didn't want that.

They came out of the elevator and walked with great purpose out of the hotel doors. A few onlookers noticed them, wondering their intent. They seemed out of place, somehow.

They walked into their own limo and gave directions to the driver. Dr. Jackson turned to him. "Now, I don't have to tell you how critical it is that this day go according to plan."

"No, no you don't. I understand."

"We cannot fail."

"I'm aware. Oh, stop here."

Levi got out of the limo momentarily, walking into a storefront. Dr. Jackson and Tyrus looked at each other, growing more impatient with each passing minute. If they didn't get there soon, all hell would break loose.

"We're doomed."

"I know."

They sat, anxious and impatient. Levi returned a moment later.

"What was so important that you risked the op to go shopping?"

He took out a small box and opened it to show him what he'd purchased.

"Nice."

He closed it again and told the driver to hurry. They couldn't fail, not today.

Honor helped Nix out of the limo, shielding her from view. If the operation was going to be a success today, no one could see Nix before she was in costume. Joy was waiting at the back entrance to the building, motioning for them to hurry. Nix stepped inside without a word, and the younger girls looked at each other.

"Have you heard anything yet?"

"On their way. Late but ready."

"I hope we can still get this done."

"Don't worry. I have a feeling everything will be fine."

They marched with the same purpose through the halls of the building until they found the room designated for Nix's costume. Looking both ways, they shut the doors and secured the lock. No one was getting past them until it was go time.

"Let's go over our strategy one more time."

The others groaned, but Levi moved the empty glasses back and began again. "You stand here. You're the first ones to move. Dr. Jackson, your job is to help Nix."

"Got it." He gave a confident look to Levi.

"Tyrus, you have the package from earlier?"

"Got it."

"Good. Now, you three." He moved the glasses around again. "Your job is to handle crowd control. You work as a team. You got it?"

They nodded. "We won't let you down."

"Good."

"One more time." Tyrus wanted to make sure this day didn't fail.

"If we don't know it by now, there's no learning it." This from Julius.

"True, but if we have any hope to succeed today, nothing can go wrong. Again."

They groaned but Levi showed them again.

They pulled up to the building a few moments later. Levi looked at them and asked, "Got everything?" They nodded again.

"Gentleman. It's go time."

They walked out of the limo, Connor yelling, "Go! Go! Go!" They ran around the side of the building and into the opposite entrance from the girls. Inside, they caught their breath. Tyrus grabbed Levi's shoulder and said, "We made it."

Levi laughed so hard he began to cough. "Yeah, well now comes the tricky part."

They walked down the hallway, into a waiting room and locked their door behind them.

"Text Team A. Let them know Team B is in position."

Seth did so. "Joy says they're in place, ready by go time."

Levi looked at his watch. "Alright, men, let's get this done. We have a half hour until the op starts. Let's do this!"

They cheered, and began to get ready.

Levi put on his costume and Tyrus grabbed his shoulder again. "You sure you're up to this?"

"If I wasn't, I would be running the op."

"Great. That's what I needed to hear."

"You good?"

"Yeah. You?"

"Never better."

They shook hands and continued to prep.

Joy rushed out of their room, frantic in her search. She looked at the crowd of people showing up. Finding her mark, she expertly navigated the crowd, blending in as she'd been shown. A man her height was sipping on a glass of champagne.

"The bird is nesting." She whispered it to him. He turned and faced her.

"Got it." Seth touched her hand.

"You guys ready?"

"You nervous?"

She nodded. "Oh, yeah. This is the highest end op we've ever done. And the margin for error is zero."

"It'll be okay, Joy."

"Your gut tell you that?"

"Yes."

"Good. That makes me feel better. Now go. Deliver the message. Hurry."

She walked away as he did, her job accomplished. Looking at a flower arrangement, she narrowed her eyes.

"This doesn't go here." She closed her eyes, and her light surrounded the flowers until they disappeared, reappearing in just the right spot. "Better." She sauntered back to the room, saying to herself, "Let's do this."

Seth walked by the door, knocking their agreed upon secret knock. Tyrus opened it for a second. "Seth! You're supposed to be out there doing crowd control. What is it?"

"The bird is nesting."

Tyrus nodded. "Oh, good. Thanks for letting us know. Now go before you blow the op."

Seth walked away, looking in both directions. No way was he going to mess up. He fixed the cufflinks on his suit and adjusted his tie. He glided down the hallway and, entering the large open room in the front, was joined by his two male companions. They looked at the crowd of people they were assigned to and at each other.

"We got this."

They nodded, showing their resolve. Walking forward, they got to work.

"What if I can't do this?" Nix turned to Honor, her eyes scared. Honor grabbed her by the shoulders.

"We can do this. You can do this. We have to."

"But what if I can't pull this off?"

"Doubts like that are a sure way for all of us to fail."

"Exactly my point. What if I ruin this, for everyone?"

Honor calmed her voice and said, "Look at me." When Nix did so, she said, "You are the reason we're here. Everything will work out well. If you're too scared, if you don't think everything is perfect, we can call the op off, walk away and try again another day. Is that what you want?"

"No."

"Then we must go forward with the plan. Just stick to it. You'll be fine. As soon as the op starts, you'll be wonderful."

"Are you sure this is on right?"

Honor double checked her work on Nix's outfit. "Yes. I'm sure."

"There's so many…"

"I know. It's a lot."

"It's beautiful though, right? Do you have the finishing touch?"

She turned and grabbed the last piece of her costume. Attaching it to the top of her head, she said, "Perfect."

Nix looked in the mirror and said, "Tell them it's go time."

She relayed the message to Joy, who relayed it to Connor. All quieted, as the ladies took their places. They were ready.

Levi grabbed Seth on his way to his post. "Get this to Nix or all is lost."

Seth bounced into the room, but finding no one there, he began to panic. If he couldn't get this to Nix, the whole op would be for nothing. Winding through the hallways, he desperately searched for them. Finding them in the entry room, he caught his breath, handing his package to Honor.

She glanced at the contents inside and said, "Oh, my god. I completely forgot. Thank you, Seth. Now get to your spot." He rushed away, and Honor turned and showed Nix the blue item inside.

"How lovely."

"He has good taste."

"I know."

"You've got this. We've got this."

Nix took a deep breath and said, "Joy?"

"Yes?"

"Open the doors. It's go time."

Gregory met his aunt as the doors opened, offering his arm and a smile. Joy obeyed, her flowers ready in her hand. A hush fell over the crowd inside, and Joy began to walk forward down the aisle. Honor was next, followed by Nix. The church was decorated with beautiful white and gold flowers, mixed with red roses. The ground at her feet was full of soft petals.

Her white dress was frilly, but beautiful. She just hoped she didn't trip on it. She looked up and saw Levi standing in the middle of the room, Tyrus at his side. She smiled at him as he smiled at her. Today was the day. It was go time. Today was their wedding day. She walked toward her future more hopeful than she'd ever been in her life. Her Leviathan, recognizing him, swam up for attention, but she quieted it back down. Now was the time for a different kind of magic.

Levi grabbed her hand gently, lifting the veil from her face. The smile he gave her was wide and full. "You look beautiful."

And that was all it took for her fears to subside. She looked at him and whispered, "We got this."

They turned to the preacher to start the ceremony, each in their heart believing that life couldn't get any better.

Tyrus found Honor at the reception, after the dancing and dining had given way to drunken fun. He walked to her and asked, "would you like to dance?"

She turned to him and said, "have you been drinking?"

"Uh, one for courage, two for strength." He took her hand and led her to the dance floor. "How do you think the op went?"

"Couldn't have gone any better, in my opinion. Very well

done."

He swung her expertly around the dance floor. Honor looked at him. "Wow. When you say you can dance you mean you can dance."

"You pick up things living for a longer time than most."

"I see that." She looked at Nix and Levi. "Have you ever been married?"

He faltered his step and said, "uh, no. This is quite unusual. Most Mythics are worried about surviving, not creating a family."

"I get that."

"Why did you want to know?"

"I just don't know much about you. I'm trying to learn."

"Well, I've never had the opportunity."

She smiled at him but didn't say anything. He tilted his head and asked, "what are you thinking of?"

"How happy they are. It makes me glad."

"Me too."

They danced together, as the night settled around them, oblivious to everyone else, until a commotion drew their attention. It was coming from the back of the reception hall.

"What is that?"

"Stay here. I'll check it out." He walked away, with the three others at his back. They walked forward, into the entry way. A crowd of people had gathered around a specific area. They shoved their way through only to find a bleeding victim on the ground.

Tyrus turned to the others and said, "Get these people out of here. No one tell Nix."

They got to work as he examined the body, looking for the point the skin broke. He turned him over, and the small black, twisted knife in his back told him all he needed to know.

He pulled it out, knowing it would be covered in poison. This man was dead. He stuck it in his pocket and walked away, outside, away from the party.

Honor found him there, looking at the knife. It was ebony, with a black blade, a small throwing knife with a symbol on top, but she couldn't quite make it out from where she stood.

"Do you know who that belongs to?" She had clearly startled him. He put the knife away and turned to her, tears in his eyes.

"What is it?" She placed a hand on his shoulder, but he pushed it away. Turning from her, he said, "Honor, I can't really explain this."

They'd learned that after their Mythics melded, that they could sense each other's emotions. She felt his sadness and wanted nothing but to sooth it.

"What's going on?"

His shoulders rose and fell as he sighed. "This knife belonged to someone I knew."

"Someone who meant a lot to you?"

"Yes."

"Whose is it?"

"I thought she was dead. She should be dead. This doesn't make any sense."

"Who?"

From behind her, Nix said one phrase that crushed Honor's heart. "The only woman he ever loved."

"And now someone is mimicking her calling card."

"Who was this?" She couldn't keep the jealousy out of her voice.

He turned to her and said, "Noémie."

"What was she?"

He looked at Nix. "The third phoenix."

Her heart sank further. "The woman who helped you when you were younger. She was a phoenix. You were in love with her?"

He nodded. "I was young and stupid, remember?"

"And she died."

"Yes."

"How?"

Nix put a hand on her shoulder and said, "maybe we shouldn't do this here, Honor."

She shrugged her friend off. Turning to Tyrus, she asked again.

"How did she die?"

The tears threatened to fall from his eyes. "I… killed her."

Honor didn't wait to be told what to do. She found her rage, suddenly, and walked away from the two, as they shouted after her to stop. She walked through the hall and out the front door. Her wings unfolding, she flew away from the party, with no one stopping her.

She flew far enough away to find some space, then set herself down on a rooftop. She breathed heavily, finding her air again. Tears seeped from her eyes, but she wasn't exactly sure why she was so upset.

"I told you."

She jumped and turned, her flame ready. Instead of attacking, the flame immediately dissolved. A shadow in the shape of a human stood in front of her.

"I told you one day you would end up alone."

"I'm not alone."

"You're very much alone right now. The man you loved murdered one of your kind. Nix knew about it and didn't tell you. They mean the most to you, and they both betrayed you."

She scoffed at him. "Right. Cause it happened to me and not actually to her."

"Rationalize it all you want. One day you will see the truth, and they you will ask for me."

The shadow held out a hand, a black talisman shimmering in it. The talisman was identical to the knife Tyrus had pulled from the body. "It was you."

"You need to know who you are in league with, and who you should be with. I didn't kill that man, but I know who did. When you want to know, break the talisman in half and I will come to you."

He faded away, as Tyrus landed on the roof. She quickly put it in her pocket and turned to him. "Honor. Are you okay?" He held her by the shoulders, and she let him.

"What happened?"

"How did I kill her?"

"Yes."

He sighed. "I will tell you one day, but today is not that day."

"Why not?"

"You're not ready to know."

"So, all that talk of us being equals, of us no longer being protected, that wasn't true?"

"No, it was. We are equals."

"Then why are you hiding this from me?"

He placed his forehead on hers. "I'm not hiding anything from you. I never have, and I never will. Except this one thing."

As she pulled away, he tightened his grip. "Please, Honor, I'm asking you to trust me this once."

"Tell me or I walk away."

"From me?"

"From everything."

"Where do you intend to go?"

She thought about what the shadow had said. "I don't need anyone but myself."

His gaze softened. "I understand and agree with that."

"So, tell me."

He shook his head. "It is the one story that I can't tell, right now."

"Why?" She shoved him, frustrated.

"Because it happened to a phoenix, Honor. A phoenix. Like you! I don't want what happened to her, to happen to you!"

"What happened?"

He sighed. "She went bad, and I had to end her."

"How?"

"That's between me and Noémie." His eyes grew angry. "When I choose to tell you, Honor, it won't be because you're forcing me to, but because you can handle it, because you're more powerful than you are now. When I tell you the story, it will be after you trust me, when I feel comfortable doing so."

An arrow of sadness pierced her heart. "You aren't comfortable with me now?"

His gaze softened. "Just give me time and trust. Please, Honor."

He flew away without another word. Honor started to shake, partly from the cold night, partly from the events that had just turned her world on its side. Who was this man she was attached to now? She took the talisman out and held it in her hand. As she did so, the black from the object danced into her eyes. They turned black and then faded.

That's odd. She walked to the ledge and glided down to the street. Dumping the talisman in the trash, she walked back to the party. She trusted him, didn't she?

The talisman in the trash pulsed with dark light once, twice, and then disappeared from the trash can. Far away, the shadow laughed.

Epilogue

The red robe flowed around her as if it were in water, but it was not. Ruby lips, painted meticulously by someone else breathed in the chilly air of the mountain. She walked with purpose into the ancient temple, guarded by holy monks. They wore robes of deep red and parted for her without a word. They avoided her gaze. To them, she was a goddess.

Still, she was only mortal. She could be killed if anyone ever figured out how to outwit her. Chimera walked into the temple, touching a spot on the far wall. It opened at her touch, revealing a staircase leading down into the basement.

She walked down slowly and approached a table with a dark figure. She sat, smoothing her robe and locked eyes with the room's occupant.

"Payment." It was a woman's voice that came from the dark, old and worn. Chimera smiled, producing a bag of gold from her pocket. It was taken, checked, and accepted.

"What do you will of me?"

"Show me my future."

The eyes blazed green, an image surrounding them both. A ghost-like version of herself came into view, surrounded by thousands of adoring subjects. She wore gold and silver, expertly crafted over her form. Below her, the other Mythics bowed, showing their allegiance to her. As she watched, waving a hand to her subjects, a firebird flew down and landed on her shoulder. Honor stood to her right, a triumphant smile upon her face.

Chimera's smile widened. She turned and walked away. Sure, she'd had to push a few boundaries, had to change a few alliances, but the end result would be the same. She was no longer some girl at the mercy of men. She was Chimera, the ancient evil that inspired the immortal's written description. She was old, powerful. She was the top of the food chain. Grabbing an apple at the top of the stairs, left in offering to her, she took a bite. She would make this world bow to her before she left it.

“All in a day’s work.” She flipped a coin to the monk standing on her right. It was a faded coin, with a Chimera on one side, and a flame on the other. She walked out, thinking on her newfound friend. The phoenix had no clue the potential destruction she could deliver, of the fates she could change. Chimera intended to sway her toward the one that was best, for her.

Urchin Queen

www.ingramcontent.com/pod-product-compliance
Lightning Source LLC
Chambersburg PA
CBHW020249030826
48979CB00030B/2679/J
9798988313533